Nunny & Cecil
A TALE OF TERROR

GAILA SWINDELL

Copyright © 2012 Gaila Swindell
All rights reserved.
ISBN:147817692X
ISBN-13: 978-1478176923

For Avalon & Alaina, my dreams come true

ACKNOWLEDGMENTS

Thanks to my brother, Kirk, and his childhood imaginary friends, Nunny and Cecil. Thanks to my daughters, Avalon and Alaina, and my dearest friends, Denise and Sue, for encouraging me to pursue my dreams. Thanks to my loving husband, Doug, and my mother, Elizabeth, for helping me live my dream.

PROLOGUE

Joe Rodman carefully made his way down the creaking wooden staircase into the basement. He toted a garbage bag and shovel in his left hand and swatted cobwebs with his right.

Giddy with anticipation, Joe and his wife Marie were childproofing every inch of the farm. Their daughter and grandchildren were coming to live with them, and they didn't want any accidents. Joe fixed old sagging steps, mended broken electrical sockets, and hung up farm tools in the barn. Marie hid poisonous cleaning fluids and stuck plastic flowers to the bottom of the slippery bathtub.

The old farmhouse hadn't seen any children since their only daughter Denise had gone off to college. Lately, they'd spent many a night lying in bed, tossing restlessly as they tried to remember what kinds of trouble kids might get into. They would rise with a purpose before sunup to repair or destroy whatever they had set their minds to the night before.

Joe had sat up straight in bed and said, "Shit!" when he'd suddenly remembered the graves in the basement: the time had come for him to remove them. Now, here he was, whistling a tune as he wandered around the basement, putting things away and postponing the chore he had come to perform. He always whistled when he was nervous; on this occasion he sounded like a canary in heat. He had wanted to perform the dreaded chore thirty-five years ago when they had moved into the one-hundred-and-thirty-year-old farmhouse, but there was something inside of him that made him uneasy about the task.

Joe didn't want those things down there under his house any longer. He had stored them away in the attic of his mind for a long time, but they had always been there just the same, making him chronically anxious about the basement, about the entire house. It was the single pea under his mattress.

He was still keenly aware of what it was like to be a boy; he knew that boys had a tendency to dig in the earth. He remembered when, as children, he and his brother Ray had dug a fort in the ground that measured four feet deep and three feet wide. He also vividly remembered how his brother had tried to bury him alive in that hole after a fight they'd had. He leaned on the shovel handle, adjusted the old pair of wire-rimmed glasses that always slid down his nose, and reflected on how life was filled with bitter ironies: it was Ray who was buried in the earth now. He allowed himself a moment to think about his brother, something he rarely did, feeling a twinge of guilt because he had never visited Ray's grave in a Philadelphia cemetery. He felt empty inside as he thought about Ray lying in the damp, cruel earth, dead before his time from sticking his knife in the toaster to pluck out toast, a bad habit their mother had always chastised him about.

Joe envisioned his grandson Adam digging up the basement floor. It would be on one of those days that Joe had experienced many times as a boy: spring fever would set in—probably sometime around the end of March—and an unexpected snowstorm would blow through, forcing Adam to play indoors. He could see Adam clearly, up to his ears in dirt, a yellowed bone in his hand, exclaiming, "Look what I found, Grandpa!"

Joe and Marie had married just before the farm went up for sale. They had driven out to look at the place the day after the ad appeared in the paper. Marie still had the clipping lovingly tucked away. They'd been living in a row house in Philadelphia, both of them feeling an urgent desire to get away from the fast pace of the city. They wanted clean air, open fields, animals in the yard, and the sound of the wind in the cornfields. They could certainly afford to escape to the country, Joe being the sole heir to his uncle's large estate.

The fieldstone farmhouse seemed the house of their wildest dreams, with twenty acres of land, including a thriving apple orchard and a thick green forest. Best of all, it was located in the heart of Cooks County, Pennsylvania, the part of the country the Amish called home.

NUNNY & CECIL—A Tale of Terror

No one had lived in the house for seventy years, the orchard being leased by neighboring farmers; the state of Pennsylvania had finally decided to sell it after much deliberation as to whether they should classify it as a historical site. There was something about the house that felt immediately like home to Joe and Marie. They saw the rest of their lives unfold before them, and it all happened right there.

The only problem with the house was minor—as far as they could see. The realtor had seemed reluctant to take them into the basement, saying, "It's a basement like any other," as they descended the staircase, and this had bothered them slightly. To make matters worse, the basement door was stuck so tight it had to be pried open. It was as if the realtor—as well as the house—had something to hide.

Joe had asked the realtor about the small, oddly shaped rocks that stuck out of the earthen floor of the basement like rotting teeth. One had "Nunny" written on it and the other, "Cecil." He had been hesitant to ask, afraid there were human bodies buried under the smooth dirt; Marie had encouraged him with a nudge to the ribs.

"Something buried there?" Joe had asked, pointing to the cursed things.

"Family pets," said the real estate agent, quickly steering them toward the new heating system.

They had already made up their minds to take the house, so Joe conveniently put those graves on his list of things to get rid of. He couldn't see anything wrong with disturbing the graves of some old, faithful pets, and he wondered why the state hadn't cleared them out before showing the house; at least they could have removed the tombstones. No one would have ever known.

He had given serious thought to getting rid of the graves when Denise was about five years old and beginning to get curious about the big house. Marie had caught her pulling up a chair to reach the lock on the basement door. Joe had gone downstairs, plucked the stones out of the ground, and thrown them into a basement closet; but he had procrastinated about completing the ugly part of the task, and now, thirty-five years later, it had to be done.

Joe's back screamed with the first shovel full of earth. He wished he had performed the loathsome task as a man of thirty instead of sixty-five. He felt the shovel hit something soft, and the hair on his head and body rose in a standing salute. On closer inspection, Joe found it was a blanket. *Good,* he thought, digging around the thing; *Maybe I won't have to see the bones.* When he uncovered the entire blanket, he picked it up carefully by both ends to avoid spilling the contents.

"Damn it!" he swore, as the bones spilled out onto the dirt making soft, unpleasant sounds. He realized with disgust that the blanket had rotted through. *Been here for a long time.* He found an old pair of gardening gloves, stiff from the dried mud ingrained in the fabric. He put them on and moved his hands around to loosen up the stiff fabric. He picked up the bones and tossed them into the plastic garbage bag, trying not to look at them. *No wonder I've put this off for so long*, he thought; *it's one hell of a nasty job. These bones must be ancient*, he thought, adding the thirty-five years he had lived in the house to the seventy that it had been vacant.

Something was terribly wrong with the bones. His first thought upon seeing them was that some sentimental old fool had insisted upon being buried with his dogs; but the grave was missing a human skull, containing only two distinctly canine skulls, much larger than the skulls of any ordinary domestic dogs. It didn't take long for Joe to figure out that they were wolf skulls—extraordinarily large wolf skulls.

Something cold and wet dripped down onto his arm, startling him; he jumped back, looking up at the low ceiling. He couldn't see any moisture; he took off his gloves and reached up to feel the wooden beam. There was no sign of a dripping fluid of any kind. He brushed his hand over the short gray bristles of his hair. He felt foolish when he realized that it was his own perspiration that had dripped onto his arm. A cold sweat had sprung out on his forehead when he'd noticed that the bones in his basement had never belonged to any domestic animal. They were the bones of wolves, but it didn't take an expert to see the bones weren't from any kind of normal wolves. He had once found the weathered bones of a neighboring farm dog out in the orchard, but these were somehow different—very different. He forced himself to examine the remainder of the bones. The spine, the ribs, and the pelvic bones all appeared to be human, but the rest were all canine bones.

He had a tremendous urge to throw everything down and make a run for it. He began whistling again. The tune of "Strangers in the Night" emerged from his dry lips. He would not allow himself to think; he wouldn't be able to finish the job if he did.

Joe threw all the mutant bones into the plastic garbage bag and began shoveling the tainted soil back into the hole. He noticed a small bundle in the loose, rank-smelling mound of earth. He didn't want to pick it up; he didn't think he could stomach any more grisly discoveries; but his curiosity won the argument with his fear, and he angrily grabbed the sack, shaking it free of the heavy, clump of earth that clung to it. *It can't be any worse than what I've already found,* he thought—*or could it?*

It was a small, rotted cloth sack, sewn shut and containing hard, little pieces of something. It clicked and clacked when he shook it, reminding him of a talisman used in some voodoo ritual. A tiny yellowish object fell out of a hole in the sack. Joe picked it up and examined it carefully. It resembled a tooth, but he couldn't figure out what it was. He impatiently ripped open the sack and emptied its contents into one gloved hand.

He studied them closely for a moment and then said, "Bird bones." He threw them into the bag with the others, feeling slightly relieved that they appeared to be the bones of a normal bird.

He quickly finished filling the hole and smoothed the earth into place. There was a sag in the perfectly level earthen floor—*as if something important is missing,* Joe thought.

Joe carried the heavy, bone-filled bag and the shovel up the stairs, trying to make as little noise as possible; he stood on the top step and listened at the door for his wife. He didn't want her nosing around in that bag. She would fly out of the house and never come back. For an instant he thought about opening the bag to check the bones again, to see if maybe he'd been wrong. But he knew what he'd seen, and the hard and ugly facts he had been trying to smooth over hit him like an avalanche, almost sending him crashing through the door from fear. They weren't the bones of any family pets he had ever seen, and though he wasn't a religious man, he prayed that they weren't the bones of any family pet he would ever see.

GAILA SWINDELL

1

Denise peaked nonchalantly into her rear-view mirror, trying to move just her eyes and not her head; she didn't want to appear nervous. Her heart slowed its rapid pace when she saw that the police car that had been tailing her was nowhere in sight. She pushed her foot down harder on the accelerator. She wanted to make it to the farm by five o'clock, as she had promised her parents; as usual, she was running late. Adam and Amy had begged her to stop for everything from roadside pumpkin patches to milkshakes and the bathroom.

She drove along the back roads to try to keep the kids interested, but they were long past bored with the scenery of dead corn stalks waiting to meet the sharp blades of the combine. Hills swelled in the distance. Women wearing simple dresses, their hair knotted under white bonnets, worked in the yards.

The sun was a dim orange glare in the sky, and Denise was thankful for its presence. Even though the kids were bored with the simple beauty of the countryside, she appreciated the rolling pastures and sighed with pleasure at the sight of the scenery she had grown up with.

"Isn't it my turn to sit in the front seat, Adam?" Amy said.

Adam looked anxiously at his mother. He wasn't adjusting to his parents' divorce as well as his sister was, and he was getting special treatment because of it.

"We're almost there, Amy. Put your headphones back on and hold tight," Denise told her.

NUNNY & CECIL—A Tale of Terror

A huge black bird careened into the speeding car's path, and Amy screamed "Mom!" Denise swerved to the right to miss it, but it was too late. An "Oomph!" was forced out of her as she came to an abrupt stop and her chest slammed into the steering wheel. Her head jerked backward and she wrenched her neck. The car had lurched over the enormous bird's body, almost sending the car out of control. A moment of total silence passed. Denise felt a cold hand of fear squeeze her stomach, a much more gut wrenching fear than the slight accident should have elicited.

This is a sign, an omen, she thought. *Remember what the doctor said, Denise: you must not cloud your head with irrational thoughts. Keep it clean.*

"Mommy! I hit my head on the window!" Adam wailed, holding his hand to his forehead.

Denise turned off the car's engine and examined her son's head as he cried all the harder. He was getting some attention, and he intended to milk the moment. He did have a slight bump on the right side of his forehead where his head had hit the window.

"It'll be all right. We'll be at Grandma's in just a little while, and then we'll put some ice on it," she said, kissing the little bump lightly, trying to hide her anguish at the sight of it.

Amy hadn't said a word; she just stared silently at her little brother. Her face was becoming red and puffy.

"Mom, what did we hit? What was that big black thing?" she finally burst out.

Denise could hear Amy's breathing become shallower. She knew that within seconds Amy would hyperventilate, something she had inherited from Denise, and right on cue, Amy began gasping for breath.

"Let's go now, Mom!" Amy grabbed Denise's shoulder and shook it furiously.

"In a minute. Calm yourself, honey," Denise told her.

She thought about the bird: there was something strange about it—besides its extraordinary size; she had to find out what it was. "I'll be right back. I'm going out to see if I can do something to help the bird," she lied. She loved animals—swerving to miss the bird was the cause of her predicament—but the thought of touching a bleeding, mangled bird made her stomach heave.

"No, Mom, no!" Amy wailed. "Let's just go!"

Amy had noticed something too, but that didn't surprise Denise; she noticed everything. Denise wondered if she should get out of the car to look at the ominous bird; maybe it wasn't such a good idea. *Oh, cut the nonsense, Denise; an oversized raven isn't going to hurt you.*

"You kids lock the door when I get out. I'll just be a minute."

"Why do you want us to lock the door, Mommy? Something bad is going to happen, isn't it? And then you'll never come back!" Amy howled.

"Then don't lock it! That's it, no more horror novels for you, Amy," she said. "Nothing is going to happen. I promise! I don't want to leave the bird here to die. Now calm down," she told them. "I'll be back in the car in four minutes. You can time me. You have your breathing under control, Amy?"

"I'm getting there. Just hurry up!"

Denise opened the door and got out. She circled the car and then looked under it. No bird. She was a few feet into the cornfield when something rustled the dry, dead stalks just ahead of her. The desolation of the cornfield, dead stalks still standing, was hypnotic. Row after row of the dirty gold plants, their gnarled roots holding onto the soil for dear life even in death, beckoned her on, deeper into the field. It was like a maze. *If I move too far into the center of this field of death, I will never find my way out.*

"Mom, four minutes is up!" Amy called, breaking the spell. Denise turned around and walked back to the car. Amy pushed the door open when she saw her mother approaching. "Hurry, Mom!"

"Cool it, you two. The big, bad bird is gone," she said, but she wasn't convinced. She was afraid her voice conveyed her uncertainty.

She wondered what had happened to the bird. She hadn't seen it fly away. *It must have crawled off, far, far away, into the cornfield to die,* she thought.

When they had driven about a mile down the road, she had a flashback of the bird's face as it careened toward the car. *My god,* she thought with a shudder—*the thing had no beak!*

NUNNY & CECIL—A Tale of Terror

2

Denise drove the car off the road, through the heavy iron gates that were pushed permanently open in a gesture of welcome, and onto the leave-matted, gravel-strewn driveway that led to her childhood home. The house had never looked so good to her. Its thick stone walls always made her feel safe and secure. She noticed someone running up to the house from the apple orchard. "Look out there! That must be Grandpa," Denise said, pointing toward the orchard.

The front door flew open, and her mother came hurrying out, drying her hands on a dishtowel.

"What brings you out to this neck of the woods?" Joe said in mock surprise, pushing a wheelbarrow toward them. "It's a darn good thing Grandma put some extra dumplings in the pot or you'd be out of luck," he said, picking Amy up off the ground in a burly hug.

Denise hugged and kissed her parents as if it had been years since she had seen them, when actually it had been only three months. She remembered sitting with them in a Philadelphia restaurant for a lunch that had barely been eaten. She had broken the news to them about the divorce, and by the looks on their faces, she'd broken their hearts.

"What's this? Suitcases? Looks like you're planning to stay a while," Joe said, heaving their suitcases into the blanket-covered wheelbarrow.

"We're coming to live with you, Grandpa. Didn't Mommy tell you?" Amy said with a worried look on her face.

"Of course, sweetheart. I was just kidding," he reached down and kissed Amy, and then picked up Adam, setting him on top of the suitcases in the wheelbarrow. "You're going to have more fun than you can handle, living with your old grandpa. Your grandma's getting old, you know, and she's not so much fun anymore."

"Grandpa, Grandma, we had an accident!" Amy told them breathlessly. "A giant black bird flew right in front of us, and we ran it over."

Marie's hand flew to her mouth. "What happened, Denise?" she asked.

"Some stupid bird flew in front of the car. I ran it over. Adam got a slight bump on his head when I tried to swerve around it," she told them, deliberately leaving out some of the details about her neck—and the bird.

"Oh, my! Let's go in the house and put some ice on that bump," Marie said, reaching out to take Amy's hand. "How about you, Amy? You okay?"

"Yes, Grandma. I was just scared."

"Well, you're safe and sound here at the house," she told her granddaughter, shepherding her toward the house.

Denise watched her father pushing Adam in the wheelbarrow and her mother walking hand-in-hand with Amy. She was happy to be there, breathing in the clean, orchard-scented air. The peacefulness of the countryside would do them all some good.

3

After dinner, the family sat down to talk and relax.

"Are you kids ready for your new school on Monday?" Marie asked the kids, who both sat curled against their mother's body.

"I can't wait, Grandma!" Amy said. "It'll be neat meeting some new friends!"

"I don't want to meet any stupid friends. We'll just have to leave them soon, anyway," Adam said.

"But, Adam, it will be so exciting. Maybe you'll even meet a new girlfriend," Denise teased.

"Maybe someone prettier than Samara Peters," Amy added.

"I don't want to meet anyone! Why should I make friends when I'll have to leave them soon? I hate everyone, so just leave me alone!" he shouted, jumping up from where he sat and then pounding up the stairs.

There was silence, as everyone looked at each other with a shocked expression.

"He'll come around. Don't worry! He's just under a lot of stress," Joe said.

"I hope so. With the stress I've been under, I really need him to be the good kid he's always been. He's been so moody!" Denise told them with a sigh.

"We'll unload his toys out of the car in the morning. That should make him feel more at home. Don't you think?" Joe asked Denise.

"I hope so, Dad," Denise answered. She was exhausted and really didn't want to talk any longer. She just wanted to sit there and meditate. Everyone seemed to sense this; talk slacked off as Marie switched on the television and they all became engrossed in a show that was on.

Denise wasn't going to let Adam's tantrum get to her; she thought his outburst was probably caused by exhaustion. She felt warm and secure for the first time in months.

Her father nodded off in his recliner. His head repeatedly fell slowly forward and then jerked back up, as he emitted a soft snoring sound.

The hardwood floor in the foyer was still shiny. The floral-patterned carpet was worn and threadbare in high-traffic areas; no prodding from Denise had ever convinced them to invest in a new one. Pretty lace curtains hung starkly white against the dark wood window frames.

This was home to Denise, someplace she would always be wanted and cared for. There were few bad memories, no ugly threats lurking in the shadows, and best of all, not a whisper of her ex-husband anywhere. Reminders of a happier time in her life surrounded her. She went up to bed trailing her hand along the smooth wooden banister, the way she had hundreds of times before, feeling as though she never wanted to leave the comfort of the old house again.

NUNNY & CECIL—A Tale of Terror

4

Denise pulled the covers up under her chin and settled into the same lumpy, old bed she had slept in as a child. She turned on the lamp on the bedside table and searched the room with her eyes, taking comfort in the familiarity of her childhood possessions.

Her worn-out, floppy-eared bunny that she could never sleep without as a child drooped over the rocking chair that had once been her grandmother's. The mauve, flowered wallpaper had faded, but was still pretty.

She reached over and turned off the light. She closed her eyes, and her mind began to race with thoughts.

"Just cut it out!" she told herself in a whisper. She jumped up and grabbed the old bunny, hoping it would offer some comfort. Denise wanted to fall asleep in a hurry; she needed to be well rested for the following day. She had agreed to meet with a group of her students at the university, even though it was a Saturday. Denise hated to work on a weekend; but she had been taking too much time away from her work to straighten out her personal life. She felt she owed it to her students to spend a Saturday with them; she was never available after class.

Denise attempted to wipe the slate in her head clean. She felt her body going limp, all the tension of the day easing out of her muscles. Thoughts floated into her mind. Moving in with her parents had been the best move she had made since her decision to get the divorce; she needed a drastic change of environment.

She felt like Donald had ripped her heart from her chest and buried it in the dirt without so much as a coffin. If she hadn't had the mental breakdown that had landed her in the psychiatric ward for several weeks, maybe then she'd feel stronger. The breakdown had hurt her more than Donald had: it had made her aware of the vulnerability of her mind and spirit.

At least now Donald was far away, working in London. She tortured herself—again—with the memory of his infidelity: she'd surprised him in his car with "the other woman." Denise's hands had locked into tight fists, her fingernails digging into her palms so hard they drew blood. He'd been lucky she wasn't carrying a weapon.

Her painful thoughts had gone around and around in her head, like a merry-go-round gone berserk, its plaster horses taking on lives of their own, jumping off and galloping into the night, taking screaming little children along for the ride. And like those merry-go-round horses, her mind developed a life of its own, over which she had no control. Her crazy thoughts had caused too many sleepless nights, finally sending her over the edge, into the murky shallows of what Dr. Crofford called a brief reactive psychosis.

Almost anyone, given the circumstances, might have reacted similarly—so the doctor said. After all, divorce was second only to a death of a spouse in the magnitude of stress on the life stress scale. If she had seen it coming, maybe she would have been even slightly mentally prepared; but she'd thought things had been good between them.

Dr. Crofford had emphasized the importance of her continuing to undergo therapy: "After a while the dust in the attic gets so thick you won't be able to breath up there; that's when the real trouble begins," he had warned. Denise had promised him she would continue to see him. And she would—when she found time. Right now she had to concentrate on starting a new life.

Donald became obsessed with winning her forgiveness. He had cried, pleaded, begged on his hands and knees, and threatened to commit suicide, but her answer to his groveling was always a firm "no!"

Enough of his guilty face, she thought. She thought instead of the handsome man who had said hello to her at the university earlier in the week. She just hoped he was a faculty member and not a student.

NUNNY & CECIL—A Tale of Terror

Denise wondered how Amy and Adam would handle her dating other men. She didn't think Amy would have a problem with it. She was always coming to Denise's rescue, saying, "Come here, Mom. You need a hug. You know what Bob Marley says, Mommy, 'Every little ting, is going to be alright.'" Her disheveled, blond hair and constant grin made her look like a wise little woodland elf. She already had all her books stacked in neat rows on a bookshelf in the corner of her room.

Denise thought about the way Adam had held her that night when she went in to kiss him good night. She had found him dozing in a pile of racecars and alien beings that her father had finally brought in from the car. From the way that he clutched onto her neck, holding on tightly when she tried to pull away, she guessed he feared she would disappear from his life, just as his father had.

She was sure the kids would be slightly disconcerted about her dating, especially Adam, but they would adjust. *They're going to have to, because there is no way that Denise Miller is going to go manless for any length of time.*

She heard her father coughing in the room across the hall. He was trying hard to hide his disappointment at her failed marriage, but she could see the pain in his cloudy blue eyes, which were almost hidden by a squint that had become increasingly worse with time. As unhappy as he was about the divorce, his childlike glee at having her and the kids move in was apparent. Denise knew that it was lonely around the farm for her parents. If they could have it their way, she and the kids would be moving in permanently. As soon as she regained her mental stamina, though, Denise planned on doing some house hunting. Her parents were her saving grace in her period of dire need, and she was extremely grateful to them, but she needed to get on with her life.

She tried again to clear her mind. Thoughts kept coming, creeping into her head, but after a while, they were deflected like bullets hitting a bulletproof vest, as she effortlessly blocked them. She felt her breathing slow down; then the subconscious material of sleep entered her mind. She was drifting, drifting, but through the fog of sleep she could hear a voice. It was Adam; he was trying to whisper but kept raising his voice.

She heard him say over and over again, "I don't want to kill my mom! Go away!"

These words entered into Denise's subconscious mind, and her dreams that night were nightmares of a most violent nature. She dreamed that Adam was chasing her down a never-ending staircase with a bloody straight razor in his hand, the kind Denise's father still used. There were words written in blood on the walls adjoining the staircase, but she was running too fast to read what they said. She knew that it was Adam only because it was his voice that emanated from the hideous, swollen, bloodied creature that was chasing her. She was running so fast down those stairs that she began to fly. She could hear the sounds of the razor slashing the air as Adam made the motions that he intended to use on her body. Denise could smell the sickeningly sweet odor of sweat mixed with blood, and she knew he would reach out and grab her at any moment. She felt her body growing heavy, and her pace down the staircase slackened. Her legs became rubbery and flopped out from under her. When Adam finally caught her by the hair with his slippery hands, he screamed, "You're a whore, and you deserve to die!"

She could hear the razor slicing the air as it approached her throat, and faster than the speed of that razor-bearing arm, she realized she was dreaming and forced herself awake.

A thousand tiny goose bumps raised their tiny heads upon her skin as she opened her eyes to find Adam sleeping next to her.

NUNNY & CECIL—A Tale of Terror

5

Adam woke up, and for a moment he wasn't sure where he was. Then he remembered the voices he had heard the night before in his room, and how he had crawled into bed with his mother. He was glad that she was already gone because he didn't want to tell her about the voices. He knew it would just upset her, especially if he told her what the voices were saying. He wasn't so sure he was going to like living with his grandparents.

The house they had just moved out of was brand new and didn't have a single creepy hiding place in it: its basement had been turned into a recreation room, and it had no attic. It had been a pretty boring house compared to this one, but at least it was safe. *Nowhere for monsters to hide,* he thought. He knew that in order to get over his fear of the old farmhouse he was going to have to explore every inch of it. He didn't want Amy tagging along; he wanted to find some places where he could go when he wanted to be alone. He thought of the barn with its dark windows, and an icy chill crawled up his back. Maybe he would ask Amy to explore the barn with him. It might have some wild animals in it, he thought, remembering the voices he had heard. Now, he was sure he must have been dreaming, but then, the night before, he had been very sure he was awake.

He decided to begin exploring the house that very day. He would start with the basement, and then work his way up to the attic. "I bet you've got some places in you where no one's ever been," he said aloud to the crack in the ceiling. He rolled over and began planning his strategy. He crawled under the covers and drew an imaginary map on the sheet with his finger. He dozed off and then woke up minutes later, startled by the feeling that someone or something was watching him. *I'll catch them,* he thought, looking quickly at the crack in the ceiling, but there was nothing there.

"What are you looking for up there?" a voice said, causing his heart to stutter. He turned to see his grandmother standing in the doorway. "I've been watching to see when you would stir," she said, coming in and enveloping him in her old lady perfuminess. He had never felt anyone quite so soft and warm—not even his mom, whose body was firm from exercise.

"Nothing," he said innocently.

"You can't fool me. I know what you were looking at. Your mother was always fascinated with that crack in the ceiling," she told him. "You get out of bed and go wash up sleepyhead," she said, giving Adam a little shove out of bed.

While Adam was brushing his teeth, a thought flashed in his head. What his grandmother had said about the crack in the ceiling made him think: maybe the voices from the night before belonged to ghosts, and maybe *they* would be his friends.

Marie bustled around the kitchen with enthusiasm. She was thrilled at the opportunity to nourish her daughter and grandchildren. The house seemed to vibrate with life, as if it was waking up from a long sleep, stretching its stiff joints. She could almost hear it, creaking and groaning with pleasure.

NUNNY & CECIL—A Tale of Terror

6

"So, what do you two have planned for today?" Joe said, looking from one grandchild to the other. "Those apples are looking pretty ripe. How about you two go out there to pick them?" he asked.

"Do we get to climb up the ladder?" Amy asked excitedly.

"Sure do," Joe said, catching Marie's worried glance out of the corner of his eye. "As long as you're very careful," he added. The one thing Joe didn't need was to get Marie's ulcer going, and he knew that with the kids living there it would be working overtime. They had managed to bring up Denise, the wiry tomboy, without damaging her in any way, but now with two of them it might be a more difficult task. "We couldn't keep your mother out of those trees once the apples were ripe. Even before they were ripe, she'd sneak up there and eat so many of the green ones that she'd be up all night, howling with a stomachache."

The kids laughed at their grandfather's musings.

"She'd bring in bushels of those things, begging me to bake her an apple pie. She sure loved those apples," Marie said, a faraway look in her eyes.

"You almost finished with those pancakes, Adam? I've never seen anyone your size put away so much food. Last night at dinner I thought I might have to go out and kill another chicken the way you were eating up those legs," he teased.

"It must be the fresh air, Grandpa. Just the other day when we were still at our house, Mom was getting worried because Adam wouldn't eat," Amy said.

A deep furrow creased Adam's brow at the mention of his old house; and then he gave Amy a dirty look. An uncomfortable silence filled the room.

"Well, let's get going before the birds peck up all our apples," Joe told them, trying to ease them back into a cheerful mood. He got up from the table and grabbed his hat from the rack. He stuck the hat on Adam's head and reached a hand out to each child. "Shall we pick?" he asked, and the tension instantly dissipated.

The autumn day was bright and crisp. Joe inhaled the fresh scent of ripe apples and clean air, his body tingling as the oxygen mixed with his blood. The sound of Amy's laughter was almost tangible, crackling in the air like electricity.

"Look, Grandpa," she said, pointing to a group of sun-glossed apples. "The sun's pointing out the pretty ones to me."

Joe had seen Adam sneak away through the trees almost as soon as they arrived in the orchard. He had opened his mouth to ask the child where he was off to, but then quickly closed it, deciding that it was none of his business. The boy was going through a difficult period and would need some special attention, even when that meant leaving him alone.

He and Marie were going to have their hands full keeping the two kids entertained. There weren't any houses for miles around, and the closest homes contained Amish people who, although they were sufficiently friendly, didn't allow their children to play with the non-Amish. Joe held the ladder firmly, looking up at his granddaughter. The sun shining in her pretty blond hair made him experience a moment of deja vu: he had stood in the exact same place holding the ladder for Denise many a time, so that she could pick Jezebel's apples. Jezebel had always been their favorite picking tree. She produced the sweetest, juiciest apples, sprouting them on the branches that were easy to reach.

"Grandpa, if I stand on my tiptoes up here, I can see the top of the barn," Amy said, breaking into his thoughts.

"I wouldn't do that if I were you. You'll get your old grandpa in trouble," he told her. "If Grandma comes out here and sees you standing on your tippy toes up there on that ladder, she'll have a hissy."

"What are those pretty decorations on the barn?" Amy asked. "Are they new? I don't think I noticed them before."

"Folks around here call those hex signs, Amy. The Pennsylvania Dutch claim those signs help ward off evil."

Do you think they ward off evil, Grandpa?"

"Evil isn't something that just comes around looking for you," he told her, "it exists inside the human heart."

Amy gave him a funny look, making him feel foolish for waxing heavy on her, and returned to her picking.

Speaking of evil, Joe thought of his ex-son-in-law; a pang of pain shot through his heart. Joe Rodman had made it through his entire life without wishing ill will upon anyone, but now Donald Miller had come along and changed all that. The way Donald had deceived Denise made Joe want to kill him. It wasn't only Denise that he had deceived, but also his two beautiful children.

Joe couldn't bring himself to think about Denise's breakdown—not even for a moment. He knew that if he did think about it, he would kill Donald. Joe was glad that Denise had decided to come home. It had broken his heart when she had gone off to college, but he had always known that there would come a time when he would have to let her go. She was a good daughter, though, always writing or calling them, and coming home to visit every chance she had.

Joe hadn't liked Donald from the beginning. He was too quiet, kept everything inside. He wasn't warm, and friendly only to that point where Joe couldn't call him unfriendly. *It's people like him—the ones who keep everything inside—who you have to watch out for,* Joe thought.

7

Adam approached the back door, moving swiftly, slyly. *That stupid girl,* Adam thought, *she's always saying the wrong thing. She had to go talking about our old house.* He kicked at the dirt. He did not want to think about his father, or all the friends he had left behind. Adam commended himself for sneaking away from his grandfather and sister so deftly. He had more important things to do than pick apples; besides, he felt a strong aversion to his sister that morning.

He peeked inside the window to see his grandmother standing at the kitchen sink, her back toward him. He decided to wait around for a few minutes until she left the room; then he would make his move, through the kitchen, into the basement.

He couldn't wait to begin his exploration of the house. The voices he had heard the night before both intrigued and frightened him. He would find out who they were and where they were hiding; he would be a hero. He had pondered the mystery all during breakfast; he was convinced that the voices had not been heard in a dream.

He reviewed the events of the night before. He had been nearly asleep when an awful smell had roused him. It was the worst thing he had ever smelled in his life, worse than the dead animal he and Evan Jambroski had found in their fort; it had burned the inside of his nose—the same way the smell of a match did when it was lit too close to his face. His father had told him it was the sulphur in the matches that burned his nose. And then came the voices—yes, he remembered it all so clearly now. He hadn't been dreaming at all.

His reverie was broken when the screen door flew open, and his grandmother came out carrying a bundle of throw rugs in her arms.

"What's wrong? You come back in to use the bathroom?" she asked him.

"No, Grandma. I was just exploring," Adam said, hurrying past her and onto the porch.

"Wait a minute!" she said, causing him to stop dead in his tracks. "Just where do you plan to go exploring?"

"Down in the basement, first. I thought I'd start with the house and work my way out to the barn. Can I?" he asked trying to sound as innocent as possible.

"Well, I do want you to be comfortable with this old place," she told him. "The old gal really gets to creaking and moaning sometimes when the wind picks up."

"Does it ever sound like someone's talking to you?" Adam asked.

"No, she never does any talking, just a lot of grumbling when her arthritis kicks in," she said. "You go in and sit down at the table for a minute; I'll shake out these rugs and then I'll pack a lunch for the great explorer to take on his trip. Ham or turkey?"

"But, Grandma, I'm not hungry," he told her. He went inside and sat down at the kitchen table anyway; he would get out of there quicker if he went along with her plan. He was impatient to get going because he was afraid Amy would come back and want to go with him. Finally, after what seemed like a year to him, his grandmother came in. "I'll have ham," he told her, having given it careful thought. He didn't want to wait while she carved a turkey.

She swept through the kitchen like a whirlwind. She was so much faster than his mother. He tapped his foot impatiently, as he watched her prepare his lunch. She put everything into an old gray backpack that looked like it was ready for the garbage can, tucked in a flashlight, and handed it to him with a smile.

"Wait one minute," she said and began rummaging through a drawer. She pulled out a frazzled map of Cooks County and added it to the contents of the backpack. "In case you get lost."

"Thanks, Grandma," he said, smiling. She reached down and gave him a kiss, and he was off on his adventure.

Adam wished he had worn a sweatshirt, as a damp chill crept slowly into his body. It didn't take long for him to decide that he didn't like the basement: the air seemed thin, making Adam feel like he couldn't get enough oxygen; there was a powerful smell of fresh dirt and minerals. The bright lights made him uneasy, making him feel as though he was under the spotlight of the enemy. He used the flashlight as a spider web destroyer, swinging it back and forth, pretending he was on safari, cutting a path through the African jungle with his machete. He moved silently and cautiously around the basement, testing the dirt walls for secret doors—a trick he had learned from spy movies. He looked timidly into the dark closets and cupboards, his confidence building each time he opened a thin plank door to find merely old tools, jars, and fruit crates and not the scary monsters he feared. He wouldn't dare venture into any of the closets, though; nothing looked interesting enough for him to risk confronting the unknown. He used the dim beam of his flashlight to peer into the darkest corners.

   The basement brought back memories of the time his friends had dared him to run through the sewer pipe that ran under the highway bordering the subdivision where he used to live. He had worked up the courage to go in, but had only traveled about ten feet into the pipe when he stepped on a dead animal, sending him running out, screaming.

   He was almost sure there would be no dead animals here—some spiders and crickets for sure, but nothing to be too worried about.

   What's that? he wondered, as the beam of his flashlight illuminated two large, gray lumps. The lumps intrigued him, but they were stuck far in the back of a very deep closet, which meant he would have to go in to inspect them. Adam pondered this for a moment; finally, his curiosity won out over his fear, and he decided to go in. He looked around the basement for something he could use to prop the door open. He didn't want to be in there for even a second with the door closed. His eyes settled on a rusty, metal footstool across the room.

   "Anyone in here?" he asked, scanning every inch of the closet. He imagined that the closet was a cave in the side of a mountain, and he was an archaeologist uncovering ancient ruins of a lost civilization. *If only I had a pick and shovel,* he thought, pretending to fight off vampire bats. He postponed entering the "cave" by hunting around the basement for a pick and shovel, or something similar. He found a saw with the blade nearly rusted through and a broom. They would do. In the back of his mind, he reasoned that at least he would be able to use them for weapons.

On his way back to the "cave," he tripped and fell in the dirt, almost doing himself in on the old rusted saw.

"Darn it!" he whispered loudly, standing up and dusting himself off. He looked back to see what he had tripped over: it was a long, thin, yellowish-white thing. Adam picked it up and examined it. It looked like an oversized chicken leg bone.

"Wow!" he said. He couldn't figure out what kind of animal it had come from, but he was in awe of the fact that he'd actually found a bone. He was the famous archaeologist, Professor Adam Miller. He turned around to the imaginary group he was leading into the cave and said bravely, "Stay back. I'll go in alone." With the saw in one hand, the flashlight in the other, and the bone and broom tucked awkwardly under his arm, he made his way in. He was no longer the brave Professor Miller, but only the frightened child, Adam Miller. The closet had a peculiar smell that the rest of the basement didn't have; as it burned his nostrils, he realized that it was the same odor he had smelled the night before. He felt like he'd been stung by a swarm of bees the way every hair on his body sprang up. *This is where they live.* He wanted to turn and run, but he closed his eyes, gritted his teeth, and summoned all his courage. He had to stay and find out who had talked to him the night before.

He knelt down on the damp, hard surface of the earthen floor and brushed the cobwebs off the gray objects. He gently pulled them out of the corner to examine them more closely and found they were light enough for him to pick up. They were large, square, flat stones. Each one had a word printed on it in black paint and an encrustation of dirt bordering the bottom edge, as if it had once been stuck in the ground as a marker of some kind. One read "Nunny" in large black letters and the other, "Cecil." Adam wondered what the words meant and what the rocks had been used for.

He looked at them for a few seconds, wondering what he could use them for, when he suddenly remembered standing in front of his Grandma Miller's tombstone. The realization of what he was holding in his hands came to him with a sickening jolt of horror; he threw the stones back into the corner with a force that broke them into pieces. He grabbed the flashlight and backpack and ran faster than he had ever run in his short life, up the basement stairs, into the warm safety of the kitchen.

8

"Professor Miller, why are we spending so much time on Freud?" Lenny Delenko asked.

Denise and her students sat around a large round table, going over whatever the students were having problems with. They missed the extra time she used to spend with them; and they had spent the entire study session firing questions at her that it would have taken months for her to answer adequately. Everything had been running smoothly, but leave it to Lenny, he had to question the curriculum. As usual, if there was something he was having problems with, he wanted no part of it.

"What's your major, Lenny?" Denise asked him.

"Psychology," he said.

"So you think I'd let you go off into the world without a thorough knowledge of Freudian theory. It would be like sending you into battle without teaching you how to fire a gun," she told him. And then in a funny voice she said, "Freud is fundamental," getting a laugh from the class and even a smile from Lenny. "Seriously, though, I'm here to teach you about Freud, because Freud is part of the study of psychology, and I am a psychology teacher. Have I answered your question satisfactorily?" she asked.

"Yes, you have. I'm going out to get a Coke, can I get anything for anyone else?" he asked. People began to fumble in their pockets and purses for change.

"It's time for a break. I'll see you all back here in about fifteen minutes," Denise told them, rising from her chair and stretching.

Lenny made for the door, and she quickly fell into step beside him.

"Lenny, are you really having that much of a problem understanding Freud? Or is it just that you don't agree with his theories?"

"I don't know, Professor Miller. To be honest, I just don't like the guy. He has a warped mind, or I should say he *had* a warped mind. I mean everything is sex, sex, sex! I'm sure there are some idiots out there who want to make it with their mothers, but those kinds of people have to be really sick. Like, every time I have a dream about flying to the moon in a rocket, does that mean I'm dreaming about my penis, or for that matter, someone else's penis? It really gets to me after awhile, you know?" he implored.

They arrived at the lunch trucks and stopped to decide which one to go to. Because it was Saturday, their choices were narrowed down to just a few.

"Can I buy you a falafel, Professor Miller?" he asked. "That truck over there makes a mean one."

"No, thanks, Lenny. I just want something cold to drink, with a strong dose of caffeine. I didn't sleep too well last night," she confessed. "If you'd like a falafel, I could get a drink from that truck."

"No, I'm not really hungry. I just want a Coke. I wanted to get you something to show my appreciation for you putting up with my crap all the time," he said, smiling good-naturedly at Denise.

"It's students like you who make teaching interesting," she said. He was a strange kid: she'd caught him looking at her in an odd way many times, studying her.

They bought a couple of Cokes, Lenny gallantly butting in to pay for hers, and slowly walked back to the classroom.

"Now it's my turn to be honest, Lenny: I don't like Freud either. He bugs the hell out of me. I totally agree that he puts too much emphasis on the sexual nature of human beings. It's true that we're all very sexual creatures, but he goes overboard. It's my job to teach his theories to you, and even though I don't care for them, I'm not going to give them short shrift. I'm sure I don't have to tell you how much he contributed to the field of psychology. Let me just say that without his work we'd still be in the dark ages," she told him.

Lenny looked disturbed.

"I don't think we can analyze our dreams in the same way he does. I don't believe that dreams have as much real meaning as he wants to give them. Hell, like what about people who don't even dream. Are they supposed to be really psychotic or really sane?" he asked.

"I'm not sure what Freud would say about it. That's a good question. But I believe everyone dreams; some people just don't remember their dreams," she told him, taking her place at the massive wooden table in her classroom.

Something about Freud was really bothering Lenny Delenko; Denise had a feeling it was based on something much deeper than what Lenny had revealed to her.

GAILA SWINDELL

9

Denise tried the front door, hoping it would be open so that she could run upstairs, change into comfortable clothes, and wash up before greeting her family. She stuck her key in the lock, but the door wouldn't open all the way: it was chained from the other side. *Since when did they start using that thing?*

She had used it once, as a girl of twelve, when she had heard that some prisoners had escaped from a North Carolina prison. Her mother had been angry when she'd come home to find the chain on the door, but laughed hysterically when Denise told her why she had chained it.

"Sweetheart, they'll never make it all the way up here to Pennsylvania," she had told Denise.

Denise rang the doorbell impatiently. She had noticed some movement in the upstairs window as she walked up the driveway. *Damn it! Why aren't they answering the door?* She set down her briefcase and hurried around to the back door, which was unlocked.

"Mom. Dad," she called out, making her way through the house to the front door to get her briefcase. There was no answer. *They must be taking a walk or something,* Denise thought. She looked around for a note, but didn't find one.

Denise ran upstairs. "Mom, Dad...Amy, Adam," she called out. As she undressed, she looked out of her bedroom window into the orchard. No one. She wondered if maybe she shouldn't have been so eager to have a few minutes of time to herself; she was slightly worried about where everyone was.

She sat down on the bed to take off her shoes, and remembered a book she had read twice; she shivered at the thought of it. It was Truman Capote's *In Cold Blood,* about a Kansas family who mistakenly thought they could leave their doors unlocked. It had been a fatal mistake. She quickly put it out of her mind; the book had scared the hell out of her.

She was a little disappointed that the kids weren't there to greet her when she arrived home, with a flurry of "Mommy, Mommy, guess what we did today!" She put on her robe and looked through the closet for something to wear. Some of her clothes were missing; she looked down to see that some her shoes were missing, too.

"All right. Who's playing games?" she asked of the empty house. She began to panic a little at the web of mysteries that she'd fallen into upon her arrival home. Her family had disappeared, they had left no note, and some of her clothes and shoes were missing.

It crossed her mind that Donald had come back from England, gone berserk, killed her parents, and kidnapped the kids. But reason told her that he liked himself too much to do such a thing.

She was thinking about how obsessed Donald had become with winning her back and wondering what extremes he might go to in his obsession, when she thought she heard a long, drawn out sigh of pleasure come from somewhere in the house. She knew it came from somewhere overhead, but she didn't want to focus in on it; she decided to pretend she had never heard it. With the funny superstition of a child, she thought if it was that monster up there looking at her through the crack, it would be better not to acknowledge its presence. It was something she had learned from her parents: *Don't acknowledge the monsters.* When she had told her father that she thought a monster lived above her bedroom, he had said something that she would never forget. She remembered his speech word for word: Monsters just want attention, Denise. If they know they can scare you, they will. So if you don't acknowledge the monsters, they'll go away and find someone else to scare.

Denise felt a sudden overwhelming urge to get out of the house. The flood of thoughts that she was trying to suppress was beginning to overflow the dam. She was scared, but she couldn't let herself think about it until she was fully dressed and could run out of the house clothed. This panic was nothing new to her; as a child she had often experienced it.

The wind in the trees outside her window would make one too many howling sounds, or the imaginary eyes peeking from the crack in the ceiling would stare down at her a bit too long, and she would be out of her bed in a flurry of blankets and into the safety of her parents' bed. While studying alone in the house, even as a college student, she would hear sounds—scratching in the walls, scurrying overhead, breathing under her bed—and she would fly down the stairs in a panic and out into the orchard searching for her father or mother. They both knew why she had sought them out without even asking; she gave herself away by being on the verge of hyperventilation. They would chastise her for her overactive imagination.

I must be losing it now. I'm a big girl, and big girls don't get scared—at least not of monsters, she thought. She threw on a pair of jeans and one of Donald's old flannel shirts, grabbed a pair of sneakers without stopping to put them on, and in seconds she was practically flying down the stairs.

The dream, the dream...don't think about it, don't think about it! Someone was behind her, or were they in front of her. She could hear breathing—loud, raspy. Three more steps to go—don't turn around. Suddenly, Adam was standing at the foot of the stairs, just as she made a bounding leap down the final three steps. They looked at each other with the terror of surprise in their eyes and braced themselves for the inevitable collision. Denise screamed as the force of her body threw Adam into the wall with a loud thud, and they crumpled—him crying more from fright than because he had hurt himself, her laughing with relief—into a heap on the floor.

NUNNY & CECIL—A Tale of Terror

10

Denise awoke to the smell of bacon and eggs wafting upstairs from the kitchen. She had slept long and deep, without the interruption of the nightmares she had suffered the night before. She still wasn't used to sleeping alone, and she felt the sense of emptiness she experienced every morning at not having a soft, warm body to wake up next to.

The day spread before her like a long cozy nap on a cold winter's day; she had nothing planned. She could lie there in bed all day if she wanted to. The sounds of little footsteps and whispering voices outside her room interrupted her thoughts.

"Darn it, Adam! You're going to make me spill this whole tray all over you if you don't cut it out!" she heard Amy whisper loudly.

"Grandma said we could both carry it, and now you're trying to hog it," Adam whispered even louder.

"She said we could both carry it *carefully*, and you're jerking it around," Amy told him.

Denise pretended she was asleep; she didn't want to spoil their surprise.

"Wake up, Mommy!" they said in unison. "We have a surprise for you."

Denise opened her eyes and acted surprised. "What a wonderful surprise! And to what do I owe this pleasure?" she asked, yawning.

"Grandma helped us cook this for you. We thought you deserved breakfast in bed for being such a good mom," Adam said, awkwardly clutching a corner of the tray.

The plate held pancakes drizzled with syrup, a heap of steaming scrambled eggs, bacon, orange juice, coffee, and even her vitamins.

"I'll be happy to accept your most gracious gift, if you would do me the honor of sitting with me while I eat, kind sir, and most gracious lady," she told them. "And where is this grandmother you speak of that you say helped make this bountiful feast?" Denise asked, as they planted the tray in her lap and their butts on the bed.

"She's downstairs cleaning up," Amy told her. "Grandpa said maybe we could go hiking in the woods today."

"Yeah, and hunt for salamanders and crawdads in the creek," Adam put in, his eyes bright and hopeful.

Denise thought it didn't sound like such a bad idea. She could empty her mind in the woods just as well as she could sitting in bed all day; in fact, it would probably do an even better job.

The family walked briskly through the orchard. In the distance lay low, rolling mountains. The sky was a clear gray; the air was fresh, cool, and invigorating.

The forest was thick with looming oaks, patches of pines, sycamores, and smooth white birch trees; from the end of the orchard, it stretched about two miles to the north, where a babbling creek bordered it. On the other side of the creek, the forest ran for about a mile north, but from that point on an Amish farmer's cornfield claimed the land.

The forest was dressed in multicolored autumn glory. The chipmunks and squirrels scurried about, preparing themselves for the winter by storing acorns in their homes and in their bellies. Birds squawked angrily at the human intruders. The family walked down the quiet wooded path, content to walk in silence. The comforting smell of dead leaves filled their nostrils.

Joe broke the spell with "Your grandma and I haven't been out here in a while. Seems like just yesterday it was ninety degrees and too hot to breathe. Besides, she's getting too old to be roaming out in the woods."

"Joe Rodman, you just pipe down about me being old. You're the one who's always complaining about aching limbs. Take me out hiking in the woods any day!" Marie exclaimed.

"Grandma, I think you look young and very pretty," Adam told her, a shy smile on his lips.

"Well, thank you, Adam. It takes young eyes to be able to see beauty clearly," she told him, grabbing his hand and kissing it.

"Ah, Marie, you know you're the sunshine in my sky," Joe said, giving her a hug.

"Grandpa and Grandma used to take me hiking through these woods every Sunday," Denise said. "Grandma would pack a lunch and Grandpa would carry it in a backpack. Isn't it beautiful out here?" She surveyed her little family, feeling like there was someone missing.

She searched the woods for the trees that had always been her favorite. When she was a child she had planted a Japanese maple in a little clearing about a mile from the creek; it served as a marker to show her how much longer she had to go to get there. Not that she wouldn't have known how far along on the path she was without the Japanese maple: Denise knew every fallen log, every curve, and every tree along that path to the creek. She had called it "Heaven Creek" when she was a girl, even though it's name was Willard's Creek; she believed that if there was a heaven, it looked like the forest along that creek.

Whenever she was afflicted with growing pains, her father would suggest a hike. She would reluctantly put on her hiking boots, not wanting to do anything but sit in her room and sulk, and she and her father would go off into the woods, fishing poles in hand.

The slow deliberate walk out to the creek, her father pointing out little things along the way—a new bird nest, a fallen tree, or some odd fungus growing on a rotting log—and sitting on the creek bank with her line in the water for hours would give her time to think or to forget, and she would feel miraculously better when she arrived home.

Adam delayed their progress now and then by stopping to try to catch a chipmunk that had scurried into a termite-eaten log at the sound of their approaching footsteps, or turning over logs to look for salamanders in the moist ground underneath.

"Where's the creek?" Adam asked impatiently. He was clearly frustrated at not having been able to catch the little creatures. "The salamanders and crawdads should be easier to catch than the chipmunks, don't you think Grandpa?"

"They don't move as fast as you do, Adam. I'm sure you'll be able to catch a few. I'd say we've got a little more than a mile to travel," Joe answered. "I've traveled this path at least a thousand times, Adam, but you're making me feel like it's all brand new again. In the spring we'll go trout fishing at the creek. You should see the beauties we pull out of there. Your mother's caught many a trout in that stream," he told them.

"Oh, Mom! Did you put worms on the hook and everything?" Amy asked in disgust.

"Sure did. Your grandpa taught me everything he knows, worm hunting and handling included," Denise said, laughing as Amy squealed with revulsion.

"Here's my tree!" Denise exclaimed, in awe at the size of her creation. "Look how big it's grown. Mom, Dad, do you think it's full grown?" It was wearing its autumn red coat of leaves. The sight of it almost brought tears to her eyes, as she pictured her innocent little self, digging the hole to plant it on her fifth birthday. Her mother had packed a special birthday lunch, complete with cupcakes and candles, and the trio had hiked out toward the woods, Denise dragging the shovel part of the way, her father carrying it the rest.

Seeing it made her feel whole again, like the girl she had been when she planted it. It was strong and healthy and beautiful, making her feel that there were still some things in life she could depend on.

"Mom, I can't believe you planted this tree. It's really pretty!" Amy's said. "I want to plant one, Mom, right next to this one. Can I?" she asked.

"Me, too!" Adam chimed in, jumping up and down. "I want to plant a giant tree like that one," he said pointing to a tall oak.

"Next time we come, we'll come on a tree-planting expedition. I'll pack a special tree-planting lunch, and we can make a day of it," Marie told them.

"There's your grandma for you, always thinking of food," Joe pointed out.

"Oh, and you're not?" Marie quipped. "Come on along. Now we know we have exactly one mile to the creek. Let's move it troops!"

When they reached the creek, Joe pulled a large, careworn quilt out of his backpack and spread it on the bank. Marie sat down on the blanket and emptied her backpack: five individual containers of apple juice, an aged Gouda cheese, rice crackers, and five Macintosh apples.

After they had their snack, Joe showed the kids how to find salamanders, crawdads, snakes, worms, and bugs of all kinds. They turned over the rotted logs that lay along the creek, and then they sat down to rest before they made the long hike back.

NUNNY & CECIL—A Tale of Terror

"You kids better rest, now. The hike back always seems longer than the hike here," Marie told them.

"How far is it from here to the house, Grandma? About ten miles?" Adam asked.

They all laughed, causing Adam to turn bright red with embarrassment.

"No, sweetheart, just about two miles," she said giving him a pinch on the cheek.

"Does the creek come from the ocean?" Amy asked, encouraging another round of laughter.

"You kids are full of funnies today, aren't you? Willard's Creek is fed by springs up in the mountains and eventually makes its way to the Conestoga River" Joe told them. "Many generations of the Amish have fished at this creek. You'll see them here sometimes," he said, rising to indicate they should go.

He sighed with relief when they finally got back to the orchard; finally, he'd be able to rest his tired legs.

Adam turned over a big rock and jumped back with a grunt. Amy began to cry when she saw what was under the rock.

"Mom, Grandpa, what is that?" Adam said, his eyes wide and his voice quiet as he tried to conceal his shock. A huge, freshly decapitated rat lay there on the ground, it's body squashed so badly that its guts oozed out its neck socket into a puddle of crimson soup, teeming with feasting bugs.

"It's a dead rat some old coon must have killed," Joe uttered, placing the rock back on top of the rat.

He knew it was unlikely that a raccoon—at least a healthy one—would have done that deed; he was confused and a little nervous at the thought of what might have. There weren't many animals that killed just for the sake of killing, at least not in his neck of the country. A weasel might; they were vicious little varmints. One of the little beasts had dug into Jake Moyer's chicken coup and killed twenty-eight chickens before Jake's dog woke up and scared it off. It left a hell of a mess. But the rat's body looked bigger and stronger than any weasel Joe had ever seen. The only other possibility sent a shiver up his spine: a rabid animal would attack any animal that crossed its path, killing just to see the blood flow. He would check with his neighbors to find out if they'd noticed anything; he didn't want the kids out there if a rabid animal was on the loose.

There was too much to eat for the animals around there for them to stoop to eating the heads off rats. The surrounding fields were filled with corn that had fallen off the stalks at harvest and hadn't been cleaned up yet; his own orchards were littered with fallen apples. He didn't understand it, and it bothered him terribly, especially since the kids would be out there playing. He would have to keep a close eye on them. He didn't want to scare them by being overly cautious.

They were all tired, and the grisly discovery had dampened their spirits. As the group silently made their way through the orchard, Joe saw something that made his blood stop flowing: there were some kind of animal tracks in the dirt that were bigger than his own size thirteen foot. On another day he might have missed them, but his senses were sharpened by the gruesome mess he'd had just seen, and like radar, his eyes had zeroed in on the unfamiliar.

"Is that the old hoot owl that's been hunting mice around this place for the last couple of years?" he shouted, trying to keep the nervous quaver out of his voice. He wanted to get the children's perceptive eyes away from those tracks, so he made a slow jog toward where he pretended he saw the bird. Looking quickly at Marie, he could see she wasn't convinced.

They walked slowly back to the house, locking the door behind them after they entered.

The children played silently the rest of the day. Everyone was tired from the outing. Joe wondered if his family was having as much trouble as he was dislodging the morbid sight of the rat from their memories. After dinner, he slipped out the back door unnoticed, his measuring tape in hand, a pistol in his pocket.

Darkness descended on the orchard at an almost unnatural rate of speed. Joe quickened his pace; he needed every bit of light he could get. He had known he was forgetting something when he left the house: now that it was too late to turn back, he realized he needed a flashlight. He thought someone was following him; a rustling sound that was too loud and heavy to be a chipmunk came from behind him.

"Who's there?" he called out. "Amy, Adam...that you?" He hoped one of the children hadn't followed him out there.

He kept moving, his hand on the heavy, bulging gun in his pocket. Whenever he would turn around to see if anyone was following him, the suspicious rustling would stop. The wind began to pick up, blowing in from the North and making the walk a bit tougher on his old frame. He was already worn out from his hike in the woods earlier that day.

When Joe arrived at the edge of the orchard, he pushed his wire-rimmed glasses up on his nose and searched the ground for the animal prints he had seen earlier. In the back of his mind, a little voice said that he was a foolish old man for going out there in the dark without a flashlight—and without telling anyone where he was going. He didn't argue with the little voice; he just grasped the pistol in his pocket more firmly.

When he finally found the prints, it was almost completely dark. He knew he should take a quick look at them and get back to the house; Marie would get crazy with worry if she discovered he was gone.

He got down on his hands and knees to examine the prints. There were two sets of them, and they were huge: he measured thirteen-inches long on one pair and twelve on the other. They were wolf prints as far as he could tell; some unusually large wolves had made them. *Rabid wolves?* he wondered.

He heard Marie calling him, "Joe...Joe."

"Be right there," he yelled back. "Damn it," he swore; he realized that she must have walked fairly deep into the orchard for him hear her calling him, especially with that wind blowing her voice away from him. *What's she doing out here in the dark?* He knew she would give him hell when he got back to the house. He yelled, "Marie, you get back to the house right now!"

It wasn't the size of the prints that concerned Joe—he had seen some awfully big wolves in his day—nor was it the fact that wolves don't live in Cooks County, Pennsylvania. It was something far more inconceivable: there were no forepaw prints, only hind paw prints; they were spaced at a man's step apart—a long-legged man's step.

He remembered digging up the bones in the basement, an experience he had almost convinced himself hadn't happened. Joe heard a rustling in the trees where the forest met the orchard. He ran back to the house as quickly as his aching legs would take him.

Joe and Marie couldn't sleep that night. They lay next to each other, each thinking similar thoughts. Neither of them wanted to mention the prints, because that would only serve to confirm their existence.

When something was wrong, they often ignored it, hoping that it would go away.

Joe felt that this time the problem wouldn't fit under the rug, but he still didn't want to tell Marie about it. He didn't want her ulcer to start acting up. He knew they had finally encountered something that wasn't going to just go away if they ignored it.

"I saw those paw prints," she said, breaking the tense silence. "How big were they?"

"How would I know how big they were?" he told her.

"You left the tape measure lying on the kitchen counter."

"They weren't there, Marie," he lied.

"We're not going to pretend they weren't there, Joe. We're not going to play that game this time," she told him.

"Marie, I told you, they weren't there," he repeated. "I looked everywhere for them, but I couldn't see anything; it got dark too fast and I forgot to bring the flashlight out there with me. If you hadn't been so foolish and come out there yelling for me, I could've looked around a little longer," he told her, hoping that would shut her up; but it just made things worse.

"What are you talking about, Joe? I didn't come out there yelling for you. I didn't even know you were gone until you came back looking as if you'd seen the devil," she told him.

Joe Rodman had never believed in the devil, and he had spent most of his life trying to stay as far away from evil as he possibly could; but he was beginning to think that it had come looking for him. It was right there in his backyard. He just hoped that it wouldn't come knocking on his door.

NUNNY & CECIL—A Tale of Terror

11

With all the excitement of a new routine, the kids getting comfortable in a new school, and a brand new life, Denise had been so busy that she'd completely forgotten about her missing clothing for weeks, until one morning, she lurched out of bed with one thing on her mind: *Where are my clothes? She reached over and shut off the ugly static of the clock radio alarm. Where in the hell are my clothes?* She had gone to sleep the night before thinking about wearing a certain skirt the next day; she had even dreamt about wearing it. She had forgotten that some of her things were missing, but her subconscious mind hadn't forgotten; it served her a reminder on a silver platter for breakfast that morning.

Maybe I just overlooked them, she thought, jumping out of bed and rummaging through her closet. But her skirt wasn't there, and some of her other things were missing, too. She pulled a piece of paper out of her dresser drawer and wrote her mother a note asking if she had seen the missing items. *Maybe she took them to the cleaners,* Denise reasoned; *she's always trying to clean everything.*

She heard her bedroom door squeak open, and her bleary-eyed mother entered the room.

"I heard your alarm go off. Can I make you something to eat?" Marie asked.

"No, thanks, Mom. I'll grab a bagel from one of the trucks at school. I'm sorry I woke you. I'll turn the volume down on my clock radio. You go back to bed now," Denise said, giving her mother a hug.

"You sure? It'll be no trouble at all for me to whip up an egg sandwich for you. You can eat it in the car on the way to school."

"Really, Mom, don't worry about me. I won't go without eating. You must have read my mind; I was just writing you a note. Have you seen any of my clothes lying around anywhere? I can't find some of my favorite things," Denise said.

"No, I haven't seen any of your clothes. Do you think you might have lost them in the move? Maybe they got stored away in boxes."

"No, I don't think so. Oh, well, be on the lookout for them, will you? I thought maybe you'd taken them to the cleaners or something crazy like that—the way you're always going into cleaning frenzies," Denise said.

"You're just lucky that you have such a clean mother. You have a nice day at work now. Don't worry about the kids, and please drive carefully," she said. "Oh, by the way, don't forget you have to be home early to take the kids to that Halloween party."

"How could I possibly forget? That's all they've talked about for the past month. I'll be here with horns on," Denise told her.

"Are you planning to dress up?" she asked. "I know Halloween has always been your favorite night of the year. I'll never know how that came to be; I think it must have come from your dad's side of the family—that love of the morbid."

"No, there's no surprise," Denise said, winking at her mother. "Everything I do is completely true to my morbid nature, and therefore, not a surprise."

"Don't get smart with me, dearie, or I'll turn you into an inchworm," Marie said. She kissed Denise on the cheek and cackled like a witch as she left the room. A second later she peeked her head back inside the room. "Denise?"

"Yeah, Mom?"

"I'm awfully glad you decided to come home for a while. I can't tell you how much it means to your dad and I to have you and the kids here. It gives new meaning to our lives."

"Thanks, Mom, and thanks for being so wonderful. I don't know what I'd do without you and Dad. You always come to my rescue, and you're always happy to do it. I just wish we'd come under different circumstances." Denise lowered her eyes, feeling the sting of tears.

"Just remember, Denise, things always get better. I'm so sorry about Donald. But you know you did the right thing. Your father and

I would have accepted whatever decision you would have made, but we both thought it best that you divorced him. Once the trust is broken, it can never be repaired. You're too good for him."

They hugged each other tightly. Marie squeezed Denise's hand, and then left her so she could get ready for work.

Denise pulled a pair of pants and a sweater out of the closet and laid them on the bed. Gathering her things together, she went in to take a shower. She looked at her morning face in the mirror and frowned. *Why do I look so terrible in the morning?* Donald had told her that one of the reasons he had married her was because she always looked beautiful in the morning.

She washed her hair and despised herself—and the world—for scheduling her class at nine a.m.; that meant she had to rise at five-thirty to get there on time—all because she had moved to the boonies. Denise wasn't a morning person.

Denise wondered what could have happened to her clothes. She had so much clothing stuffed in her closet; it wasn't that unusual for her to have trouble finding things. She often had to search hard, but she always found what she was looking for. This time they appeared to be gone. She turned off the shower and dried herself off with a thick, fluffy towel that smelled like home.

She slipped the sweater on over her head. As she smoothed it down over her body, she noticed it was covered in hair.

"What in the hell is this?" she asked aloud of the empty room. She took the sweater off and examined it more closely under the light. It was animal hair. She hadn't had a pet since her dog Sammy had died when she was eleven.

Denise was childlike in her excitement about Halloween. She pulled up the long, winding driveway at a speed that her father would disapprove of, sounding the horn of her car to get everyone's attention; she jumped out of her car and ran up to the door with a broom between her legs, disguised as a witch and shrieking.

Amy and Adam, partially dressed in their Halloween costumes, came racing down the steps to greet her. They stopped dead in their tracks when they saw Denise, their eyes wide with fright.

Denise burst out laughing at the looks on their faces: "Don't you know your own mother?" She chased them through the house on her broom, shouting "Double, double, toil and trouble, fire burn and cauldron bubble."

Amy and Adam laughed as they ran from her, but then Amy stopped suddenly and began to cry, "Mom, you're scaring me. Now stop it!"

Denise had to bite her tongue to keep from laughing. She remembered when she was a child and her father had dressed as Count Dracula for Halloween; a similar scenario had taken place. Part of her had known that it was her father in a costume, but then there was that other part that wondered if her father was not who she thought he was: a real vampire could have bit his neck in the middle of the night and turned him into a vampire.

Denise bent down to hold Amy in her arms, but Amy cried harder and ran to her grandmother, who had just entered the room.

"Denise, look what you've done; you've scared Amy!" her mother said.

"How do I know that's really Mom?" Amy said.

Denise pulled off her wig and hat, revealing her blond hair, and said, "Look, Amy, it's really me." She still found the episode extremely funny and had to force herself not to laugh.

"Come on, honey. I'll help you finish getting ready," Denise offered.

"I want Grandma to help me," Amy said. She was not acting like her usual brave self; but then, Denise was beginning to realize that although Amy was brave in the face of matters of the heart, she seemed to take a chicken stance when it came to matters seemingly supernatural. Denise decided it was because Amy read so many horror novels.

"Amy! Now, cut it out. Grandma's busy; besides, I want to talk to you," Denise told her. Denise held out her broom, and said, "Here, you can ride the witch's broom."

A bright smile slowly appeared on Amy's tear-stained face. She grabbed the broom, stuck it between her legs, and ran up the stairs laughing.

Denise turned to look at her mother, who gave her a look of mock disapproval and said, "I told you that you have a morbid side to your personality. Scaring your own child that way—now what would your father have to say about that."

NUNNY & CECIL—A Tale of Terror

They both laughed at the memory of a ten-year-old Denise being frightened out of her wits by her own father. She had avoided him for a good week after that incident.

Her father came in from the orchard just then.

"What would you say about that, Count Dracula?" she asked him.

"What would I say about what?" he asked.

"About dressing up in a costume and scaring your daughter?"

"Why, I'd say a person should be damned to hell for such a thing," he said.

Denise practiced her witch screams on Amy and Adam as they approached the school. The school held an annual Halloween party in the gym because many of the children lived too far out in the country to trick-or-treat from house to house.

Denise felt the kids were really missing out on the fun that came from trick-or-treating from house to house: walking the eerie, leaf-strewn streets at night, with only the street lights and the moon to light their way. The bushes took on strange and ghostly shapes, while the bare trees cast bizarre shadows across their paths.

And then there was the feeling of being at one with the mystery of the night; costumed as someone or something other than a child, walking hand in hand with phantoms and goblins.

Marie had been right in her observation that Halloween was Denise's favorite night of the year. It was the one night when she could pretend to be someone else. She had always nursed a secret desire to act, but opted for the more secure and more reliable career of a psychology professor.

Amy wore flowing white gauze, white face paint, and blue lipstick, her interpretation of Poe's dead Annabel Lee, and took a pedantic satisfaction in having to explain who she was to everyone: "You don't know who Annabel Lee is? Well, you should read the poem; it's by Edgar Allen Poe, my favorite writer."

Adam was dressed as a werewolf. It was the first Halloween that he had asked to dress as something other than his usual pirate. He was very precise in what he wanted his costume and makeup to look like. He said that he had recently watched a werewolf movie on TV, and he wanted to look exactly like the werewolf in the movie. Denise found it odd that he wanted only his head, hands, and legs to be those of a werewolf; he refused the fur suit his grandmother had offered to sew for him.

Denise pulled the car into the parking lot. No parking spaces were available, so she parked on a patch of dirt where the parking lot met the woods.

The party was just getting started. Amy and Adam rushed off to compare costumes with their schoolmates as soon as they entered the gymnasium. Huge black spiders, complete with bloody fangs, hung from rope webs; ghosts and witches flew through the air on cables; and stuffed wolves howled at a huge white moon that was suspended with fishing line.

Most of the parents came in costumes and stood around the edges of the gym with bags full of candy to pass out to the children. A witch cackled in the corner while stirring a concoction in a huge cauldron; an attached sign read "Brumhilda's Brew." The witch waved in greeting at Denise.

"A cup of the brew, sister?" the woman asked, smiling to reveal her blackened teeth.

"As long as it doesn't contain the skin of the bat; I'm allergic, you know," Denise said.

"It does contain a pinch of powdered goat skin, but no bat," she said, laughing and extending her green hand in greeting. "I'm Dana Barrow, but you probably know me as Mrs. Barrel—that's what I get for marrying a man with a last name that the children can make fun of, and taking his name. Please call me Dana. I'm an English teacher here at the Grove School."

"Well, it's a pleasure to meet you; I've heard so much about you. I'm Amy and Adam Miller's mother, Denise Miller. Amy raves about you."

"Ah, yes, the well-read Amy. You've quite a girl there. A born English teacher, I say; but she insists she is to follow in her mother's footsteps and become a psychology professor. Amy's one of my favorite pupils; sometimes she even teaches me things I didn't know."

Denise laughed. "Me, too. I'm afraid, though, that Amy's sacrificing her childhood in the pursuit of knowledge; she's also following in my footsteps as a loner. I was the same way as a child, but I gave as much time to play—even though it was usually solitary play."

"I think she'll be fine," Dana told her. "Once she becomes interested in boys, she'll pull her nose out of the books. My advice to you is to just be happy she's acquiring all of this knowledge instead of wasting her time on internet, like a lot of the kids I teach."

The woman studied Denise for an uncomfortable moment and said, "I can't pass up this opportunity to talk about your son; has Adam been giving you a rough time at home?"

"Yes, he has. Has he been behaving strangely at school?" she asked, a frown furrowing her brow.

"Yes, in fact, I've been taking notes on his behavior. I was waiting for the parent-teacher conference to discuss it with you. If you'd like, I could see you one day after school in my office," Dana offered.

"That would be great. Could we make it on a Tuesday or Thursday, though? I teach in Philadelphia on Monday's and Wednesday's."

"Is this Tuesday at three forty-five all right with you?" Dana asked.

"Perfect," Denise told her. "I'd better be going; it looks like it's almost candy distribution time. It was nice meeting you, Dana. I'll see you Tuesday."

Denise made her way over to a small clearing and stood waiting to distribute her candy. She could see Amy and Adam standing in line at the apple-bobbing station. She waved at them, but they didn't see her.

Adam and another boy were trading dirty looks. Denise watched as the other boy, dressed as a punk rocker, approached Adam. The boy said something to him and then cut in front of him in the apple-bobbing line. Adam pushed the boy out of his way, and the boy turned around and pushed him back. Just as Denise was about to run over to see what was going on, a woman dressed as a cave woman—obviously the punk rocker's mother—came running over to chastise the boys. She plucked her son out of the line and forced him to stand at the end, while a man dressed as a caveman stood nearby giving the boy a dirty look. Denise realized that the punk rocker must be the infamous Jeffrey Abrahm, the boy who incessantly teased Adam.

Watching the mothers and fathers dressed in funny costumes made her suddenly feel very lonely; she seemed to be the only single parent at the party. The familiar, choking balloon of anger and pain rose in her throat as she thought of Donald; if he hadn't screwed up so badly he would be there with her. Actually, she realized, she wouldn't be there at all; they would be taking the kids trick-or-treating near their home in the Philadelphia suburbs.

Denise passed out candy, thinking about what Adam's teacher had said about him; the idea that she was going to raise the two children alone, with no mate to help her, hit her like a baseball bat in the gut. She had never given it much thought, always thinking she could handle whatever came her way, but she was suddenly frightened at her singular state, surrounded by couples who had each other to turn to. She had no one.

   Denise felt someone staring at her; she looked around the room and saw two people dressed in shockingly realistic werewolf costumes staring at her. They looked oddly familiar, and she laughed at the absurdity of the idea that two people in werewolf costumes could look familiar; but the way they were watching her made her think that maybe she looked familiar to them, too, and it was also making her nervous. One of them was actually panting, his tongue lolling out of his mouth. Denise noticed the extreme length of the thick pink tongue, the drool gathering at the tip, and the fang-like teeth that looked real enough to chew her to pieces.

   Damn it, Denise thought, *those aren't costumes they're wearing; they're real!* They appeared to be some kind of freakish wolflike creatures. The sight of them had a strange effect on her. Denise felt like she was alone in the room with them; she imagined them pouncing on her and ripping her throat open. She was curiously aware of her bodily functions: her blood raced, thin and hot, through her veins; her heart slammed wildly in her chest; her throat constricted; her muscles quivered like congealed fat; and her mouth seemed as dry as powder.

   Just as the room began to spin, one of the creatures turned its back to her; she saw a zipper running up its furry back. She felt a cool rush of air flow into her lungs, expanding them with relief; she felt like the most foolish person on earth. They were *people* wearing costumes. She hoped they hadn't noticed her panicked terror.

   Denise felt her blood rush to her face. She wanted to leave. The room was too warm, and the deluge of people in costumes was beginning to seem like a horror movie or some cult gathering of devil worshippers. She wouldn't have been surprised if they all turned on her with their ghoulish faces and started chanting her name.

   Amy and Adam rushed over in a whirlwind of chatter, proudly displaying their bags full of candy.

   "It's time to go," Denise told them. "Have you had enough fun for the night?"

   "But, Mom," Amy whimpered, "the party hasn't ended yet."

NUNNY & CECIL—A Tale of Terror

Denise looked around the room uneasily and saw that many of the people were gathering their things to leave. The people dressed as werewolves were nowhere in sight, and she hoped they had left. She was too embarrassed to face them; she was sure that her fear of them hadn't gone unnoticed. They were probably laughing hysterically at her behind those gruesome masks.

She looked at her watch. "Come on, you guys. It's almost nine o'clock. You have to get up for school tomorrow, and I have to get up for work."

"All right," Adam and Amy moaned in unison.

They began the long walk to the back of the parking lot, Amy skipping most of the way.

"Who was that boy you were arguing with, Adam?" Denise asked.

"That was stupid Jeffrey. He was trying to take cuts," he said, and then mumbling, he added, "He's asking for it."

"Asking for what?" Denise asked.

"Asking for trouble," Adam said.

"Well, you just ignore him. I was watching the two of you. He's a troublemaker," she said.

"He took cuts! How am I supposed to ignore him when he does something like that?" he asked.

"If you ignore him, you'll take the thrill out of his bullying. Don't you see he's trying to get a rise out of you? You're just falling into his trap—doing exactly what he wants you to do. I don't mean that I want you to let him push you around, but if you can, try to ignore him. Alright?" she asked, getting in the car and opening the passenger door for the kids. The door was broken and could only be opened and locked from the outside.

"He'll get his," Adam mumbled.

"What did you say?" Denise asked.

"I said alright," he lied.

"I hope that's what you said."

Denise closed the door on Amy's long flowing wig, and Amy yelled, "Mom!" Denise reopened the door to let Amy pull out her hair.

"Sorry, Annabel," she said, chuckling.

As she walked around to her side of the car a sudden brisk wind blew in, knocking her hat off her head and blowing it toward the woods. Denise gave chase, and as she bent over to pick it up, she heard a cracking sound, as if someone broke a tree limb in half. She picked up her hat and stood very still, listening.

Crack.

Crack.

She heard it twice again, but it wasn't the sound of wood breaking in half, it was more of a snapping crack, like something brittle—a bone, maybe, breaking in half. Then she heard a gnashing and grating sound, as if someone with very big teeth was eating crunchy cereal in the woods.

She couldn't move; she was both curious and petrified. She stared hard into the dense thicket of trees from where the brutal sounds emanated. A low, unearthly growling sound issued forth from the thicket and then Denise saw them: two phosphorescent yellow eyes, burning like yellow flames.

The force of her survival instinct broke through her fear and moved her legs—slowly, awkwardly, one after another, like a paraplegic suddenly gaining the power of mobility—toward her car.

The keys, she thought, fumbling through her purse. *Where are the damned keys?* She was startled by their cold metallic presence in her hand, where they had been all along.

She heard the growling sound again, but this time it seemed to be coming from all around her. She jumped into the car, slammed the door shut, and punched the lock down with her fist. The kids hadn't noticed a thing; they were busy trading candy.

"I'll give you this pack of baseball cards for your candy necklace," Amy said. "There's bubble gum in there with the cards, you know."

"What do you think I am, stupid or something? You think I don't know that there's gum in there, asshole," Adam said.

Denise turned around without even thinking and slapped Adam in the mouth, then looked at her hand like it belonged to someone else; she rarely hit her children.

Adam looked stunned.

"Who do you think you are—talking to your sister like that? I never want to—," she stopped in mid-sentence; the cave woman was running hysterically toward the car. Denise stopped the car and opened the window.

"Have you seen my son, Jeffrey? He was dressed..." she stopped to catch her breath. "He was dressed as a punk rocker, with green spiky hair," she looked into the car and recognized Adam in the back seat.

"You know my son, have you seen him?" She sobbed convulsively for a moment and then turned and screamed at the woods, "Jeffrey! Jeffrey!"

Denise shook her head and said, "I'm sorry. I haven't seen him."

The woman ran off, screaming. Denise wondered then and all the way home—and for the rest of her life—if she had heard him, heard his bones snapping in two, his child's body being pulverized by sharp teeth in the dense woods beyond the parking lot.

And in the days and nights that followed, she was troubled by the memory of the people dressed like wolves; it was as if—for what reason, she didn't know—they had come to the party just to see her.

GAILA SWINDELL

12

Not hide nor hair of Jeffrey Abrahm was ever seen again. The disappearance of Jeffrey gave that Halloween a mystery and significance that put it in the Halloween Hall of Fame for all of the children at the Grove School and the entire community.

Some speculated that Jeffrey's father, who had run off with another woman years before, had come back and kidnapped the boy. That was the theory that allowed Jeffrey's mother to stay sane the rest of her days.

Others entertained a more grisly explanation for Jeffrey's disappearance, whispering that they saw the boy being whisked through the air, a goblin holding him by the collar with one long bloody talon. They presumed he was going to be turned into a goblin because of his devilish nature.

This rumor, which the people of Cooks County took great precautions to never let reach the suffering ears of Jeffrey's mother, became something of a legend in the area; whenever a child was naughty, the locals would admonish him or her with tales of Jeffrey Abrahm.

Denise never mentioned the yellow eyes she had seen or the sounds she had heard that night in the woods. She managed to convince herself that it was nothing more than some woodland animal walking through the brush; and because it was Halloween night, she supposed she had let her imagination get a little carried away—just as she had with the people in werewolf costumes.

NUNNY & CECIL—A Tale of Terror

The Amish people fascinated the children, whose school bus had to pass the Amish horse and buggies every day on the way home from school. They couldn't understand why anyone would want to live without phones and electricity and wear such ugly, black, old-fashioned clothing. They had grown up in the conventional arena of the Philadelphia suburbs, where everyone lived a cookie cutter existence. Denise was glad that now they could experience such a different way of life and see how others lived, so different from themselves.

Amy was adjusting wonderfully to the old house and her new school. Denise never had any problems with her daughter; as long as Amy had plenty of books to read she was content. Amy actually seemed happier living on the farm: she was no longer forced to go outside and play with the other children, especially since there were none within miles of where they lived. Amy was free to follow her nature as a loner.

Adam had been involved in some altercations with classmates: his gym teacher, Mr. Babford, had called Denise a number of times about Adam's violent nature. Mr. Babford said he had never had a student who was as "hateful" as Adam.

Dana Barrow had much to tell Denise during their meeting. She said that Adam was mean to the girls in his class.

"I've wanted to pick up the phone and call you so many times," Dana said, "but I hesitated to bring it up before the parent-teacher conference. It was not an overt behavior that I could put my finger on; it's more of an underlying rage that I sense inside Adam whenever he comes in contact with a member of the opposite sex, including myself. It's grown worse in the time I've known Adam. I know Mr. Babford has called you several times already."

"I don't understand. What is it that he does?" Denise asked. She knew that Adam had been in several fights with other boys; this was out of character for Adam, but Denise felt it was a fairly normal under the circumstances; this "underlying rage" aimed at women was something far more difficult to deal with.

"Well, for one thing he seems to snarl at girls as they pass by. I'm sorry if what I'm telling you is upsetting to you," she apologized, "and I know some of what I'm saying may even sound crazy...but it's all true. Look, this is my notebook." She gave Denise a red notebook. "Go ahead and read some of the things I've written."

Sept. 28--Adam making angry faces at me when he thinks I'm not looking.

Oct. 5--Adam seething with anger today. Looked like he wanted to hurt Madison Butler as she walked by his desk.

Oct. 8—Thought I overheard Adam telling Davis Jenks that he wants to stab one of the girls with his pencil. When I called him over to ask him what he and Davis were talking about, he said they were discussing soccer.

Oct. 17--Adam knocked Danielle Stetell's books off her desk as he walked by. I had to force him to apologize. He said it was an accident; therefore he shouldn't have to say he was sorry.

Oct. 23--Adam snarled at me. He said his nose itched.

"You see, they're mostly things that I can't be sure about, although I think I am. I don't want to accuse Adam of lying. At times I've even wondered if this snarling expression was a nervous tic of some kind. It's the frequency of the problems and the way that they all seem to be against women that makes me think he has a deeper problem," Dana told her. "One other thing that I should mention. I haven't noticed Adam doing this, but I've heard the children teasing Adam. They say he talks to himself."

Denise looked out the window, gathering her thoughts. "Adam's father and I were recently divorced," she said. "I think Adam blames me for the divorce, even though he knows that his father was unfaithful to me. I suppose it's his inability to adjust that's making him angry with women. I'll definitely have a talk with him, and if this poor behavior keeps up, I'll take him to a counselor. Adam never gave me any problems before the divorce; both of the kids have always been easy going. I'm sorry about the problems he's caused you."

"I have two boys of my own, Denise, and, believe me, they're not that angelic. I'm sure this must be a difficult time for you all."

Denise had sensed that there was something more that Dana wanted to tell her; she had a feeling the teacher was withholding something because she was afraid of offending Denise. "Is there anything else? Please don't be afraid of offending me," Denise had finally said, but Dana had looked down and said no, there was nothing she had to add.

Denise knew without a doubt that she was lying.

NUNNY & CECIL—A Tale of Terror

It was the Saturday before Thanksgiving; Denise sat alone in her office, trying to work but mostly thinking. She had papers to grade, and knowing the kids wouldn't give her any peace at home, she had escaped to her sanctuary.

Hearing a noise, she looked up to see Hillary Brannom standing in the doorway of her office. Hillary was new to the university faculty, but she acted like she had worked there since birth. Denise doubted that Hillary had a social life: the woman seemed to live at the university and made everyone's business her own.

"Catching up on some work, I see. What's wrong, kids running you ragged at home?" Hillary asked.

"Not really, Hillary. I just needed to do a little research, and the texts I needed were here in my office," she lied.

"What are *you* doing here on a Saturday?" Denise asked, trying to appear preoccupied.

"Working as usual, that's all I do anymore," she said, staring at the spot on Denise's desk where the picture of Donald used to be. *Oh shit!* Denise thought. *She notices everything.*

And right on cue, Hillary asked the question that Denise knew was forthcoming: "Where's that picture of Donald you used to have on your desk? You two aren't having problems, are you?"

Why do I put up with her? Why don't I just tell her to get the hell out of my office? She didn't want the woman to know that she'd touched a nerve, so she said as nonchalantly as possible, "Oh, Donald and I are divorced. Didn't you know?"

"Well, I had a feeling you two were having problems. You were spending a lot of time away from the university, and I asked myself, what would make Denise spend so much time away from her work? And the answer I came up with was marital problems," Hillary babbled stupidly, the way she always did. "So, you must be taking it pretty hard?" she said, in a concerned tone.

"No, not at all. Actually, I'm very happy to be single again," Denise lied—again. She could see where the conversation was going. In a minute Hillary would sit down, make herself comfortable, and—pretending to lend a sympathetic ear—try to suck out every dirty detail. *Why doesn't she just wear a T-shirt with "Roto Rooter" written in big red letters across the front of it?*

"Listen, Hillary, maybe we could talk about it some other time, over lunch, maybe, but right now I've got to get this work done and get home in time for dinner," she told her. *That's it, give her permission to clean the septic tank of my mind at a later date, and she'll go away happy.*

"Okay, Denise. You take care now. And if you need a shoulder to cry on, you know where to find me," Hillary said, leaving the office. Denise fought an urge to throw a book at her head and resumed grading papers.

She came to Lenny Delenko's paper and read it twice. It was pitiful. He usually did very good work, seeming to have a deep interest in psychology. She knew he was having problems with Freud—and apparently some other aspects of his life—and feeling sorry for him, she thought about giving him a better grade on the paper than he deserved. Finally, after reading the paper a third time, she slapped a big red D on it. If she gave him a merciful C, she would be doing him more harm than good; she sensed that Lenny could use all the good he could get.

Denise lost herself in the ride home. The sun sank slowly behind the rolling hills in the distance; flocks of starling rose abruptly out of fields of pale dead corn stalks that looked as dry, brittle, and barren as her heart felt.

Denise had a long distance to travel to and from the university, but she only had to be there two or three days per week; the time spent in the car gave her some very necessary time to think. She wanted to start dating immediately and get the movie starring Donald Miller off the big screen in her head.

Most of the people she associated with didn't know she was divorced, although many of them had probably guessed, as Hillary had; she had been so busy that she hadn't had time to enlighten them. *Maybe it was a good idea to let Hillary know that I'm a free woman,* she thought; *she'll do a great job of spreading the news.*

She didn't want to date any of the other professors at the university; she knew one or two of them were only hungry for young, female students. She snuck a look at herself in her rear-view mirror. One thing she was sure of: it wasn't her lack of beauty, intelligence, or personality that had sent Donald in search of someone new; it was his insecurity, his need for a constant ego boost.

Denise felt guilty for ignoring all the messages Dr. Crofford had left for her to call him. She felt fine—most of the time. Her brief reactive psychosis had been just that: brief and reactive. As long as she could maintain a fairly normal level of stress, she would probably never suffer another episode of severe mental illness. *That's it, Denise—ignore it and it will go away. But remember what Dr. Crofford said: After awhile the dust in the attic gets so thick you won't be able to breath up there; that's when the real trouble begins.*

"Later," she said aloud to a mental picture of Dr. Crofford. "Give me time to get my life together."

What perfect timing, she thought, tuning her satellite radio to a station playing the band Cake's rendition of the disco anthem "I Will Survive." She sang along, singing the pain right out of her heart.

13

The phone rang as Joe Rodman was making his way from the yard into the house; after the fourth ring he realized that no one else planned to answer it.

"Hello," he said gruffly into the receiver. "Hold on a minute. Adam!" he called up the stairs to his grandson. "Adam, it's for you!"

Adam came running downstairs wearing his winter coat and carrying his hat. "Hello," he said, out of breath from running. "Oh, okay. See ya," he said gloomily, putting the receiver back onto its cradle.

"That one of your new school friends?" Joe asked, noticing Adam's disappointment.

"Yeah," he scowled, kicking at the floor angrily.

"What happened? He cancel your plans?" Joe asked him.

"Yeah. He said he doesn't feel good," he said. "He and his dad were supposed to pick me up, and we were supposed to go fishing."

"Well, what do you say about us going for a ride? Just you and me. I'll go put a few things away, and then we'll go. Sound good?" Joe asked.

"Yeah, Grandpa," he said, a smiling tugging at the corners of his mouth.

The old Chevy truck grumbled slowly up the steeper hills, jerking occasionally to let them know it was too old for hill-climbing expeditions. They passed fields of fat, dirty brown sheep, and big black and white cows, Adam exclaiming, "Look, Grandpa!" so many times,

Joe thought his head would swivel off. When they got higher up in the mountains, a few people even had goats tied to trees in their front yards. The truck ran smoother once it loosened up a bit and whined only on the toughest hills.

"I bought this old truck when your mother was only about fifteen years old. She'd get me to let her ride in the back when we'd go for ice cream. But after a few carloads of boys pulled up next to us, hooting and hollering at her, she decided she liked it better up here in the cab. I guess she felt like she was on display. It wasn't too long after that she wouldn't be caught dead riding back there. She packed up all of her tomboy clothes and toys and started asking us to buy her high heels and earrings. I'm telling you, it was a lot less expensive when she was a tomboy," Joe told Adam.

"Grandpa, how come we don't have a pond?" Adam asked. Joe had noticed Adam looking at the smooth, round ponds in many of the yards of the small farms and country houses they passed. "I sure wish we had a pond."

"Well," Joe said, stalling for time while he thought it over, "maybe in the spring we could dig a pond out in the yard somewhere."

"If we had a pond, we could dig it next to a tree and then put a swing over it," Adam said.

Joe didn't know what to tell him; he knew Denise planned on moving back to the city in the spring. He was surprised that Adam wanted to stay on the farm; Adam had given him the impression that he hated it. "I guess you really like living on the farm," he said, waiting to see what Adam would say.

"I love it! I have my new friends, and I really like living with you and Grandma," he said enthusiastically. "Especially since mom doesn't have time for us anymore."

There was the stinger. Joe's ears turned red with anger. *Damn that Donald Miller!* He wanted to strangle him with his bare hands. He bit his tongue to keep from yelling at the child. *Can't he see? Is he so blind— even in his youth—that he can't see that his mother is doing the best she can under the circumstances?* Joe couldn't wait for Denise's Christmas break; maybe that would give her time to heal the wounds of her children. He wondered about the friends Adam had mentioned. He wasn't sure what new friends Adam was talking about; the boy moped around the house much of the time. He was touched that Adam said he liked living with them, but the biting comment about Denise crowded out the compliment...

"This looks like a good place to stop," Joe said, pulling the truck onto the shoulder of the road. "There's a path right there that goes into the woods."

Adam started to jump out of the cab of the truck, but Joe caught him firmly by the arm.

"Before we go I want to say a few things," Joe began. "Now, you know what happened between your mom and dad, so you know it wasn't your mother's fault. I'm not trying to badmouth your father, but you don't see him here trying to take care of you. Your mother has to work to support you and your sister, and you should be happy that she has the job that she does; it leaves her more time to spend with you and Amy than a lot of other jobs would. She's doing the best she can, Adam. Can't you see that?" Joe asked him.

"Yes, Grandpa," Adam answered with lowered eyes.

"Your mother is going to have a break coming up at Christmas, and then she'll have lots of time to spend with you. For now you'll have to make do with your mean old grandpa and grandma. Okay?"

"Okay," Adam agreed in a tiny voice.

"Come on! Let's go for a hike!" Joe said.

They walked along the path, talking occasionally. Adam overflowed with energy and pulled Joe along with the force of it.

"I miss my dad, but you're almost as good, Grandpa," Adam said. "I can talk to you about boy stuff—not everything, but most everything—and not worry about any old girls listening."

"Why, thank you, Adam. I consider that one of the greatest compliments I've ever received. These sure are some beautiful woods, aren't they?" Joe asked.

"Sure are, Grandpa. Where does this path go to?"

"I think it goes farther on up the mountain we were just driving up. There's a hawk refuge somewhere up here, but I don't think this is the path that leads to it: I think that path is marked with signs. See how they've got the trees marked so you don't lose your way," he said, pointing to some white marks painted on the trees bordering the path. "Your mother and your grandma and I used to drive along until we found a path that looked good, and then we'd get out and hike it," Joe said, feeling slightly guilty that they hadn't asked Amy to come along. But he could see how Adam was enjoying the one-on-one male contact, and he appreciated it too. Joe had always been somewhat of a loner and hadn't had many friends in his day. As long as he had Marie to talk to, he was happy.

The cool late autumn day was perfect for a hike. They walked in silence, each one content with his thoughts. Adam wasn't bothering to turn over any rocks, and Joe hoped that their previous expedition hadn't scared him too badly. That rat under the rock had been a shock, but Joe wouldn't allow himself to dwell on it; it was too nice of a day to be thinking about all the things that were bothering him.

A small stream ran out of a pipe on the side of the path; they cupped their hands to drink the icy-cold mountain water. Adam got a kick out of drinking water right out of the mountain.

Adam began collecting leaves along the path. He walked along picking them up and smoothing them out into a little pile in his hand. He squatted down to pick up a bright red leaf and said, "Look, Grandpa, horseshoe prints."

Joe bent down next to him to look at the prints.

"Looks like they just went through here; those prints are pretty fresh," he told him. The sight of the horseshoe prints forced him to think about the mysterious paw prints.

"Grandpa, do wolves talk?" Adam asked him, as if reading his mind.

Joe was startled; he didn't know what to say. *Has the child read my mind? Why would he ask such a question?* Joe thought that might be a normal question for a four or five year old, but Adam was eight, and surely he must know that talking wolves did not exist. Joe's stomach became queasy when he thought of the tracks and then of the bones he had dug up in the basement. *Talking wolves?* A cold breeze suddenly blew in from the west, making him pull his cap down tighter around his ears.

"Not any that I've ever seen, Adam." If he didn't talk about it, it didn't exist. *Don't acknowledge the monsters.* But the horror of what might exist, and the image that formed in his mind when he put all that he knew together, made his skin shrink around his bones and aged him twenty years.

He had to ask Adam why he had asked the question; it was his duty. He couldn't—as much as he wanted to—shrug off Adam's question, pretending that it was just a child's wild imagination.

"Have you ever seen a—uh—wolf that talked, Adam?" Joe asked him, bracing himself for the answer. If it weren't for those bones and those prints—and even the rat (*what in the hell decapitated that rat?*)—he could walk away from the question. But he had to get to the bottom of what was going on; he thought it might save his family if he opened his eyes this time, instead of closing them to problems as he usually did. *Save us from what?*

"No, Grandpa," Adam said. "I haven't seen them—yet."

"What do you mean 'yet'?" he asked.

"Nunny and Cecil told me that they're wolves. But I haven't seen them because they're invisible."

Joe snapped the branch he was holding in two. His mind raced to make sense of what the boy was saying. It was all very simple: Adam had seen those names on the tombstones in the basement and he was so lonely that he was using the names for some imaginary playmates. That was it. But how could he know about the wolf part?

"Invisible, you say, and they talk to you?" Joe asked.

"Yeah, Grandpa. They're my best friends; they said they'll never leave me."

"When do you have time to talk to them, with school and homework and everything?"

"That's a secret, Grandpa. They said if I tell all their secrets, they won't talk to me anymore."

"Did they? Well, I can understand that." Joe didn't want to press the issue. *The boy is obviously under a lot of pressure. Imaginary playmates are just that: imaginary. Or are they?*

NUNNY & CECIL—A Tale of Terror

14

Adam sulked around the house. After the excitement of his morning outing with his grandfather, the routine activities of racing toy cars and video games seemed boring in comparison.

His grandmother noticed that he had been acting bored, but she had expected that to happen sooner or later. He'd been spending much of his time in the attic, which she didn't like because of the dust and drafts; but more than that because she thought it was unhealthy for an eight-year-old boy to be spending so much time alone, in an attic. She decided she should rescue him before he got himself into trouble.

Marie went up to Amy's room and knocked quietly on the closed door. She hoped she could talk Amy into abandoning her books for a while to play with her brother.

"Come in!" she heard Amy say. Amy's face brightened when she saw her grandmother. "Hi, Grandma! Do you know when Mom's coming home?" she asked.

Marie walked over and sat down on the bed. "She should be home by supper time. Are you getting hungry? It's going to be a few hours before we eat," she told her.

"No, Grandma. I'm not hungry. I just wanted to ask Mom about this book report I have to write," Amy explained.

"Can I help?" Marie asked her.

"No, Gram. It's about psychology and since that's Mom's specialty, I'd better wait for her."

"What are you reading?" Marie asked.

"*Sibyl*," Amy stated nonchalantly. "The teacher said we could do a book report on any book we're interested in."

Marie thought the book was over her granddaughter's head. "Wow, that's an oldie. Does your mother know you're reading that?" she asked.

"I guess, but I don't know for sure."

"Well, we'll just have to ask her when she gets home. Don't you think that book is—well—a bit over the heads of many of your classmates?"

Amy looked very serious with her thick glasses and messy hair, and a little lost among the heaps of pillows on her bed. A frown appeared on her smooth brow as she concentrated on her grandmother's question.

"Maybe for some of them, Grandma."

Marie laughed softly at her granddaughter.

"I came in here to talk to you about Adam. I know you're busy studying, but he seems awfully lonely. Do you think you could go down and play with him for a while?" Marie asked.

Amy opened her mouth to voice what Marie was sure would be a big "No," and Marie reached out and put her hand over Amy's mouth, and said for her, "Sure, Grandma. Anything for you."

When she took her hand away, Amy burst out laughing and said, "Sure, Grandma. Anything for you."

Adam was sitting in his room playing with his toy cars. In his frustration at having no one to play with, he had wrecked the cars many times: the tiny cars were heaped in four and five car accidents. When Amy entered his room, he ripped off a piece of the bright orange racetrack. Jumping up off the floor, he brandished an orange, make-believe sword at her and shouted, "En garde!"

"Cut it out! I came to see if you want to play. I'm bored with reading," she lied.

"Okay. What do you want to play?" he asked her.

"How about psychologist? You lie on the bed, and I'll ask you questions," she suggested. She was determined to follow in her mother's footsteps, but she didn't want to teach, she wanted to analyze.

"Psychologist? No way! Let's play hide and go seek!" he said.

"All right. Where do you want to play?" she asked, giving in because she loved him.

NUNNY & CECIL—A Tale of Terror

"The basement. It's the best place in the world to play," he said, donning a devilish grin.

"Okay. Let's go," Amy agreed, wanting to get it over with as soon as possible.

Amy had never spent much time in the basement before; upon descending the staircase into the cold, damp, musty room, she was almost sorry she had agreed to play the game down there. She was deathly afraid of bugs, and she knew there must be a million of them, springing out of the earthen floor by the minute. She wouldn't let even the thought of rats or mice enter her mind; she knew she would run away screaming if she did. The headless spectacle of the fat-bodied field rat still haunted her late-night thoughts.

"Maybe we should play upstairs, Adam. It's too damp down here, and we might catch colds," she said, trying unsuccessfully to hide the fear in her voice.

"No way! I told you this is the best place to play. It has the most hiding places. Nunny and Cecil like to play down here; they're going to play with us. Now you go hide, while I cover my eyes and count to fifty," he demanded.

"Nunny and Cecil? What are you talking about?"

"Nunny and Cecil are my invisible friends. They're only *my* friends; they said that they don't want to be your friends," he told her.

"Who said I wanted them to be my friends? Besides, there is no such thing as invisible people," she told him.

Adam stood thinking for a moment; he looked like he was going to say something, but didn't. Amy felt she could read him so well.

"Count to one hundred," she told him, not wanting to spend any more time than necessary down there talking about fictional characters. "I don't know this horrible place as well as you do." Her eyes scanned the room for a place to hide, while her body refused to move.

"One, two, three, four, five..." she could hear him counting from somewhere in the room, but she couldn't see him. *Why did I agree to do this?* She walked slowly, her footsteps soundless on the damp, hardened earth floor of the room. She opened a small closet door, but it squeaked, giving her whereabouts away. *Actually,* she thought, *that's just what I want—Adam to find me right away.*

"Sixty-one, sixty-two, sixty-three..." he counted, as Amy eased her body in through the little door. She stood there, touching nothing, with her arms wrapped tightly around her. The closet was pitch black, and she closed her eyes tightly to block out what might come out of that blackness. *Never again,* she thought, as she heard Adam finally reach one hundred.

Amy began to sniffle and sigh loudly, hoping Adam would hear her and find her quickly. She could hear a slight scuffling noise; she assumed it was Adam searching the basement. Her teeth chattered; she wasn't sure if it was from cold or fear.

Nunny and Cecil—how did he come up with such ridiculous names? Will he never find me? she thought. A noise came from inside the closet, a muffled pounding that she realized was the beating of her own heart. It seemed like she had been closed up inside the room for an eternity. *Adam, where are you?* She became aware of an odor that was vaguely familiar. She had smelled it upon entering the room, but now it was overwhelming. *It smells...like...like cold metal,* she thought. *Like rust. What is it?*

The scuffling noise was getting louder, coming closer. *Good, Adam's approaching,* but no, the scuffling was in the room with her. *Adam's not coming!*

Then she heard breathing, loud and raspy breathing coming closer to her ear, drowning out the sounds of her drumming heart and chattering teeth. *This is a dream,* she thought as she opened her mouth to scream, but no sound emerged. *This has to be a dream! Adam isn't coming, ever. He has left me to die at the hands of some creature.* And then she couldn't move; she was paralyzed with fear. *Maybe his invisible friends aren't just figments of his imagination. Nunny and Cecil like to play down here; they're going to play with us.* Something growled like a dog, and then she felt something cold and wet touch her hand, sniffing at it, licking it with a sandpapery tongue. Her legs moved to run, but then buckled out from under her. She fell. Her face hit the thin wooden door and, finally, she screamed louder and harder than she had ever screamed, and then she fainted.

Her next conscious observation was that she was being carried over the shoulder of the monster, carried away into the dungeon where it lived. She kicked and screamed as hard as she could.

"Calm down, Amy, it's only me," she heard a voice say. It was not a monster, but her grandfather. She buried her face in his soft flannel shirt and cried an ocean.

NUNNY & CECIL—A Tale of Terror

Joe put Amy into the care of her grandmother, who insisted he go down into the basement to find "the monster," so down he went. He didn't find the monster, but what he did find made his brow break out in a cold sweat: a long, thin, yellowed bone lay in the corner. *How could I have missed this, the very thing I didn't want the kids to see?* He realized that in his haste to dig up the mutant bones, he must have thrown one and missed the bag.

"Damn it!" he swore, wanting to kick himself. *I have to be more careful with the kids here. I don't want them getting scared of the place, especially Amy, with all those books she reads.*

He threw the monstrous thing into an old canvas lawn mower bag. *Hell! The damned thing is longer and thinner than any bone I've ever seen. Must have had some real strange kind of family pets back then,* he thought, moving up the stairs at a pace his old legs hadn't seen in a while.

GAILA SWINDELL

15

Adam was banished to his room until Thanksgiving Day, and then he was to emerge for dinner with an apology to his entire family. When Denise slipped into his room on Thanksgiving morning with news of an early reprieve, he did not seem the least bit remorseful.

"What would make you do such a horrible thing to your sister?" she asked him.

"My friends told me to," he answered.

"What friends?" she asked.

"Nunny and Cecil."

"Nunny and Cecil? Are those some strange kind of nicknames? I've never hear such odd names. Are they your new friends at school? Why would they tell you to do such a thing?"

"They don't like girls," he answered half of her question.

Dana Barrow had not been wrong in her assumption after all: Adam was having a problem with the female sex. Things were coming together, even as they were falling apart.

"I asked you if they're your friends from school. Who are they?" she asked, wondering how boys Adam's age could be so mean. Amy had been traumatized by Adam's prank.

"I know them from school," he told her.

"I want to know their last names. Something is extremely wrong with those two boys. I hope you're aware of that. A practical joke is one thing, but you really hurt your sister. Now tell me their names."

He sat without talking, his lower lip trembling, defiant.

"They don't have last names," he said, his voice barely audible.

"What do you mean? I don't understand. Everyone has a last name, except maybe some celebrity like Cher or Sting or Bono. Now what is it?"

"They don't go to my school," he confessed. "They live here."

She could feel her temper rising, along with an unmistakable feeling of fear that Adam was going off the deep end; she struggled against an overwhelming urge to slap him into reality.

"This conversation is going nowhere. No one lives in this house but your family. How can you tell me that they live in this house?" she shouted at him.

"They're invisible," he told her, this time looking her straight in the eye. "And they're the only friends I have."

Denise's head began to reel, and the painful reality of what he was saying hit her like a truck. *What have we done?* she thought; *or better yet, what did Donald do to our son by screwing up our marriage? Invisible friends!* So that's who Adam was talking to when his schoolmates accused him of talking to himself. But Adam was eight years old, a bit old for having invisible friends: the trauma of the divorce was forcing him to regress. *Stay calm, Denise, he'll get over this.* Monday, after the holiday weekend, she would take him to see her friend Paul, one of the best child psychologists on the East Coast; he could help Adam. *In no time, the invisible friends will be shot back to hell where they belong.*

16

Denise and Adam sat in the waiting room of Dr. Paul Raison's office. Children's artwork of all medias filled the walls. Denise's favorite was a crab made from a tuna can.

Adam didn't seem nervous; Denise had finally convinced him that he wouldn't be getting any shots. Denise was terrified at the thought of what his diagnosis might be. She knew the psychology of children quite well, but the guilt she felt had strangled her logic.

Hell, why should I feel guilty? It's all Donald's fault. The bastard, she thought, fighting an urge to scream the words.

Paul came out of his office with a wide smile on his face. He'd lost most of his hair, but it hadn't taken away from his boyishness.

"Hey, Denise! It's great to see you," he said, giving her a quick hug.

"Hello, Adam. It's a pleasure to meet you," he said, shaking Adam's hand.

"Hi," Adam said shyly.

The two of them entered Paul's office, leaving Denise alone in the waiting room. After an hour of sitting there, she dozed off. She fell asleep for what she thought was only a few minutes and had a dream so horrible she would never forget it.

In the dream, Denise was sitting in front of a roaring fireplace drinking cappuccino with a handsome man. They were laughing because every time Denise took a sip from her mug, she would get foam on her lip. Amy sat by the fire, reading quietly; Adam wasn't there. She went over to where Amy sat and began to smooth back her daughter's hair. The back of Amy's head was wet and seemed to sink in when Denise touched it. As she pulled her hand away in disgust, tufts of sticky hair clung to Denise's hand; she shook her hand violently in a desperate attempt to shake the oozy mess loose. A mass of the vile hair flew from her hand and stuck to Amy's face. Amy appeared to be sleeping; Denise shook her, screaming "Amy, wake up! Wake up!" She continued shaking her until Amy fell out of the chair, hitting the ground with a sickening thud of dead weight and sending a foul smelling cloud of dust into the air.

When Denise woke up, trembling and sweating, Adam was sitting in the chair facing her, a sly grin on his face.

GAILA SWINDELL

17

Denise sat in her car, furious at the traffic. The center city traffic drove her crazy, and she knew it would take an hour to find a parking spot once she reached her destination.

She was sure she had spotted Lenny Delenko behind her in the swarming mass of traffic. She kept checking her rear-view mirror to see if it was him.

She turned right on Walnut, and then left on Seventeenth. When she slowed down to look for a parking space she saw him. He turned onto Seventeenth from Walnut, pulled into a "No Parking" space, and just waited there.

Great, just what I need: Lenny Delenko stalking me around Philadelphia. She was not in any mood to tolerate any crap from a psychotic student.

Denise was pissed off at Paul for not giving her any information about Adam over the phone or by email. He wouldn't say a thing except, "When can you come and see me?" She had gone through two days imprisoned in the hell of ignorance while she waited for him to get back from a psychology conference in Los Angeles. She couldn't even confide in her parents; she didn't want them to know what was going on. She had to lie to them about where she was taking Adam; and the worst thing about the entire situation was that she had to tell Adam to lie, too. It would only make them worry, and they didn't need that kind of stress at their age.

Denise's bout with the dark side of the mind had both of her parents spending countless hours in the bathroom, building their relationship with the toilet. They had treated her gently since then, as if one false word from them would send her down the road of no outlet. They had never really understood psychology, always thinking treatment was reserved for the truly psychotic. If they knew Denise was taking Adam to a psychologist, they would probably spend the rest of their days in diapers.

Their lives were stressful enough, caring for her and the kids. They acted like second parents to Adam and Amy; they did everything possible to try to relieve Denise of all of the pressure of single parenthood. They fed them, dressed them, played with them, and helped them with homework.

Denise was there as much as she could be for the kids, but she was beginning to notice some resentment from them. Even Amy was starting to get bitchy. They ignored her when she was around, and they had quit coming to her with their problems. Denise's mind was in such turmoil over the invisible playmates incident that she couldn't reach out to them, at least not until she met with Paul. Luckily, she still had another month before Donald came back from London. She wanted him as far away from her as possible, for as long as possible.

She finally found a parking spot after circling the block four times. Each time she passed Lenny's car, he hunched down further in his seat. She pulled into a spot three spaces up from where he was parked and searched her purse for the handful of quarters she had grabbed out of her father's old bottle filled with change.

She walked past Lenny's car, while Lenny tried desperately to hide behind a cup of coffee. He obviously hadn't mastered the fine art of spying. She decided the best way to deal with him was to ignore him.

Paul's receptionist greeted her with a tense smile and ushered her into his office. He was sitting at his desk, looking out at his wonderful view of the city.

"Hi, Denise. How's it going?" he said, jumping up and giving her a hug, to which she stiffly gave him one back. "I can feel the tension. Loosen up; everything is fine. Please sit down," he told her, indicating a plump, green suede chair next to his. Both chairs were turned to face the window.

"So, tell me about Adam," she said anxiously. The room was like a padded cell: soft, noiseless, and oddly comforting.

"He's fine. He's been through some stress—as I'm sure you're painfully aware of—and he's lonely right now. He needs some playmates—real, live kids—and a lot of love and attention, that's all. It's really very simple," he said.

Denise could feel her body relaxing for the first time in two days. Those were the words she had been hoping to hear. She knew that Adam's behavior was relatively normal considering the circumstances, but she had been blinded by her fear.

"He's having a very normal reaction--guilt, anger, jealousy. But he's going to be fine, Denise. Trust me. I don't mean that his condition isn't serious—he's a very angry young man—but I've seen this happen many times as a result of divorce, and the problem is usually resolved with the all-time greatest psychological healer: time. I know you think I'm a prick for not giving you this information over the phone, but even though you're a friend, your son is now my patient and I have to stick to the policies I've established. One thing I never do is discuss my patients over the phone. Besides, now I can get you to go to lunch with me. So what do you say, still mad?" he asked.

"Who could stay mad at an imp like you? No, I understand, even though I don't want to. That's the same line of bull about sticking to policy that I feed my students," she confessed.

"Well, the reason I have that one particular policy is because many parents think that if they take their kids to the shrink, they can wash their hands of the problem, especially people with a lot of money and little time."

"I understand perfectly, and I think it's a terrific policy. Now, I haven't eaten in two days—thanks to a certain child psychologist I know—and I'm starving! Where would you like to eat?" she asked.

"South Philly, of course. I know a great little Italian place, actually I know a hundred great little Italian places, but this one has quiet little booths where we can discuss Adam and catch up on each other's lives," he said, jumping up and putting on his hat. "Got to protect this valuable brain," he winked, taking off his hat and rubbing his bald head.

Denise felt comfortable and happy again at home that night. She spent time with Amy and Adam making plans for the weekend. Each one had made out a Christmas list. They gathered in Denise's room with a large bowl of popcorn to share.

"I'm really sorry that I've been spending so much time at work lately, but the end of the term is coming up and I do have to spend time with my students. If I don't please them, I don't pay the bills. And working so far away doesn't help matters much. I know you might be afraid that because Daddy is gone, I might go away, too. You can trust me: I'll never leave you. Divorce is a traumatic situation. You two will probably feel anxious and unsettled for some time to come, but I hope those feelings will go away as we adjust to our new and different lives. I love both of you more than anything or anyone in this world."

"I love you, too, Mom," Amy said.

"Me, too," Adam said, looking up at the ceiling.

Denise took note of his distraction. Paul had said that Nunny and Cecil were projections of Adam's anger. They gave him permission to lash out, to misbehave. He had also said that of all the imaginary playmates children had described to him, Adam's were the most vivid. When she had asked him what they looked like, Paul said that it wasn't important.

She gathered her children into her arms and lay back against the headboard of the bed, enjoying the moment.

She hadn't told them her news. It could wait until later in the week; she didn't want to ruin the peaceful moment. Paul had arranged a blind date for her with one of his colleagues. It wasn't totally a "blind" date; Denise had seen a fuzzy online photo of the man. He looked all right—nothing spectacular; she was so grateful of the chance to get out and socialize that she wasn't going to be finicky.

"I can assure you, Denise, that he is a gentleman and a scholar," Paul had said in a fake English accent, "and the picture doesn't do him justice."

He had pressed a small plastic package of condoms into her hand when they had said goodbye, and, a wicked grin taking over his face, said, "Enjoy."

"You're a pig, Paul! Some things never change," she said, laughing at his little joke.

The sound of the children's soft, even breathing lulled her to sleep, and all seemed right with the world.

GAILA SWINDELL

18

The world outside the breath-fogged window was covered in a thick, white blanket of snow. The list of school closings flashed across the bottom of the television screen. Adam jumped up from eating his bowl of cereal and ran over to the television.

Upon seeing the name of their school, the children gave a resounding "Yes!" They took each other's hands and jumped up and down, swinging in a circle, in celebration of the three-day weekend that spread before them.

"Well, we have the whole day to do anything we want. What's it going to be? Play in the snow or go back to bed? I know some great sledding hills, and I'm sure Grandma and Grandpa have that old sled of mine somewhere around here. They never throw anything away, " she told them.

"Let's go sledding!" Amy shouted.

A few moments passed and then Adam spoke up: "I want to stay home, Mom. I don't feel good," he said unconvincingly, while putting his hand on his stomach.

"Oh, honey! Come here; let me feel your forehead. Tell me what's wrong," Denise said, putting the back of her hand on his forehead. His forehead was cool to the touch. "I don't feel any fever, Adam. Does your stomach hurt?" she asked.

"Yes," he whined.

Amy stood there with a look of disgust on her face; she could see through Adam's facade. "Adam, you're lying! You just want to stay home and play with your stupid imaginary playmates, Runion and Weasel, or whatever their stupid names are."

"Amy, that's enough," Denise insisted.

"I'll go up and get the thermometer. You sit down and rest on the couch," Denise told him, knowing that the threat of the thermometer would get him to feel better.

"That's okay, Mom. I'm starting to feel a little better now. Let's go sledding," he said without enthusiasm.

"Are you sure, Adam? I don't want you getting any sicker. You don't have to go if you aren't feeling up to it," she told him. "Grandma and Grandpa will be home from the farmers' market soon."

"I want to go," he told her, brightening his tone.

"Alright. Bundle up good," she said, kissing him on the cheek.

Denise sat on a bench, sticking her tongue out to catch the falling snowflakes. She was tired of sledding, so she sat and watched Adam and Amy take turns with the one sled they had to share. Amy tripped and fell in the snow as she was running back up the hill to where Adam waited impatiently for his turn on the sled.

Adam roared with laughter.

Amy obviously didn't see any humor in her tumble: she wiped the snow from her red and frozen face and shouted up the hill at her laughing brother, "You shut up—you weirdo!"

"Come on, you guys! Don't start fighting, or we'll go home," Denise shouted. "Are you okay, Amy?"

"Yeah, Mom, but Adam's not going to be when I get my hands on him."

"Amy, that's enough!" Denise said.

Denise was disturbed about Adam feigning illness that morning. She thought he would jump at the chance to go sledding.

She wondered if she should go see Dr. Crofford. The dreams she had been having were enough to send her back to the hospital for another one of Dr. Crofford's nice little vacations. She leaned back on the bench and wrapped her blanket securely around her body. She contemplated the nightmare she'd had the night before, attempting to understand it; it had haunted her from the moment she had opened her eyes that morning.

She remembered sitting in a courtroom for most of the dream. She sat on the witness stand, while the attorney, whom she recognized as

Bruce, the man she was going on a date with the following night, interrogated her. The judge was the same fat man who'd presided over her divorce proceedings.

"Do you feel that you are fit to raise these children?" Bruce asked her as he pointed at Amy and Adam, sitting huddled in the corner of the courtroom.

"Yes, I do," she responded.

"Are you a slut, Denise Miller?" he shouted at her, spraying spittle into her face.

Denise wiped her face with a tissue that she was suddenly holding and looked up at the judge for help; she was astounded that he hadn't threatened the prosecutor with contempt of court. She looked around the courtroom to see if there was an attorney there to represent her; there wasn't.

Suddenly, a horrible smell overwhelmed her. It was so bad that it burned her nasal passages—like sulphur. She looked up at the judge and cringed in horror when she saw that he had turned into a large, wolflike creature, who stared intently at her with yellow, glowing eyes. The sound of his raspy breathing filled the courtroom and made the walls seem to move in and out.

"Answer the question, slut!" the judge shouted down at her.

"No!" she screamed defiantly, almost jumping down from the witness stand. She thought about taking the children and making a run for it, but when she looked at the judge again, she decided that it probably wouldn't be a good idea: one false move and he would probably tear them all to pieces with the sharp, curling claws that protruded from his paws.

The rancid odor was like a poisonous gas, gagging her. It seemed to get worse whenever the judge opened his mouth to speak. The hideous creature began to ask questions; Bruce disappeared. She was alone in the courtroom with the creature and her children.

"How many men have you slept with since your divorce?" he shouted down at her. His lips smacked when he spoke, and a thick, red drool dripped slowly from his fat pink tongue out onto his desk.

"How is that in any way relevant to this case, your honor?" she asked him.

"We are here Denise Miller, to judge your fitness as a mother. Answer the fucking question, please!" he demanded.

"The answer is zero," she shouted, looking over to where Amy and Adam sat. They seemed strangely composed, and Adam was even smiling.

"How many times have you fucked your father?" his voice boomed into her ear. His fetid breath came down like a fog, settling around her.

"What a sick question!" she shouted, and then realized that the faster she answered the questions, the sooner she would get out of there. It dawned on her that she might never get away, and she began to panic. They could lock her up for life if they found her guilty, and at the hands of such a loathsome creature, she wasn't sure what horrible fate awaited her. She began to vibrate with fear, but managed to whisper a feeble, "No, never," in answer to his question.

"Remember, Jenna Jerrel, you are in a court of law. You have sworn to tell the truth," he bellowed down at her.

"I see what the problem is. You have the wrong person. My name is Denise Miller.

"It doesn't matter; you're all the same. Now answer the question."

"No—never!" she shrieked, struggling to control her fear and anger.

"But isn't that how you conceived Amy?" he asked, pointing to Amy.

"No. Where would you ever get such an idea?" she implored.

"Look at her, an obvious product of inbreeding," he said, pointing to Amy again, who had turned into a wolflike creature, similar to the judge. Then he pointed to a page in a small black leather-bound book and said, "It's written right here, in your diary. We have written evidence, in your own hand, that you're lying."

She tried to protest that it wasn't her diary, but it was too late; he was delivering her sentence. He pounded his gavel on the desk, and as he rose from his desk she saw that his body was covered with matted, gray fur, and that although his head and appendages were wolflike and he had paws instead of hands, his torso seemed human under the thick fur.

"The sentence has been delivered to me from the fiery depths," he said, pulling a flaming piece of paper from beneath his robes, "You are sentenced to die by the hand of your son!" he roared.

"This is a horrible mistake!" she shouted at him, unable to control herself any longer. "Please let me go!" she shrieked. "You'll pay dearly for this!"

"I already have," he told her, smiling to reveal yellowish-brown fangs and pushing his horrible face down close to hers. "I already have!"

NUNNY & CECIL—A Tale of Terror

19

Lenny Delenko opened the door of the dark house and walked slowly to his bedroom. He put his backpack full of books on the floor next to his desk, sat down on the edge of his bed, and pulled off his shoes. His stomach growled so loudly it startled him.

"All right, all right, supper's on its way," he said, heading toward the kitchen.

He was surveying the contents of the refrigerator, when he heard his mother's voice say, "You're home," almost sending him head first into a bowl of leftover spaghetti.

"It looks that way, doesn't it?" he said sharply, purposely not turning around to look at her and continuing his search for food. He was surprised he hadn't smelled her standing there; she took a bath in cheap perfume every day before Lenny arrived home.

"I made you a nice dinner," she told him, coming toward him and rubbing his shoulders. "Your favorite, vegetable lasagna," she said, as Lenny pushed her hands off of his shoulders.

"Sorry, but I'm not hungry," he lied, grabbing a soda and slamming the refrigerator door.

"Where's dad?" he asked, turning around, trying not to look at her as he walked quickly past her. He couldn't help noticing the flame-red, see-through nightgown she was wearing.

"He's out of town, again...Boston, I think. I worked so hard to make your favorite dish, and you're not going to eat it! You don't appreciate a damned thing, do you?" her voice was rising to its usual high-pitched screech.

She opened the cupboard, pulled out a bottle of scotch, and poured some into the empty glass she was carrying.

"Look at the table, just look at the table I've set, and I know you won't be able to resist," she said, her voice softening. "Please have dinner with me, Lenny. I'm so lonely!" she whined.

"If you get rid of the candles," he told her. There was no way in hell he was going to have a candlelight dinner with his own mother.

"All right. If you insist," she told him.

"And put on a robe," he added.

"What, you don't like my gown? It's a hundred-and-fifty-dollar gown," she told him.

"I don't care how much you paid for the thing, if you don't put on a robe, I'm not eating with you," he told her, wondering why he still had an appetite.

Lenny sat at his desk, his stomach and his mind full and churning. *What in the hell has got into her? Is she fucking crazy?*

Speak of the devil: his mother slithered into the room. She had lost her glass in favor of the entire bottle, and she had also lost her robe. *Freud never said a thing about this,* Lenny thought, as Sheila Delenko stood in front of the desk where Lenny sat typing at his computer. She bent over and leaned on the desk, her large, sagging breasts almost flopping out of the top of her gown.

Lenny was mortified. *She's going too far with this. What would Freud have called it? Reverse Oedipus complex, that's it,* he thought—*or maybe just plain old sexual abuse.*

"Is studying all you ever do, Lenny?" she asked, slurring her words. "All work and no play make Lenny a smart but dull boy."

"Yeah, Mom. Why don't you go to bed? It's late," he told her, keeping his eyes on the computer screen and his fingers going at a steady pace.

"But it's no fun to go to bed all by myself. Maybe you'd like to come cuddle with your mommy," she said in a baby voice.

"Mom, just go to bed! I'm too busy to be bothered with this kind of shit. Now, please, just leave the room! I have to have this finished by tomorrow morning," he told her. And he had thought Mommy

NUNNY & CECIL—A Tale of Terror

Dearest was a horror story. Sheila Delenko was making Joan Crawford look like June Cleaver.

"Don't you use that kind of language around me, mister!" she said, pointing her finger at him as she backed up and hit the wall with a bang. She turned around and looked at the wall as if it had no business being there. "I won't have it!" she yelled. And if you don't start cooperating, if you don't start doing more for your mother, we'll just have to take you out of that school. Do you hear me?" she screeched.

Lenny stopped typing and just stared at her in amazement, shaking his head. Her moral compass was broken. She was pitiful, standing there in a see-through gown in front of her only son, trying desperately to get him to sleep with her. He was so repulsed by the sight of her, that he wanted to kill her. *But you're even more repulsed by your desire for her, aren't you, Lenny?* There was that goddamned voice in his head again.

She just stood there screaming nonsense at him until finally he couldn't take it anymore. Lenny jumped up from his chair and then pushed his mother out the door of his room. She tried to hit him with her bottle of scotch, but he managed to pull it from her grasp. She was holding onto the bottle like it was a life preserver.

He slammed his bedroom door with all of his might and turned the lock. After she was done throwing her tantrum, she'd fall asleep, a bottle cradled in her arms like a teddy bear.

Lenny finished typing the paper, printed it out, and turned off the computer. He stood up to stretch. The glowing red numerals on the clock read 3:07 a.m. Lenny was wired from typing and the ordeal with his mother; he felt like going out for a run to unwind.

Better get to bed, he thought, knowing that his nine a.m. class was less than six, short hours away. Professor Miller wouldn't be too happy if he was late, especially since there was a paper due. If he came in late she would think he was typing it right up to the minute that he had to leave for class, and she would scrutinize it more carefully. She wouldn't stand for any hastily researched, last minute garbage thrown at her.

Lenny pulled off his clothes, turned off the light, and lay down on his bed. He thought of his mother, remembering a time when he would have been thrilled by an invitation to sleep with her. When Lenny was about four years old he had begun begging his mother to let him sleep with her when his father was away on trips. She would always give in. He would lie in his father's place, secretly praying that his father would never return home. He fantasized that his father had been killed in a plane crash, or run away with another woman, and then Lenny became the man of the house, sleeping with his mother every night.

His mother had let him sleep with her until one humiliating night when he was twelve years old. He had been awakened in the middle of the night by the feeling of something wet and sticky between his legs. He panicked when he felt that it had seeped out of his pajama bottoms and onto the sheets. It was everywhere! He had run crying into his own bed.

The following morning he was out of bed and off to school before his alarm went off. He never wanted to face his mother again. When he finally returned home and saw his mother, she never mentioned the previous night. Lenny never slept with her again.

Revulsion at the memory still choked him. When he was fifteen years old, his shame at this memory had caused him to burn his penis with a cigarette.

He remembered another hellish summer night that had branded itself on his memory. He had been roused from his light sweat-drenched sleep by moans and heavy sighs coming from his parents' room. Thinking a prowler had broken in and was hurting his parents, he had grabbed his baseball bat and run groggily down the hall. After listening at their door, he decided that the prowler must have tied up and gagged his father, because it was his mother who was making all the noise. Lenny ran into the living room and called 911. He unlocked the front door for them as he had told the operator he would. Then he had run back down the hall and burst through his parents' bedroom door, brandishing the bat.

He would never forget what he saw and did that night. His mother and father were naked; his father lay on top of his mother, doing what Lenny had only seen dogs do. His mother screamed so loud it hurt Lenny's ears. His father shouted, "Get the hell out of here, Lenny!" But Lenny just stood there, mesmerized by the terrible scene before him. His father jumped out of bed, his penis red and swollen, and grabbed Lenny by the shoulders. At the same time, Lenny swung at his father with the bat and cracked him in the ribs.

"You stay away from her! You stay away from her!" Lenny screamed.

NUNNY & CECIL—A Tale of Terror

His mother sobbed. His father grabbed the bat, wrestled it from Lenny's grasp, and threw it on the floor. He picked up the struggling Lenny, carried him to his room, and laid him down on the bed.

Lenny surrendered, his skin stinging where his father had touched him. He was asleep by the time the police arrived. He spent the next week in the hospital with a 106-degree fever, which the doctors could find no cause for. Lenny couldn't remember the events of that hot summer night until one night when he was seventeen years old and saw his naked father walking down the hall with an erection.

Now he wished his father never had to travel. His mind was a turbid river of polluted thought when he finally fell asleep. He bobbed along in the murky current, twitching so violently during the night that he knocked his bedside lamp off the table; he was so sound asleep that he didn't hear it crash to the floor. His dreams were vicious.

In Lenny's first dream, one of his reoccurring dreams, he was a little boy again. He was lying in the bunk bed he used to have, trying to fall asleep. He imagined that the super heroes on his sheets were in a war against each other, but that wasn't why he was having such a hard time falling asleep: his parents were arguing again. Their voices rose and fell, drifting in from their room down the hall; he drifted along with them, out on the waves of the ocean of falling sleep. Fragments of his parents' conversation floated into his mind, which was somewhere on that unexplored continent between the land of Sleep and the land of Awake.

"You're never here to give him any attention. He's always my responsibility, and I'm sick of it!" his mother said.

"Don't give me that shit, Sheila. It's not my fault I have to travel. You signed on the dotted line just like I did. If you didn't want to adopt Lenny, you should've just said so." That was his father talking.

"You just wanted to adopt him so I'd have to stay at home while you're on the other side of the country, fucking some broad. Well, don't be surprised if you open your suitcase to find the little bastard packed along with your underwear. I've had it!" his mother screamed. "I never wanted a damn kid."

"You're a cruel bitch, Sheila. You're right—we never should have adopted Lenny; you're not fit to be anyone's mother!"

Lenny was on a boat, drifting away from their voices. That was the end of his first dream—a dream he often had, but never fully remembered. When he was awake, fragments of the dream would pop into his head like soap bubbles, but the moment he touched one, almost grasping its contents, it would burst.

In the next dream, Lenny was a little boy again, walking home from school in the snow. When he came to his house, he was afraid to go in. Soon it would be dark and he would have to go in. He could see his mother's eyes looking at him through different windows of the house, but he just stood there. First, he could see her eyes in the upstairs window, then through the dining room window, and then through the living room window. Finally, the front door opened, and his mother was standing there, completely naked.

"Come in, Lenny. It's getting dark out there," she told him, her eyes looking wide and strange.

Lenny started to cry, and ran down the street as fast as his little legs would carry him. He didn't know where to go. It was getting so cold and dark, and he couldn't see because the snow was beginning to blow in his eyes.

The next thing he knew he was at the university, sitting in Professor Miller's class. He was still a little boy. There were kids in the class from his grade school, but most of the students were the people who were actually in Professor Miller's class with him.

Professor Miller was talking about Little Hans and the Oedipus complex. She looked directly at Lenny during the entire lecture, and he could feel people staring at him. He raised his hand, but Professor Miller ignored him and kept on talking.

Lenny got up to leave the room and Professor Miller said, "Lenny Delenko, just where do you think you're going?"

"I'm tired of listening to this stuff," he told her, running out into the hall and then out of the building.

He could hear her calling him, "Lenny, get back here right now."

Everything on campus looked so big—the buildings, the people, the bell tower. Lenny tried to find his car. He walked for blocks and blocks, moving deeper into the run-down neighborhood that surrounded the school. He saw his house down at the end of the street. He wondered why his house was in that neighborhood, but he was so tired, it didn't matter.

He walked into the house and went straight to his room. He lay down on the bed, and his mother came into the room. She was wearing her old quilted robe with the never-ending supply of tissue in the pockets.

"Is my baby boy tired?" she asked, stroking his hair off of his face.
Good, he thought, *she's back to her old self again.*

She stood up, and the robe fell open to reveal a black bustier, complete with garters, fishnet hose, and spike-heeled shoes. Her flaccid breasts spilled out of the top of the bustier, and she rubbed a bottle of scotch between her legs.

"Daddy's going to be home soon, so we have to hurry," she told him. "Let me help you off with those things," she said, pulling off his shoes and then tugging at his pant legs.

"Leave me alone," he said. "Please, Mommy, I'm tired. I just want to go to sleep." He was so tired.

"But Mommy's so lonely, and she's been waiting all day for you to come home," she told him. "Now lift up your arms so I can take off that shirt."

"Please leave me alone," he begged. "Why are you doing this?" he asked her.

"Cause Mommy doesn't have anyone else to play with," she told him, trying to pull his underwear off.

Sheila grabbed Lenny's little hand and pulled it toward her breast. Suddenly Lenny realized he was holding a butcher knife in his hand, but Sheila didn't see it. She screamed when the cold metal tip of the blade touched her breast, and Lenny knew what he had to do. It was the only way to get her to leave him alone.

He plunged the knife into her heart again and again, the horrible sound of metal breaking through flesh and bone exploding in his ears, hot wet blood squirting into his eyes, blinding him for a moment.

He wiped the blood from his eyes and got up from the bed. He looked down at his mother lying there in a pool of blood, but the person lying there wasn't his mother at all: It was Professor Miller.

Lenny screamed until he woke himself up. For one terrible panicked moment, when he felt the wet and sticky fluid between his legs and thought it was blood, he wondered if the gruesome events of the dream had actually occurred. When he realized that it was semen, he almost wished the dream would come true; but it wasn't Professor Miller who he wanted dead.

20

The wind nipped at Joe's face as he walked toward the barn. He had just finished another one of Marie's breakfasts fit for a king, and he hoped the walk to the barn would help him burn off a few pancakes. The blood in his body was concentrated in his stomach, helping with digestion, and left the rest of his body empty of its warmth.

The barn, in all its stone glory, was magnificent against the backdrop of the bright blue sky. Its enduring strength at such an old age was an inspiration to Joe. He doubted he would see eighty.

Joe felt a renewed sense of purpose since Denise and the kids had moved in. He had wondered how he and Marie would adjust to a houseful of people after being alone for so many years; now he wondered how they would adjust after Denise and the kids moved out. He hoped they would stay a while.

Joe picked up a stone that had fallen from the barn and put it back in its place. He would remortar it in the spring. He pulled the heavy set of keys from his pocket, and looking out toward the forest, he took the barn door lock in his hand. Something wasn't right: he could feel the raised insignia of the padlock on his hand; usually the back of the lock was smooth. He looked down to find that the lock was on backward. Someone had been in the barn. Joe was compulsive about consistency; he always put the lock on with the insignia pointing outward.

He walked inside, shutting the door behind him in a futile attempt to keep the cold air outside. The barn was silent except for an occasional scamper of a rat, mouse, or cat alarmed by his presence. A whiff of rancid air stung his nostrils and he decided it was time to check the rattraps. It wasn't his favorite thing to do, especially after a big breakfast; but with odors like this one wafting through the air, the job had to be done.

He came to the first trap and, finding it empty of a victim and unsprung, the blob of peanut butter still stuck fast where he had put it, he moved on to the next one. He could see his victim as he approached, so he turned and walked to his supply shelves to get a garbage bag. He pulled a plastic bag out of the box, donned a pair of disposable plastic gloves, grabbed a shovel and the jar of peanut butter he kept in the barn, and walked back to the trap.

He felt uneasy and wondered which of his two previous experiences were responsible: the last time he had used a garbage bag and shovel had not been pleasant; and the last time he had seen a dead rat, its head was missing. *And surprise, surprise, this one's head is missing, too,* Joe thought, looking down at the decapitated rat. Maybe it had rolled away, or maybe the cat had got it; but Joe couldn't find the head anywhere, and the cut was as clean as if someone had chopped it off with a butcher knife. Somehow the precision of the cut made him feel slightly better: the rat that Adam found in the woods had its head torn right off; although it was odd to suddenly begin to find decapitated rats, at least they seemed to be the victims of different executioners. This one seemed to be the job of a human being, knife in hand; and the door lock being on backwards made it even more likely that this was the deed of a human. But why, he wondered, would anyone want rat heads?

He pulled back the bar on the trap and wiggled the rat's bloated, stinking body free with the shovel. It had been there a couple of days and was stuck fast to the trap. It was hard and stiff. Joe was glad it was almost winter and there were no flies. He shoveled it up and into the open garbage bag, and then reset the trap.

He approached the next trap. He felt like he might lose his breakfast when he saw the decapitated rat that lay there; a man could only take so much.

The third trap was empty—even of peanut butter—but the fourth one did make Joe lose his breakfast. He ran outside and just made it out the door before he vomited the entire contents of his stomach.

Three decapitated rats in one morning were a bit much for Joe to handle. Something was definitely wrong.

He buried the rats, reset the traps, and cleaned up around the barn. He walked around the barn looking for evidence that someone had been there: a cigarette butt, a footprint, a candy wrapper, a wad of chewing gum. He found nothing.

He grabbed his keys and started for the door, but a peculiar sound stopped him dead in his tracks. It was an angry, scratching sound. He followed the sound to its source: the old barn cat, its fat body packed into a small space in the wooden frame of the barn, scratched frantically at the wooden slat on which it sat. There was a space underneath the platform made by the slats, into which a grown man could stick his entire arm; and there was something in there that the cat wanted. Whatever it was, it smelled ripe. Joe looked into the hole and the cat crouched low, hissing at him.

"Get out of here!" Joe said to the cat. "I'll catch you in one of those traps if you don't watch out." The cat hissed again, but didn't move an inch. Joe grabbed a hoe and swung at the cat with it; the cat ran away.

Joe put his arm into the hole and pulled out a navy blue drawstring sack trimmed in gold thread. The sack read "Seagram's Crown Royal." Joe knew he had seen the sack before; he just couldn't remember where. He emptied its contents onto the floor: a plastic zip-lock baggy, containing the most gruesome sight he had ever seen: rat heads. He had to look closely to determine what they were; they looked like triangular balls of dirt and fuzz, with a light covering of mold beginning to form. But when he looked close he could see the hard, little black eyes, the whiskers, and the sharp teeth that jutted out over the lower lip. He was glad he had already lost his breakfast; he didn't think he could have made it outside so quickly this time.

He stuffed the plastic baggy back into the sack, pulled the drawstring tight, and put it back in its place. He didn't want the culprit to know he had discovered the cache. Joe was halfway back to the house when he remembered where he had seen the drawstring sack: tied to Adam's belt loop.

"I have nothing to wear," Denise told her mother. She stared at the clothes hanging in her closet. "You know, Donald and I didn't get out that much...and after losing some of my nicest things in the move, I'm left with nothing. I still wonder if I really lost those clothes, or if

Donald stole them. They were my sexiest things; maybe he was afraid they'd help me attract other men," she said.

"Speaking of Donald," Marie began, "he called earlier from England while you and the kids were out. He wanted to talk to Adam and Amy. I didn't want to tell you because I thought it might ruin your evening, but you know me—I can't keep a secret." She chuckled nervously. "He sounded kind of depressed," she added, as if she thought that might make the bad news somehow better.

Denise suddenly had the urge to rip up every piece of clothing in the closet. It was his fault, his crime that had forced her into the mess she was in. There she was, a thirty-five-year-old woman with two kids trying to find something to wear on a date. She tried to control her rage; she didn't want to upset her mother.

"What in the hell am I going to do? I don't have a damned thing to wear," she said slamming the closet door.

"I knew I should have waited to tell you. Now you aren't going to enjoy yourself tonight," her mother said apologetically.

Suddenly, without warning, Amy burst into the room sobbing hysterically. Blood streamed down her face from a small cut on her forehead.

"Mommy, I fell and hit..." she stopped to catch her breath; she was hyperventilating. "I fell and hit my head! Take me to the hospital!" she wailed.

Denise ran to her daughter and gathered her up in her arms.

"Shh, Shh, quiet down. Now, let's see how bad it is. Hold still," she told the squirming child. The cut was just a tiny surface scrape, but it was really spitting out some blood. Denise's stomach turned and she fought to stay conscious: the sight of blood made her faint.

"Mom, it's that smell. The blood smells like that room in the basement!" she wailed even harder.

Denise wondered why the basement incident had been so traumatic for Amy. She sat rocking her daughter, wondering if maybe she should take her, too, to see Paul.

"It's all right, honey. It's just a little cut. You'll be fine," Denise told her, stroking her soft hair.

Marie had run to the bathroom for some towels and bandages. She rushed in and handed Denise a cool washcloth, which Denise applied to Amy's head to stop the flow of blood. Then Marie began cleaning Amy's bloody face and hands with a warm, wet towel.

"Thanks, Mom," Denise said, rocking Amy. When Amy stopped crying, Denise gently placed her in her grandmother's arms.

"Come here, you," Marie said, smoothing Amy's hair back from her face.

"It's the smell, Grandma—the smell of the monster in the basement," Amy whispered to Marie, as if it were a secret.

But Denise heard her loud and clear as she started out of the room to rinse out the towels; she stopped dead in her tracks hoping Amy would say more. Joe and Adam arrived on the scene to survey the commotion. Adam's eyes were round and frightened; Denise could see that he felt guilty. He walked over to where his sister lay huddled in their grandmother's arms and reached out to take her hand.

Amy's reaction surprised everyone: she pushed him away as hard as she could, shouting, "You get away from me! You're friends with the blood monster."

"Amy!" Denise said. "That wasn't very nice. You accept your brother's kindness. I'm sure he feels terrible about what happened."

"He does not!" Amy said. "He's not my little brother anymore."

Denise closed the bathroom door behind her, and then rinsed the towels in the sink. The warm water felt good on her hands. *My God*, she thought, *what's happening to us. Six months ago we were a normal, happy family—or so I thought.* She wrung out the towels, pretending they were Donald's neck. She felt the passion of her hatred flow through her veins like adrenaline, making her want to punch the mirror in front of her.

Amy seemed to be regressing. *Actually*, Denise thought, trying to rationalize the situation, *she's only acting her age—something she hasn't done in a long time.*

Denise could smell the iron sweet odor of her daughter's blood as it flowed from the towel into the sink. *The smell of the monster in the basement:* her daughter's words echoed in her head, *geez, what an imagination—damn it!* A realization knifed through her mind: the judge in her dream, the hideous wolflike creature—it had smelled like blood. She wondered why she hadn't realized this before; the smell of blood had been fairly significant in her life, always causing her to faint, dead away.

Why did her monster have the same smell as Amy's?

21

Denise examined her naked body in the mirror: front, then side, then back. *Good,* she thought while slipping on the matching black panties and bra, *it's not perfect but close enough.* Those spin classes and the weight training are really paying off. She thought she looked better than most of her female students, many of whom subsisted on nothing but junk food. She saw them downing candy bars and coffee for breakfast. But she had been like them at one time: wearing too much makeup, eating the wrong foods, placing importance on the wrong things in life—she had been so out of touch with herself.

She slipped the black mini dress over her head and stuck her feet into the black high-heeled pumps. There was a knock at her bedroom door as she was plucking the curlers out of her hair.

"Come in," she called out.

Her mother entered, carrying something behind her back.

"Wow! Don't you look gorgeous!" she exclaimed, circling her daughter and letting out a whistle of appreciation.

"Thanks, Mom. What have you got?" she asked.

"When we moved into the house, I found these earrings in an old chest in the attic. I thought they'd go well with your outfit," she said, handing a Denise a small yellow box, while staring at the hemline of her dress.

"Great! I was just hunting through my jewelry box for something to go with...this...dress," she said, faltering as she pulled the earrings out of the box. They were dangling wooden ravens.

"Thanks...Mom. It was...so nice of you to think of me," she said, not quite grasping what it was that made her feel uncomfortable at the sight of the ravens.

"You don't like them?" her mother said.

"Oh, yes, I do. It's just that they remind me of something I can't quite put my finger on. That's all. Sure, I'd love to wear them!" she lied, not wanting to hurt her mother's feelings. "Wow. I can't believe you found these in the attic. They must be antiques." She put them on. "What do you think?" she asked.

"Perfect," Marie answered.

Denise picked up a bottle of lemon perfume from her dresser and sprayed it on her neck, arms, and then, with gusto, behind her knees and between her breasts.

Denise!" her mother said in mock disapproval, and the awkward moment was immediately forgotten as they both broke into silly giggles.

Denise arrived five minutes late at Bruce's front door. She felt extremely lucky when, after she had driven twice around the block, a car sidled out of a space right in front of his home.

He lived in an old row home in the Old City section of Philly. His polished marble steps gleamed white as ghosts in the darkness. A brightly colored stained-glass window was set into the brick above the lacquered wooden door.

The door swung open, and a handsome man beamed down at Denise. He said, "Hello. You must be Denise."

She stifled a "wow" and said, "Yes, and you're Bruce?" She suddenly felt like a sixteen-year-old girl.

"Yes—come in, come in. It's getting really cold out there," he said, beckoning her into the warmth, and then closing the door behind her. "Let me take your coat. Sit down," he said, indicating a black leather sofa.

She gave him her coat and sat down. The man was beautiful; the picture Paul had shown her hadn't done him justice. He didn't look anything like the formidable attorney in her nightmare.

"Would you like a drink?" he asked. He took her icy hand in his warm grasp and sat down next to her. "You must be chilled to the bone. Here sit by the fire." He pulled a chair close to the crackling fire in the fireplace. "What can I get you?" he asked.

"Wine?" she asked.
"White or red?" he asked.
"Red," she answered.

"This place is really nice, Bruce. Do you know in all the time I've lived here in Pennsylvania, I've never seen the inside of one of these places? Oh, wait a minute...yes, I have. Some of the people I went to school with lived in row homes, but they were really terrible inside. Clothes and junk everywhere," she said, beginning to relax. "I remember one of my friends used to have mold growing in cups left around her house."

"I had a few friends like that, too," he said, chuckling.

While he was off in the next room getting their drinks, Denise took the opportunity to check the place out. The roaring fire was framed by a artfully carved, wooden fireplace mantle, decorated with an odd collection of rocks and broken sea glass; her eyes rested on a framed photograph of a beautiful woman ensconced by two equally gorgeous children. *That must be the ex-wife Paul mentioned,* she thought, with a funny pang of emotion she couldn't name.

The place was immaculate. *He must have a maid,* she thought, noticing that the woodwork shone brilliantly, as if recently polished. She was almost hypnotized by the warmth of the place. She wondered if that was Bruce's goal. She pictured him reading a book called *Hypnosis Through Interior Decorating*; but then she remembered that Paul had said Bruce was "a gentlemen and a scholar," and even though he had said it in jest, she knew there had been some truth to the statement.

Noticing several pieces of art hanging on the walls, she decided it would do her good to get up and take a look at some of them—get the little people in her brain who were responsible for conversation moving again.

"Are you interested in art?" he asked, handing her a glass of wine.

"I love art. Lately, though, I haven't had much time to get around to any of the local museums. I did recently drive up to New York for a Gauguin exhibit at the Met," she told him.

"Paul said you moved in with your parents for a while. How do you like it?"

"It's nice living with them right now," she said.

"It must be a long drive from Cooks County to Philly, but then you probably don't teach every day. How many days a week do you teach?" he asked.

"Two days a week, but I have other obligations at the University, so it really comes out to about three and sometimes four days per week. And sometimes I just drive down and lock myself in my office; it's the only way to get any work done. You'll have to come out and see the house sometime. My parents love to show it off," she said.

"Are there many children for your kids to play with out there?" Bingo, he'd asked the wrong question, and she was sure it must show on her face. The wine had gone straight to her head, and she felt suddenly awkward.

"No, that's the big problem with the whole situation. By the way, whose party is it we're going to?" she said, trying to change the subject. Adam's ridiculous imaginary playmates had immediately come to mind; her mind grasped the thought and held on tightly. Just then the smell of wet dog wafted into the room. She pretended not to notice.

It was becoming difficult to steer the conversation. She felt like she had to be careful of what she said, especially because of the woman staring at her from the picture on the fireplace mantle.

"One of my patients is having the party. I've been to several of his parties, and they're usually very interesting. Is that all right with you? I mean—we can do something else if you'd like."

"No, I'd love to go," she insisted. "I haven't been to a party in a long time." The wet-dog smell was suddenly so strong she thought she might vomit. It was as if the thing was right under her feet. She looked around for some sign of a pet. "Do you have a dog, or a cat?"

"No. Why do you ask?"

"I just wondered. It must get lonely here without..." She felt that the cover-up was too stupid and too obvious to finish. She hoped he didn't think she was suggesting anything. He didn't seem to notice the smell.

"Yes, it certainly does. I miss the kids so badly I could die," he said. An awkward moment stretched between them. "Well, then, we'd better be on our way. I'll get our coats," he told her. "Oh, by the way, do you like sushi?" he inquired.

"Love it," she told him, glad to be going.

The party was at an estate in Villanova, which was closer to Cooks County than Philadelphia was; so—unromantic as it was—they did the practical thing and took both of their cars to make Denise's drive home shorter.

Bruce apologized profusely for not having asked her to meet him there, but Denise was happy that she had a chance to see his place; it really gave her more of a sense of what he was like.

A garish woman with her black hair done in a beehive, a slash of red lipstick on her lips, and painted black eyebrows greeted them at the door. She was obviously drunk and took an annoying liking to Denise.

"Where did you get those earrings? I must have them!" she exclaimed.

"They're antiques. I really doubt that you could find any like them around here," Denise said, grabbing a glass of champagne from a tray carried by a woman dressed as a geisha girl.

"I'll pay you for them! Name the price—I'll pay it. I must have them!" she demanded, slurring her words.

Denise would have gladly given her the dreadful things, but if she went home without them, she would surely hurt her mother's feelings.

The woman, Bernadette, followed Denise around, demanding that she sell her the earrings. Bruce tried to rescue her from Bernadette several times and was successful—several times. But she was like a bad cold: every time they thought she was gone she would come back again.

In their final confrontation, Bernadette grabbed Denise's arm as Denise walked past her and in a voice different from her own, she said, "I am the messenger."

Denise jerked her arm away from the irritating woman and fighting a tremendous desire to slap her, said, "Just what in the hell is that supposed to mean?"

Bernadette bent close to Denise's ear, reached over and tweaked one of the birds dangling there, and said, "I am the messenger of doom." Then, with an outburst of hysterical laughter, she stumbled away.

Denise was not only furious, but also frightened. *Why would she say such a thing to me? She must be insane.* But Denise was determined to have a good time, so she tried to ignore the ugly incident.

Finally, Bernadette passed out in a chair, spilling the drink she had been holding all over her red taffeta dress.

"You should slip her one of your cards," Denise said to Bruce, lightening the tense mood Bernadette had generated.

After they were rid of the "messenger," the party went well. There was an abundance of excellent sushi, as well as a lot of other great food. The host, Marvin, said he had originally planned it as a "sushi and sake only" party, but then decided that some people might go hungry and thirsty.

Bruce was intelligent and thoughtful. They sat alone by the fire for most of the night. He wanted to know everything about her, and she was suddenly aware of the scar that Donald's infidelity had left on her mind: she was uneasy about revealing too much of herself to Bruce. The easy bond of trust she had always felt with people had been given a good beating.

"So how's it feel to be single again?" he asked her.

"I've been too busy to even think about it," she told him; but realizing that busy could be misconstrued to mean busy dating, she quickly added, "I mean, with my work, my kids, my students, and driving back and forth to Philadelphia—it's enough to make my head spin. How about you? Do you like being single again?"

"Actually, no, I think it's kind of weird. Even though I was slowly preparing myself for it—because of the circumstances—I was still shocked when I found myself out there on my own. Sometimes I feel like I'm in a movie, like this isn't really my life. Do you know what I mean?" he asked.

"I know exactly what you mean," Denise said, thinking she could write a book about all of the weird things that had been happening to her. It all seemed so crazy. "I look back at the person I was just seven or eight months ago, and I think, was that really me? Everything seemed fine then, but it was so damned normal. I guess I really liked that normalcy, but I've learned so much since then, about people I thought I knew so well, and just about life in general," she told him.

"Was your divorce pretty traumatic?" he asked.

She hesitated for a moment before speaking. She could feel herself holding back, consciously keeping her distance. She decided to let her old friend intuition guide her, and she slowly became her usual candid self again. She had never been one to think before she spoke—before the divorce, when she trusted people.

"It was very traumatic. It's strange the way your life can change completely in a matter of minutes; in one single moment it can go from one extreme to another. One minute I was living this fairy tale life of happiness and the next I was plunged into the depths of hell," she said, imitating Rod Serling, and making them both laugh.

"It is spooky...the way life is. I don't believe we're the masters' of our own destinies. Just when you think you have everything under control, something or someone comes along to prove you wrong," he said.

"You're so right," she told him.

The conversation kept going off the deep end: they would start out talking about something lighthearted—their tastes in art and music—and end up talking about serious issues like religion and politics.

"It seems like we've both been starved for serious conversation for a long time," Bruce told her. "Can you drive home safely after all that sake? I feel like I'm in high school. I don't want my date's parents to get the wrong impression of me."

"You think *you* feel like you're in high school," she told him, "the whole brood will probably be up waiting to smell my breath when I get home."

They both laughed at the thought, and then he reached over and kissed her—a kiss so soft and filled with emotion that she wanted to plant it in her memory forever.

"Adam," a voice said, waking the sleeping boy out of a dreamless sleep.

"Adam." The voice was a raspy whisper in the quiet darkness of his room, startling him to attention. Even though it was there, in his room nightly, he still wasn't used to it—the sudden voice in the darkness.

And then there was the smell—the rancid, metallic, sweet smell of blood that stung the inside of his nose. It made Adam aware of their presence sometimes even before they spoke. He was growing used to it, and he no longer covered his nose with his blanket. He was even beginning to welcome it: it was rather soothing—comforting even, because it made him aware that he was among friends.

He wished they would let him see them. They had told him he would have to wait, but he was growing impatient. He thought excitedly of the little tidbits he had hidden in a little sack in the barn: he would use them as an offering to get them to show themselves.

"Yeah?" he said, cranky from having been woken up. "I'm awake."

"Where is she, Adam?" the voice was slow and drawn out; it sounded like the speaker was gargling gravel. It was Nunny's voice.

"Yes. I'd like to know where the slut has gone off to now," another voice wheezed out of the darkness. It was Cecil, who had a breathing problem.

"She went to a party," Adam told them.

"The slut lied to you, Adam. She's with a man. Aren't they all the same, though—lying whores?" Nunny asked him.

"Yes. She's probably fucking him right this minute, don't you think Nunny?"

"I'd say so. After all, we saw her putting perfume between her breasts and behind her knees, and we all know what that means," Cecil pronounced each word slowly and deliberately. "How do...you...feel about that, Adam?"

Adam wanted to throw up at the thought of it. *My own mother, performing that filthy, vile act with some man, who isn't even my father!* Nunny and Cecil had described it to him in detail, the writhing and moaning and sweaty grossness of it. He cringed and clinched his fists, his little nails digging hard into the flesh of his hands, drawing blood.

"I hate it! I'll kill her—I will," he told them, struggling to keep his voice low.

"Not yet, Adam—not yet," they said in unison. And then they were gone, leaving Adam alone with his anger.

NUNNY & CECIL—A Tale of Terror

22

Judy's eyes were human again.

Night after night, as soon as Amy was alone in her room, her stuffed dog Judy's eyes, which were normally large, round, black-and-white button eyes, became slanted, with yellowish-green irises and lids that blinked. They would stare at her for as long as she would stare back at them. But when her mother or grandmother came in to check on her, the eyes turned back into the lifeless eyes of a stuffed animal.

She had told her mother, but her mother had just laughed and said what Amy had known she would say: that Amy read too many horror stories. So she just lay there, night after night, staring into the thing's eyes. Finally, she decided she couldn't take it any longer and began turning Judy toward the wall when she went to bed at night.

But that led to something just as unexplainable, something she was sure was not just her imagination. A shadow in the shape of a large wolf's head with a very long snout would appear on her door every night. Sometimes it looked like the wolf's mouth was slightly open, and she could see the shadow of a long fang and a lolling tongue.

And then sometimes...there was the breathing.

23

Adam woke up with a start. The sun had already risen; he had meant to beat it. He was surprised that he had even fallen asleep; especially with his excitement over his plans for the day and the anger he felt at his mother.

The house was quiet; everyone was still asleep. If he hurried, he could run out to the barn, carry out his plan, and be back in bed before anyone stirred, as he had so successfully done once before.

Adam tiptoed out of his room and down the stairs. He checked his pajama-top pocket for the plastic bag he had put there the night before. He went into the kitchen, picked up a chair, and carried it over to the wall next to the sink. He climbed up on the chair and took the spare set of keys off the hook high up on the wall. He climbed down off the chair and carried it back to its place under the table. If anyone got up before he returned, they wouldn't notice that anything was amiss.

He took his winter coat down off the hook in the back foyer and put it on. His coat was cold. The house was cold. He slowly and carefully unlocked and opened the back door and slipped outside.

A fog lay thick as pudding on the orchard, dampening the cool air. Adam couldn't see the barn; he had to estimate where it was in relation to the house. He ran through the orchard in the direction of the barn.

It felt strange and different in the fog, as if he was on another planet. The trees looked stark and alien. Adam wondered if he was still dreaming. He heard sounds behind him, the rustle of leaves, a snap of a twig. He stopped dead in his tracks, listening intently for just a moment; he had no time to spare. If someone were following him, he would have to give up his plan. But he heard nothing but the rush of his own breathing and the pounding of his heart in his ears.

He was upon the barn before he saw its great presence through the fog. He opened the large padlock on the door and stepped inside. It was so quiet and peaceful inside, a different world. He could easily make it his home and never see another human form for as long as he lived; and maybe someday he would. It would be just him and Nunny and Cecil. After he collected what he needed, he would have something to offer them as barter: he would give them what they loved to eat and they would show him what they looked like. At first it had been kind of neat that he couldn't see them; no one else that he knew had invisible friends. He hadn't even known there was such a thing. But he was growing weary of this game. He wanted flesh-and-blood friends to play with.

What he saw before him made his heart beat with excitement: the rats were there in the traps, two big fat ones. Adam ran to the back of the barn and took the butcher knife from its hiding place. He heard a loud purring sound and looked up to see the cat watching him. He wondered how Nunny and Cecil would feel about a big, fat cat head; but he didn't think he could catch the thing. It was as wild as a panther and probably meaner. Adam swung at the cat with the knife, and it took off running.

He had a job to do, and it had to be done quickly. He looked at the first rat, its fat body locked in the jaws of the trap, and it looked back at him: the rodent wasn't dead yet. Adam stood as far back from the thing as he could, while still being able to reach it with the knife; its blood would probably squirt out all over the place because it was still alive. He had never killed a mammal before; chopped the heads off of some already-dead rats, sure, but this was different: it was looking at him; he would be the executioner. He thought about why he was there: it was all his mother's fault. He wasn't exactly sure about why he was angry; he was confused. Nunny and Cecil had told him she would abandon him, and they seemed to know so much. They knew about things before they happened. Adam didn't know what to believe. A feeling came over him, as if there was someone else in his body. He picked up his arms and brought the knife down hard on the rat's neck.

He looked at the sight before him. He thought about when he had found the decapitated rat under the rock not so long ago, and how it had terrified him. Things had changed so much since then. He felt like another person. Sometimes, lately, it was as if there were other people inside his head, all talking at once.

The rat head looked so strange separated from its body, almost unidentifiable: a fuzzy arrowhead with whiskers. He thought about what the skull would look like free of flesh.

"Adam," a voice behind him said. The hair on his head felt like it had abandoned ship; it wasn't a voice he recognized.

"I suppose you'll be needing this," the voice said. Now, he knew who it belonged to. He had been followed. Adam turned around to see his grandfather standing there holding his blue drawstring sack.

Adam's head spun with excuses. But there was no denying what he had done; his grandfather was not a fool. Another way out of the situation struck him: he did still have the knife; he doubted if his grandfather had told anyone where he was going or why. But Adam wouldn't even let the thought fully come to mind; it just hung there on the edge, its cruel claws pawing at the dirt in his head. He looked up to see his grandfather watching him. He said something that made Adam believe that he had at least guessed at Adam's thoughts: "I hope you're done using that thing. It can be a dangerous weapon. Hand it over."

Adam gave him the knife. *Great*, he thought. *Now I'll have to go back to that stupid psychologist.* Adam didn't think Paul was such a bad guy, but Nunny and Cecil had told him that Paul was just trying to keep him calm and rational until his mom had time to make a getaway.

"What's going through that head of yours, little guy?" his grandfather asked. "Just what did you plan to use these for?"

Adam stared down at the ground.

"You'd better answer me, or you'll have to answer to your mother," his grandfather warned. "This little game you're playing has got to stop. Now, you'd better start talking."

"What?" Adam asked.

"What are you using these for? Why are you doing this?"

"Nunny and Cecil want them."

"For what?"

"To eat."

"You know these things carry diseases of all kinds. I think you'd better let Nunny and Cecil fend for themselves. If I catch you doing anything like this again, I'll cut *your* head off. Do you understand me?"

"Yes, Grandpa."

NUNNY & CECIL—A Tale of Terror

"Just who are Nunny and Cecil?"

"They're my friends. They're invisible. They live in the house with us."

"Enough is enough. I don't want to hear another word about that Nunny and Cecil. There is no such thing as an invisible person. You got me?"

"Yes, Grandpa. But Grandpa, they're not people. They're..."

"That's enough, I said," his grandfather interrupted. "One more thing, Adam. Did you chop the head off that rat you found under that rock in the woods?"

"No, Grandpa."

"Adam, it's important that you tell me the truth about this."

"I didn't do it, Grandpa. Honest!"

"I guess I'll have to take your word for it. Now you get back to the house and clean up."

"Grandpa, are you going to tell Mom?"

"I don't know, Adam. I'll have to think about it."

It was clear to Adam why his grandfather didn't want him to have invisible friends: his grandfather was afraid.

Denise woke up to the sound of the rain on her window and the smell of bacon wafting up from downstairs. The first thing that entered her mind was the memory of the previous evening: Bruce's handsome face and warm embraces.

She felt strangely guilty when the kids, seeing that she was awake, came clamoring into bed with her.

"Good morning, Mommy," Amy greeted her. "Did you have fun last night? We missed you."

"Speak for yourself." Adam spat the words at his sister.

"Adam! What would make you say such a nasty thing?" Denise demanded.

"Where were you last night?" he asked.

"Just who do you think you are, mister? You have no right to speak to me with that tone. Now go to your room. Right now!" she screamed.

Adam jumped off the bed and ran to his room like a bullet, slamming the door behind him.

"I'm sorry, Mommy," Amy apologized for him. "I don't know what's wrong with him this time. I think he's spending too much time with Nunny and Cecil."

"Amy! You speak as if they're real people. We must not feed his imagination. And don't apologize, honey. It's not your fault," she said, sighing and pulling her daughter tightly to her. She would let Adam sit in his room and steam all day, until he decided to come out and apologize.

She really wanted to be able to enjoy the day, but she would never be able to do that without first having it out with Adam.

As she was putting on her robe, she felt the first dull throb of an after-a-night-of-wine-and-romance headache. She searched the medicine cabinet for ibuprofen, and then, after scrubbing her face, brushing her teeth, and swallowing two Excedrin Migraines, she prepared to enter the den of the fire-breathing dragon.

She knocked on the cave door, and the dragon emitted a tiny sound that she couldn't quite make out. She entered.

"What's up, Grendl?" she asked, hoping the touch of humor would change his attitude and her own.

"Nothing."

"Why are you so mad at me all the time? What was the reason for that mean and nasty outburst a few minutes ago?"

"Where did you go last night?" he pouted.

"I went to a party—just where I said I was going. Do you have a problem with that?"

"Someone told me you were with a man."

"Who told you that?" she asked, amazed that he knew and feeling like a guilty child.

"Nunny and Cecil told me," he said. *Nunny and Cecil are projections of his anger; they give him permission to lash out and misbehave*—Paul's words echoed in her head.

"How did they come by this information?" she asked, wanting to scream, "There is no such thing as a Nunny or a Cecil!"

"I don't know, and yes, there is," he said.

"Adam, I did go to the party last night…with a man. His name is Bruce, and he's very nice. He is divorced and has two children, too—just like me. I'm sorry I didn't tell you before I went, but I was afraid you would lie awake all night, upset that I was out with a man. I was planning to talk it over with you today," she confessed, feeling guiltier than ever. She had withheld the truth to avoid a hassle, something she had told her children never to do.

"Listen, I'm going to be totally straight with you. You know why your father and I got a divorce. It wasn't my fault! Now, if you think I'm going to stay home for the rest of my life crying over your father, you're crazy! I'm going to date other men, Adam," she was on the verge of crying and blinked her eyes rapidly to hold back the tears.

There was suddenly a peculiar odor in the air. It smelled like blood. "What's that horrible smell?" she asked. It was there, and then it was gone. *Friends with the blood monster,* Amy had said of Adam. She looked at Adam, trying to conceal the horror that was creeping into her mind, but then the smell was gone, and she wasn't sure whether she had smelled it at all.

"I don't smell anything," he said innocently.

"Adam, Paul had a long talk with you about Nunny and Cecil, and he told you not to talk about them to anyone, because—as he explained to you—that will only reinforce their imagined presence in your mind."

Adam gave her a funny look, as if he didn't understand what she had said.

"Why don't you talk to us about how you're feeling? Have you been practicing the exercises Paul gave you for when you feel anger?"

"No," he said.

"Well, I want you to do those exercises. I'll plan a special surprise for you if you'll do them."

His face lit up at the mention of a special surprise. "But if you talk about those imaginary playmates again, you forfeit the special surprise. Do you understand me?" she asked.

"But they're real, Mom!" he told her. "I'm not lying!"

"Adam!" she said, clenching her teeth and fists.

"Yes," he said, bowing his little head.

"Yes, what?"

"I won't talk about them anymore. But how do I know I'll like the special surprise?"

"I'll make it worth your while—don't you worry. Look, I know there aren't any kids around here for you to play with, but Amy told me just this morning that she wishes you'd ask her to play with you more often," she lied. "She's lonely, too, you know. Soon we'll move back to the suburbs, and you'll have a lot of friends to play with. Just bear with me through this. I need some love and understanding, too!" she told him. "Alright? Is there anything you'd like to say, now that I'm through with my speech?"

"I'm sorry for being mean," he apologized.

"I accept your apology," she told him, hugging and kissing him.

While Denise was squeezing Adam, she noticed a gray clump of hair on his pillow. She picked it up and looked at it.

"What is this, Adam?" she asked, bewildered.

"I don't know," he said.

"You *do* know, Adam. Now tell me what it is! It's horrible and it stinks!" she said. It smelled like a dirty, wet dog.

"If I tell you, you'll get mad," he said.

"You're darn right, I'll get mad. But if you don't tell me, I'll get even angrier. Did you sneak a stray dog in here?"

"No," he said.

"Adam, what is this?" she asked.

"It must have come from Nunny and…" he started.

"Don't even it say it!" she interrupted. "Now this isn't our house, and you can't have any pets here. Believe me, you don't want to make Grandpa angry. If he found some filthy dog in here, he'd have a fit, and Grandma would too. Now tell me, did you bring a dog in here?"

"No, I didn't!"

"Then what was it? A cat?"

"I didn't bring any kind of animal in here!"

"I can't take this anymore. I thought we were friends, but I guess I've let you down somehow. Go on downstairs. I think breakfast has been ready for a while now. I'll be down in a minute, after I clean up this mess," she said, pulling the bedding off of Adam's bed and throwing it into a heap on the floor.

Denise pulled off her nightgown and put on a sweatshirt and pants. As she was leaving the room to go downstairs, she noticed the bird earrings lying on her vanity. *I'd better put those things away,* she thought. They made her uneasy, reminding her of something. *I should have given them to that awful Bernadette,* she thought with a laugh. But as she picked them up to put them into her jewelry box, the laugh turned into a grimace of horror as one of the little black beaks fell bouncing clickety-clackety onto the smooth white surface of the vanity, forcing her to remember what she had tried to forget: the bird that had almost caused her to lose control of the car—it had no beak.

I'm the messenger of doom, Bernadette had said, reaching up to touch one of the ravens dangling from her ear.

24

Denise walked slowly down the stairs to the breakfast table, where everyone sat waiting for breakfast. She was tired.

"Fried, scrambled, poached, or boiled," her mother called out. "Hmm," she muttered, opening the egg carton. "Has anyone been into these eggs?" I just bought this carton yesterday, and there were twelve little, bald, white ones."

There was a unanimous "no" from the family, but Denise noticed that Adam scrunched down further in his seat.

"Must have been a mouse," Marie said. Everyone wanted scrambled, so she broke all the eggs into a bowl, and then went into the refrigerator for more.   Denise popped toast into the toaster and watched her mother scramble eggs. There were dark circles under her mother's eyes, and she clutched her stomach when she thought no one was looking—a sure sign that her stomach was acting up.

"Mom," Denise said, "you didn't wait up for me last night, did you?"

"Oh, no, Denise," she said, not meeting Denise's gaze. "I slept like a baby."

"Grandpa and Grandma let us stay up to watch the late movie, *The Ring*," Amy said.

Denise told them about the party, carefully leaving out the most important part, which was Bruce. It was difficult for her to leave him out; she wanted to tell them everything about him.

"Mom, you don't look so hot," Amy told her.

"You do look rather peaked," Marie told her, looking concerned.

"I guess I'm just getting to old for partying," she told them, looking out the window for the umpteenth time that morning at the enormous raven, sitting atop the scarecrow's head, staring at the house. She took her first bite of the eggs on her plate; they were cold—cold as her trembling hands.

25

Adam rushed upstairs immediately after breakfast. He opened his sock drawer carefully and spied the eggs. He looked around the room for something to carry them in: a sock would be perfect. He carefully placed the eggs inside a white athletic sock, and then listened at his door for sounds of his family, but heard nothing. He walked out into the hall and stood at the top of the stairs, listening to make sure everyone was still downstairs. Satisfied that he wouldn't be disturbed, he put his hand on the cold doorknob of the attic door. As he was opening the door, he nearly dropped his sockful of eggs as a voice behind him said, "Just where do you think you're going?"

Adam swung around to see his sister standing there with her hands on her hips, playing the mother hen.

"Where does it look like I'm going?"

"It looks like you're going looking for trouble," she said snottily. "What's in your hand?" she asked.

Damn it, he thought, beginning to hate her. *Why do I have to have a stupid sister, anyway?*

"None of your damn business!" he told her.

"You're not allowed to swear. Now if you don't tell me what's in that sock your holding, I'm going to tell on you—immediately!"

"Take it and see for yourself, nosy!" he said, shoving the sock at her. "Be careful! I'll kill you if you drop it," he told her.

"Adam!" she exclaimed, peering into the sock. "You're a liar, and a thief too. Boy, Adam, I don't know what's gotten into you. Lying, swearing, and being mean to everyone—you're just asking for trouble!" she told him, shoving the sock at Adam. "What are you doing with these eggs? Feeding your monsters?"

Adam smiled at the thought of how horrified she would be if she knew how right she was.

"If you know what's good for you, you'll mind your own business!" he told her. Closing the door quietly behind him, he tiptoed up the attic stairs.

"Nunny? Cecil?" he called out in a whisper. "I have a present for you."

"I have a present for both of you," he said into the empty air of the cluttered, dusty attic.

"What do you have?" Adam recognized Nunny's gravelly voice.

"You know what it is: your second favorite thing to eat. But I'm not going to give it to you unless you let me see you. I'm tired of having friends that I can't even see."

"But if you see us, you might not want to be our friend. We told you before, we're not very pretty to look at," Cecil wheezed.

"I don't care what you look like. I'm not afraid. You're the only friends I have, and I want to see you. Now, I'll give you these eggs if you show me what you look like," he said, presenting the eggs like precious gems, one in each hand. He wished he had the rat heads; they would be so much more enticing.

Cecil said, "All right, we'll do it. But you mustn't be afraid. We might be horrible to look at, but we would never hurt you."

"I told you," Adam insisted, "I won't be afraid. Nothing scares me." There was a scrambling noise in a darkened corner of the attic; a dark form approached the boy. It was partially covered by an old, torn blanket. Adam could see the hands that held the blanket together, but they weren't hands: they were more like paws with thick, black, curling claws extending from them. *I'm not scared*, he told himself, although he was repulsed at the sight of the pawlike hands.

Slowly, they lowered the blanket to reveal themselves. Adam took a step backward and thought fleetingly of running down the stairs screaming. He could feel the hairs on his arms rise to the occasion and the adrenaline surge in his veins; but he had given them his word that he wouldn't reject them. They couldn't help it if they were ugly, he reasoned. He put his hand on an old chest in order to steady himself, to give him something solid and real to hold onto. They had told him that they looked somewhat like wolves, but Adam never dreamed they could be so horrible. He'd seen werewolves in horror movies, but Nunny and Cecil were more human than the werewolves he'd seen, which made them all the more repugnant.

"Still friends?" Nunny asked, extending his grotesque paw-hand for Adam to shake.

Adam hesitated, taking a few seconds to look at it, and then, taking hold of the paw with his small hand, he said, "Still friends."

"And now the eggs," Cecil said, a thick ooze of drool dripping from the corner of his mouth onto the wooden floor.

Adam gave them the eggs, which they devoured, crunching into the shells and gnashing their pointed teeth. They licked the yolk from their black lips, smiled at Adam, and then turned and disappeared into the dark corner, wagging their tails behind them.

NUNNY & CECIL—A Tale of Terror

26

Christmas morning arrived in a flurry of wrapping paper and laughter. A goose was in the oven and a fire was on the hearth.

After all the presents were opened, Amy and Adam broke into the brightly colored, cellophane-wrapped popcorn balls that were hanging on the tree. Their grandmother had said, "No popcorn balls until Christmas day," and she had counted them daily to make sure the kids didn't try to sneak one.

"Don't eat too many of those things," Joe told them. "You'll spoil your dinner, and you might even get sick."

"Listen to your grandpa; he's speaking from experience. One Christmas he ate so many of them, he got really sick," Marie told them.

"I remember that, Dad. Your face turned the same shade of green as that popcorn ball," Denise laughed.

"That's why I don't eat them anymore," he muttered, clearly embarrassed.

"That was the same Christmas you bought me my first car. That's probably why you got sick, Dad, from worrying about me having my own set of wheels. You should have seen that car: a red Chevy Camaro. I thought I was so cool in that car. That was one of my best Christmas days ever!" Denise reminisced.

"My best Christmas is right now! I love all my presents, especially my books!" Amy told them, looking at the huge pile of books on the floor.

"My best Christmas was the year we went to the mountains, with Daddy," Adam said, looking hard at Amy, trying to make her feel guilty. "I like the presents he sent me the best," he added, making everyone uncomfortable.

The aroma of roast goose and stuffing was beginning to permeate the air, making everyone's mouth water. Marie brought out a tray of tiny sandwiches for lunch and informed them that dinner wouldn't be served for another three hours.

The phone rang. Marie got up to answer it.

"I'll bet I know who that is," she said, hesitating a moment before going into the kitchen to answer it.

"Merry Christmas," she said into the receiver.

"Same to you, Marie. How are you?" It was Donald.

"I'm fine. Hold on, and I'll get the kids," she said, purposely dropping the receiver onto the counter.

"Amy, Adam, it's your father," she said.

The kids rushed into the kitchen, excited about speaking to their father. They both missed him terribly. Amy didn't like to admit it, but Adam made sure everyone was aware of his feelings on the subject.

Marie busied herself in the kitchen, and then went back into the living room to face her daughter, who sat on the couch with an afghan on her lap, staring silently at the fire. She looked up at her mother with one of her don't-say-anything-cause-I'll-cry smiles. Marie sat down beside her and began stroking her hair.

She and Donald had been so happy together. She would never understand why he had an affair. He had been on a losing streak in the courtroom, which damaged his ego, but Denise had always been there for him, encouraging him on.

She wished that she could erase what he had done and that it was him who was sitting there with his arms wrapped around her instead of her mother. *But no*, she thought, *he's a thousand miles away, probably in the arms of some woman.*

"Thanks for being here for me, Mom! Don't worry. I'll be fine," she said, smiling sadly. "Now, let's go see what's cooking," Denise said, throwing off the afghan and getting up to stretch. *Now, if the kids don't tell me too much of what their asshole of a father said,* she thought, *I'll be fine.*

Marie must have read Denise's mind: when Amy and Adam flew into the kitchen, chirping about what their father had said, she told them to get upstairs and make their beds, allowing Denise to get lost in her cooking.

After making her bed, Amy decided to put her new books on her bookshelf. She went downstairs and gathered them awkwardly in her arms, dropping several of them on her way back upstairs.

She thought about the conversation she had just had with her father. He always seemed so preoccupied, like he wasn't really listening to her when she spoke.

He had been such a great father…before, but now he seemed so different. He used to talk with her about what she read as if he was genuinely interested; but this Christmas he had sent her some books that were for kids younger than she was, and a stupid doll—of all things. She had a feeling that he hadn't even done the actual shopping for the presents, that he had probably sent his secretary.

Amy decided to go find Adam. She looked in his room; he wasn't there, so she made her way slowly up the creaking attic staircase. She wanted to be generous of spirit because it was Christmas day; she would play with her brother if he liked. The new hockey game their grandparents had given him for Christmas looked like it might be fun to play.

"Adam," she called out into the dimly lit room. "Adam, it's me, Amy. Do you want to play?" she called, expecting Adam to jump out from a dark corner and scare her.

She listened for movement but heard nothing. The sun burst through the fortress of the gray winter sky; a beam of sunlight passed into the room through a small window, illuminating the darkened corners Amy had been so afraid of.

She walked carefully around the attic, taking advantage of the suddenly available light and peeping into every corner where something or someone could hide. There was nothing there, no monster of any kind, so she eventually began to relax.

She surveyed the lamps, boxes, and dozens of chests that covered the dusty wooden floor of the attic. There was even a beautiful antique birdcage, with golden bars and a mirror for the bird inside.

The old chests were incredibly intriguing to her, but she wondered if her mother and grandparents wouldn't want her going through them, thinking she would mess everything up. *But they let Adam hang out up here. He probably doesn't go rummaging in the chests, though,* she thought, running her finger through the thick dust on some of the chests, an indication that they hadn't been touched in a very long time.

Amy decided that she'd better hurry up and do it; she might never get a chance to do it again, once her mother or grandparents found out. Someone would soon be looking for her.

Excitement and fear flowed through her veins, filling her with nervous energy. She made her way to the farthest corner of the room, the corner most likely to contain the oldest, most interesting chests. She brushed the dust off an old sea chest with her hand, sneezing from the particles flying helter-skelter into the air.

It was a huge effort just to unbuckle the thick leather straps that bound the old chest. One of the straps was so stiff that it broke when Amy tried to unbend it.

"Great", she said aloud.

The chest didn't want to open. She used all of her strength to try to push open the lid, but it wouldn't budge; finally, as she was about to give up and try another one, it opened with a "thunk" so loud, she was sure everyone downstairs must have heard.

She dove in. Her excitement was somewhat diminished as she went through the trunk finding only neatly folded dull colored dresses. She wanted letters and books and love notes. She pulled out one of the dresses and held it up. "Yech!" she exclaimed in disgust at both the plainness of the dress and the odor of mothballs that filled her nose. The dress was made of an ugly green material, threadbare in some places. It was very long and had a high collar.

She had noticed a large old mirror with a gilt-edged frame over near the birdcage. She wanted to get the total effect of the dress and the person who had worn it, so she decided to put it on. She shook it out, hoping to rid it of the odor and any bugs that might have made it their home. *It sure is a heavy dress for being made of such lightweight material,* Amy thought, rubbing the flimsy material between her fingers.

She put the dress on over her own clothes and walked over to the mirror. She noticed a pile of old hat boxes in the corner and opened each one, searching for a hat to go with the dress.

She decided on a bright red one with a net that hung over her eyes and a smashed feather that she imagined had once stuck out boldly. It was quite a vivid contrast to the dull green of the dress. The hat didn't look like it was from the same era as the dress; it had probably been her grandmother's; the dress could have belonged to her grandmother's grandmother.

She twirled around in front of the dusty mirror, laughing at how silly she looked. The dress hung down heavily on one side, as if something was weighing it down. Amy pulled up the hem to examine it and felt a heavy, square-shaped object inside of it. She hurriedly took the dress off and turned it inside out, knocking the hat onto the floor in the process. The hem of the dress was expertly sewn, except for the section just above the object, which was sewn haphazardly.

"Amy, is that you up there? It's almost time to eat," her mother yelled up the stairs to her, almost giving the girl a heart attack.

"Yeah, Mom, it's me. I'll be right down. I was just...I was just looking for Adam," she shouted, her heart beating like bongos in her chest. She stood perfectly still, listening for her mother to ascend the staircase, praying that she wouldn't.

Tap, tap, tap. She heard the footsteps on the staircase and quickly looked around for a place to hide the dress and hat.

Denise," she heard her grandmother's muffled voice from downstairs.

"I'm up here, Mom," Amy's mother yelled down. Amy's grandmother had yelled something about potatoes boiling over.

Tap, tap, tap. The sound of her mother's footsteps descended the stairs, and Amy sighed with relief.

She wanted to stay in the attic and open the hem, but she was afraid that once her mother had things under control in the kitchen, she might come back up. She folded the dress neatly and stuffed it under everything else in the chest. She put the hat back in its box.

She took a handful of dust from the floor and spread it over the top of the chest. Then she blew on the dust to even it out. She looked around to see if everything was in place and scampered down the steps with the joy of her newfound mystery.

Denise sat on her bed reading, trying not to doze off. The hustle bustle of Christmas day was behind her; she was glad for some time to herself. She looked up from her book to see her father standing at her door, his finger to his lips, signaling her to keep quiet.

"Do you have a minute to talk?" he whispered.

She shook her head yes.

He came into the room and sat down on her bed.

"I don't want anyone to hear us, especially Adam, and he's right above us," he said, pointing up at the ceiling.

"I'm going to tell you something that's really going to upset you," he said. "I should have told you before, but I kind of promised Adam I wouldn't. You can decide whether or not you're going to talk to him about it. If you do, he might not trust me anymore. But I'll let you decide."

"What is it?"

"This is going to sound really strange. I was out checking the rattraps one day in the barn...and the rats that were caught in the traps were missing their heads. I found the heads in that blue drawstring sack that Adam carries around with him."

Denise could feel her skin begin crawl away from her bones. She was afraid of what he would say next.

"I heard Adam get up real early one morning, so I followed him. He went out to the barn and chopped off a rat's head with your mother's butcher knife. If your mother would have seen him, she would have cut *his* head off."

"So he knows you saw him?"

"He knows it, alright. I asked him why he did it..." he began.

"And?" she prompted.

"He said the heads were for Nunny and Cecil—to eat. He asked me if I was going to tell you, and I said I wasn't sure."

"What about that rat he found under that rock in the woods? Did he chop its head off?" she asked, finding it hard to believe they were having the conversation.

"He said he didn't know anything about that one."

"Why did you decide to tell me now, Dad?" she asked him, feeling sick to her stomach.

"Because he's up in the attic right now talking up a tornado with his imaginary buddies, and I'm a bit worried about the boy."

Amy spent that night in the attic—at least in her dreams she did.

In a dream, she heard a voice calling her name, "Amy...Aammyyy."

She got up from her bed and went out into the hallway. The voice called again, "Amy...Amy."

The unfamiliar, girlish voice was coming from the attic. The attic door was slightly ajar, and a bright, unnatural light seeped through the opening. Amy ascended the staircase, her nostrils filling with the heavy scent of ammonia. The wooden floor had been swept and polished, and everything in the attic had been dusted and neatly arranged.

A phonograph was playing old-fashioned music. She was suddenly cold. The windows were open; a cold breeze gently blew the filmy white curtains into great billowing curves.

She liked the music. She wanted to lose herself in the feelings it aroused, but she was distracted by an odd, scratching sound in the corner of the room. She turned to see a huge raven in the gold birdcage. It stared intently at Amy through large, coal-black eyes that glowed with an unearthly light. It looked like the monstrous bird that had swooped in front of their car, almost causing them to have an accident.

Amy looked at the chest that contained what she had come to find; it opened slowly with a loud grating noise. She was walking toward it, the phonograph music getting louder and faster by the moment, when suddenly the bird flew out of its cage and swooped purposefully into her path, its wings beating the air with hard downward strokes.

Amy ducked to avoid the bird, but it continued cutting her off from her destination. She began to swing her arms wildly at it, and the bird, in turn, began to peck at her head and arms. The music grew louder and more erratic. She was about to turn and run back down the stairs when, with a final determined swing at the vicious bird, she knocked its sharp beak from its face, causing it to fly—screeching in pain—into a corner of the room.

Amy walked over to the chest, marveling at its eerie attraction. She bent over to look inside, but recoiled in horror as a tremendous heat flowed out of the aperture. The chest contained a pit so deep that she could barely see what lay at the bottom. When she strained her eyes to look, she saw creatures—half wolf, half man—dancing in a fire.

Something cold and wet touched the back of Amy's neck and pushed her so hard that she fell head first into the pit in the chest, the lid closing with a "thunk" as final as the closing of a coffin lid. Amy slowly tumbled, screaming, into the fiery depths; the strange wolflike creatures danced in a frenzy, their faces pointed upward, their mouths stretched wide open to reveal razor sharp teeth.

Amy knew that at any moment they would rip her flesh into pieces.

"Amy, Amy!" someone called her name from above. "Amy!" It was her mother's voice, forcing her awake and pulling her back into the land of the real.

27

Bruce was fifteen minutes early. He didn't want to risk being late to meet Denise's family, so he had given himself plenty of time. He stood outside and gave the place a once over. Two figures looked down at him from the attic. *That must be the kids,* he thought, waving up at them. But they didn't wave back. He waved again, thinking maybe they were shy. Again, there was no response. He shaded his eyes with his hand and strained to see who it was. Maybe it's just some boxes stacked up there, he thought. But then he noticed the eyes. One of the figures had glowing, yellow eyes.

That's odd, he thought. And he thought it even odder when within the next few seconds Amy and Adam came running around the side of the house.

"Well, hello!" he said to them, glancing up to see that the figures were no longer there. *It could have been Denise's parents,* he reasoned, wondering why they were up in the attic, and if it was them, why they didn't wave.

The children stopped in their tracks and surveyed Bruce from head to toe. Adam pushed the hair out of his eyes and turned around to look up at the attic window.

This is getting stranger by the minute.

"I'm Bruce, your mother's friend," he said, extending his hand to Adam, who just stared at Bruce's hand.

"I'm Adam," he said glumly, and turned to look at the attic window again. *He must have some friends up there,* Bruce thought.

"And you must be Amy," he said, extending his hand to her. She hesitated for a minute, and then shook his hand firmly.

"Our mom's upstairs getting ready, and Grandma's setting the table. Do you want to go in?" Amy asked.

He was about to speak when the front door opened and Marie came out of the house to greet him. She shook his hand warmly.

"Hello, Mrs. Rodman. It's a pleasure to meet you."

"Hello, Bruce. Please call me Marie. It's so nice to meet you. I see you've already met my grandchildren," she said. And then turning to Adam: "Why just look at your hair! You run upstairs and have your mother fix it for you," she said, giving him a little pat on his shoulder to get him moving.

"Well, come inside. Dinner's almost ready," she told him. "I hope you like shrimp."

"I do," Bruce said.

They all walked into the house; Joe met them at the door.

"This is my husband, Joe. Joe, this is Bruce," Marie said.

"Bruce, it's nice to finally meet you. Can I get you a beer?" Joe asked.

"I'd love one."

They sat and talked, the kids watching Bruce's every move. Denise came downstairs and they sat and talked until dinner was ready.

Bruce looked around the table at everyone and was both surprised and relieved that no one had glowing, yellow eyes. He thought about asking if they had any ghosts in the house, but decided that it probably wouldn't be a good idea. *That's all I need,* he thought, *to come over for dinner and scare the hell out of everyone.*

They were in the midst of eating dinner, when Adam excused himself and left the table. He never returned, and no one said anything about it. Denise had mentioned she was having some problems with him—without going into any detail—so he guessed the boy's sudden departure from the dinner table had something to do with his problems.

After Bruce had looked at Adam's empty chair for about the seventeenth time, Denise leaned over and said softly, "We're ignoring his bad behavior. I think if he doesn't get the attention he's seeking, maybe he'll wise up and be a good boy."

Bruce shook his head and said, "I see."

28

Amy peeked into her brother's room; he wasn't there. She hoped he wasn't in the attic; she was on her way up there and didn't want him nosing around in her business. She had put off going up there, waiting for it to be vacant, waiting for the residue of fear from her nightmare to go away. She was impatient to find out what was hidden in the hem of that dress, even though she felt her nightmare was a warning to stay away from it.

She was relieved to find dust on the attic stairs. If they would have been clean, as they were in her dream, she would have hightailed it out of there and forgotten about what was in the dress.

"Adam, are you up here?" she called out, but there was no sign of her brother. One thing she didn't want was for him to find out about her secret. She had no time to waste. She headed straight for the old chest and pushed it open with every bit of her strength.

Amy reached deep into the chest and pulled out the dress. Her heart almost beat itself right out of her chest in anticipation. She ripped the hem open and gasped with delight when she saw it was a small, black, leather-bound book with gilt-edged pages. She knew that it must be a diary; no one would have gone through so much trouble to hide anything else—unless, of course, they were love letters.

She pried the book open to one of the first few pages and read: "Diary of Jenna Jerrel, 1874." She had to separate the pages with her fingernails; they were glued shut from being compressed for so long.

Amy heard a tapping noise; she slammed the little book shut and quickly looked around the room, but she couldn't locate the source of the sound.

She neatly folded the dress and put it under the other dresses in the chest. She closed the lid of the chest; it resounded with a thud that brought memories of her nightmare. *The closing of the coffin lid.*

Tap...tap...tap--there it was again.

Amy's mouth went suddenly dry. She stuffed the diary down her pants and ran as fast as she could down the attic stairs, fearing that she would be sucked back into the chest.

She was in such a hurry that she failed to see the huge raven that sat just outside the attic window, tap, tap, tapping at the glass.

Amy kissed her grandparents goodnight.

"Amy, you look so tired. And you have a test tomorrow, don't you?" her grandmother asked.

"Yes, I do, Grandma. It's only a spelling test, though, and they're so easy I could take them in my sleep."

"What did you do today to get so tired? Were you wrestling with boys in gym class?" her grandfather asked.

You know me, Grandpa—I'm always wrestling with boys," she said with a tired laugh, walking slowly toward the stairs.

Amy hadn't had time to read the diary earlier that day, and now she was dead tired and had to get to sleep.

She took off her clothes and put on her pajamas. Her room felt oddly warm; it was usually the coolest room in the house, being in the northwest corner. She turned Judy toward the wall, looked in the closet and under the bed for monsters of any kind, and then turned out the light and crawled into bed.

Amy's mind raced with thoughts of the diary, but her body was beginning to feel weightless and unconnected to her head, the way it always did when she was very tired and had a lot on her mind. As her conscious thoughts began mixing with her subconscious thoughts, creating that elusive state at the midpoint of consciousness, she heard the heavy, raspy breathing sound that she always attributed to the wind and the age of the house. Her grandmother had explained away every odd noise that way: the house was old and had a right to wheeze and knock and sputter and cough, especially at night.

The sound woke Amy, and she sat up wondering if she had been sleeping. It was gone now, and all that remained was the misshapen shadow of the wolf's head on her bedroom door. She looked around the room, as she always did, for the object making the shadow; and, as usual, there was nothing there to make such an odd-shaped shadow.

She had seen the shadow many times, but tonight it seemed larger and more threatening. She was tired of it being there, tired of explaining it away as nothing.

"Grandma," she called out as loudly as she could. "Grandma, come here!" Amy thought about jumping out of the bed and running for the door, but she was too scared to move. She was surprised that she could even call out.

Amy thought she heard the sound of her grandmother's footsteps on the stairs, but she wasn't sure. The door suddenly opened, a cool whiff of air blew in, and Mr. Wolf vanished. Amy's grandmother stood at the door.

"Grandma!" she said, throwing her arms around her grandmother's neck. "Will you sleep with me tonight?"

"Why, Amy? What's wrong? Did you have another bad dream?" Marie asked.

"It wasn't a dream, Grandma—it was real. There was a wolf in my room," Amy told her.

"Well, he's not here now," Marie said. "There's no wolf, honey. Are you sure you weren't dreaming?"

"It was the shadow of a wolf—the shadow of its head there on my door," Amy told her.

"Let me turn off the light and close the door. I'll lie here next to you, and we'll see if he comes out," Marie said, crawling into bed with Amy. "I'll lie here real still and quiet so it won't know I'm here."

Marie lay there until she heard Amy's breathing turn into the soft, slow breathing of sleep, and then she eased herself out of the bed.

She tiptoed down the stairs. Joe was asleep in front of the TV, his head lolling to one side, a soft snore escaping his lips.

Marie nudged him awake, and walked over to turn off the TV. "Wake up, Joe. It's time to go to bed. You'd sleep there all night in that chair if I'd let you, and then I'd have to listen to you complain all day tomorrow about your backache and the crick in your neck."

"Alright," he said, rising from his chair and stretching.

"What was wrong with Amy? A tummy ache?" he whispered as they climbed the staircase.

"No, it was just some shadows in the dark. She's always seeing something. She reads too many horror stories," she told him.

"Shadows? What kind of shadows?"

"She says that there's a shadow in the shape of a wolf's head on her door some nights," Marie told him, pulling her sweater up over her head. "I stayed in there with her until she fell asleep."

So, did you see any wolf shadows?"

"No, I didn't. But I did see the shadow of a great big chicken," she laughed. "You'd think this house was haunted the way those kids act sometimes. If it were haunted, it would have started being haunted a long time ago. We never had any problems with shadows and ghosts and monsters when Denise was growing up," she told him, pulling down the covers and crawling into bed. I mean, what could have happened between when Denise was little and now to make this old house so spooky?"

"You've got me," he said.

Joe lay awake for a long time that night, thinking about the bones he had dug up. *A shadow of a wolf's head, he thought; somehow it fits right in.* A lot of things had changed since he had dug up the mysterious bones and taken them out into the woods. He had thought he would rest easier knowing they weren't down there, in the earth below his house, but that wasn't the case. He had disturbed the spirit of the place when he dug up those bones, and the house no longer felt like an impregnable fortress.

He lay awake that night until Denise was home and safely asleep in her bed, and then he fell into a shallow, troubled sleep.

Denise stood outside on the balcony adjoining her bedroom. Her breath smoked the freezing winter air. The moon was full, illuminating the orchard with its unearthly light. She was too excited to sleep, thinking about her night with Bruce. He had met her halfway for dinner.

"What would you like to do after we eat?" he had said between bites of his fettuccine.

"Let's just go sit in the car somewhere, and make out...or whatever," she said.

"A toast to whatever," he said picking up his glass and clinking it lightly against hers.

Denise was thinking about how they had made love in the backseat of her car, how bitterly cold it was outside, how toasty warm it was in the car, the fogged windows providing all the privacy they needed, when she saw something move down in the orchard.

She watched for a moment; seeing nothing out of the ordinary, she slipped back into her reverie.

Denise leaned against the railing. The moon was more beautiful and full of light than she had ever seen it. The apple trees looked wild. Something moved in among the trees; this time she was certain. She strained her eyes to see. The cold had worked its way under her skin, making her teeth chatter. Turning to go into the house, she heard something rustling in the orchard.

She turned around just in time to see them: two men danced among the trees, slipping in and out of the shadows, their bodies moving rigidly, arms jutting out ritualistically. She stared down at them, trying to see who they were. As they danced out of the shadows of the trees, into the bright light of the moon, she could see clearly that they weren't exactly men: their heads were wolflike, as were their appendages, and yet they danced on their hind legs. Their glistening tongues lolled from their mouths, their tails wagged, and their sharp teeth gleamed. She had an odd feeling that she had them somewhere before.

Just then a smaller figure joined the two. She thought for a fleeting moment that it was Adam and her heart jerked in her chest. It was a young boy, about Adam's age, dressed like a punk rocker. The boy was missing one of his arms and a piece of his torso, but he danced with a smile on his pale lips. Denise knew the boy: It was Jeffrey Abrahm. He looked up at her and laughed.

Denise bit her lip in fear and gripped the railing so tightly, her nails sank into the rotting wood. As she wrenched her hands free of the railing and turned to run into the house, she could smell the blood. The smell was all around her, suffocating her. *I must not faint*, she thought; the door leading from the balcony into her bedroom seemed hours away. *If I can only reach that door, lock it, then, fall inside, I'll be fine. I must not faint...yet.* The smell of the blood was overwhelming. *So much blood, and just from biting my lip,* she thought. She could hear the creatures' feet pounding the frozen ground, or was it her heartbeat in her ears; she wasn't sure. She knew only that the sound was getting closer...they were getting closer.

Her hand fell upon the icy handle of the storm door, and she wrenched the door open. Her vision was closing down like the aperture of a camera. *Lock the door...can't faint until I lock the door.*

She locked the door, stumbled to her bed, and fainted, dead away.

The alarm clock's blare of static-charged music filled Denise's aching head. She cursed the still-dark sky outside her windows; she hated to rise before the sun. A vision of the wolflike creatures and the butchered boy flashed in her mind. She comforted herself for a full two minutes with the rationalization that it must have been a dream. Even as she looked at the blood-encrusted cut on her lip in the bathroom mirror, she told herself it was a dream; but the broken chips of white paint beneath her torn fingernails did not lie.

GAILA SWINDELL

29

Denise closed her office door behind her and walked over to her desk. She picked up the handful of messages that lay in the basket, and then settled into her comfortable chair, turning it around to face the window.

It felt so good to be totally alone in her haven, the only place she could truly escape. The campus looked so pretty with the light blanket of snow that covered it. Luckily for her, it had stopped snowing; she hated to drive in the snow. She knew she could stay with Bruce if the weather became too hazardous, but that would just cause problems with her loved ones.

Her parents had always been open-minded, but they were becoming increasingly more uptight and overprotective every day. Her father had exercised his temper when she took a walk out by the barn without telling anyone where she was going. Denise had never seen him so angry. It was probably the second time in her life that she had ever heard him raise his voice.

"Don't ever let me see you out there alone. Do you hear me, Denise? You could fall and hurt yourself, and we'd never even know you where you were. From now on, I don't want anyone going back there without me," he had yelled at the entire family, who had come running to see what all the commotion was about. "The barn is off limits, is that clear?"

Denise had asked her mother about her father's outburst: "What's got into Dad? I've never seen him act that way. I've been wandering around on this land without supervision since I was old enough to walk."

"Your father's under a lot of pressure right now. He feels very responsible for everyone. That barn is old; it could come toppling down any time. You just never know," Marie had told her.

They had been alone for so many years, and now they had a family to raise all over again. It was all too much for them to handle, and with Adam misbehaving all the time, they were probably going crazy. *Maybe that's why they had only one child,* Denise thought; *they couldn't handle more kids.*

When she was a child, Joe would let her go up to Willard's Creek alone, and now as an adult, he didn't even want her going as far as the barn by herself.

It all became suddenly clear to her that the pressure was getting to them. A sign reading "Guilt Trip" flashed before Denise's eyes. They had pleaded with her to come and live with them after the divorce; she had warned them that it wouldn't be easy.

Denise wanted the kids to finish the school year at their school; it would be too traumatic for them to be pulled out before the year ended. In the meantime, she would start looking for a house. Just knowing that they had a place to go to in June would ease the burden for all of them. She had hoped they could spend the following summer on the farm, but it could get lonely playing with the apple trees, and Adam seemed desperate for friends. Denise couldn't take hearing anything more about Nunny and Cecil; she was afraid of what she might do if Adam mentioned their names again. Lately, she had even caught herself wondering if they were real.

Denise picked up the pile of pink slips on her desk and quickly leafed through them. One read, "Professor Miller, Please call the university counseling center at ext. 9712. Ask for Edith." Maybe this Edith person was calling to thank her for sending someone her way.

Denise put the little pile of notes back in the basket on her desk. She had to get some work done before she headed home, so she took off her shoes, leaned back in her chair, and began to grade papers.

It was hard to concentrate with that message glaring at her from the basket. She was dying to know what this Edith person wanted. She had a funny feeling it had something to do with Lenny Delenko, possibly because the paper she was holding in her hand at that very moment was written by Lenny, and it was about how unethical it was to use rats for laboratory experiments.

Denise dialed the extension and the person on the other end identified herself as Edith, Denise said, "Edith, this is Professor Denise Miller. You wanted to discuss Lenny Delenko?"

The surprised voice on the other end said, "Well, yes, how did you know?"

"I'll be right over," Denise said, folding Lenny's paper and putting it into her purse.

Catherine Hall, the building that housed the university counseling center, was a behemoth of a building. Denise looked around before entering the building, not wanting Lenny to see her going in. She walked down a flight of stairs into the basement of the building, and down the hall to the counseling center. A receptionist directed her to Edith's office.

"Hello, Professor Miller," Edith said, standing to shake Denise's hand.

"Hello, Edith. Please call me Denise," Denise said.

Edith shut the door behind Denise.

Denise took off her coat and sat down.

"Is it still snowing out there?" Edith asked.

"No, it finally stopped. It looks like it could start up again at any moment, though."

"So, Denise. Tell me, how did you know I was calling about Lenny Delenko?" Edith asked.

Denise told her about how Lenny had been acting strangely, staring at her, following her around center city.

"A few weeks after I caught him following me, I copied one of your counseling center fliers and passed it out in a few of my classes; I was hoping Lenny would get some help. And when I received your phone message, I was reading a very strange paper he wrote for an assignment I had given," she told her.

"Did Lenny know that you saw him following you?" Edith asked her.

"I'm not sure. I didn't look directly at him, but out of the corner of my eye I could see him trying to hide behind a cup of coffee," she told her.

"Hmmm, that's interesting. Well, I'm sure you know the policies of the counseling center. We guarantee the patient that we will not give information regarding his or her treatment to anyone. We are not even allowed to mention that someone was here. But we had a meeting about Lenny's case and decided that we have to break our rules in this instance, and now, after hearing this, I feel it's imperative I discuss this with you. I must have your word, though, that you will relate none of what I'm about to tell you to anyone—ever," she said firmly.

"Oh, of course. You have my word," Denise assured her.

"I know this might seem unprofessional, a breach of confidentiality, but we're afraid your life could be in danger. Lenny came to us last week and said he'd been having some bad dreams in which he murders you," Edith told her.

Denise took a long, slow sip of coffee and swallowed hard. Edith's words were going down the wrong way.

"He's had several, and they're starting to become more frequent," Edith told her. "It's the nature of the dreams that's so bizarre. Lenny's first visit was on the seventh. He said that the reason he'd come to the counseling center for help was because he's having dreams about killing his mother.

"He said his father goes out of town on business trips quite often; he's done this ever since Lenny was a child. Lenny said his mother gets very lonely when his father's away, and she drinks. Lenny thinks she's an alcoholic.

"Lenny feels very responsible for his mother when his father's away; his father always tells Lenny that when he's out of town, Lenny is the man of the house. He said that as a child he liked it when his father said this, but now, as an adult, it makes him feel uncomfortable—resentful. He said he doesn't know why it makes him feel uncomfortable.

"He said he spends as much time as possible away from the house when his father's away, and his father gets very angry at Lenny because of this. Lenny said he stays away from the house because he hates to see his mother so lonely and drunk all the time. I asked Lenny if he stays away because he's afraid he might hurt his mother, and he said that wasn't the reason. That concluded the first visit, and Lenny made his next appointment for today.

"The morning after his first visit—the eighth, I received a call from Lenny. He asked if there was any time I could see him that day; he said it was urgent.

"He came in at one o'clock, looking like he hadn't slept at all. He said that he couldn't bear another night of those dreams; he had stayed up all night drinking coffee. He drank four cups during his session that day. He acted as though he were on amphetamines, but when I asked him if he'd taken any drugs, he said, 'No, I would never do that.' I asked what was wrong, and he said he'd get around to it soon enough. He said that the dreams were driving him crazy, and he just couldn't take it anymore.

"I taped part of the session with his permission" Edith said, and pressed the button on the tape recorder that sat on her desk.

Denise sat back and listened to Lenny's voice emanate from the little black box. He talked very quickly: "I'm always a little boy in the dreams. I'm walking home from school in the snow, and it's getting very dark. When I come to my house, I stand outside looking at it. I'm afraid to go in, but I don't know why. I know it has something to do with my mother.

"All of a sudden, while I'm standing there, I see her eyes looking at me through different windows of the house. First they're in the upstairs window, then in the downstairs window, and then my mother's standing there in the front door. I run away and it's getting dark, and the snow's getting in my eyes.

"I end up here at school, in Professor Miller's class. The class has some of my classmates from grade school and some of the people who are really in that class. Professor Miller is lecturing, and she keeps looking at me. Everyone starts to stare at me, so I get up and leave.

"I wander around the school—everything looks bigger than normal—and then I start looking for my car. I start walking through the crummy neighborhoods around school, and finally I come to my house. I go in. I'm very tired, so I lie down on my bed. My mom comes in and starts bugging me, and all of a sudden I have a knife and I stab her. That's it, that's the dream. It's always the same. Listen, I have to go now."

The tape recorder clicked off.

"I'll play part of the next day's session now," Edith said, pulling the tape out of the recorder and putting in another one.

"Lenny made an appointment—at my insistence. I was afraid he wouldn't come back. He wouldn't look me in the eye after he'd told me the dream. I felt that he was leaving something important out, and I found out that I was right.

"By the way," Edith went on. "I checked Lenny's school records to see if there was anything significant. I thought there might be some problems at home, perhaps recorded by a high school counselor or something. It turns out that Daniel and Sheila Delenko adopted Lenny when he was only seven months old."

"Does Lenny know that he was adopted?" Denise asked.

"The records indicate that he doesn't know, and when he came back the next day, I asked him if the Delenkos are his real parents, and he said they are. I knew the records said that he didn't know, but sometimes the parents feel the need to tell their child that he or she was adopted," she said clicking on the tape recorder.

"Lenny, why did you run away from your house? You said you were afraid of something, but you didn't know what. Was it your mother's eyes? Was it your mother?" Edith asked.

"I was afraid of the house, but I didn't know why. There was something about the house," he answered.

"But you said that when your mother appeared, you ran away. Think very hard, what was it about your mother that made you run away?" Edith asked.

"Sh...she was naked," he said.

"And that made you afraid?" she asked.

"Yes," he answered.

"Why?"

"I don't know."

"Do you always stay a child through the entire dream?"

"Yes."

"What was Professor Miller lecturing about? Do you remember?"

"Little Hans and the Oedipus complex."

"Do you think that you might be suffering from the Oedipus complex?"

"No! I think it's bullshit. I hate Freud!"

"Have you ever felt any sexual attraction to your mother?"

"Are you kidding?"

"No, I'm not kidding at all."

"The answer is a definite no."

"You said you finally found your house in the bad section of town. Do you feel that there's any significance to this?"

"Could be. I live in a really nice section of town, so if all of a sudden my house is in the bad section—it must mean the house is somehow...bad."

"What do you feel in your dream right before you kill your mother?"

"Tired."

"Anything else? Are you mad at your mother?"

"Yes."

"Why?"

"Probably because she's wearing sexy clothes under her robe."

"I thought you said she was naked."

"She was when she was looking out the window, but not when I go in."

"So there were certain things about the dream that you didn't tell me yesterday? Why did you withhold these things from me?"

"Because they're so ugly...it's hard to tell someone about them. I'm afraid you might think I have some subconscious desire for my mother or something, which is the furthest thing from the truth."

"I'm here to help you, Lenny, not to judge you. I can't help you if you don't tell me everything. Promise me you won't withhold anything more from me," Edith demanded.

"I promise."

"What kind of sexy clothes is your mother wearing?"

"One of those black things, you know, with the garters attached; black fishnet stockings and black high heels. If you turn your head away, if you quit looking at me, I'll tell you the rest. I can't do it with you sitting there looking at me. Alright?" he said.

"Sure Lenny, that's no problem," Edith said.

Lenny began speaking in a much louder, thinner voice; he sounded like he might cry. "She's wearing her robe, the robe she always wore when I was little—with the tissue in the pocket. Whenever I needed tissue, she'd always reach in the pocket of that robe and pull some out; she'd blow my nose, or wipe my eyes, or whatever. She was always a good mother...except for the drinking. Anyway, her robe falls open and I see what she's wearing; I get really scared.

"She starts pulling off my clothes, and saying that we have to hurry because my dad will be home soon. She tries to pull off my underwear, and I tell her to leave me alone. She grabs my hand real tightly and pulls it toward her breast, which is practically falling right out of that thing she's wearing, and all of a sudden, I have a big knife in my hand.

"Right then, I know that the only way to get away from her is to kill her; I push the knife into her chest again and again. It's really horrible—the sounds and all! I have to go now; I'll come back tomorrow."

"Lenny!" Edith called.

Denise heard the door slam shut, and then the machine clicked off.

Denise felt slightly relieved, but only for a moment. "So you think my life could be in danger because I'm lecturing in this dream? I don't understand," Denise said.

"I'm sorry to say that there's more. You see, Lenny came in the following week and revealed one more important detail that he'd left out of his account of the dream. After he kills his mother, he gets up out of his bed, wipes the blood out of his eyes, and looks at his mother lying there dead on the bed—only it's not his mother lying there in a pool of blood: it's you."

The snow was beginning to come down heavily in huge, silent flakes; the kind that build up quickly, turning the road into a dangerous white slide. Denise struggled to see through the blinding whiteness, thinking sadly of Lenny.

Just when she thought it couldn't possibly snow any harder, it did. The sky was getting darker by the minute; Denise started thinking about the possibility of finding a hotel for the night.

Dreams are funny things, she thought. *Why me, though? Why is it me who's lying there dead, night after night in Lenny's dream when...*the association came to her like a bullet to the brain: she saw herself clearly, sitting in the court of the monstrous wolflike judge, and she could hear him as clearly if he were bellowing into her ear at that very moment: you are sentenced to die by the hand of your son! And then she thought: Lenny's mother, dead by the hand of her son... The association was farfetched, but it was close enough to make her sweat.

Denise got off at the next exit and headed back to Philadelphia, to the safety of Bruce's home. Driving all the way home in what was evidently a blizzard was risky, and the conditions at home could prove to be downright dangerous.

GAILA SWINDELL

30

Amy pulled the tiny flashlight out of her drawer and climbed into bed. She could stay up as late as she wanted to. With her mother spending the night in Philadelphia and the big snow outside her window piling higher by the minute, Amy could sleep until noon if she wanted.

She pulled the covers up over her head, and then she heard it: the sound of the breathing filled her room, louder and raspier than ever. *Why is this happening?* she wondered, peeking out to see the wolf's head shadow on the door.

It's trying to punish me—whatever it is. It's trying to punish me for finding this diary. She hoped that if she ignored it—if she could ignore it—it would go away.

She pulled the covers up over her head—to hide and to drown out the awful raspy breathing sound her grandmother swore was made by the heating pipes that snaked through the old house; she turned on the tiny flashlight, opened the diary, and began reading:

Diary of Jenna Jerrel, 1874

April 7-The smell of spring is in the air, and it is as sweet as the flowers that hang heavy from the trees. Father spends most of his days in the orchard and his nights by the fire, for although the days are getting warmer, there is a chill in the night air. He sits and drinks his whiskey, staring into the fire, mumbling and shouting out in anger.

NUNNY & CECIL—A Tale of Terror

He never asks me to read to him anymore, and I fear that he is sinking deeper into his black moods. I am afraid of him, so I stay away. He looks at me in the strangest manner, as if he's seeing someone else, as if he doesn't know me. I am hoping the change of season will lighten his heart, and therefore his moods, but I am losing faith daily.

April 21-Father is at the tavern again. I am alone in this big house again, with nobody but my little bird Mina to keep me company. Today, I taught Mina to say "father." She is so black that she is almost blue and preens herself constantly. She looks beautiful in her golden cage.

Father stays at the tavern every Saturday night until the darkness of the night becomes the dawn of Sunday morning. I hear him come into the house, knocking things over as he finds his way to bed, swearing and shouting until I fear for my life. He is no longer himself; I fear the devil has taken his soul.

April 22-Maybe I was wrong about Father, for this morning he took me to church; although his behavior is still horrendous, the fact that he wanted to go to church at all shows there is some hope. I don't know how he managed to wake up after having come home not three hours before; perhaps God woke him. He barely spoke a word as we walked along the dusty road, his dull eyes staying clear of mine.

It was a wonderful day, though, with flowers everywhere and the sun shining brightly. I saw a very handsome boy looking my way as we stood outside the church. He was tall and muscular, with golden hair and soft brown eyes. Father saw the boy looking at me, and he grabbed ahold of my arm until I almost cried out in pain, pulling me away to the other side of the crowd that was gathering. I was very embarrassed and both sad and angry that Father would behave in such a manner. I hope the boy did not notice Father's behavior; if he did, he surely will not look my way again.

The schoolteacher, Miss Moyer, came over to talk to me. She said that she thought my dress was very pretty. I was glad she said this because I was ashamed to wear it, and she made me feel better, as she always does. The dress is so small and tight and faded. It's bad enough that my skin is much darker than that of the other girls. They stared and snickered at me as usual, and I heard Rebecca Toban making sounds like that of an Indian on the warpath as she passed me. It hurts me terribly when they do this, but it is my own fault, for I should have never told them that Mother was an Indian princess. I know it was a lie, but I thought that it might make them see my Indian heritage in a different way. I thought that maybe it would make them respect me, but I can see that it only added fuel to their fire. I am very proud of my Indian blood; I only wish that I knew more about it. Father becomes very angry whenever I ask him about mother, so my efforts are fruitless.

Miss Moyer said that she was sorry that I couldn't attend classes any longer, and she looked at Father with angry eyes when she said this. She does not like Father; that is clear. She said that she had something for me and went inside the church. I was so happy that I almost cried when she came out with a parcel of books for me. Father told her that we would accept no charity from her. Miss Moyer said that it was not charity, but a gift. Father said that he could not afford to have me waste my time with books when he needed me to labor on the farm, and then he said good day to Miss Moyer and forced me away from her.

I was sick at heart from his behavior, and I had the most terrible urge to run away from him. But I know he needs me now. I must work hard and be good to help keep his soul away from the devil.

May 3-I am so thrilled. Miss Moyer stopped by when Father was in the orchard. She gave me the parcel of books and asked if there was anything I needed. She said that she would be moving to a new town in the fall, but she would be back to check on me before she left. She said she would bring more books.

I laughed so hard I thought I would cry when Mina screeched, "Father...Father" and scared Miss Moyer half to death. She thought Mina was especially beautiful, and fed her some crackers that she had in her pouch.

I love Miss Moyer, and I am ever so grateful to her. I think I might die without the books she gives to me, for they are my only escape from this dreary existence, from my struggle to make Father well again.

May 5-The orchard is abloom with fragrant white blossoms, and Father seems happier. I knew the change of season would help lift his spirits.

The books that Miss Moyer brought are enough to make me weep with joy every time I see them. The book that I will read first is entitled Paradise Lost, and it was written by a man named John Milton. I have read some of his poetry in one of the books that Miss Moyer gave to me last year. I am reading it first because it appears to be the most difficult, and also because of the title, which makes me want to cry: it's so bittersweet, like life itself. I cannot believe that someone would throw these books away: Miss Moyer found them in a pile of rubbish behind the church, or so she said. There are about five others, but I will have to write about them later, dear diary, as I hear Father's heavy footfalls upon the stairs.

May 23-I found a box of letters in the attic. The handwriting is so small and cramped that I can hardly read it. But what pleasure they will bring to me, as they were written from my mother to my father. It is a pity that Father cannot read; I guess Mother was not aware of this when she sent him the letters. Finally, I will know what she was like. I am so excited; I live to read them! Father is keeping me so busy cleaning, cooking, sewing, and working in the orchard, that I fall dead asleep as soon as I lie down.

May 26-I asked Father if we could go to church again tomorrow, as it will be my sixteenth birthday, but he said that he cannot tolerate the way everyone tries to poke into our business. He said he wants to be able to worship the Lord in peace, and the only place he can do that is right here in our own home.

Oh, how I cringed to hear him speak those words! I am trapped forever inside the stone walls of this house. I sit in my room, staring out over the orchard, wondering what is beyond the forest and Willard's creek. Sometimes, when the weather is warm, I sleep out on the balcony. I look up at the heavens and pray for something to happen, that somehow I can go away from this place. I am dreadfully lonely. I grow older with each passing day, and I would just as soon die as stay here for the rest of my life with Father; but the way he keeps me locked up here, I will never meet a young man who will take me as his wife; and with nothing decent to wear, no one would want me anyway.

This dark Indian skin has become my curse, for I can't imagine anyone wanting me when they have dozens of fair-skinned beauties to choose from. But that young man at church that day, he seemed to like me; maybe he was just staring at me because he felt sorry for me, or because he thought I was ugly.

Father has not bought a piece of fabric for me since my fourteenth birthday, and the seams of my dresses can be let out no more. I tried to think of a way to cut several of them up into pieces and then use the pieces to make one dress that fits properly. But then it would look like a patchwork quilt.

For my birthday today, Father gave me a pair of earrings that he carved in the image of Mina. They are very beautiful, as Mina is.

I think Father intends to keep me here forever. It would break my heart to leave him, but it will kill me to stay.

June 4-I cannot believe my luck in finding those letters that Mother wrote. I do so wish I could have known her; I feel as though I do. She began writing to Father because of an ad that he placed in the newspaper for a wife. Father must have had someone write his letters for him, for Father cannot write and it is clear from Mother's letters that he did correspond with her.

She is so different from Father; I wonder what she saw in him. I have a feeling that the only way she could have properly escaped her Indian family was through a marriage, and this is why she married him. She was probably in much the same predicament as I am now. If only I had access to a newspaper, for sometimes I think I would gladly marry anyone to escape this house and Father's rampages, which only get worse with time. I can thoroughly understand how mother must have felt, trapped in a small house with a large family.

Mother was a very intelligent woman; she wrote so beautifully. I am very surprised and happy at all of this. If only she hadn't died when she gave birth to me. She wrote that she was from the wolf tribe of the Ipaki Indians; she wrote that they worshipped the spirit of the wolf. She wanted Father to know this before they were married; although she did not believe in the religion of the Ipaki, she did practice it out of respect for her people and their traditions. Father must have asked her if she would attend the Christian church with him, because she indicated that she would.

Father must have loved her dearly and her death must have ruined him, for he is only a shell of the man she must have married: I cannot believe she would have married him if she knew him as he is now, no matter how badly she wanted to escape from her family.

I do believe that it was necessary for her to leave the family, for she indicates in one of the letters that there were too many mouths to feed and her mother was pressing her to find a husband.

How sad life can be! Poor mother: to die so young, and with so much of life yet to live. We would have been such good friends, as well as mother and daughter; Father would probably be a good and happy man. We would have such happy times together! If she were alive, she would show those terrible girls at school. They would be in awe of her intelligence (and beauty, as I can tell just from her writing that she must have been beautiful), and then they would accept me. Mother would have made me go to school and taught me all of the Indian traditions and rituals; my life would be rich, instead of dull and so dreary that sometimes I no longer wish to live.

Amy was fascinated. The diary was more interesting than any book she had ever read, especially because it was about someone who was once real, who had lived in the very house she lived in.

She was so tired. She wanted to read it in its entirety, but her eyelids were heavy.

One more entry, she thought, *I'll read one more.*

August 10-It is so hot that sometimes I must sleep on the balcony just to breath. I am sorry that I have not written in so long, dear diary, but Father works me until I am weary. He drinks all night long, now. As soon as he comes in from the orchard, he orders me to bring him his bottle of whiskey. I poured some out the other day and added some water to make it weaker in strength, hoping against hope that he would not notice. But he did. He screamed at me and threw the bottle against the wall. What a horrible mess! He said that the whiskey was expensive and he would make me pay for wasting it the way I did.

I am so frightened, for now, as soon as he begins to get drunk, he gets that notion in his head that I must pay for that bottle of whiskey. He says that he hasn't forgotten, and, one of these days, he'll think of a punishment to fit the crime. I live in fear and dread of that day.

Poor Jenna—poor, poor Jenna, Amy thought. She couldn't wait to find out what her fate would be, but she had to go to sleep. She remembered the dream she had about the attic and was fascinated by how much it had foretold: the black bird in her dream must have been Mina, and for some reason Mina didn't want Amy to read the diary; and the dancing wolves at the bottom of the fiery pit might have had something to do with Jenna's mother being in a tribe that worshipped wolves.

It was all somehow connected—however loosely—to the strange things happening around the house. Amy was dying to find out what that connection was.

31

The alarm clock screamed. Denise woke up in a panic, until she realized where she was.

"Bruce, please turn that thing off," she mumbled.

He continued to lay there with his head under the pillow. Denise clambered over his lifeless body and struggled with the clock, finally managing to silence its deafening blare.

"My god! I woke up, and for a minute I didn't know where I was," she said, pulling the pillow from Bruce's head. "You'd better get up Dr. Bruce; you don't want to be late for your first patient."

"My first patient isn't scheduled until eleven-thirty," he told her.

"Then why did you set the alarm for seven?"

"So that I have time to appreciate your morning presence," he confessed. He kissed her neck until her body melted in his arms.

It had been so long since she had woken up to a man's body—hard and strong and magnetic. She wanted to wake up to him every morning, but that would come in time. For now, she wanted to savor the moment.

Denise suddenly pulled away from Bruce. She jumped out of bed—to Bruce's protestations—and ran to the window.

"I want to see the snow," she said, pulling up the shade to see the great, billowing drifts and survey the quiet, gray sky. "This is wonderful, and it looks like it's going to snow some more. I'll be trapped here for at least another day," she said gleefully, pulling the shade down with a laugh and running and jumping into the bed.

"There's a crazy, gorgeous woman running naked around my room. What a way to start the day!" he said, capturing her in his arms.

"Why don't you cancel all your appointments today? We'll just stay in bed until tomorrow," she said.

"I'd love to, but I can't. Mrs. Jergenson is coming in today for an emergency appointment. She called yesterday and begged my receptionist to schedule her for sometime today. Besides, I thought you had some things that you wanted to accomplish today," he said.

"I do, but I'd rather stay here with you," she said, thinking about her plan for the day. She had to call Paul: she wanted him to use his influence to get her in to see one of his psychologist friends. She felt too guilty to go back to Dr. Crofford. She looked at the clock again: seven-twenty. She had plenty of time to put it out of her mind—for a few hours, anyway.

"Before we begin the morning exercise program," Bruce said slyly, running his hands up and down her legs and pressing his hard body against hers. "You seem especially eager to get away from the farm. Any particular reason?"

"Well, if you must know—now—of all times, it's Adam and his imaginary playmates." There, she had said it.

Bruce pulled away from her slightly so that he could look at her face. "How long has this been going on?" he asked, suddenly serious.

"Since around Thanksgiving, about the time I met you. In fact, that's why I just happened to run into Paul—our matchmaker. I took Adam to see Paul about these ridiculous playmates. By the way, that woman Bernadette at the party, do you know what she does for a living?"

"She's a psychic," he said. "Why?"

"I was just wondering," she said.

"Why haven't you mentioned this imaginary playmate thing to me before?" he asked. "Maybe I could help you with it?"

She was quiet for moment, thinking about what Bernadette had told her. The senseless words of a drunken woman now made perfect sense: she'd encountered the raven—"the messenger of doom" according to Bernadette, a psychic, of all things—on her way to move in with her parents, and since that day, her life had become hellish.

"Denise…"

"I don't know. I was hoping they'd go away...I mean, that Adam would forget about them. He hasn't mentioned them lately, but I know they're still around."

"What do you mean they're still around? You talk as if they're real."

Damn it, she thought; *why did we have to get into this conversation.*

"You're sure they're imaginary?" Bruce asked.

"Bruce!" Denise said, clearly disturbed. She wasn't sure what was real anymore, but she wouldn't tell him that.

"I'm sorry, Denise. I was only kidding," Bruce said. "I just can't wait for you to find a place closer to the city, a place we...I mean you could call home," he said, slipping and saying "we" again.

"Me, too," she told him. There was nothing that she wanted more than to get away from the farm and find a home with Bruce.

All of the ghosts in her head were quickly exorcised with one velvety soft kiss; Bruce slipped his tongue into her mouth, and they began the long, slow dance of love.

32

When Denise woke up in the huge bed, Bruce was gone. She looked at the clock: ten-thirty-three. She inhaled the potent aroma of coffee, went into the kitchen, and poured some of the steaming brew into a cup. She searched through a few cupboards for the sugar before realizing it was right there in front of her. A note bearing her name was attached to the refrigerator with a magnet in the shape of a fish: "Neecy, please call me this afternoon. It's snowing like a blizzard as I write this. Damn! Looks like the naked, crazy woman will have to spend the night, again. I love you, Bruce."

Denise pattered back to the bedroom, coffee cup in hand. She pulled her wallet out of her purse and hunted through the small pile of cards that she kept there. "Paul Raison, that's the man I want to talk to," she said.

She dialed the number on his card. "Is Paul Raison there? This is Denise Miller calling."

"One moment, please," the voice on the other end said.

A few seconds later, Paul clicked on. "Denise, how's it going?"

"Fine, but not great. How are you doing?" she asked.

"Just great. Business is booming. We're raising a generation of lunatics," he laughed.

"Very funny. You're talking to the mother of one of those lunatics," she said without much humor. "I'm sorry to bother you, Paul, but I have a favor to ask," she said.

"Shoot," he replied.

"I was wondering if you know a psychologist that might have time to see me today. I'll understand if it's too much to ask, but I'm kind of stuck in the city today, and I really could use a good shrink."

"I know just the person for you to see. She's new, but she's good. I know you'll like her. I'll give her a buzz and get right back to you."

"I knew I could count on you, Raison Man," she said, using the pet name she had called him during their college days together.

"Hey, hey, no name calling, now," he said, feigning indignation. "I'll call you back in a flash," he said.

Dr. Laneforth's office was in a charming old building on Market Street. Denise opted for the stairs rather than the elevator, but changed her mind when she saw the steep, narrow staircase.

"Dr. Laneforth will see you now, Ms. Miller," the plump, chipper little receptionist said as soon as Denise walked in.

Dr. Laneforth was a pretty woman trying desperately to hide her prettiness: her dark hair was pulled back into a bun, and her small features were hidden behind a pair of too-large glasses with dark, thick frames.

"It's a pleasure to meet you, Denise. I'm Susan," she said, shaking Denise's hand with enthusiasm. "Please sit down. I can't tell you how flattered I am that Paul asked me to see you. When a colleague asks you to see a close friend, you know that he or she has faith in your work."

"It's a pleasure to meet you, Susan. Thank you for seeing me on such short notice," Denise said. She could feel her body relaxing in the pale orange and yellow office; she forgot about the blizzard raging outside the window.

"Now, what I want you to do is to just sit back, relax, and tell me what's going on in your life. I'll listen and take notes until you're finished. I'll try and save any questions until you're finished talking. Are there any questions I can answer for you, now?" she asked.

Jeannie came into the room carrying two cups of steaming, fragrant tea and placed them on the desk.

"Thank you, Jeannie," Susan said.

"Thank you," Denise said. "I don't have any questions right now, Susan. I'll start from the beginning—the beginning of my problems, that is. Last summer I found out my husband, Donald, was having an affair. I was shocked to say the least. Our relationship was good; we were happy—at least I was. We have two beautiful, healthy children. I couldn't for the life of me imagine what would make him do such a thing.

"He's a lawyer, and he'd lost a few cases just before I found out that he was having the affair, so I think that he might have done it to boost his self-esteem, although I'm not sure if that was really the reason. It could have been just plain old-fashioned lust. Anyway, I immediately filed for divorce.

"He begged me to give him another chance, to the point that it almost became an obsession with him. I never gave it a second thought; divorce was the only answer for me.

"We were living just outside of Philly at the time, in Villanova. I decided to sell the house and move in with my parents; I wanted to erase Donald from my life completely, and that meant getting out of the house where there were so many memories of him.

"My parents live way out in Cooks County in an old farmhouse. I thought it would be good for the kids to live on the farm for a short time; and my parents wanted to help out until I could adjust to being a single parent.

"My son, Adam, is taking this divorce very hard. He's angry and disagreeable all the time, and he claims to have invisible playmates named Nunny and Cecil. He does horrible things, and then says that Nunny and Cecil told him to do them.

"I've been having crazy dreams about my children. I'm beginning to have hallucinations, and I just can't take it anymore. To top it all off, one of my students at the university has been following me around town." She could save the rest for later; that was Lenny's problem, not hers—at least it wasn't her problem, yet.

"Are you dating anyone?" Susan asked her.

"I'm seeing a man who I'm very much in love with. Our only problem is that we don't get to see enough of each other, with me living out in the boonies," Denise told her, realizing that Susan probably knew Bruce; they were in the same profession, and they were both friends with Paul.

"Oh, one more thing. There's this monstrous black bird that sits on a scarecrow out in the orchard behind my house; it just sits there and stares at the house. I feel like it's watching me; I feel like it's some kind of harbinger of doom. I have to use all of my willpower to keep from pulling out one of my father's guns and shooting it," she confessed, laughing at how ridiculous she must sound to Susan. There was more to tell about the bird, but she didn't want to sound completely crazy—at least not yet.

She felt better already: *confessing even a small piece of one's soul works wonders for the psyche,* she thought.

"I'm so glad I came to see you; I've had no one to talk to for so long. I don't want to unload all of this on my parents; of course, they are aware of the problems with Adam, although they don't know that I took him to see Paul for counseling. And I can't tell my boyfriend, Bruce. It's a new relationship, and I don't want to scare him off," Denise told her.

"You have another child, a girl?" Susan asked her.

"Yes, Amy. Amy has been so good through all of this. She's only eleven years old, but she's very mature for her age. She's very supportive," Denise told her.

"I have a few questions for you. You said that you didn't think twice about divorcing Donald after you found out he was having an affair? Why was that?" Susan asked.

"I put so much value on truth, and I knew I wouldn't be able to ever trust him again. Part of me wanted to pretend that I never saw him with the other woman; for the first couple of days after I saw him with her, I would wake up in the morning thinking it had all been a bad dream. I loved him so much!" she said. She wanted to cry, but the tears wouldn't come. "I did, however, suffer a brief reactive psychosis. I was hospitalized for a short time. I don't know if the hallucinations I'm having now are an overflow of that. I don't know anything anymore."

"Do you still love Donald?" Susan asked her.

"I don't think so. I never allow myself to think about what I feel for him. I vacillate between an overwhelming hatred for him and a distinct numbness. I do feel a terrible sadness for the loss of what I thought we had together, our family life," Denise said. "Sometimes, something will remind me of some intimate moment he and I shared, and I think that if I allow myself to cry, I'll never stop."

"You said that your relationship with your boyfriend is free of problems, and that you love him very much. Why aren't you able to talk to him about your problems?"

"I've only been seeing him for a few months, so I'm not that secure in our relationship. I really do think he'd want to help, but I'd like to handle this myself—first. I think I'll come out of it a stronger person. Bruce—that's his name—is recently divorced, too, and he's going through a period of healing just as I am. I don't want to burden him with my problems," she said. "Also, as I said, I don't want to scare him away."

"You said that you've had no one to talk to. Don't you have any friends?" Susan asked.

"Yes, I do. But I'm so busy with my own life that I suppose I'm letting my friendships dwindle and die out. I haven't seen any of my friends since around the time of my divorce; I do call, text, email them occasionally. Between driving to and from the university, spending time with Bruce and my children, and working, I don't really have time for friends right now. I've always been one to withdraw from the world when I'm having problems," Denise told her.

"Why do you withdraw?"

"I just need time alone, I guess, to heal. I do wonder if the way I handle things is backfiring. Something happened the other night that made me think that I really need some help. It concerns the hallucinations that I mentioned. Well, actually it is the only hallucination so far—since the brief reactive psychosis, that is. I want an objective opinion about what's happening to me. I have this awful feeling that it's all some sort of premonition of doom," she told her. "And…I just wish my life were normal, again. I never had to analyze life before, it was all so…so perfect," she added.

Denise told her about the nightmares she'd been having, and then about seeing the dancing wolfen creatures in the orchard.

There was a moment of silence as Susan studied her notes. "You often mention the sense of smell—in your dreams and in your hallucination. You said that when Amy fell onto the floor, a cloud of dust that smelled like death rose into the air. Can you put into words what that smell was like?" Susan asked.

"It smelled like something rotten. It smelled like—like dirt, decay, and blood."

"You said that the wolflike judge had a foul smell; what was that smell like?"

"Blood."

"And when you bit your lip, the smell of blood was so overwhelming that it caused you to faint?"

"Yes. It was a very strong smell of blood. I know what you're going to ask me next, and no, I've never fainted before from biting my lip, not even when I used to faint from the sight of blood."

"Have you ever seen a wolf before?" Susan asked.

"Only on TV, on some animal show," Denise told her.

"Do you remember anything about the show, about what the wolves were doing?"

"They were caring for their young. It was about how wolves take care of their children."

"How do you distinguish a wolf from a dog—say a breed of dog that looks something like a wolf?"

"Wolves have bigger heads, and they have bigger teeth. I think their eyes are more almond shaped. They look wild."

"Did you get a good look at these wolflike creatures? Could you see their teeth?" Susan asked.

"Yes. I could see them very well; I could see their teeth and their tongues hanging out of their mouths. The moon was very bright that night."

"Were they wearing clothing?"

"No, they weren't. One of them looked just like the creature from my dream, all furry. And the other one wasn't hairy at all, in fact, its head and face had very little fur; you could see the skin right through any fur that it did have."

"This is very interesting, Denise."

Denise looked at her watch; she looked out the window at the blizzard that seemed to be getting even worse.

"I really have to go, Susan. I have to run over to the university to take care of some business," Denise told her.

"When can you come back for your next appointment?" Susan asked her.

"Is next week all right?"

"I should have some answers for you by then. I'm so glad you came in. One more question before you go: what did you and Bruce do on your date the night you saw these creatures?"

"We made love in the back seat of my car."

Lenny sat in the library, looking at a book but not reading it. He didn't want to go home, but he was tired of sitting there and just plain tired. He felt on the verge of a breakdown. He wanted so badly to talk to Edith, but she wasn't in her office.

"Would you like to see another counselor, Lenny?" the guy at the desk had asked him.

"No, thanks," Lenny had told him.

He was ready to tell Edith the truth about his mother—how she had been trying to seduce him. He really liked Edith.

He looked up from his book to see a lone figure trudging through the snow toward Paley Hall, the psychology building. He stared at the figure, thinking a person had to be crazy to be out in that stuff. He smiled to himself at the irony of his thought: *That's why I came out in it,* he thought, *because I'm crazy.*

He could tell by the blond fringe of hair hanging from under the scarf on the woman's head and the way she moved that it had to be Professor Miller. He winced as the image of her in his dream flashed into his head: she was lying there on his bed, the red blood that splattered her body contrasting with her beautiful snowy white skin and pale blond hair.

He wondered if she would have time to talk to him about his paper. Even if she didn't, the walk over there would pass some time; he never wanted to go home again. He felt physical as well as mental pain at the thought of seeing his mother. A hot flame of shame engulfed him— *mother, yeah...right. The bitch...the whore...I should kill her and be done with it.* That was his voice. But another voice, one he was becoming increasingly familiar with, one he wanted desperately to silence, chimed in: *Admit it,* it said. *The real problem is that you want her just as much as she wants you.* Lenny slammed his book shut and flung it across the room. He could feel people looking at him, but no one commented.

Professor Miller would be happy to see him. She always had a kind word and a sexy smile for him. He was suddenly afraid for her: maybe he would tell her about the dreams; maybe he should. He felt like he had to protect her; maybe even from himself. He felt such a strong connection to her, one he didn't fully understand.

He gathered up his books and notebooks, stuffing them into his backpack. He put on his coat and made his way out of the library, into the snow. The cold, hard pellets of snow stinging his face were invigorating.

He looked up as he saw the light in Professor Miller's office go on. He decided to get some hot chocolate for the two of them; it would give her time to settle in. He hoped that she would have a good word for him about his paper, which he could not remember writing. He hoped that she would be glad to see him.

Denise shook the snow from her coat and hung it on the rack. The university had canceled classes for the day because of the blizzard; the campus looked like a ghost town.

She called Bruce's cell.

"Hello." His voice sent a warm surge of comfort through her tense body. She wiped the fog off the window and peered out over the campus. She could see someone swaddled in a heavy coat approach her building, and then, stop, turn, and walk away.

"Are you busy?" she asked Bruce, although she knew he wouldn't have answered if he were.

"No, I was just sitting here studying my next patient's folder," Bruce said. "Did you get your business taken care of?"

"Yes, I did," she said, thinking guiltily of Susan. *Should I tell him: no I won't.* She would have to think of a good lie, one that she wouldn't get caught in: "I just went over to the Gallery and did a little shopping."

"Did you buy me anything?"

"No, I didn't buy anything, really." She felt uncomfortable lying, but she was entitled to her secrets.

"Where are you, now? What time do you think you'll make it over to my place?" he asked.

"I just stopped by my office to take care of a few things. I should be at your place by six. Would you like me to pick up something for dinner?" she asked.

"No; I'm going to show off my culinary skills tonight."

"That sounds great. What are we having?"

"It's called...surprise a la Bruce," he teased.

"Come on. Tell me what were having so I can think about it. I'm starving already," she said.

"You'll see when you get there. Denise?"

"What?" she asked, knowing what he was going to say.

"I love you."

"I love you too."

Denise hung up the phone and leaned back in her chair. Her feet were frozen. She reached down and turned on the little space heater that she kept under her desk.

There was a message on her desk that said for her to call Edith. She dialed Edith's number: no answer. She threw the pink piece of paper on her desk.

Denise was a little uneasy about being in the building; there didn't seem to be anyone else there, except the guard on duty in the lobby, checking student and teacher I.D.'s.

Denise heard the whirring sound of the elevator as it made its ascent. A spitting, purring sound came from the area of her feet, frightening her so badly that she nearly fell backward in her chair: it was only the space heater, which produced steam heat; every once in a while it would hiss like a fire-breathing dragon.

There was a hard knock at the door. Denise looked at the door, then at the phone. *I should call the guard,* she thought. But no, he would have checked the I.D. of anyone coming up in the elevator. Thoughts began to race through her head: *what if there was someone hiding in the building; what if the guard was in the bathroom when this person came in; what if this person killed the guard?*

Denise sat frozen in her chair, wondering what to do, when a voice called out, "Professor Miller, are you in there?"

It was Lenny. *Great.*

"Come in,' she said, trying to sound normal.

"Sorry I had to kick the door, but, as you can see, my hands are full. I was in the library studying; I saw you come in and I thought you could probably use some hot chocolate," he said nervously.

He really was a sweet kid—always so thoughtful. She didn't want to be afraid of him, but she was. "Thank you, Lenny. You're always thinking of others." And dreaming of others, she thought. "Please sit down. What are you doing out in weather like this?" she asked, immediately wishing she hadn't. She knew damn well why the poor kid wasn't at home.

As Lenny turned and reached for a chair, his coat rode up to reveal the dull glint of metal in his back pocket.

Her heart beat faster and the air in the room suddenly became very hot. She reached down and switched off the space heater.

"I had to do some research at the library," he said, pulling the chair up to the front of her desk to face her. "I was wondering what you thought of my paper. I can't remember what I wrote," he said, chewing his lip and drumming her desk with his fingers. Just when she was about to tell him what he'd written, he blurted, "Oh, yeah, now

I remember. I know it's a little strange, but the idea struck me one night, and I felt it would be a good topic for a psychology paper," he said, brushing a thick lock of black hair back off his forehead. His eyes were so blue and penetrating that he almost looked unearthly, like some alien being.

Denise's eyes suddenly focused on the pink piece of paper on her desk: the message from Edith. It read "Call Edith Tailor" in big black letters. She quickly looked up into Lenny's eyes. No, he hadn't noticed her looking at it. She had to get that piece of paper out of his range of vision without being obvious.

Denise took a sip of the steaming hot chocolate, stalling for time while she pondered different angles for critiquing his paper. She had to be truthful, but she didn't want to make him mad. She realized that she could lie and say that she hadn't read it yet.

"Well, Lenny, to be perfectly honest with you..." *Now isn't the time to be honest Denise, now is the time to humor him.* "It wasn't really what I was looking for. I wanted you to do some research on a particular paradigm and then write about it. I thought you might write about behaviorism since you seem to be so interested in that school of psychology. You are very creative, but as I said, that wasn't what I was looking for," she said, putting it mildly.

Lenny sat very still, not saying anything. He looked very troubled, very angry. He chewed on the lip of his Styrofoam cup.

Denise's armpits were suddenly hot and soaking wet with perspiration. She was using all of her self-control to hide her fear.

"So, did you grade it yet?" he asked.

"No, I didn't. I'd like you to write another paper. I don't want you to think that you wasted your time on what you wrote. I've been giving it a lot of thought, and I think you could submit this paper, 'If God is a Rat, We're All in Trouble,' to a magazine that's looking for new creative writers." *Well said, Denise.*

He was scanning her desk. *No, don't do that.*

"Lenny, could you get that sweater up there for me," Denise said, pointing to a sweater hanging on the coat rack.

He jumped up to get the sweater, while she snatched up the message from Edith and threw it on the floor under her desk.

"Wow. I don't know what to say," he said, handing her the sweater. "I've been having a hard time at home, and I don't know how I'll find the time to write another paper."

"Well, I'll tell you what. You can have until two weeks before the end of the semester to hand it in. I'd give you until the end of the semester, but I don't want this to interfere with your studying for final exams. What made you write about something that was so totally different from what I asked for?" she said, smiling to temper her statement.

"I just thought it had to be written," he told her.

"Please keep this between the two of us. I'm giving you a second chance because you said you're having problems at home. I don't want everyone asking for a second chance. Does it sound fair to you?" she asked.

Lenny stood up, a funny look on his face; he slowly reached around to his back pocket.

Denise's felt giddy and lightheaded; she wondered if she was dreaming. She looked quickly around the room for something to defend herself with, and still sitting, she pushed her chair back against the wall.

"Life is never fair," Lenny said.

Denise saw his hand touch the smooth piece of sharp metal in his back pocket. It was all happening so quickly. When Lenny pulled the silver iPod and headphones out of his back pocket, Denise burst out laughing in surprised relief.

Lenny gave her a confused look and said, "But that doesn't matter now, does it?" He stuck the headphones into his ears, and as he was turning to walk toward the door, something on the floor caught his eye. He reached down under her desk. Denise jumped out of her chair when she realized what he was going to do. She was no longer laughing; she felt like she had swallowed a cork, as the dry lump of fear stuck in her throat. Lenny popped up with the pink message from Edith in his hand.

"Dropped something, Professor Miller," he almost shouted, as most people do when listening to music through headphones. He handed it to Denise without looking at it and walked out the door.

Not until she heard the mechanical whir of the elevator did Denise unclench the hand in which she held the piece of paper: the message was now a small, hot, wet ball.

33

With her mother away in Philadelphia for two days and a secret knowledge tucked away in her mind, Amy felt somehow older, wiser. She knew something that no one else could know, except the dead, and they didn't matter—not now.

Amy crawled under the covers, making a small air tunnel for herself and began reading Jenna's diary.

Nov. 1-I am sorry for staying away from you so long, dear diary, but the harvest was very good and it kept me busy. Some days it was all I could do to crawl up the stairs to my room.

Father is putting the rewards of the harvest to ill use, spending it all on whiskey at the Inn. His moods grow worse daily. I stay as far away from him as possible, and I no longer take my meals with him, as he requested that I leave him to eat alone. I live for the day I will leave this wretched place.

Nov. 5-I shall die! Father came into my room tonight smelling of whiskey. He told me that now I am a woman, and I shall do a woman's work. He forced himself upon me, and I begged him to leave me alone. I screamed at him as he took me with such force, that I am surprised I am not dead. I prayed aloud until he slapped me so hard I thought my jaw was broken. I vomited afterwards and all through the night. I am sick to death, and I pray that death shall overtake me. Who can I tell? Who will save me from this hell?

Amy's little heart beat so loudly, she was afraid her grandparents would hear it and come upstairs to see what was wrong. She had to read the entry twice to believe it; it was too horrible to even imagine. She felt suddenly sick to her stomach. When she felt she could go on, she returned to deciphering Jenna's cramped script that became more illegible with each entry.

Nov. 7-Father broke the beak from Mina's little black face. I buried her in the cellar after I found her twisted body on the path that leads to the creek. I tried! I tried so hard to quiet her, but she would not listen. She had overheard me as I screeched in agony and imitated my cries: "No, Father! No, Father!" she piped over and over again. Yesterday, I tried to teach her something new to say, but I was weak and could not spend much time at the task. I am sorry, Mina! You were my only friend. May you rest in peace.

Nov. 10-I live in fear of Father's wrath. He will not look at me, nor speak to me, which I am glad for. His soul is with the devil now, and I will not look upon his feet for fear that they are cloven. Why has death not taken me? I am regaining strength and that is the last thing I want. I want to wither and die! I thought that Mother's spirit might come down from the heavens and whisk me away; but then I realized that heaven is not for those who have sinned as severely as I have. Surely God will blame me for taking part in Father's sin, no matter that I was unwilling. I should have left long ago, long before I blossomed into a woman.

Nov. 14-When father went to the tavern last night, I crept into the attic. I was desperately afraid that he would try to lie with me again, and I know that it will kill me if he does. He will have to kill me; I would gladly die before submitting to his evil. I took my blanket and pillow and prayed he would not find me there. I thought of running away, but I have no money and no place to go. In the summer I will leave, but now, winter is on its way. My only prayer is that the days will pass quickly.

Nov. 21-I slept in the orchard last night, with nothing but a blanket for protection from the elements. The barn was locked and I did not dare enter the house in search of the key. Father came home from the tavern in a drunken rage and chased me through the house. I fled into the orchard and found the blanket wrapped around the trunk of a failing tree. I will not let him touch me again! When I was hiding in the orchard, he yelled to me that the demons of the orchard would get me; but I was not afraid, for there is nothing more frightening than Father.

Amy jumped out of her bed and put the diary back in its hiding place. She couldn't take anymore of Jenna's cruel world; she dreaded the hellish dreams that might come to her in the night. She could see the familiar shadow on her door, and she wanted to slap it, or even laugh at it. After what she'd just read, the shadow seemed silly in comparison.

34

Denise arrived home to a flurry of hugs and kisses, the smell of roast pork and sauerkraut filling the house. It was good to be home, but her problems hit her smack in the face again: Adam did not come down to greet her and acted like he hadn't noticed she had been gone. She had hoped he had miraculously changed while she was away. He stared at her through dinner as if she were an impostor, or an unwelcome guest.

"Did you enjoy your time off from school?" she asked him. He was trying to make her feel guilty for staying in Philadelphia.

"Yes," he said, stirring his sauerkraut and applesauce together on his plate. "I drew some pictures for you while you were gone," he said proudly.

Everyone turned to look at Adam in surprise. Any happiness Denise would have normally felt at his announcement was tainted by a nagging suspicion.

"They've been so good. I was surprised that they didn't get bored," Marie said. "Amy helped me clean the house yesterday just like you used to do when you were little, Denise."

"And Adam helped me shovel the walk," Joe added.

Denise looked at the children; even Adam beamed. She had missed them so much during those two days, but the time away had given her some time to think and cleanse her mind, something she had desperately needed to do.

Denise finished the dishes and washed her hands. She walked into the living room where her parents were watching TV.

"Did you have any time to look around for a place?" her father asked her.

Denise felt a hot flush of anger sweep over her skin.

"Now, Dad, when do you think I had time to do that?"

"Well, I thought maybe you'd have found some time in the last few days."

"In the blizzard?" Denise asked.

"Now what kind of thing was that to say, Joe?" Marie asked.

"It was a simple question. I'm sorry I asked. Geez! I just thought she might have taken a drive into the suburbs."

"If I would have been able to drive around, don't you think I would have come home, Dad? Are you in a hurry to see us go?"

"Not at all. Now, just forget I asked. I guess I just wasn't thinking," he said.

Denise got up and left the room. *As if I don't have enough problems,* she thought.

Denise finished grading the papers and put them neatly into a folder. She got up from her chair and walked over to the window. The orchard looked peaceful. Her previous vision of the wolf creatures seemed a muddle, like a far away dream, dreamt in another lifetime. She walked across the hall to Adam's closed door and knocked.

"Go away; I'm busy," Denise could hear him say.

"It's me, Adam. Can't I come in?" she asked.

"I guess so, but only for a minute," he said.

"What are you so busy doing?"

"I'm building a bridge," Adam told her.

"I thought you had some pictures for me," she said. She felt so strange; Adam was so cold to her. She wanted to weep, to beg him to come back to her.

"They're upstairs in the attic," he told her.

"Well, let's go get them," she said.

They ascended the staircase, Adam first. Denise thought of Lenny's dream and a cold wind, coming from the rafters of the attic, blew across her face, chilling her. She wondered if Adam ever dreamt of killing her, or if he ever fantasized about it during his waking hours.

Denise suddenly realized, with a horrible sense of foreboding, that she was afraid of Adam—her baby. He looked different to her, like somebody else's child. He had become a stranger to her, the workings of his mind, a mystery.

The attic was musty and cold.

"Here they are," he said, standing on tiptoe to reach the top of a low rafter in the corner. He pulled out some pieces of paper and then handed them to Denise.

They were simple crayon drawings of a woman. The woman's hair was colored in with a gray crayon; there were lines drawn in around her eyes and mouth.

"They're...they're very nice, Adam," she said. "Are these pictures of grandma?" she asked.

"No, they're pictures of you," he said.

"But I don't have gray hair and lines on my face, do I?" she asked.

"You will someday," he said.

She thought it very odd, but she didn't want to press the issue. "Well, thank you, Adam. It's nice to know that you were thinking about me," she said, trying to keep the sarcasm from her voice.

She bent down to give him a hug, when she noticed a pile of something—old rags maybe, on the floor in the far corner of the room.

"What's that?" she asked, walking over to the pile. On closer examination it looked like a nest of some sort, a giant nest made out of *her* clothes—the clothes she had been unable to find!

Denise picked up some of the items of clothing from the nest. A flurry of hair that reeked of old, wet dog flew into her face making her sneeze. It looked like the same filthy animal hair she had found in Adam's bed.

"Adam, do you know what this is? Do you know how these things got here?" she asked.

"No," he said.

"Have you been bringing some old, stray dog up here?" she demanded.

"Mom...Dad," she screamed down the stairwell, "would you come up to the attic please. You too, Amy."

Adam tried to scoot past her to go back downstairs. Denise caught him by the collar.

"You're not going anywhere, mister," she told him. "I'm going to get to the bottom of this now."

Adam turned around and looked her in the eye with a look that said he had murder on his mind. Denise could feel the child's hatred for her shoot into her heart like a bullet. She slapped his face. "Don't you ever look at me like that again! Do you hear me?" she seethed.

"Yes," he said through clenched teeth.

She was grateful for the sound of footsteps pounding up the stairs; Adam's features distorted to make him unrecognizable to her, like some fiendish gargoyle. His hatred was like a hand at her throat.

"What's all the racket about?" Joe asked. Marie and Amy were right behind him.

"It's about that—that filthy nest of my favorite clothes! Does anyone know how they got there?" she asked on the verge of hysteria. It was too weird of a thing to do. She could see why one of the kids might sneak a poor lost dog into the house, but she couldn't imagine why they would use her favorite pieces of clothing for the thing to sleep on—unless, of course, they felt a vengeful hatred for her.

Joe walked over and picked up Denise's sweater like it was a dirty diaper. "Looks like a dog or a cat has been sleeping here," he said. "I sure don't know anything about it."

"Me either, Mom," Amy said.

"Mom?" Denise looked at her mother.

"I haven't been up here in ages, Denise," she said, bewildered.

"We all know who spends the most time up here, don't we?" Denise said, as all eyes turned to Adam. "You can all go back downstairs," she began gathering her things, trying to hold them away from her. "You stay here and help me, Adam."

Joe skulked down the stairs, with Marie and Amy pushing behind him. Marie gave Denise a look that seemed to say don't be too harsh with the boy.

"Honest, Mom. I swear I didn't put them there!" Adam exclaimed.

"I just don't know anymore, Adam. What's gotten into you? You used to be such a good little boy; now, you're angry and mean and deceitful. I'm taking you to see Paul, again," she said, noticing a smirk suddenly cross his face at the mention of Paul. "You think it's funny? Well, you'll continue to see him until you're over this... this insane phase you're going through. I just can't take this kind of behavior anymore! I suppose you're going to tell me that Nunny and Cecil did this," she said.

"But they did, Mom...they did," he insisted.

She was going to explode. She wanted him as far away from her as he could go. "Go to your room, and stay out of my way," she screamed, and she meant it.

Joe lay in his bed staring at the ceiling, a position he assumed often lately. The sandman had put Joe last on his list of customers in Cooks County.

He felt guilty about hurting Denise when he'd asked her if she'd looked for a house, but he had to get her and the kids out of the house. He had decided to pretend he had no patience with them and act like he wanted them out of there.

He could imagine the look on Denise's face if he told her the real reason: he had disturbed the graves of some evil wolflike creatures, who were now out to destroy his family. Denise would think he was senile. *The hell with senile,* he thought—she would think he was insane.

He had missed Denise so much in those two and a half days that she was gone, that he had almost abandoned his plan, but the nest in the attic reaffirmed his decision to go through with it. He knew that those creatures had made the nest; and when Denise had blamed Adam, he had to use all of his control to keep from interfering. Whatever connection Adam had with the creatures was a mystery to him, and he wanted to keep it that way. The connection would soon be broken and Adam would grow into a normal young man with dim memories of his days on the farm; he would store Nunny and Cecil away with all of his other childhood fantasies. He decided to keep a closer eye on the boy and try to keep him out of the attic; that would help to keep the monsters away.

35

The day was gorgeous: bright sunlight, blue sky, and an icy cold wind that cleaned the air and mind of debris. Great heaps of dirty snow lay everywhere. The sun wasn't strong enough to melt it; not with the thermostat reading zero.

Denise stood outside Susan Laneforth's office, thinking about what a difference a week's time could make in weather and disposition; although it was still winter, it was spring in her mind. She felt confident that she wasn't losing her mind; she hoped Susan would confirm her belief.

Susan's receptionist said, "Go right in, Ms. Miller. Dr. Laneforth is expecting you."

"How are you, Denise?" Susan said, rising to shake Denise's hand.

"Much better, thank you. I think this great weather has something to do with it. It might be cold, but the blue sky and sunshine sure beat that blizzard," Denise said.

"I agree. Would you like a cup of tea or coffee?"

"No, thanks. I just finished lunch."

"Is there anything new that you'd like to fill me in on?" Susan asked.

"Not really. I'm feeling much better. The problems haven't really gone away; I'm just handling them better. In fact, our session last week worked wonders; I've felt better ever since. I even had lunch with an old friend the other day. I realized that it's not fair to cut off my relationships with friends just because I'm having problems," Denise answered.

"Did you talk about any of your problems with your friend?"

"No, I didn't. I carefully avoided them. Someday when everything is fine and dandy, I'll spill my guts, but not now."

"Well, I've been studying your case and I've come to some interesting conclusions, but then your mind works in interesting ways, Denise. I'd like you to participate in a little word association. I'm going to say a word, and I want you to tell me everything that comes to your mind when you think of this word."

"Shoot," she said.

"The word is wolf," Susan said. "What do you know about wolves?"

Denise thought for a moment. "Wolves make excellent parents. They supposedly take very good care of their young—they're known for this. They're also the subject of horror novels and movies in which people turn into werewolves when the moon is full, and they can only be killed by a silver bullet. They run in packs."

Susan laughed and then asked, "Do you see what I'm getting at?"

"Not really," Denise said.

"Wolves make excellent parents. They are known for the care they give to their cubs. Your subconscious guilt feelings of not being the best parent you can be right now are taking on the form of wolves in your imagination. You don't have a lot of time for the kids and you feel guilty. You're also feeling guilty about Adam's problem adjusting to the divorce. Your subconscious mind is projecting images of wolves in front of your eyes—when you're awake and when you're sleeping—to purge itself of your repressed guilt," Susan said.

"I see," Denise said.

"You said that you and Bruce made love in the car the night you had the vision of the wolves dancing in the orchard. Your subconscious guilt feelings about indulging in self-gratification instead of being home with the kids must have been at their peak for those feelings to escalate into a full-scale hallucination. Or you might have been feeling guilty, thinking that a good mother wouldn't have done such a thing—that it might be perceived as out of character by your children," Susan told her.

"Very good, Susan. I would have never thought of that, but it certainly makes sense."

"Your life was so normal before, that you never had to analyze it; now you're superstitious about under analyzing life; subconsciously and even consciously you might think it got you into trouble, so now you're overanalyzing—reading too much into everything.

"There's a bird that's been sitting on a scarecrow on your parents' farm for years, and if not that bird, another one, but now you think it's a harbinger of doom. You're looking at everything under a magnifying glass," Susan told her.

"I hadn't expected you to come so far in your conclusions, but this is amazing," Denise said.

"The boy in your hallucination was your subconscious warning you of what could happen to your son if you don't give him more attention. You have to talk to people about your problems, and I know that you know how important it is do that; that's what friends are for—to share the good and the bad. If you don't share the good and the bad with friends, you end up either sharing only the bad with people in my profession, or in the psyche ward of your local hospital.

"Adam is obviously suffering because of the divorce. But you have to ask yourself, are you being the best possible parent you can be under the circumstances? And if the answer is yes, then absolve yourself. You are not superwoman. If necessary, spend a good twenty minutes a day blaming Donald. Pick up the phone and scream at him, even if there's no one on the other end. *Do* you feel like you're being a good mother?" Susan asked.

"Yes, I do. I usually don't go out with Bruce until the kids are getting ready for bed. I spend lots of time with them when I'm not working," Denise said.

"You're going to have to try to stop worrying so much about Adam," Susan said. "I'm sure Paul must have told you that Adam is reacting to the divorce the way many children would. He'll grow out of it; give him time. Don't cater to his black moods. He'll eventually see that he won't get any attention that way, and he'll change his behavior."

They sat and talked for a while and then Susan said, "I hope our sessions have helped you. Here's my card; my home phone number is on the back. Don't hesitate to call any time you need me."

Denise rode up the elevator to her office, steeped in deep thought. Everything Susan had told her had made such perfect sense.

If only Adam would get better, everything would get better. Denise didn't want to talk with Susan about Adam. She went to see Susan for herself, not for him. She would save any talk of him for Paul. She had tried to call Paul earlier in the day; his secretary had said he was out of town. Denise wasn't able to schedule an appointment with Paul until the week after the kids had spring break. They would be with their father for their spring break, and Denise hoped that by then Adam wouldn't need to see Paul again. She hoped Adam would come home with a new attitude after his weeklong vacation with his father.

Hillary swayed toward her, her arms full of books, her face beaming. "Hello, Denise," Hillary said. "One of your secret admirers was up here looking for you earlier—a kid named Lenny. I thought you'd gone home, and when I told him, he seemed to get very angry. I think he has a crush on you. He's a cute kid."

Cute but dangerous, Denise thought. "He's not my type, Hillary. Thanks for the information," Denise said, pushing past her.

Denise just wanted to get what she needed from her office and drive home. There was another message on her desk to call Edith. Denise picked up the phone and dialed Edith's number.

"Hello, Edith. This is Denise."

"Hello, Denise. I was wondering if you could find time in your schedule to come over to the counseling center. It will only take about fifteen minutes."

Denise looked up at the clock on the wall: three o'clock; she could spare fifteen minutes. "I'll be right over," she told her.

Walking quickly, she scanned the campus for Lenny, but he was nowhere to be seen. She didn't want him to see her going into Catherine Hall. She could make up a dozen reasons for going into that particular building, but she didn't want to make Lenny even slightly suspicious: he might abandon his psychological counseling; and she didn't want to even try to imagine what might happen to him—or herself—then.

"Hello, Denise. It's good to see you," Edith said. "This won't take long. I just want to fill you in on a few things."

Denise took off her coat and sat down.

"So how's Lenny doing?" Denise asked.

"He's still having the dreams, but not as often. I think that's a bad sign; I think he's actually thinking more about the content of the dreams during his waking hours, now, whereas before, he tried to keep the dreams out of his head while he was awake. I'm afraid he might be contemplating making his dream a reality.

"He denies this whenever I ask him about it, but he also seems cockier; his eyes are beginning to take on the glint of insanity.

"Has he made any contact with you?" Edith asked.

"Yes, he has," she said, and told Edith about Lenny's visit to her office.

"Denise, you're going to have to be more careful," Edith told her. "I don't think Lenny would hurt you...I'll explain in a minute, but you never know.

"Lenny admitted that his mother, Sheila Delenko, has been blatantly seducing him. You can imagine what this is doing to poor Lenny. He's ashamed and grief stricken. He said that he feels no animosity toward you; in fact, he admitted to having a crush on you; he hates his mother with a passion, but he also loves her very much. He's terribly confused.

"Lenny seems to think he's something of a psychic, now," Edith said. "He says that he's the messenger of doom."

Denise felt a cold finger of fear caress her spine. She had a vague feeling that she was dreaming and shook her head as if to jar something loose. She could hear Edith talking, but she didn't seem to be there in the same room with her: Denise felt like she was having an out of body experience; she was floating somewhere above the room, looking down.

"Denise, are you all right?" Edith asked.

*Messenger of doom...messenger of doom...*Denise nodded her head yes, but she was lying: she felt she was not and never would be all right again.

"He said that he thinks you're in grave danger, and he wants to warn you. I discouraged him from doing this; I think it's best that you have as little contact as possible with him. Are you sure you're all right, Denise?" Edith asked, while Denise nodded her head, again.

"You don't look well. I hope you're not taking him seriously. His so-called premonition is the raving of a lunatic. He's lost all touch with reality."

But as Denise walked slowly out of the building, she wondered if Lenny was more in touch with reality than any of them.

Lenny sat studying in Carver Hall. He loved the massive building: the vaulted ceilings and granite walls gave it a medieval ambience; the quiet echo of footsteps on the polished wood floors made him think of a library he had loved to visit as a child.

He looked up from his book to see that it was three-thirty. He glanced out the window just in time to see Professor Miller walking slowly out of Catherine Hall, which was directly across from Carver Hall; she looked like she had just been told she had only six months to live. Edith stood at the door, waving goodbye to her.

36

Fear ran hand in hand with revulsion through the darkest corridors of Amy Miller's mind. She was deeply troubled by the little black book of horrors that Jenna Jerrel had packed away in the attic. She had eaten the forbidden fruit, and it was stuck in her throat, choking every bit of innocence from her child's mind.

Amy had always been aware that evil existed, but never had she been so intimate with it. What made Jenna's story so horrible was that it was not just imagined: it was real and had taken place right there in the very house she lived in.

It was still early in the evening when Amy had kissed her mother and her grandparents good night. They had looked at her curiously, wondering why she was going to bed so early; she had said that she had a rough day and was very tired. Her grandparents were on edge that night, but since reading the diary entries, the whole world seemed to be on edge to Amy. They almost seemed happy that she was going up to bed, getting out of their hair, and that was unusual for them.

Amy had studied her family members carefully. Her faith in human beings had diminished with her father's infidelity, and after reading about what had happened to Jenna, it was close to disappearing. She found herself being more suspicious, more guarded—*like Adam,* she thought.

She wondered if he had experienced any of the things she had. Maybe his stuffed animals were suddenly sprouting human eyes in the night, or maybe the shadow of a wolf's head was appearing on his wall too. She had never discussed it with him. They had grown so far apart; he seemed like a stranger to her. She was afraid of him and kept out of his way.

She wanted to finish the diary that night. She had been putting it off, thinking maybe she might never finish it, but she had to find out what happened to Jenna.

She would be gone the following week, staying with her father—something she wasn't looking forward to. She was afraid that if she didn't finish the diary now, she might never finish it: someone might find it while she was away, and then she would never know what happened to Jenna.

She burrowed snugly into her bed with her flashlight and the diary; just as she was about to begin reading, she heard a knock on her door. She quickly turned off the flashlight and stuffed it and the diary under her pillow.

"Amy," her mother said, opening the door slightly. "You asleep?"

"Not yet, Mom," Amy feigned grogginess.

"Mind if I come in for a minute?"

"No."

"Why are you so tired, honey?" her mother asked, a worried edge to her voice.

"Uh...I ran around a lot in gym class," she lied.

Denise sat down on the bed and said, "Can I have a hug? You know I really miss you and your brother when I'm at work, and I'm really going to miss you next week when you go away with your dad."

"Mom, do we have to go with Daddy next week?"

"Amy! You know you'd really hurt your father if you didn't go. Is that why you went to bed early—because you're upset about going? Don't you miss your father?"

"I just don't want to be away from you, Mom, and I'm still mad at Daddy," she said.

"Well, I don't want to be away from you either, but your father will be devastated if you refuse to see him. You don't want him to be hurt, do you?"

"No, I guess not. But Mom, will you call every day?"

"I'll call often. You can call me anytime you want," she said. "Okay?"

"Okay," Amy said sullenly. "I'm tired, Mom. I want to go to sleep now."

NUNNY & CECIL—A Tale of Terror

"I love you, Amy," her mother said, kissing her on the forehead.
"I love you, too, Mom."

Amy lay very still for a few minutes. She pulled the flashlight and diary out from under her pillow, burrowed under the covers, and began to read.

Dec. 20-Christmas is almost here, and I still have not had my monthly. Please, Lord, save me from this evil! Father has not been to the Inn, as he stays sober for the Christmas season. He will not meet my gaze, and I do not speak to him, except to answer his questions about dinner or chores. He has not approached me again, but I still fear him as I fear nothing else, for I would rather die than have him touch me again.

Feb. 10-I am with child, and my belly is swollen. I am sick in the morning, and I am constantly hungry. Every night I pray that I will die in childbirth, as mother did.

I have read more of Mother's letters. She was a beautiful person; how could she have loved someone as depraved as Father? Dear God, how could he have committed such an act, an act unsurpassed in the pure evilness of it. He has murdered my spirit; he has murdered my will to live.

Apr. 13-I am in such pain; it feels like there are snakes in my belly, slithering toward my heart, their darting tongues injecting it with poison. I will surely give birth to a monster. It is a sin for a father to lie with his daughter, and the fruit of Father's madness will be cursed.

May 13-My belly is formidable in size, and I must hide within the walls of this house and wait for the birth of my child and the death of myself. I welcome death with open arms, for life is no longer worth living. There is nothing for me; life is a black void. I do nothing but sleep and weep...and wait.

August 7-What monsters have sprung forth from my womb! They are hideous creatures— two of them—with the faces and appendages of wolves and the torsos of men. Why am I still alive? At three days old they are not helpless infants, but can scramble up my legs; it seems that they are trying to force their wretched way back into my womb. They grow threefold daily, and already are as tall as myself. I feed them eggs, as my breasts are dry and sore, and they eat them whole with their sharp teeth. But they are never satisfied, and I fear they will turn on me.

One day I found them feasting on rats and mice, smearing themselves in the hot blood. I vomited upon seeing this, and they hurried to get at it, salivating ravenously.

I call them Nunny and Cecil. Nunny is very ill. He does not breath properly, but seems to always have a cold.

I keep them in the attic and pray that Father does not find them; he would surely kill them. They are restless; I sing and read to them to soothe them, a book of children's tales. Their favorite tale is Jack and the Beanstalk. They sit silently, looking up at me with such love and devotion, that I find myself loving them back. I wonder if I could find an abandoned cabin in the woods, where the three of us could live. I could teach them to be civilized, and I'm sure we could be happy in our own way. I could plant a garden, and we could hunt small game together...but if their thirst for blood is as strong as they have demonstrated, then maybe hunting would only serve to undermine my teachings.

If only I could trust them.

This is too spooky, Amy thought—Nunny and Cecil! Everything was suddenly so obvious, so horribly clear. Amy remembered catching Adam taking a sockful of eggs up to the attic; she remembered the awful look on his face when she had asked him if he was going to feed his monsters. *What am I going to do? No one will believe me. They'll think I wrote the diary myself in an effort to get us out of this house. They'll laugh at me and think it's cute. They'll take away my horror novels.*

She continued reading.

August 8-Nunny and Cecil have committed an act so abominable, as to be unforgivable. I could not find them early this morning; I feared that Father had found and destroyed them. I was beside myself with worry and dread, praying that they were still alive—that is, until I found them.

I found their paw prints outside the front door, and I followed them for what seemed like several miles. Before I could see them, I could smell their carnage: they were in a feverish ecstasy, oblivious of my presence, feasting on a neighbor girl.

I have been spared my life in order to take their lives. They are evil and cannot be allowed to live. I should never have expected otherwise:

evil begets evil. I will kill them tonight with the poison Father uses for rats.

August 9-I have lain with my father and taken the lives of my children. In a moment, I will take my own life. Lord, please forgive me and welcome me into your arms. I know that to take one's own life is a sin, but I know that you only spared me in childbirth to perform my duty.

Last night after Father went to bed, I took their bodies down into the basement. By candlelight, I dug their graves in the hard soil next to Mina's grave and placed them inside. I had no box in which to place them, so I wrapped them in my blanket, as I will no longer need it. I painted their names, Nunny and Cecil, upon two stones and marked their graves.

And now it is time for me to die. Forgive me, Lord!

Amy shut the book and wiped the tears from her eyes. *I never should have read it,* she thought, thumbing wildly through the remainder of the diary, hoping to find that Jenna had not gone through with her suicide. But there was nothing more. Amy jumped out of her bed to hide the diary in the hood of her coat.

Her mind was weary. As she lay there trying to sleep, she thought she would never stop crying. Jenna's story was too horrible to have happened. Amy thought she should burn the diary, so that no one would ever have to be subjected to its horror again.

She realized with an overwhelming feeling of dread that burning the diary would not rid the house of the evil it contained; it was all suddenly as clear to her as the sky had been that day. They were doomed: Nunny and Cecil hadn't died for good with that rat poison. They were there in the house, still. The shadows of their hellish heads were on her wall; her own brother had befriended them. There was nothing she could do; if she told anyone they wouldn't believe her.

GAILA SWINDELL

37

Elam Riehl carefully took another sip of the steaming hot chocolate that Mrs. Stoudt had been filling his cup with for the last hour and a half; he pulled back quickly as the hot liquid burned his lips.

"Hot enough for you?" Mrs. Stoudt asked.

"Hot enough to burn the skin right off my lips," he said.

"Well, if you get your inside hot enough, your outside won't get so cold. If you get any closer to that wood stove, we won't have to worry about you walking home in this blizzard. You're going to catch on fire if you don't watch out," she warned him.

Elam smiled and moved his chair even closer to the stove, absorbing its heat. At that moment he felt as though he never wanted to leave the warmth of that room, the comfort of his friend's home.

Elam's friend, Jerod Stoudt, sat staring out the window at the blizzard. Jerod looked as stiff as a statue the way he sat there, rigid and silent.

"What are you thinking about, Jerod?" Elam asked.

"You know what I'm thinking. I'll say it for the last time, Elam. You just stay here with us until the storm is over. You'll freeze to death in this blizzard. Just look at it out there. That snow must already be five inches deep, and it just started coming down not an hour ago," he said.

"I only have three miles to go, Jerod. Once I cross Farmer Jacob's field, my family will be able to see me coming."

"That's a lie, Elam. Why...I can't even see our barn through this stuff, and it's right there—a hop, skip, and a jump from the house," Jerod said, pointing out the window. "I wish my father were here. He'd make you stay."

"Elam, you know Jerod is right," Mrs. Stoudt told him. "You really should stay. We have plenty of room, and the girls will be so tickled that you're staying with us, they'll bake you something good to eat. Maybe Gerta will even make her potato filling to go with the chicken I'm roasting. There's not a boy in the land who'd turn that down."

"Mother," Gerta called down from upstairs.

Elam smiled and his heart beat a little harder at the sound of Gerta's voice. "You know I'd love to stay, Mrs. Stoudt, but if I don't get home soon, my folks will be worried sick. You know how my mother is. Thank you for offering to let me stay, but I really must go home. Elam put on his coat, scarf, and gloves.

"Here you go," Mrs. Stoudt said, putting an old wool cap on his head. "This one's just not practical for weather like this," she said, putting aside the broad-brimmed black hat that he usually wore. "We'll keep it here for you so you won't have to carry it." She filled a paper bag with cookies and handed it to Elam. "Put this in your pocket just in case you get hungry on the way."

"Thank you, Mrs. Stoudt. I appreciate your kindness. Tell the girls hello for me, please," he said loudly enough so Gerta would hear him. Elam walked over to Jerod and gave him a soft punch on the arm. "I'll be all right, Jerod. Don't worry about me."

"Sometimes I wish we could have a telephone, then we wouldn't be going through all of this. You could just pick up the telephone and call your mother," Jerod said. "If anything happens to you, it's all because of our stupid religion."

"That's enough, Jerod. Mind your mouth! Your father would take you out behind the barn for talking that way!" Mrs. Stoudt said.

"I'll be seeing you," Elam said, walking toward the door. He opened the kitchen door, letting in a cold gust of air, and as he was about to walk out into the snow, he heard Jerod call his name.

"Elam."

Elam turned to look at his friend.

"Take the road, why don't you."

Elam smiled and saluted in reply, and then walked out into the blizzard. He hesitated, looking toward the road and then back toward the fields. He knew that if he took the road it would take him a good forty-five minutes longer to get home, but there was always the chance that someone would come by and offer him a ride; he doubted anyone would be out in the storm. He decided to take the back way; he didn't want his mother to worry one minute longer than she had to.

Something swooped down at him from out of the snowy sky. He didn't see it—his eyes were looking at the ground in front of him as he concentrated on his walking—but he heard its wings beating the frigid air. He couldn't imagine what kind of bird might be out in that blizzard; he searched the white curtain in front of him in hope of seeing it again. He thought it might do him some good to know that he wasn't the only creature dumb enough to be out in the blizzard.

Swoosh...

He saw it: a huge raven, bigger than any bird he had ever seen.

Elam had always attracted wild creatures.

Swoosh...

He hoped the raven would take refuge from the storm on his shoulder; he could use the company; but instead, it continued to swoop down at him, always heading back toward the Stoudt's house. It seemed to be telling him to go back. He would have loved to turn around and head back to the warmth of that kitchen—and Gerta—but he had to go on.

He pulled a cookie out of the bag in his pocket and held it up in the air for the bird. The bird did not return, so Elam ate the cookie, which was now slightly soggy from being covered with snow.

He crossed the remainder of the Stoudt's land with no problem. The snow was hitting his back, which made the going easier. It was only three o'clock, but the blizzard made the sky almost as dark as night. The snow was hard and firm already, crunching loudly underfoot as he walked through the bleak field.

He hoped his mother might have some hot soup for him when he arrived home. He hoped she wasn't worrying about him. Elam knew she was probably attempting to make dinner and having a rough time concentrating on her task; her little round face constantly at the window, her eyes searching the whiteness for her boy.

Elam thought the blizzard was beautiful in its quiet splendor, draping everything in a white shroud. The edge of the forest, where it met the clearing, was like an immense white wall, acting as Elam's guide home.

He got lost in his thoughts and the sound of the snow crunching under his feet. He was excited about the baptism that he would undergo in a few short months. He would feel better once it was over, more sure of himself and who he was, more sure of his devotion to his religion. He wished that Jerod wouldn't voice his doubts about being Amish; it only made Elam wonder what life would be like as one of the non-Amish—the "English." It was a sin to even wonder about such a way of life, and he always felt a heavy burden of guilt whenever his mind did wander in that way.

He reached the halfway mark in Farmer Jacob's field: a pine that stood taller than any other tree on the edge of the forest. It was barely visible, covered in snow against a backdrop of whiteness, but Elam could make out the outline of its majestic form.

He contemplated the high suicide rate among the Amish youth; he could feel his stomach tense and his fists clench in an involuntary response. It made him physically ill to think about it. He understood their tortured minds: torn between living by the Amish law or abandoning their families and going to live among the English, they chose death instead.

He had never thought of suicide, even though he was sometimes frustrated with their simple existence. That was the way it had to be, and the only way to live with it was to accept it—wholeheartedly; and he did. He believed the old adage that one had to accept what one could not change.

Elam heard something else crunching in the snow besides his own lonely footsteps.

He stopped and looked toward the woods and then out into the empty field; but he could see nothing through the veil of snow that hung before his eyes. It was enough to drive one mad, that veil: he could not pull it back like a curtain; he could only strain his eyes to try to see through it.

"Who's there?" he called out, but there was nothing to be heard but the crackling of his own words in the icy air. It seemed that he had been walking for miles and was getting nowhere. A chill was suddenly crawling through his flesh into his bones; he had been so deep in thought that he hadn't thought about the cold for a while.

A shrill howl, like that of a coyote or wolf, pierced the quiet. It sounded like it was right at the edge of the woods, which was only several hundred feet away from him. He was surprised and frightened all at once. He knew the Pennsylvania woods as well as he knew his own home; wolves did not live in those woods.

He continued walking, trying desperately to go back to what he had been thinking about. He wanted to rid himself of the panic that had suddenly overtaken him. He thought of the warm wood stove at Jerod's house and Mrs. Stoudt's steaming cups of hot chocolate. But that didn't help to ease his mind; it only made him wish all the more that he hadn't left.

More crunching in the snow somewhere behind him...or maybe it was to his right, just north of him. Whatever it was that was following him was trying to step into the crunching snow at the same time he did, or so he thought; but he could still hear a crunch in the snow even after his foot had already hit the ground, almost as though the sound of his footstep had an echo.

He couldn't see a thing through the dense sheet of snow that surrounded him; the darkness didn't help matters. Elam had traveled that same path at least a thousand times. He and Jerod had been best friends since they were old enough to speak; the three-mile walk between their houses never stood in the way of their being together. It was rare that they had time to see each other lately: they were always busy working their parents' tobacco farms, running errands, and in Elam's case, since he had no sisters, helping out around the house. Sometimes they would agree to meet halfway at a certain time to see each other for a short while.

There it was again, only this time it was more of a cry than a howl, a cry of excitement rather than pain, followed by a strange kind of panting. Elam had never seen any strange animals on that path, at least not the kind that his imagination was conjuring just then.

He started a slow jog. It was very difficult to run through the snow; it had probably reached seven inches high in some places. Elam was suddenly very sorry about his decision to begin jogging: he had excited his hunter, like the desperate flailing of a frightened swimmer excites the shark, and now it ran parallel to his path, where the forest met the field. He could hear it breaking through the dense low-lying brush that was tangled there. The stuff was almost as hard to get through as barbed wire; Elam realized that whatever it was that was running there must be tough; the thorny thicket didn't seem to impede its progress.

If he could only see, his fear would be allayed, or so he hoped. He strained his eyes so hard that they hurt, but he was as good as blind.

Elam picked up his pace, but his lungs were filling with icy cold air, tightening up on him, forcing him to slow down as he gasped for oxygen.

He heard it coming toward him, crunching in the snow as it ran, but he still couldn't see it. Now it was going out and away from him, circling him. There was a crunching in the snow behind him and a crunching in the snow in front of him, and suddenly, an evil, low growling seemed to come from all around him.

He had no idea how many there were, but he did know that they were hunting him, cruelly determined to make him their prey.

Why didn't I stay at Jerod's? Why didn't I listen? He hadn't listened because he knew the blizzard would not be a problem for him—and *it* wasn't: he never expected to be hunted down like a frightened deer.

He suspected his hunters to be canine in species because of the low growling sounds they made and the howling he had heard before. They were probably just stray dogs that had become lost and confused in the blizzard—or so he hoped. He whistled to them, pulling out his bag of cookies at the same time.

"Here, boy. Here, boy," he called. "I've got some cookies for you," he said, slowing to a walk and holding out the cookies, hoping they would smell them and come near. He whistled, hoping the animals—whatever they were—would be charmed by him as wild creatures always were.

A dark form leapt out of the blinding whiteness in front of him, its jaws clamping down on his wrist, ripping off his entire hand. Elam screamed and something grabbed his leg at the calf, snapping right through the bone with its powerful jaws.

The last thing Elam was aware of, before he fell face first into the frozen snow and became lost in the murky sea of unconsciousness, was pain...burning, ripping, killing pain.

38

March blew in like a nest of angry bees, hurling it's last of winter wrath at the Pennsylvania countryside. Schools and businesses closed as roads turned into ice-skating rinks for cars; smart people huddled indoors, drinking hot tea, sitting by the fireplace. They had suffered their fair share of blizzards that winter.

The wind howled like it was the end of the world and herded the frenzied snow into great white bluffs. The sun hid its shining face from the world for two whole weeks, seemingly lost to the people of Pennsylvania, and then burst forth like brand new in the third week of March, melting the frozen ice that clung to the earth and revealing a horror to the residents of Cooks County that made all previous horrors look like cartoons.

The doorbell rang at the Rodman farmhouse, startling Joe, who had his straight razor perched just over his left cheekbone; he ran downstairs with a towel around his sun-leathered neck. Two policemen asked if they could come in and talk to Joe.

"Sure. Come on in and have a seat right in there," he told them, pointing to the living room. "Let me go up and finish this mess. It'll just take a minute; I'll be right down."

Joe took his time finishing his shave and rinsed his face in icy cold water. He would have liked to stay up there, pretending that the officers had never come. But he knew that wouldn't do. He knew why they had come: they must have found the young Amish boy who had been missing since the first day of their recent snowstorm.

Joe knew the whole story. Reuben Beiler, the farmer who owned the land adjoining Joe's, had told him everything; at first reluctantly. Folks were beginning to think Elam Riehl had grown bored with being Amish and had run away to enjoy the good life. But then others said no, he wouldn't have run off for any reason. His friends said that he would never have even thought about violating the Ordnung in any way; they said he had feared the meidung—which was the shunning that took place when someone violated the Ordnung—more than anything. He was just three short months from being eighteen and very eager to be baptized.

Joe slowly descended the stairs, listening to the muffled voices of the policemen who sat waiting. "Joe Rodman," he said, extending his hand for the officers to shake.

"Good to meet you, Mr. Rodman. I'm Officer Harred," the older of the two said, shaking Joe's hand, "and this is my partner, Officer Zinn."

Officer Zinn shook Joe's hand and said, "Nice to meet you, Sir."

"What can I do for you, officers?" he asked as he settled himself into his chair, preparing for something ugly.

"I'm sure you read in the paper—or maybe you heard it on the news—about that young Amish kid, Elam Riehl, the one who has been missing," Harred said

Joe nodded his head yes.

"Well, now that the snow has melted, we've been able to locate him," Harred went on. "We found him in Farmer Jacob's field. I know Farmer Jacob is down the road a bit, but we felt you should know, just the same," Harred told him. "We found the boy's bones, Mr. Rodman. Some animal got at him, left his bones completely bare. Every bit of flesh was eaten," he told him matter-of-factly.

"Excuse me a minute, please," Joe said, rising and making a dash for the kitchen. He filled a plastic cup with ice water and drank it down quickly. The water was so cold it froze his throat. Then he reached up on the top shelf of the kitchen cabinet and pulled down a pint of whiskey—something used only for hot toddies in the Rodman household—and after taking a big whiff of the stuff, he drained a quarter of the pint. It was like fire running down his throat, burning the frozen membrane. His head began to clear, and he wiped his sweating face with a towel.

"You okay in there, Mr. Rodman," Harred called to him.

"Yup. Be right there." Two words ran through his head: Nunny and Cecil. And then, *it's all your fault.*

"I'm sorry," Joe said as he reentered the living room. "I have a question for you: How do you know the flesh was..."eaten" off the bones?"

"The bones have been gnawed on," Harred told him. "It looks like an awfully big dog had a field day with the boy. We think some starving animal did it—something strong with very big, very sharp teeth. When the snow melted, so did the tracks of the animal that ate—uh—killed him. This boy was no weakling; he was a strong, well-muscled young fellow."

"How did you identify him?" Joe asked.

"That's the most bizarre part of the crime. They left his head intact. Didn't touch it," Harred told him.

"That must have been a sorry sight, indeed," Joe said.

Officer Zinn took out a pad and pencil and asked, "Have you seen any stray animals wandering around here? Maybe out back in your orchard? Or have you noticed anything strange lately, like have any of your fences been knocked down or any of your animals killed? Think carefully, have you seen anything out of the ordinary?"

Joe didn't even have to think about an answer to Officer Zinn's question; it was already there, waiting to roll off his tongue. "Uh...no," he lied, "can't say that I've noticed anything amiss."

"Mr. Rodman, are you sure you haven't seen anything that could help us with this case? This is some serious business, you know," Zinn said, both officers staring hard at him. Officer Zinn began to scribble furiously on his pad.

"Sorry, I can't help you. If I say I haven't seen anything, then I mean what I say. Now, you officers can just leave me your cards, and I'll call you if anything comes up," he said rising. He didn't feel like being friendly any longer.

"We'd really appreciate that, Mr. Rodman," Harred said, handing him a card. "Would you mind if we took a look around your property?" he asked.

The two policemen stood up. They were both tall and muscular. They towered above Joe, so much so that he had to look up at them.

"Not at all. Go right ahead," Joe told them.

"One of the boy's leg bones was missing," Zinn said. "It was the large bone—the femur. We'd appreciate it if you'd be on the lookout for it. And there was some silvery-gray hair, canine in origin, scattered near the boy's bones. Let us know immediately if you see an animal that color."

"Before you go, has anything like this ever happened around here before?" Joe asked.

The two officers looked at each other, and then Harred said, "Way back in 1875, a crime of a very similar nature took place just a few miles from here; the only difference was that in 1875, the victim was female. The records of that particular crime are a bit fuzzy, but it seems to me that the two crimes are exactly the same, even down to the silvery-gray hair found near the body. In the 1875 case, it was evident that the animals that killed the girl were of a canine nature; their paw prints were found in the soil near her body."

"What do you mean, 'canine nature'?" Joe asked.

"Well, that's what I meant when I said the records were a little fuzzy. 'Canine nature' was all that was written in the records to describe the perpetrators. It was never explained. Anyway, the animals or killers—whatever you want to call them—were never found. I have a sneaking suspicion that this is going to be the case this time around."

Harred nodded toward the pictures of Amy and Adam on the fireplace mantle. "Those youngsters come to visit you often?"

"They're living here...right now," Joe told him.

"I'm sure I don't have to caution you to keep them close to the house, preferably inside. Thank you for your cooperation, Mr. Rodman," Harred said with a wave of his hand. And then they were gone.

Marie pulled into the driveway just as a patrol car was leaving. Both of the officers inside gave her a saluting wave and a false smile, which alleviated the vise of fear that had tightened around her heart when she first saw the car leaving her house.

Nothing could be too wrong if they waved and smiled. She came bustling into the kitchen with her arms filled with groceries, a worried look in her eyes.

"What's wrong?" she asked. "They find that boy?"

"Sure did. They found him out in old Farmer Jacob's field," Joe told her.

"Was he dead?" she asked, noticing that her husband wouldn't meet her gaze.

"Sure was. Why don't you go up and put your slippers on, sit down, and relax for awhile?" he said giving her a kiss on the cheek. "You work too hard."

"What's going on, Joe? You tell me, right now. Quit trying to put me off," she told him sternly.

"If you sit down in this chair, I'll tell you," he said, pulling out a chair.

She sat down. "Now, tell me, Joe. You're making me crazy with waiting," she demanded.

"They found the boy's bones," he told her.

"What do you mean they found his bones?" she said. "Why, he was in the flesh just two weeks ago. A body doesn't decompose that fast."

"I know that, Marie. Some animal ate the flesh off his bones—all except for the head. That's how they knew it was him right off."

She was silent for a few minutes, a furrow growing deeper in her smooth brow as the horror of what he was saying sunk in.

"What kind of animal do you think it was, Joe? I've never heard of such a thing happening in all my life. It's so...it's so...horrible! I can't...I can't even imagine such a thing," she said, tears falling from her eyes.

"Don't you cry, now," Joe said, bending down to hold her. "They'll find that miserable animal. It was probably starving to death."

"That poor boy! What are we going to do? I mean with the children and all and Denise coming home so late all by herself," she said in between sobs.

"Well, it's still winter, and that's a good enough excuse to keep those children in the house. And Denise is a reasonable girl; she'll understand why we don't want her coming into the house, alone, at three o'clock in the morning. She can beep the horn for us if she does have to stay out late, and we'll go down to meet her, bring her in the door safely.

"I'll go down in my truck every day to get the kids when the bus drops them off. Now, stop crying. There's nothing to worry about," he told her, holding her small, cold hands in his own large, warm ones. Marie saw him looking at their hands; she knew what he was thinking: how old their hands looked—old and powerless and weak.

"I guess you're right. We'll just keep the kids inside and the doors locked," she said, wiping her eyes and nose with a tissue. "They'll be safe in the house. No animal is going to get them in here."

NUNNY & CECIL—A Tale of Terror

39

It was Saturday and much too lovely a day for Denise to be anywhere near the university, but she'd had to go in for a few hours. It was over now and she was on her way home. She was at the City Line exit when she suddenly decided to turn around and head over to Bruce's house and pay him a surprise visit. She hoped he was home; she was in need of a love fix.

There was no answer when she knocked and rang the doorbell, so she let herself in with the key Bruce had given her. It was strange in the apartment without him, quiet but still alive with his energy, as if he were in the next room. "Bruce," she called out. Maybe he hadn't heard the bell. For some reason she felt like an intruder. But if he didn't want her there when he wasn't home, he would have never given her the key.

She was disappointed that he wasn't home. She wished she'd called to let him know she was going to be in the city, but it was early morning when she'd left home and she didn't want to wake him with a phone call.

She was almost to the door when she decided to get a drink of water and leave him a note. She opened the refrigerator and poured a glass of water. She opened the junk drawer and pulled out a pad of paper and a pen. Dear Bruce, she wrote, and then set her glass down on the counter. Denise was surprised to see another glass on the counter; Bruce never left dishes out. He must have been in a hurry this morning, Denise reasoned. She started to write again, but the glass caught her eye. There was lipstick on the rim, in a shade quite different from Denise's. She picked up the glass and examined it, her pulse, rapid, her heart in her throat. The breakfast she had eaten earlier decided it wanted to make a dramatic reentry into the world. She wasn't sure she could make it to the bathroom, but she felt it was worth a try. She ran to the bathroom and vomited into the toilet.

She was sure Bruce could explain the glass; she *hoped* Bruce could explain the glass, but it still worried her sick. All her sick, suspicious fantasies featuring Bruce and the "other woman" were suddenly there on the screen in her mind's eye. She washed her face, concentrating on the cold water, splashing it into her eyes to erase the erotic film fest running through her head: Bruce and some woman, the same woman she'd found Donald with, going at it on the kitchen counter, the couch, the weight bench.

If she was going to confront him about his infidelity, she needed evidence. Denise ran to Bruce's bedroom and threw back the covers on the bed. She looked under and on the pillows, under the bed, on the bedside tables, in the wastebasket. The next thing she knew she was emptying his drawers, his closet, his medicine chest. She examined the hair on the bathroom floor, in the bathtub, and in Bruce's brush. She inspected the clothing in the laundry hamper. She was in the kitchen next, searching the drawers, the refrigerator, the garbage can. In the living room she removed all the cushions from the furniture.

She was combing through the ashes in the fireplace when the sound of the doorbell brought her back to the real world. She looked around, disbelieving what she'd done to Bruce's home, his things. Her hands were covered with soot. *Who could possibly be at the door?* She brushed off her hands and looked through the peephole. A young boy stood on the stoop. Denise opened the door.

"Is my dad home?" the boy asked.

"Bruce?" Denise said.

"Yes," the boy said.

"No, he's not here."

"Who are you?" he asked.

"I'm his friend, Denise."

"Can I come in?"

"No, I mean...not now. It's not a good time. I was just leaving," she said.

"What are you looking for?" he asked.

"What are you talking about?" *What in the hell is going on here,* she wondered.

"You'd better let me in, or I'll tell my dad," he said.

"I said I was just leaving."

Denise looked back inside the house to see how much damage she'd done. The place looked like a pack of wild toddlers had been set loose to roam at will. Her eye happened upon the picture of Bruce's children on the mantelpiece; the boy on the stoop was not the same boy who was in the picture.

She slammed the door shut, cutting off the boy's fingers in the process. He screamed, "You bitch!" And then, "Mom, let me in."

Denise looked down at the bloody fingers scattered on the tile floor of the foyer. "What have I done?" she screamed. She ran to the kitchen and grabbed her purse. She shoved the note she'd begun and the glass she'd drunk from into her purse. She had to get out of there as quickly as possible. *To hell with the boy,* she thought. *You know who he is, Denise. Think about it.*

She ran to the foyer. The fingers were gone; but she'd known they would be.

She opened the door and looked around. No one. She walked as nonchalantly as possible to her car and drove home.

When she arrived home she immediately went upstairs and found Adam's class picture. She wanted to be sure. She found the picture of the boy on Bruce's stoop. His name was Jeffrey Abrahm.

This is one more reason to hate living in a small town, Amy thought, as she entered the library that was just slightly bigger than her bedroom. She was used to massive libraries that covered whole city blocks.

Her grandmother had dropped her off saying, "Now don't take home more than you can handle." She said she would be back to pick up Amy in an hour.

"May I help you, young lady?" the librarian asked, looking down at Amy through bifocals.

"I'd like to get a library card," Amy told her.

"Do you live in Cooks County?" the woman asked her.

Amy said, "Yes," refraining from asking the woman why she, a ten-year-old girl, would have come to that particular library if she didn't live nearby.

"Well, then, fill out this form and bring it back when you're through. You'll need a parent or guardian to sign it for you."

Amy hastily filled out the form and took it back to the woman. "My grandmother will sign it when she comes to pick me up."

"I'll have your card ready for you when you check out. Can I help you find anything?" the woman asked.

"I'm looking for books on Indians."

"Right over there," the woman said, pointing to a shelf over by the window. "In the nine hundred and seventies."

"Thank you," Amy said, hurrying over to the bookshelf.

Jenna Jerrel had never actually written that her father had forced sexual intercourse upon her, but through the strange terminology that Jenna had used to describe what he had done, and because the act had resulted in pregnancy, Amy was sure that the mysterious dance had taken place.

She understood that much. But she didn't understand how a human being could give birth to the wolflike monsters Jenna had described. She had felt foolish asking her mother if human beings could give birth to other animals. Amy knew about incest. She knew it was taboo and it often produced children that weren't quite right—but with the heads of wolves and the bodies of men...she didn't think even the horror of incest could produce that. She was reasonably sure that the form of Jenna's children had something to do with the Indian blood Jenna had inherited from her mother, especially since Jenna's mother had been a member of the wolf tribe of the Ipaki. Amy was there at the library hoping to enlighten herself in the ways of that tribe.

The shelf contained seven books on Indians. Amy looked through three of the larger, nicer looking volumes; the books were full of information on the Ipaki, but not the kind of information she was looking for.

Amy looked at the clock: she had thirty minutes before her grandmother would be out in front of the library honking the car's horn. She was becoming discouraged. Amy put the three books back on the shelf. There, at the very end of the books on Indians, was a thin, tattered book, barely discernible in its emaciated state; she pulled it out. The print was worn off the side of the book, and the title, *Indian Customs*, was scarcely legible on the front. The book looked as though it had been dragged through the mud.

Amy skimmed through to the index, and seeing the Ipakis listed there, she eagerly took it over to a table in the corner of the library. She found that the book actually had been dragged through the mud; some of its pages were glued together with the stuff. Amy temporarily rid herself of her aversion to dirt and plunged headlong through the book as if she were searching for the secret to surviving adolescence.

Twenty-five minutes to go. Hopefully her grandmother would be late; but Marie had expressed some concern about leaving her granddaughter alone at the library, and more likely than not she would be early.

Amy's eyes flew over the pages:

The Ipaki, whose name translates to 'the ancient people,' were divided into three main tribes, according to the form taken by their individual gods, the Great Spirits; the worship of a Great Spirit and eleven demigods was universal to all three. The eleven demigods were the sun, moon, earth, fire, water, house, corn, east, west, north, and south. The number twelve was sacred to each of these tribes, hence the one main god and eleven demigods worshipped.

The three different Ipaki gods or Great Spirits were the wolf, the pheasant, and the deer. The Ipakis felt it a great taboo to hunt any of the animals they or their Ipaki neighbors worshipped; hunting the ground hog, wildcat, and rattlesnake was also prohibited.

The wolf tribe claimed a dominance over the pheasant and deer tribes because of the superiority of its warriors and because the wolf was the benefactor of all the Ipaki. It was the wolf, which, after being offered the Indian princess Sasquatow, was said to have led them out of the interior of the earth, where they had dwelled for centuries without the benefits of their demigods.

The wolf tribe has some peculiar legends surrounding it. Ipaki legend has it that once a month when the moon was full, the wolves would howl incessantly until a virgin Indian maiden was sent to their den in the forest to mate with their leader. The Ipaki referred to this prolonged howling as "the calling." They never dared to refuse to appease the Great Spirit, as they feared they would be banished to the center of the earth for eternity.

The holy man of the tribe would choose twelve Indian maidens at the beginning of each year and assign each maiden a month of the year. All of the virgins of the tribe would gather together at the celebration of the New Year, each hoping to be chosen to mate with the Great Spirit; it was of the highest honor to be chosen for this position.

The preparation of the Indian maiden was a lengthy ritual during which the maiden was kept inside her family tent for a month before the full moon of her designated month. With each phase of the moon she was given a different treatment to make her more attractive to the wolf: her family would rub her skin daily with turkey fat, and they would paint her face, a few brush strokes each day, so that eventually she would resemble a wolf.

On the final day, before the moon was at its fullest point, the holy man of the tribe would visit the Indian maiden to purge her of any fear she might have and pray for her fertility.

When the wolves began the calling, the maiden would either go naked into the forest, or if the weather were harsh, she would dress in a special garment made from the skins of freshly killed beavers. She would follow the sound of their baying until she found their den, where she would mate with the leader of the pack.

After the mating, she would pray in the den until the sun began to rise, and then she would make her way back to her camp, chanting all the while. The rest of the tribe would stay inside their homes until they received word from the maiden's family that she had returned to camp.

This mating ritual was supposedly the reason for the superiority of the wolf tribe warriors. The maiden would give birth to a male child nine months after her mating with the wolf, and the child would have the sharpness of perception and the shrewdness of mind that the wolf was believed to possess, making him the most revered of warriors. These warriors were known as the Munsquay, which meant Son of God in the Ipaki language.

After the birth of her child, the Indian maiden would have the honor of selecting the Munsquay of her choice as a husband. The Munsquay were immortal because they were said to be the sons of god; after their mortal death their ghostlike images appeared with the head and appendages of a wolf and the torso of a man. They were said to wander the earth and assist the Ipaki in battle.

The current inhabitants of southeastern Pennsylvania claim to see the ghosts of the Munsquay and to hear wolves howling on certain nights of the year when the moon is full, although the last wolf seen in Pennsylvania was in Clearfield County in 1892.

Amy was suddenly aware of the blaring sound of a horn, and she looked out the window to see her grandmother waving at her to come out. She slammed the book shut, not bothering to put it back on the shelf, and flew past the librarian who said, "Wait...wait, don't forget your library card."

Amy didn't stop and didn't look back at the old woman, but ran out to her grandmother's car, jumped in, and slammed the door.

"We should have your hearing checked. I sat out here and beeped this horn for five minutes before you looked up. Didn't you hear me?" her grandmother said.

"Sorry, Grandma. I was concentrating on what I was reading," Amy told her.

"Didn't you take out any books?" Marie said, looking around.

"No, Grandma. I didn't see any that I wanted."

Her grandmother began to talk, but Amy wasn't listening; she was deep in thought about what she had discovered. The revelations of her detective work surprised, pleased, and horrified her all at once. She was pleased that she was correct in her hypothesis about Jenna's Indian blood being the culprit in her defective children, but she was also deeply disturbed at why it was correct. The idea that people could do such things—even if it was only legend—repulsed her.

She looked out at the Pennsylvania landscape that she had always found so beautiful and wondered if the legend was true. When she thought about the terrible secrets that lay hidden in the hills and dales of that lovely countryside, it shook her until her bones rattled.

GAILA SWINDELL

40

It was cold. The frozen ground crunched under Joe's feet; he could see his breath in the clear, crisp air. The day itself seemed unaware of anything wrong in Cooks County; the sun was shining brightly. The cold brought with it a certain sense of peace.

The first thing on his agenda was to find the pit he had thrown those bones into. He felt his coat pocket to make sure he hadn't forgotten the heavy-duty lawn and garden bags. He wondered why the pit was there at all. *Must be six feet deep,* he thought. *Some kids playing out here must have dug it, or someone with something big to bury.*

He walked along, his eyes and frozen ears alert to anything out of the ordinary, his body taut with cold and apprehension. As he found himself deeper in the woods, he began to relax. The rush of fresh air around him helped him to push his troubles into the back of his mind. It was so peaceful with the trees all leafless and stark, the ground barren and hard, and the frozen creek resting its voice.

He walked along this way for a few miles, forgetting himself, until he came upon the massive hole. He had thrown branches down into it to cover the bones, but he hadn't wanted to camouflage the hole, thinking it was too dangerous; a person might fall in and it would surely be a trap for animals.

When he jumped down into the hole, he fell to his knees, sobbing and flinging his body against the earthen walls of the pit: the bones were gone. He thought for an instant that the police search parties might have found them, but if they had found them, it would have caused quite a stir—more of a stir than the dead boy had caused, and he would have certainly been made aware of it.

An image of the Amish boy lying in his casket flashed before him; the boy's head left intact like some cruel joke, something to be viewed by his loved ones as they said their final farewells.

The words of some children's fairy tale popped into his head when he thought of the boy: *Be he live, or be he dead, I'll have his bones to grind my bread. What in the hell are those words from*, he wondered.

The words echoed in his mind; the voice in his head kept repeating the words like a loathed pop song overheard while changing radio stations. He got up off his knees, brushed himself off, and began walking at a fast pace down the forest path toward home.

He turned abruptly and walked back to the hole. He had to check it again.

This time, there were no bones, but the pit was not empty: the limbless body of a boy about Adam's age rested at the bottom, his bloated blue-white face looking strangely happy. His pale, thin lips were stretched into a smile.

Joe held his nose to block out the slightly sweet, gamy reek of rotting flesh. He recognized the boy even though his face was distorted by decomposition: it was Jeffrey Abrahm. The boy's eyes popped wide open, and, gnashing his teeth and barking like a dog, he wormed his torso up the side of the pit. Joe screamed and aimed his gun at the thing, but it laughed like a hyena and disappeared before he could fire. The sound of its wicked laughter resounded through the forest for longer than it should have.

Suddenly, the words that Joe had heard only in his head seemed to be coming from somewhere outside of his head, somewhere in the trees, down near the creek; he didn't really care where they were coming from, he just wanted to get out of those woods.

Be he live, or be he dead, I'll have his bones to grind my bread.

He walked fast, as fast as he could without actually running. The forest that had always been his friend, the place where he had always felt so comfortable and safe, had become his worst enemy.

The sun disappeared, and he looked up to see a singular black cloud in the otherwise flawless sky. He began to run, his old heart racing to keep up with his legs. The voice in the forest whispered louder—or so it seemed—to be heard over his thumping heart. His heart sounded like the beating of tribal drums in his ears, the cannibals right on his heels.

Be he live, or be he dead, I'll have his bones to grind my bread. BE HE LIVE, OR BE HE DEAD, I'LL HAVE HIS BONES TO GRIND MY BREAD!

He thought for a second that he was losing his grasp on reality: there were no voices in the forest. But he heard them loud and clear; it was like the wind was speaking, the words whipping around his head, disorienting him. He heard someone running behind him; there was no mistaking the sound of footfalls on the frozen earth. Joe felt like he was in a movie—a horror movie entitled *Let's Scare the Shit Out of the Old Man.*

He couldn't run any faster. He felt something brush against his leg, and when he looked down to see what it was, his glasses fell off. He couldn't stop the forward motion of his body, and his right foot came down on the wire-rimmed glasses with a sickening crunch. He reached down and scooped them up with an agility that he didn't think he still possessed. Now he was nearly blind and still running.

Something grabbed him, ripped through his coat and shirt and held fast. He opened his mouth to scream, but his lungs held no air to push out any sound from his parched throat. He tried to pull away without facing his attacker, but whatever held him did so with an iron grip. He could feel its steely claw against his soaking-wet-with-perspiration skin. His heart stopped dead, and he turned to face his attacker: a tree branch. He broke it off, threw it down, and started running again.

The trees and other landmarks he had always used as mileage markers were nowhere to be found; unfamiliar in their winter nakedness, they did him no good. Or maybe it was his feverish rush to leave the woods that obscured them from his sight. And then he remembered he was not wearing his glasses: He wouldn't have recognized the landmarks if someone had pointed them out to him.

Whatever had been running behind him now ran in the brush alongside of him. He strained to see it, but it was so well camouflaged that it seemed to be the brush itself. It broke through the dense brush like a tornado.

Be he live, or be he dead...

He could smell the thing contaminating the frozen air with its stench. He had forgotten that he was holding a gun, and he was suddenly aware of it in his hand. It didn't matter though; it gave him no comfort; he sensed that it was useless against whatever was chasing him. He couldn't kill the thing; it was already dead.

Finally, he could see the orchard, his own barren apple trees motioning him to hurry: Come home old man, they seemed to say. His trees had never looked so good to him, not even when they were heavy with the crimson jewels that had been his gold for so many years.

When he tripped and fell, he was almost grateful; the obligatory commercial would come on and he would be able to rest. But in the back of his mind he knew that it didn't happen like that in the land of reality: in the land of reality the attackers pounce on you when you fall, and rip the flesh from your bones—at least that had been the violent reality for the poor Amish boy.

Joe fought the urge to curl his body into a ball and surrender to the teeth of the enemy.

"Fool," he said, getting up quickly, grateful that the gun hadn't gone off when he fell. He had unlocked the safety when he started running.

He looked around to see nothing but his beloved orchard and the giant hedge of the forest where it met his land.

He looked down to see what it was he had tripped over; he hoped that none of the roots of his trees had popped out of the ground to play traitor. It was a long, thin, dirty-white bone—a femur bone. For an instant he pictured the Amish boy—tall and strong and alive, *reduced to this,* he thought, *this bone.*

He thought of Marie, and then he thought of his beautiful Denise and Amy and Adam; a surge of anger, and with it, adrenaline, coursed through his veins like an electrical current; he picked up the bone and broke it in half like a toothpick.

"Damn them—damn the evil things!" he said. But when he looked down and saw the paw prints in the frozen earth near where the bone had been, he realized it was he who was damned—damned on this hell called earth.

GAILA SWINDELL

41

Paul Raison drove down the turnpike a little faster than he liked to drive. He wanted to get home in time to get a few hours of rest before he went to work. He had been away too long; he had probably lost a few patients because of it.

It was downright irresponsible on his part; but it was worth it.

He would have been home three weeks before if he hadn't met the lovely Rita at the psychology convention in Pittsburgh. It had happened so fast; he couldn't believe that he, Paul Raison, the ultimate cynic in matters of the heart, could fall in love so quickly. He had fallen so hard and so fast, he was surprised he hadn't broke something—like his heart.

There wasn't a car on the highway, it being two a.m. on a lonely Sunday morning, with only an occasional truck to pass in a hurry.

The roadside signs indicated he was approaching a rest area. His vision was getting blurry. He pulled into a turnpike rest station to get some coffee. He thought there was nothing more desolate than a turnpike stop at night, nothing more macabre than the occasional pale face of a night traveler in the unflattering glow of fluorescent lighting, an advanced five o'clock shadow making every man look surly and desperate.

Paul ordered a cup of coffee from the fat woman with the sagging lower lip and the penciled-on eyebrows behind the counter. He was hungry, but the thought of eating something prepared by the toothless souls he saw cooking the food made his stomach lurch. He decided to get something out of the snack machine on his way out; maybe a chocolate high would help him stay awake.

On the road again, he thought about what lay before him: mentally ill children with mentally ill parents. He felt extremely guilty about not contacting Denise while he was away; she was his friend and he had disappointed her—one of the drawbacks of treating your friends' children. His secretary had said that Denise had called for him several times and was upset that he wasn't available.

Paul was really worried about Denise; her judgment and reason were faltering. Adam's antisocial behavior was scaring the shit out of her.

Paul remembered his visit with Adam quite vividly. The boy seemed perfectly normal, until he described his imaginary playmates: a look came into his eyes, a lunatic stare, a wide-opened hysterical assurance that gave him away—all this in the eyes of a face that was almost cherubic in its innocence. Like the calm in the eye of a hurricane, it could fool you into thinking it was safe to go inside. For a boy with a face like that to have that kind of look in his eyes, Paul was almost convinced that he had indeed seen the hellish creatures he had described.

The memory of what he had seen in Adam's eyes made him shudder. But he had used his reason and experience when diagnosing the boy, and his reason and experience told him Adam was going to be just fine; it was his intuition that told him otherwise, and he couldn't let that influence him. He had seen many cases of children with imaginary playmates; it was a phase many children went through. With the trauma of his parents' divorce, and the disrupting move to the farm and the isolation Adam experienced there, Adam was reacting in what could be called a "normal" manner. He would get through it.

Paul's car plunged into a patch of fog so thick that he couldn't see to drive. He didn't know what to do. He wanted to pull over, but he was afraid to. He knew that the wisest course of action was to keep moving; to pull over would be like asking for someone to hit him. He couldn't see what was in front of him until he was right up on it, and if a trucker decided to pull over right where Paul's car was sitting.

Something crossed the road in front of him; he swerved to miss it, almost losing control of the car.

"Damn it!" he said.

He wasn't sure what it was, possibly a deer. All he could see was a brown shape. Something crossed the road in front of him again; this time, he hit it. He slammed his foot on the brakes and flew forward, hitting his head on the windshield. He was slightly disoriented and very dizzy. He wasn't even sure if he was still headed in the right direction.

That thing I hit, Paul thought—*whatever it was, it was definitely not a deer; it was walking upright. Why would anyone be crossing the road in this fog?*

A truck came barreling by, its horn blaring, almost skinning the side of Paul's car. Paul realized that he was driving on top of the dotted line instead of to the side of it.

He panicked at the thought of having hit someone, but he panicked even more at the memory of what he thought he saw. It looked like something out of the imagination of Adam Miller: half wolf, half human.

I've had too much coffee, Paul thought, rolling down his window and pouring out the remainder of the wicked brew. Something reached out of the fog and grabbed his hand; it was padded like a dog's paw, with scratchy fur and long claws. Screaming like he didn't know he could scream, he jerked his hand away from the vile thing's grip and pressed his foot down hard on the accelerator. He quickly rolled up the window.

Paul could feel his heart beating like a heavy metal drummer. He pressed the automatic door lock and heard the gunshot sound of the doors locking in unison. He felt adrenaline rush through his veins like a brush fire; there was something out there that wanted him. He could almost smell it—whatever it was—or maybe it was the smell of his own fear.

He felt a warm wetness between his legs and realized that he had pissed his pants when that thing had grabbed his hand. He had seen it clearly: it was a big hairy paw with talonlike claws. He looked down at his hand to see he was bleeding from a long thin scratch.

Get hold of yourself, man! Paul began to try to make some sense of what had happened, organizing the facts: *I was thinking about Adam's imaginary playmates; I hit a patch of fog; an animal of some sort ran out in front of me; another animal ran out in front of me; I panicked; I poured out my coffee; I scratched my hand on something outside; I hallucinated because I panicked.*

That explains everything.

The fog broke up, and Paul relaxed. He grabbed a napkin from the glove compartment and dabbed at his bleeding hand. He was so tired.

Another patch of fog. Paul could see it in the immediate distance. It swirled and gyrated in the glare of his headlights like it was alive.

"Damn it!" he said, as the fog overwhelmed his car. There was something there on the side of the road. It was a man waving Paul down. Paul slowed down and pulled over. *This is crazy,* he thought; *I should just keep going. But the man obviously needs help.*

Paul waited for the man to approach his car, realizing that he had not seen the man's broken down vehicle; but who could see anything in that fog. The man, a tenebrous figure in the fog, stood outside the car. Paul heard him say something, but it was difficult to understand him with the window rolled up. Paul started to unroll his window, when suddenly the fog shifted and the man was as clear as day to him—only it was no man: it was a wolflike creature from hell, similar to what Adam had described, covered with blood and missing half an arm. It was shouting at Paul in a voice that seemed to come from a deep tunnel: "You sorry bastard! You ran me over back there, and now I'm going to run you over!" It laughed darkly and pressed its bloody stump against the window.

Someone was pounding on the passenger window, and Paul turned to see a young boy pounding his fist on the window, screaming for Paul to let him in.

"My god! What are you doing here?" he said. He reached over to unlock the door, but then stopped in mid action as the boy opened his mouth a bit too wide, revealing long yellow fangs.

Paul pushed the accelerator to the floor and the car took off with a screeching of tires. He pushed ahead through the fog at eighty—and then ninety—miles per hour, an insane speed for the conditions at hand. He kept his eyes firmly glued to the white lines in the center of the highway and his foot pressed firmly on the accelerator. His fingers gripped the steering wheel so tightly, that he wondered if he could ever pry them loose.

Something bolted into the path of the speeding car, but Paul didn't let off the gas for a second.

"Fuck you if you think I'm falling for that again!" he said. He heard hysterical laughing; he unglued his right hand from the steering wheel for a moment to make sure the radio was completely shut off, but the laughing wasn't coming from the radio.

He vowed to never see Adam Miller again, if he ever made it home alive. It was the boy's fault—surely what was happening was the boy's fault. Paul knew this was an irrational thought, but reason played no part in this nightmare of nightmares.

Finally, the fog cleared, the fiendish laughing stopped abruptly, and Paul relaxed slightly. The winding Pennsylvania turnpike was no place for a car to go ninety miles per hour, especially in the fog, but Paul kept up the same pace. He wanted to make it to the next rest stop, where he planned to stop, get out, and be among human beings until the sun raised its burning face.

Another patch of fog rose up. Paul tensed and scanned the side of the highway looking for a sign that would indicate a rest stop was close by, but the only sign he saw read "S Curves." *Great,* he thought, *dense fog and S curves—a fatal combination.*

He heard a strange noise, and he prayed that he wasn't getting a flat tire. But the noise wasn't coming from outside the car, it was coming from the vicinity of the back seat. It was the sound of asthmatic breathing, agonizingly deep and forced. The horrible unmistakable metallic odor of blood filled his nostrils. *What in the hell could that be?*

He wanted to turn around to look, but he was paralyzed with fear. The S curves were getting hairier by the minute and he had to fight to maintain control of his car. If he took his eyes off the road for an instant he would surely be a dead man.

When the thing in the back seat pushed its bloody stump into the side of Paul's face and shouted, "Look what you did to me, Paul," the car veered off the dark highway into a vast, black valley and Paul was...a dead man.

42

Denise relaxed in her room. Earlier that day, Marie had told Denise about the Amish boy. Marie talked as though the killers were there in the room with them; she kept looking around the room and jumped up off of her chair when a tree branch blew against the window.

"Mom, take it easy," Denise had told her as she took her gently by the shoulders and sat her back down.

"But, Denise, we have to be more careful around here. Amy and Adam aren't allowed to play outside unless one of us is out there with them. And you..." she said, shaking her finger in Denise's face, "you aren't to be coming home so late at night. When you come home after dark, I want you to beep your horn until your father comes out after you. Do you understand?" she shouted in a harsh voice, her eyes darting from Denise's face to the window.

"Yes, Mother. Whatever will make you comfortable," she told her.

"Don't you patronize me! I won't have it! Now, this is a serious matter, and I want you to take it seriously!" Marie had roared at her daughter before stomping off down the stairs.

Denise still couldn't get the hysterical look of her mother's eyes out of her mind. It was probably just a hungry pack of wolves or a dog of some kind, Denise had told her, but that only seemed to make Marie crazier.

"There are no goddamned wolves in Pennsylvania, Denise!" her mother had screamed.

The sheriff had told her father that they had found some tufts of hair near where the boy was killed—silver-gray, canine hair. Joe had cursed the Cooks County Police Department, saying they were backward in their investigation.

She looked out the window to see a huge raven sitting on the balcony. Denise looked at the thing and saw its beady black eyes studying her. She was sure it had come to jog her memory; the loose ends she was trying to tie together were suddenly tied into elegant knots: the color of the hair they had found near the dead Amish boy was silver-gray, just like the hair she had found in the nest of her clothes in the attic and in Adam's bed. It was probably just a coincidence, but she made a note to question Adam about the animal he had been harboring. She didn't want Adam befriending some possibly rabid dog who ate the flesh from a person's bones.

Denise picked up the newspaper and began reading. On the second page, Denise read, "Philadelphia Psychologist Killed in Auto Accident."

A gasp escaped Denise's lips as she read the name of the dead man: Paul Raison. She recalled something Adam had said: I wish Paul were dead! And I wish you were dead, too! She remembered the sly look on the child's face when she told him that he would have to go to see Paul until he discontinued his bad behavior.

Don't be crazy, Denise! That's an irrational thought! She wanted to slap herself into sanity. She knew it was preposterous for her to think Adam could have caused Paul to fall off a cliff on the Pennsylvania turnpike.

But nothing seemed impossible anymore. Reality was no longer the solid, reliable world of the absolute, but a dim mockery of life filled with shadows lurking in dark corners and nightmares that didn't end when she woke up.

NUNNY & CECIL—A Tale of Terror

43

Adam lay awake thinking of his mother. He looked at his clock and saw that it was two-thirty a.m. He was so angry he wanted to scream. She had a lot of nerve, brazenly flaunting her sexual escapades in the face of the whole family; *what else,* he wondered, *would she be doing out at this time of night?*

Just then, he heard the front door click shut and the dead bolt snap into place. *She's in the kitchen,* he thought; he could hear the water running through the old pipes of the house. He heard her trying to climb the creaking wooden staircase quietly and then his grandmother's voice say, "That you, Denise?" He heard his mother say, "Yes, Mom. Go to sleep!" And then he heard her in the bathroom, washing up, alerting everyone to the fact that it was two-thirty in the morning, and she was just getting home.

He heard a muffled knocking on the bathroom door, and his sister whispered, "Mom, can I sleep with you tonight?" and then his mother whispered, "Sure, Honey. Are you having bad dreams?" And then Amy, "No, Mom. I just can't sleep. Maybe I'll sleep better with you."

The rest was a muffle as Adam seethed with anger. And then, catching a whiff of the unmistakable aroma of Nunny and Cecil, he felt better. At least he had someone to talk to.

"Adam, we've come to tell you a bedtime story..." Nunny told him. Suddenly, they appeared at the bottom of Adam's bed. "About why women are all the same."

"Yes, they are all the same," Cecil wheezed. "You'll soon come to find out that your mother is a wretched, lying whore, and she wants nothing more than to be rid of you and your sister so she can run off with some man."

"How do you know that?" Adam asked, tired of them telling him what women were like, but not telling him what fueled their beliefs.

"Be patient, my friend. We'll tell you everything in a moment. Do you remember those two rocks with our names painted on them that you found in the basement?" Nunny asked him.

"Yes," Adam told them, remembering the feel of the smooth, cold stones in his hand, and how they had broken in half when he had thrown them down.

"Well, those stones were once stuck into the earthen floor of the basement to mark our graves. Your grandfather—dear man—set us free the day you came to live here. He dug up our bones, releasing our souls from that cold, damp prison. He reburied our bones in the woods behind the orchard, but he didn't rebury our spirits. Why do you think that we were buried in the basement?" Nunny asked him.

"I—I don't know," Adam was confused.

"Mothers can be so evil. Our mother—the woman who gave us life—also gave us death. She poisoned us and then buried us in the basement so that she wouldn't be found out and taken to prison for the murder of her precious children," Cecil told him. "She kept us hidden in the attic until she murdered us. You're lucky that your mother has allowed you to live for so long. We were only three days old when our mother brought us that fateful dinner. She loathed us because we were the product of her sin. She was a whore, and she wanted us out of her way so that she could continue in her sinful ways. Your mother will do the same to you one day, Adam. Mark my words: she will do it. Maybe you'll get lucky, and she will just leave you here with your grandparents."

"But if your grandparents are not here to care for you, then she will either have to kill you or take you with her," Nunny added. "And you know what her decision will probably be?"

"Then, what should I do?" Adam asked them desperately.

"Just wait and see what happens," Cecil told him. "Watch her closely and do not—I repeat—do not trust her! We'll think of something."

"In the meantime, we have a new friend to keep us company," Nunny said. At that moment, Jeffrey Abrahm appeared, looking like a shark had eaten most of him for lunch. A huge piece of his rib cage was missing, as well as the right side of his head and his left leg. He hopped over to the bed on his right leg and sat down.

"Jeffrey!" Adam gasped. "What happened to you?"

"Don't act like you don't know, asshole. It was all your fault," Jeffrey said.

"What are you talking about?" Adam asked.

"I pissed you off at the Halloween party, so you sicced your friends here on me. Well, now they're my friends. And if you don't hurry up and get rid of this shitty family of yours, you're going to be out of the picture."

"Jeffrey!" Cecil said. "That's quite enough."

"We'll leave you to rest, now, Adam," Nunny said. "Goodnight."

"But...but..." Adam began. But they were gone.

GAILA SWINDELL

44

When Joe woke up it was still pitch dark outside; the clock mocked him with its fluorescent green display of 3:17 a.m. For Joe it seemed more like seven—time to rise and deal with the day. He hadn't had a decent night's sleep in he didn't know how long.

Until recently he hadn't noticed the effects of age: the sleepless nights and sudden urges to nap during the day; the slow degeneration of his memory, which was marked by an uncertainty as to whether some incidents had even occurred, or whether the fogginess surrounding them indicated they were figments of his gray imagination; and worst of all was the deterioration of strength—in mind and body. His eyes, his legs, his ears, his brain, his goddamned penis—nothing worked as well as it used to.

He had enjoyed a good life, but time was a thief in the night, and life was too brief. It was as if one day he was a strapping young man, and the next day he was a feeble old man. He was like an old piece of farm equipment: still doing the job, but taking more time and effort to do it, and breaking down a hell of a lot more in the process.

He lay there squinting into the darkness, listening to the sound of his wife's breathing. The rain spattered hard on his window and the wind gusted angrily. The spring had brought with it an abundance of rain that fed the thirsty earth.

Joe had always said he would die in that house; the condo life was not for him. He and Marie had decided to live the remainder of the time they had together there in the farmhouse. But Joe hadn't planned on encountering the strange and disturbing incidents of late.

He could hear the wind growing stronger, but hard as it tried, it couldn't rock the old farmhouse. The house was old, like Joe, but unlike him it was sturdy and solid. And unlike him it seemed to grow stronger with age, the elements working to cement the old boards and stones together, instead of tearing them apart. Its many sounds—creakings, whistlings, grindings—were all like sighs of contentment, as it happily settled more permanently onto the earth on which it stood.

He ground his teeth together so hard that he was sure the grating sound in the darkness would wake Marie. He wanted to kick himself for digging up those ungodly bones. *Why couldn't you let them be? Why didn't you leave them there to rot in the soil?*

Joe lay there, cursing himself and listening to the rain and the wind, when suddenly he heard another sound—a knocking.

He listened intently to the chaos of the night, trying to hear the sound again, but he heard nothing unusual.

He settled into his pillow, hoping the knocking wasn't a loose barn door, banging and splintering against the barn.

Bang...bang...bang.

There it was again. He wasn't sure if he should be relieved to hear that the sound wasn't coming from the direction of the barn, or be worried to hear that it was coming from somewhere downstairs. It had to be something that had come loose in the wind.

Bang...bang...bang.

"Damn it," he whispered in the dark, "what in the hell could that be?"

He didn't want to go running down there like a fool in the dark, but the sound was beginning to worry him; it sounded more like someone knocking than something loose and banging.

He looked at the clock and wondered who would come knocking at that hour and in that kind of weather. No one else in the house seemed to be disturbed by the noise. Marie lay there breathing as peacefully as a child.

A dark shadow cut off the beam of light from the night light that shone into his room from the bathroom down the hall; Joe's heart skipped a few beats as he quickly reached behind the headboard of his bed and fumbled for the key to the nightstand where he kept his handgun. If it had really been a prowler, Joe realized his action wouldn't have been quick enough.

The shadow had a voice: "Grandpa...you awake?"

It was Adam, standing there in his bare feet and pajamas.

"Grandpa, someone's knocking on the door," Adam said as if he was in a trance; the voice coming from him didn't sound like his own.

Joe had to ask himself if he was dreaming; nothing seemed real in the darkness. Adam seemed almost transparent, his body wavering like a specter. Joe realized that it was probably the way Adam was blocking the light, causing a weird glow to radiate around his dark image, that made him appear so. But Adam's voice was so strange—almost ghostly.

Joe felt silly, suddenly realizing that he was afraid of the boy, his own grandson. Adam was no longer the innocent child Joe had always known: he seemed to be part of the unholy alliance—part of the evil that was gradually possessing the very ground that had sustained the family for so many years.

Joe rarely operated on instinct or intuition, but something told him that Adam's strange behavior was more than an eight-year-old boy's inability to adjust to an ugly divorce, and the result of Adam's experience could possibly prove fatal for the rest of them. But he couldn't bring himself to tell the family that he thought Adam was capable of sudden violence; they would condemn him as a senile, raving lunatic.

He had to ask Denise and the kids to leave—politely, but firmly. No more hinting around. It would rip his heart in half to do the dirty deed, but it was for their own good.

Bang...bang...bang.

"Don't you hear it, Grandpa?" Adam said calmly. He didn't seem afraid of what the noise might be; fear would have been a normal child's response.

Joe was unsure about what to do. "I hear it loud and clear, Adam. I'll take care of it; you just go back to bed," he whispered to him.

"All right, Grandpa. Please go see who it is. The noise is keeping me awake," Adam said in that alien voice. His words had a hollow, robotic sound. He turned and walked silently from the doorway, the ray of light he had been blocking slipped back into the room.

Joe got up from the bed and put on his slippers. He walked over to the window to see if he could see anything; if someone were there, there would probably be a car out front. But there wasn't.

He started toward the nightstand to get his pistol, but then, as an afterthought, he went into the closet for his shotgun. He thought perhaps just the sight of the long cool barrel might give him additional protection; from what, he didn't know. Anyway, it would definitely give him confidence.

As he shuffled out of the room, he expected Marie to call out to him, asking him where in the world he was going at that time of night and with his gun. But she continued dozing. He wondered if he should wake her: if he didn't come back right away, she could call the police.

What in the world has got into you, man? he asked himself. *There's nobody out there. Probably just a loose shutter.* But as he walked down the stairs...

Bang...bang...bang...

He thought he could hear the sound coming from inside the house; he proceeded slowly, cautiously, step by step, his slippers padding softly on the wooden steps. He walked through the foyer to the front door and stood there listening.

"Who's there?" he called out.

Nothing. No one.

"Who's there?" he called out with slightly more volume.

Again, no answer.

He turned and headed through the hallway, looking into the living room as he passed; the house seemed different somehow—unfamiliar.

Bang...bang...bang.

It was coming from the basement door; someone—something—was standing at the top of the basement stairs, pounding on the door. Joe could hear them breathing; the thickness of the door was the only thing that separated him from them.

He stood there listening.

Bang...bang...bang.

Joe could see the door vibrate; he could see the key quiver.

Am I dreaming? Could someone really be there?

Bang...bang...bang, was the answer to his question.

A surge of fear flowed through his body, making him want to hightail it out of there. And after the fear had run its course, an even fiercer surge, this time of anger and adrenaline, coursed through his veins.

He turned the key in the lock and flung open the door, jumping back and aiming his gun at the empty air. There was nothing there but a gust of cold damp air and the stench of something dead and rotten.

Joe awoke to a cool hand on his forehead. He opened his eyes to see Marie, fully dressed, sitting on the bed next to him. He immediately turned to look at his enemy, the clock: nine fifty-five the display read. He had never liked the dimension of time, even when he was young and time seemed to go on forever, but lately he had grown to hate it; it was slowly but surely ticking away the moments of his life. One of the many reasons he loved farming was because time was told gently by nature—the bloom of the trees, the tender green of young crops sprouting through the red-tinged soil, and the song of the rooster—and not by some pasty-faced company president who didn't give a damn about the lives of his employees, or the quality and quantity of the time they spent with their families.

He had escaped the rat race all right, but he was paying for it now in the strangest ways.

"Aren't you feeling well, sweetheart?" Marie said, a worried look in her eyes. "You haven't slept this late since the last time you had the flu. You're usually up and running before the rooster crows."

He remembered the events of the night before, and for a relieved instant he thought it had all been a dream; but it had been too real to be a dream. The way things had been going, unreal described the events of his conscious state better than real did. He was confused, and Marie was looking at him, waiting for him to speak.

"I...I was awake most of the night. That wind and rain had me worried for a while. I guess lying here worrying got me all tuckered out."

She looked like she didn't believe him.

"Joe Rodman, are you telling me everything?"

"Have I ever lied to you?" he said, suddenly very grateful that she was sitting there in front of him, holding his hand, giving him strength. He was dying to tell her everything—about the bones, the voice chasing him through the woods, the nighttime basement visitors, and his fear of Adam—but he couldn't bring himself to do it. It wasn't that she wouldn't believe him—although he would have a terrible time convincing her that Adam might do them harm—he just didn't want to make her worry.

"Well, you've never actually lied outright, but you've withheld the truth to save me pain, and even though you meant well, withholding the truth is just as much a lie as a lie is."

They both laughed at this.

"You're feeling frisky today, aren't you?" he said. "I don't usually hear that many words come out of your mouth until around noon. But if I were you, I'd feel frisky, too; you slept like a baby through that storm last night. You left me to sit up alone and worry about a tornado. And if a tornado had blown through here, I don't think even that would have disturbed you. They'd find you someplace over in Berks County—still sleeping."

"I'm sorry, Joe. Why didn't you wake me? I'd have been happy to sit up and worry with you," she laughed. "It would have been romantic, and then we could have...well, you know." She raised her eyebrows.

"My god," he said, pinching himself on the arm. "Either I'm still dreaming, or you've been downstairs taking vitamins. You really are frisky this morning."

She gave him a sly smile; he reached out and put his arms around her, hugging her like he would never let her go.

"I love you, Marie. If anything happens to me, I want you to know that you've made me the happiest man on earth."

"What do you mean, if anything happens to you? You've got another good thirty-five years left to live old man; that's a long time. You aren't going anywhere, so don't even talk like that," she said. "Besides, when you go, I'm going with you."

"What's for breakfast?" he asked. "I worked up quite an appetite through the night." Actually, he wasn't the slightest bit hungry, but Marie would definitely think he was sick if he told her that.

"Sorry. You slept right through breakfast. I suppose I could salvage up a piece of old toast or something," she kidded.

"That would be just fine," he told her.

"Would that old toast sound better to you if it were French?" she asked.

"Oh, Marie, that's all right. I don't want you to go making breakfast twice in one morning..."

"You shush. I wouldn't dream of making breakfast twice in one morning. I really meant it when I said old toast; I saved some for you when I made breakfast for the kids. It might be a bit soggy, but I think you'll like it anyway."

"Anything made by the hands of such a woman would be heavenly—even soggy," he told her, taking one of her hands and kissing it.

"My...for that, I'll even heat the syrup for you," she told him. "You take a shower and get dressed, and I'll have everything ready for you when you come down."

He looked at the clock again and it told him—with its swift flipping of numbers—that his days were numbered.

Joe walked outside to survey the damage; he squinted hard, the bright sunlight hurting his eyes. The place looked like it really had been hit by a tornado. There were boughs and twigs scattered everywhere.

He started toward the cellar door; if anything had come down into the basement during the night, that would have been its only point of entrance, unless it had broken a window to get in. He stopped in mid step, turned, and headed for the barn, postponing the possible confrontation with an ugly reality. He wanted to see how much damage—if any—had been done out there. He could handle a wind-damaged barn better than evidence of an intruder in his home.

He could see that he would have to clean up the orchard; the wind had played havoc with the apple trees, probably hitting them harder than most because of their unwillingness to bend and sway. *And that was the way with all things that refused to bend and sway: they were always hit the hardest.*

Joe was happy to see that the barn had withstood the storm, even the door had held tightly onto its hinges. The once-colorful hex signs he'd put high up on the wall of the barn were faded and worn, looking somehow ominous to Joe—maybe because they had failed him. He had never really expected them to ward off evil spirits, but he had hoped they might do something in the face of evil, besides chipping and fading in the sun.

He took out his keys and opened the big padlock on the barn door. He walked inside and looked around. It was quiet and peaceful in there. Everything was as it should be.

When he walked back to the house and saw the huge paw prints leading from the woods on the west side of the house to the cellar door, he wasn't the least bit surprised.

45

Lenny Delenko walked swiftly down Broad Street. People stared at him as he passed; only a very crazy or a very poor person would be out in the cold wearing nothing but a thin T-shirt and jeans. His eyes glowed like gems, and a tie-dyed knit cap topped his unruly black hair. He muttered to himself as he walked, oblivious to what was going on around him.

He didn't know what to attribute his bursts of energy to; he rarely needed sleep or food, and when he did sleep, his dreams were always premonitions. He would dream something—a burning building, a town flooding, and even something as quotidian as cutting himself on the chin while shaving, or a pimple on a particular place on his face—and soon afterward his dream would come true.

Edith had looked at him like he was insane when he told her that he knew Professor Miller was going to die before her time; he hadn't told Edith that he thought Professor Miller's son was going to be the one to commit the murder.

He turned left onto South Street and walked east toward the river. He didn't know which was bleaker, the empty lots strewn with trash or the sterility of the new brick row homes. He blocked it all out, focusing instead on the visions in his mind's eye.

An image of Professor Miller, the same one that always flashed in his head, appeared before him as if on a movie screen. Her soft white flesh was torn; blood splattered her body like thick globs of red paint.

Lenny shook his head frantically as if trying to escape a giant spider's web; he shook his fist and screamed "No" at the gray sky. His mind was becoming more like a computer every day: he quickly deleted the file featuring the dead love of his life and replaced it with another.

All of his senses were sharp; he could see things from miles away—well not actually see things, but know they were there. He could smell them. He could smell his mother—his only natural enemy—whenever she was anywhere near him; and then he would move, move as quickly as possible away to where he could no longer smell her.

He couldn't believe she was doing this to him. Every so often the fog in his brain would clear and he would be just plain old Lenny again—without the energy, without the super senses—and then he would realize what was going on; then, he didn't feel so good. He would understand the extreme horror of it all, and it was worse than any horror he had ever known. He would feel like he was suffocating, become short of breath for days on end.

His own mother wanting him in that way—it was enough to make him want to destroy the world; when a mother's love for her offspring is tainted by lust, the world is a dark tunnel. There could be nothing more forbidden, nothing more unconscionable.

Yeah, but what about a son's love for his mother, Lenny boy? Shouldn't that be lust-free, too?

"Fuck you!" Lenny screamed out at the voice in his head. "You fucking demon, fuck you!"

Lenny felt he was the prophet, and it was up to him to save the world. He would be hailed the king of the world. His mother would contaminate mothers everywhere with her sickness if he didn't stop her. She had to be eliminated; she was defective. He had to wait for her to make her move; he knew she would soon.

Lenny arrived at his destination: Juniors Occult Shop. He stood outside for a moment absorbing the aura of the place, calmed by the sight of it. It contained powders, herbs, and charms that could make his world a better place to live. He walked inside, people turning to stare at him as he moved his lanky body jerkily to the beat of the reggae music coming from somewhere in the back of the shop.

He scanned the shelves, not looking for anything in particular. He read the labels on the cans of aerosol spray: "Jinx Away," "Spell Breaker," "Love Aura"...

He took down a can of "Evil Away" and took it up to the counter. A man behind the counter shoveled something that looked like marijuana into a plastic bag for a customer.

"I have you to thank, Junior. You have saved my life, for I was about to die of loneliness," she told him as she handed him some money. "You keep the change, Junior. If I could, I would pay you in gold for what you have done for me."

"Don't thank me. I am merely the middle man," he said. "And what can I do for you, young man?" the man said, turning his attention to Lenny.

"Just this," Lenny said, putting a can of aerosol spray labeled "Evil Away" on the counter. Lenny paid the man for the spray. "Thank you very much," he said, turning to leave the store.

He stopped suddenly and turned back to face Junior. "Do you have anything to make nightmares go away?" Lenny asked.

Junior's eyes grew wide as he stood staring, seemingly entranced by Lenny's sapphire eyes. Lenny became nervous as he waited for what seemed like an eternity before the man spoke.

"I have just the thing," Junior said, pulling a ladder along the shelves and climbing up it. "I give you a little to try, and then you come back and buy some if it helps." Junior scooped a blue powder into a small plastic bag and climbed back down the ladder. "Put this under your bed at night, and ask the spirits to heal you before you go to sleep. Just a little every night—a fingernail full. This should last about two weeks or more, and if you notice a difference, come back for more. But if it fails to work, I have other things. Don't worry," he said, handing the bag to Lenny.

"How much do I owe you?" Lenny asked him.

"You owe me nothing. It is a gift."

"Thank you!" Lenny said, walking toward the door.

"Good luck," Junior called after him.

NUNNY & CECIL—A Tale of Terror

46

The market was bustling with activity. Amish merchants stood behind glass freezer cases filled with chickens, baked goods, vegetables, cheeses, meats, and sausages. Denise walked through the din with Amy holding one hand and Adam following close behind.

Denise had been so worried about the kids when they were away with Donald that she vowed to spend every minute she could with them when they came home. She even let them take the day off from school to go to the Amish market with her; it was only open on Friday.

Adam tagged along behind, acting like he didn't want to be seen with his mother and sister. Now that Paul was dead, Denise didn't know who to take Adam to for counseling.

Amy insisted they stop at a stand where fresh-baked cookies were sold.

"Look, Mom, six for a dollar," Amy told her, pulling a dollar bill out of her coat pocket. "I want to buy some for Grandma and Grandpa with my own money."

Denise was so glad to see Amy had returned to normal that she would have probably agreed to anything the child asked. Amy had seemed to be slipping away for a while, into a dark little world of her own. She had dreaded going away with her father and practically begged Denise to let her stay on the farm.

Donald had tried to talk to her on the phone about the kids, but she refused to take his calls. He had finally broken down and written her a letter, which she had reluctantly read; after all, he would never actually have the satisfaction of knowing that she had read it if she didn't respond. In the letter, he asked why the kids were so quiet all the time. He had accused her of trying to turn them against him. She had promptly torn the letter into tiny pieces and threw it in the trash.

Amy had finally abandoned her black mood when Denise told her that she had gone to look at a few houses in the Philadelphia suburbs. Denise could see that the isolated farm life was taking its toll on her daughter.

Bruce wanted to get married in June, and then take a summer-long honeymoon exploring Europe. But Denise couldn't leave the kids there on the farm all summer, it wouldn't be fair to her parents or the kids—and she couldn't live without them for that long.

Her parents and Amy had responded to Bruce's proposal with a rousing round of happy cheers. Adam had shouted, "You won't succeed in your plan," and then he'd run up to his room where he stayed for the rest of the day.

He was becoming impossible to deal with. She had used all her expertise as a parent and her knowledge of psychology in trying to deal with him, but he was beyond her.

She had started writing a letter to Donald about Adam; she hated to admit defeat, especially to someone she considered her enemy, but she didn't know what else to do; she needed more than a psychologist's help in dealing with Adam. In her letter, which she hoped she would never have to send, she asked Donald for a complete family history. She was beginning to wonder if there was any history of antisocial personality in his family; Adam's weird behavior wasn't coming from her side.

On some dark and gloomy nights when she lay crying into her pillow, she even thought of letting Adam go live with Donald. The thought was like a monster in the night, nudging her in the ribs with its prickly elbow, saying, "you would really like to just be rid of Adam, wouldn't you?" But when the morning came, and the sun came dancing its rejuvenating dance inside her bedroom, she banished the monster to the dungeon of her mind and vowed never to give up her son. She loved her children more than life itself, and she would go to any lengths to keep them by her side.

"I want chocolate chips...and some peanut butter, too," Amy said pressing her hot little hands against the glass-enclosed cookie case that bore a sign reading Please Do Not Lean On Glass.

NUNNY & CECIL—A Tale of Terror

The Amish woman behind the counter seemed too harried to even notice Amy. Denise gave the woman their order and turned around to ask Adam want kind he wanted.

"Peanut butter," he muttered.

At least he still has an appetite, Denise thought.

"Smile, sweetheart," she told him.

His response was to turn and walk to the door, where he stood waiting for them.

They paid for the cookies and walked out the door to the next building. There were some food items there, but it contained a variety of goods—books, jewelry, long underwear, boots. As they passed a stall where cages full of birds sat atop one another, Adam paused to look at the birds.

Denise was drawn to a bookstall across the aisle. She heard a whirlwind of wings and turned to see Adam standing there looking at the birds, his hands in his pockets, the birds flying crazily around in their cages, chirping madly. The entire display of birdcages was moving, swaying back and forth; seeds and feathers flew everywhere.

"Adam," Denise called out, "come over here right now."

He didn't move; he didn't seem to hear her above the commotion.

"Adam!" she called again.

He turned to look at her, a funny smile on his face.

"Come here, now!" she demanded, motioning for him to come to her. She noticed that something shot out of one of the cages onto the floor. The birds were being driven wild by something.

Still, Adam didn't move.

Denise ran over to where he stood and grabbed his arm.

"What's wrong with you, Adam? You come to me when I call you. Do you understand me?" She had to practically yell to be heard over the ruckus of the birds. Maybe he couldn't hear her over the ruckus of the birds, but he had to have noticed her body movements.

Just then, something on the floor caught her eye. There was a thin, scarlet stream of blood running along the straw-scattered concrete floor. It had just missed splashing onto Adam's shoe. She looked up at the cage to see a yellow bird thrashing its body against the wire bars of its cage. Its head had split open; one of its eyes dangled free of its socket and blood covered its feathers.

A Mennonite woman came hurrying over.

"What is going on here with my babies?" she asked, her hands on her hips. When she saw what had happened, she let out a wild shriek. "What have you done?" she turned to face Adam. "I saw you over here antagonizing them, you wicked little boy! Go away from here and never come back!"

"How dare you say those things to my son! He was just standing here...he didn't do anything at all," Denise said, taking Adam in her arms and pulling him away.

All the people had stopped what they were doing to gawk at the scene unfolding before them. All was quiet, even the birds had stopped their rioting.

The woman glared at Adam as though she would hit him if she could. "Just go!" finally issued from her lips, and she waved her apron in a shooing motion.

Denise suppressed a desire to shout obscenities at the woman, and then she hurried Adam away, while Amy waited just ahead for them, hunkering low from embarrassment.

"Let's go, Mom," Amy said. "Everyone's staring at us."

"Ignore them," Denise told her. "Hey, look at that book stand up ahead. Looks like a good one, doesn't it?"

"I don't feel like looking at books today, Mom," Amy said, surprising the hell out of Denise.

"But Amy..." Denise started to question her, but then felt like she just didn't have the energy. Everything was changing in ways she didn't understand.

A blast of cold spring air smelling of honey and hay hit Denise in the face as she exited the building. It was exhilarating. She hurried along, not paying attention to whether or not the kids were following, just wanting to get away from the place.

"Mom, slow down," Amy told her.

Denise turned around to see her children skipping along behind her, almost running to keep up with her, Amy looking sad and bewildered, Adam looking angry and mean.

"Come on," she said, holding out both hands for them to take hold of. Amy quickly caught up to her and took her hand; Adam stayed behind, which tore at her heart.

"Mom," Amy cried, pulling her hand away, "you're hurting my hand."

Denise eased her grip on the child's hand, realizing that she had been squeezing it in her anguish.

"I'm sorry, sweetheart," Denise said.

"Mom, where are we going?" Amy asked.

"For a walk," Denise told her.

They walked across the street to a stone bridge that crossed a narrow muddy river. The river moved rapidly with a torrent of new spring rain. The date on the bridge read 1874.

"That's when Jenna was alive," Amy blurted out; her hand flew to her mouth as if she had said something wrong. She quickly ran to the other side of the bridge.

"Who's Jenna?" Denise called out to her, noticing a dark shadow cross Adam's face.

"Jenna was a whore," Adam said.

Amy flew around from where she was standing and directed a mean look toward her brother.

"Adam, I've had about all I'm going to take of your foul language. I don't ever—do you hear me—ever, ever, ever want to hear you talk that way again," Denise told him. "Amy, who is Jenna?" she asked.

Denise wondered if Jenna was a schoolmate, but then why would Jenna have been alive in 1874. And if Jenna were alive then, how would either of her children know her. Some vague memory flashed in her mind, but then darted away like a skittish cat. Why did the name sound familiar? It wasn't really the name that sounded familiar, but the flash of a memory—a fragment of a dream or something—that it evoked.

"She's someone we read about in school," Amy said.

Denise decided to let the matter go. Amy's answer didn't satisfy her; she couldn't imagine why the kids would be reading about whores in school; but Jenna was obviously someone who the children disagreed about, and talk of this person would only cause an altercation.

"You two wear me out," Denise told them. "Come on, let's go home."

Later, when she thought about what occurred when they left the bridge, it seemed as though it had happened in slow motion. Every detail of those few moments was permanently ingrained in Denise's mind, the bizarre incident playing over and over on the movie screen in Denise's head, as she searched for some clue as to its significance.

The three of them had made their way back over the bridge and were attempting to cross the street. Denise grabbed the children's hands before Adam had a chance to protest. Amy was whistling a familiar tune; Denise realized later that the song she had been whistling was "Buffalo Girls," a tune that was sung in elementary school even when Denise was a child. The sun was bright, causing Denise to squint as she looked at the approaching cars, and she didn't want to use her hand to shade her eyes because then she would have to let go of the children's hands.

Cars passed at what seemed like too rapid a rate of speed for a section of the street frequented by pedestrians. Denise could see an Amish horse and buggy approaching. There was a break in traffic; the kids moved forward as if to cross the street, but Denise pulled them back.

"Wait a minute. Here comes a horse and buggy," she told them. "We'll get a close-up view."

The carriage rolled easily on the pavement; the sun glinted upon the reddish-brown coat of the horse as it strutted proudly, its head held high, a powerful hot breath blowing like smoke into the brisk air from between its large, equine teeth.

Adam moved out toward the street to see around his mother and sister so that he was facing the horse.

The horse turned its head slightly, as if to get a better view of the three of them. Its large black eye gleamed like onyx; it seemed to be looking at Adam—maybe not directly at Adam, but just past him, as if someone else was standing there next to him. The horse slowed its pace slightly. Denise marveled at the beauty of the animal and the enormous amount of life that emanated from its gleaming, muscular body.

It looked as though the boy and the horse were having some sort of private, silent duel. The sardonic smile Adam used so frequently of late scarred his sweet lips, his eyebrows arched like a villain's. The horse bared its teeth and a thousand demons danced in its huge black eye.

A thin strap hit the horse's back with a cruel snap. The horse reared, its hooves working frantic strokes in the air as its eyes bulged from their sockets and a strangled whinnying sound came from its throat. It twisted its magnificent body in the air and came down in an unnatural position to its left, smack in the line of the oncoming traffic.

The strap hit the horse's back again and before the creature could get up and move out of the way, a speeding van slammed into it. The grotesque thud of metal against flesh and bone filled the cold spring air.

Denise screamed, high and thin. Amy clutched onto her mother's leg, her nails digging through Denise's jeans into her skin. Denise pulled the children forward, practically ripping their arms out of the sockets, and began running toward where she thought she had parked.

The only thing that ran through her mind was an imaginary newspaper headline: Young Boy Burned As a Witch by Amish. She had to get Adam away; if the woman who owned the birds came out and saw him standing anywhere near the mangled corpse of the horse, all hell would break loose. That imaginary headline might just become a reality.

GAILA SWINDELL

47

The first thing Denise saw when she entered her office was a can of aerosol spray, on her desk, smack on top of Lenny's paper. The can was labeled "Evil Away"; the instructions said to spray the stuff on one's body, avoiding the eyes, nose and mouth, or in dark closets, under the bed—anywhere one might think evil was lurking. It was no doubt from Lenny. She thought about using the spray for some kind of practical joke, but then tossed it into the garbage can. It would give the custodian something to think about.

She picked up Lenny's paper, hoping that this one wouldn't be quite so insane; she dreaded the thought of possibly having to fail Lenny—not only because she knew he was a smart and previously conscientious student, but also because she was afraid of him. If she gave him a bad grade—or failed him completely—he might decide to get revenge in some way. She hated to think that way about Lenny, but he had been exhibiting some pretty bizarre behavior, excluding what she had learned of him from Edith.

The paper was entitled "Behavioral Techniques," and it looked like any normal student's paper except for the tattered, coffee-stained front page.

Denise sat down in her chair and looked at her watch. She had a good thirty minutes to spare before class started; what better way to spend it than reading Lenny's paper. She was relieved to find that it was very good, but Lenny's doodles on the last page were enough to make her stomach lurch. Perfect images of black birds adorned the margins of his paper—*the messenger of doom;* but it was the bird on the back of the final page that made her spill tea all over her desk: a large black bird, with eyes that were piercing even in the crude drawing, stood perched upon a scarecrow that looked remarkably similar—right down to the black button eyes and the faded red bandanna that it wore around its waist—to the very one that was nailed upon a wooden plank, like a crucified sandbag, in her own backyard.

After drawing a big red A on Lenny's paper, Denise shoved it into her bag. She would give it back to him without a word; she didn't want to deal with Lenny Delenko—not that day, not ever.

He might be the messenger of doom, but he couldn't tell her anything she didn't already know.

GAILA SWINDELL

48

Denise stood waiting outside the Continental waiting for Bruce. He had seemed surprised when she suggested they meet there for dinner; she usually liked to go somewhere away from the crowd—someplace intimate and serene; and the Continental was anything but that.

She didn't want to be too alone with Bruce; he might start pestering her about the wedding. She couldn't make any decisions about such an important event; she didn't even want to begin to think about it. There was too much happening, too much to figure out. Denise loved Bruce with as much of her heart as she could give at that time, but he couldn't help her go through what she was going through. No one could. Misery in its truest form cannot be shared.

She waited patiently, thinking about her day. Lenny's insanity haunted her. She wanted to reach out to him, help him, but she knew that she couldn't.

Her mind shifted to her problems with her son, but that was too dark, too close to home on this bright day; *besides,* she thought with unusual optimism, *Adam's going to be fine; he's just a baby.* Her thoughts shifted back to Lenny. She thought of his mother, Sheila Delenko, and the way she had killed Lenny—the Lenny that Denise had known—by pretending to be his mother for so many years, and then attempting to be his lover. The role of the mother is everything to a child: Lenny's mother made him what he was, gave him his identity as her son, and then to take that identity away from the boy...she might as well have put a gun to his head.

Lenny had to have already had some minor psychosis to fall over the edge as easily as he had. His mother's apron strings must have been the only thing keeping him tied to his sanity. Denise hypothesized that Lenny subconsciously feared or knew he was adopted, and when his mother seduced him, she confirmed his worst fears.

She could see Bruce walking quickly toward her. His eyes met hers and his face lit up. She was torn in two: part of her wanted to run to him, throw herself into his waiting arms; the other part wanted to take off running as fast as she could in the opposite direction.

She didn't understand why he was being so persistent. It was almost as though he was afraid of losing her, as if he could see into the future, and in that future he had lost her.

"Hello there, handsome. Can I buy you a drink?" Denise asked Bruce as he walked up and stood beside her.

"Well, I don't know. I mean, I barely know you, and I'm not that kind of guy," he said with an effeminate wave of his hand.

Denise whispered into his ear, "I know just what kind of a guy you are." They both laughed, and Denise kissed him.

"I'm sorry I'm a few minutes late," he apologized, "but I had an emergency call from one of my patients just as I was leaving the office."

"Let's go inside," Bruce said.

They sat in a booth, ordered martinis, and talked about their days. Denise drank her martini down like it was water. She put down her empty glass and asked, "Do you believe that people can become possessed by evil spirits?"

He looked at her and then at the glass in her hand, and then back at her; his eyebrow arched.

"Cut it out," she said. "It's a serious question."

"You mean like in *The Exorcist*?"

"Well...kind of. I mean, in your work, have you ever studied or heard of any cases in which someone was possessed?"

"Not really," Bruce said. "Of course, I'm dealing mostly with neurotic patients. I don't encounter the extremes. I have heard of schizophrenics who believe they're possessed and family members of schizophrenics who *think* the schizophrenic is possessed. But I don't believe that evil spirits can possess people, because I don't believe in evil spirits. Do you?"

"No," she said, "I don't.

"Then, why did you ask me that question?"

"I don't know; I was thinking how much one of my students has changed this semester," she lied. It was true about the student, but that wasn't why she had asked the question. She was really thinking about Adam and how animals were suddenly afraid of him. The incidents with the bird and the horse were just too bizarre. But she couldn't understand how her cute, little, eight-year-old son could scare anything.

"So you think this student might be possessed?" Bruce said, breaking into her thoughts. "Come on Denise, that's a pretty big jump in thinking. Actually, it's downright irrational. The student's changed a lot this semester, and so he must be possessed? Are you leaving something out?"

"All right, you don't have to get sarcastic, Donald."

"What did you say?" Bruce's face turned bright red with anger.

"Oh my god! I'm sorry—really. I don't know why I said that. I guess it's the martini. Really, I wasn't thinking about him or anything."

"You must think I'm a fool. Admit it. You were thinking about the asshole, or you were thinking I was an asshole, so you called me his name."

"Bruce, I swear I wasn't thinking about him, and maybe I was a little mad at your attitude, but I wasn't thinking you were an asshole."

She could feel a volcano of anger beginning to erupt inside of her, but it was quickly extinguished as Bruce reached out and took her hand and said, "I'm sorry. I didn't mean to be sarcastic. And I believe you if you say you weren't thinking about him. I just feel like there's something you're withholding from me. Tell me, are you? You know you can share anything with me."

"No, I'm not withholding anything. I wasn't actually thinking that the kid is possessed. I don't know what I was thinking; although I do kind of believe in ghosts, not necessarily evil spirits, but just...ghosts," she confessed, and then wished she hadn't. *Why did I even start this conversation?*

"Why do you think I'm withholding something from you?" she asked, trying to change the subject.

"For one thing, you keep staring into space, and you keep skipping from one thing to another, like there are some things you have to leave out. Don't forget that I study people for a living. I make it a point to watch and really listen to people when they're talking."

"Well, maybe that's why I love you so much. I haven't ever had someone pay such close attention to what I'm saying and how I'm saying it," she told him.

"And now I can see that you're trying to get out of all this with flattery. Don't think for a minute that I'm going to fall for it," he said. "But maybe we should save your secrets for a time when we're both perfectly sober. I can see that the martini is getting to you; your face is very pink."

Denise was relieved to go on to something else. She was afraid that she might tell all about Adam, in an alcohol, garlic-induced spell of some sort. She was also very sorry that they had even had the conversation: it had confirmed her suspicions that Bruce would think she was crazy if she ever told him about Adam and all the bizarre things that had been happening; and even though she had expected him to act in just that way, she was hoping that he would understand. She just couldn't picture the logical, sensible Bruce saying, "Oh, sure I believe people could become possessed by evil spirits." And although her own logic and reason told her it was a ridiculous thought, her intuition told her that something just as farfetched as possession was exactly what was happening to her baby boy.

GAILA SWINDELL

49

The enemy had changed its strategy.

Joe walked through the orchard. When Marie had asked him where he was going he had told her he wanted to check on the trees.

But that was a lie.

He needed to get out of the house; get some fresh air, find somewhere to be alone, somewhere he could think. The stars were just beginning to show in the blue-black sky. The roaring chaos in his mind seemed a dark contrast to the quiet of the country night.

It didn't seem like his orchard anymore; the trees he had known and loved for so many years were almost sinister with their twisted limbs and gnarled shapes, bearing flowers as if for a funeral. There were things out there he didn't understand, things that had sprouted from the same soil that had sustained Joe, his family, and others before them.

Dinner had been unbearable; he had barely touched his fish. The change in the enemy's strategy was so obvious; he was surprised that they would think him so stupid that he wouldn't see it. But then, he realized they had every reason to think him stupid: he had freed them from their muddy graves.

Adam was trying to pull the wool over his eyes. A kid his age didn't have the cunning of an adult; he didn't have the intelligence to manipulate his family the way he was trying to; and Joe knew without a doubt that someone had to be influencing the boy. He didn't trust him—he couldn't trust him. He was ashamed at this mistrust; he realized that Adam was only the tool of the enemy, and he was acting on the instructions they—whoever *they* were—gave him. Joe knew that the boy couldn't help himself.

Joe had never been to war; his poor eyesight had made him ineligible for the service. Even if he had fought in a war, he would have no idea how to fight what was trying to destroy him now; how could he fight something when he didn't have a clue as to what it was he was up against? He had only one plan of action: to eliminate the tool of their destruction—Adam.

50

Joe sat underneath an apple tree looking up at the house. Denise's bedroom light was on. Asking her to leave was going to kill him, but it was better that he die than her and the kids. If they left, they could go on with their lives and forget the nightmare of the farm. If they stayed, well...

He reached up and picked a twig loaded with blossoms off one of the trees. Perhaps the offering would soften the blow.

He knocked softly on her door.

"Come in," she said.

"Hey, Neener," Joe said solemnly.

"Hi, Dad," she asked.

"Here," he said, handing her the stem of flowers.

"How sweet of you, Dad!" She got up from her chair and hugged him. "You and mom were right: I should be more worried about the kids. I'm just so tired of living under this black cloud of fear. I know how hard it must be to have us here. You're not used to all of this commotion, and all the problems that go along with raising a family—again. But I'm glad you came up, because I want you to know that we'll be moving out of here as soon as we find a place. I'm going to start doing some serious house searching."

Joe felt relieved; he took a deep breath. He didn't have to say a word, but he wrestled with saying something—anything—to let her know that he really hoped that she meant what she said.

"Denise..." he began. He had to choose his words carefully; he didn't want to offend his darling daughter, whom he loved more than anything. "Denise, you know I don't want you to go. But this is rough for two old folks like your mother and me. We worry constantly about you and the kids. I rarely sleep at night. I'm not trying to make you feel guilty. I guess...I guess I just want you to know that when I do get angry and start yelling, it's because I love you and those kids—and your mother, of course—more than anything; there's just too much happening around here, too many things I don't understand.

"I know there's a lot happening everywhere these days, but it's just not as spooky somehow as some wild animal tearing all the flesh from a body. And they have only one clue as to what the damned thing was...and they have no idea where it is.

"Adam needs to go someplace where he'll have friends to play with. I don't know the boy anymore! He scares me with the way he acts. I know he seems to be getting better, but I really believe that the only way he *will* get better is if he gets away from here."

He would leave it at that. He hoped that he hadn't hurt her feelings; he hoped she knew that they would always welcome her into their home. Nothing would have made him happier than if Denise and the kids could stay there at the farm with them forever. But they had to leave; their lives depended on it.

51

"Your grandfather is trying to interfere," Nunny said to Adam.

"If he succeeds in his plan, you'll be moving any day now," Cecil said.

"And then we'll be separated?" Adam asked.

"You know we can't come with you. This is our home—forever," Cecil said.

"Well...can't you do something?" Adam asked.

Nunny and Cecil looked at each other for a long moment. "We'll think of something, Adam," Nunny said. "Don't worry. Trust us."

Jeffrey Abrahm appeared. He said, "Your time is running out, Adam Miller. Hit the road..."

Nunny put a large and hairy paw over the bloody boy's mouth, and said, "Shut up, Jeffrey."

52

Denise practically skipped down the hall to the elevator. Not even her heavy bag loaded with completed final exams could weigh her down. She would drive away from the university in just a few short minutes, and she wouldn't see the place again until the fall term—if she could help it.

The whole world seemed to feel as she did. Groups of students sat talking and laughing, people rushed by with smiles on their faces. Birds played games in the air, racing around, chirping happily.

"Have a good summer, Professor Miller," Valerie Simpson, one of Denise's students, said as she passed.

"Thanks, Valerie. I hope you have a great summer!" Denise said.

Denise walked through the heart of the campus, seeing buildings that she had passed almost every day as if for the first time. Everything looked fresh and new and different. The healthy scent of spring was invigorating. Denise felt like she could breathe again. It had been a long, tough school year. It was never easy, but she usually didn't have a million problems of her own to deal with to make her work seem that much more difficult.

"Denise," someone called from behind her.

Denise turned around to see Edith hurrying up to her.

"Hello, Edith," Denise said, fighting an urge to turn and run. She didn't want to hear anything about Lenny. She was tired of seeing his deranged face, his empty, dazed expression.

"How have you been, Denise?" Edith asked.

"Fine, thanks, and you?"

"Great. I'm so excited. I just received an invitation to work at a clinic. It's with Dr. Freese, Dr. Kartowski, and Dr. Yeng. Do you know any of them?" Edith asked.

"If that's Ed Freese, yes, I went to school with him. Congratulations, Edith! Are you going to take the job?"

"You bet I'm going to take it. I can't wait! By the way, have you seen Lenny around?" Edith asked.

"Yes, I have. In fact, he just finished taking my final exam. Is he still coming in for treatment?" Denise asked.

"No. He hasn't been in since...well, since the last time you came to see me. It's been that long. I've left several messages for him, but he's never returned my calls. How's he doing? I mean, as far as you can tell."

"He's not well, Edith," Denise told her. "I'm surprised he was able to make it through the entire semester. I've never seen anyone change like that—so quickly." *Well, except for my son,* she thought.

"Well, I guess his identity was so tied up with his relationship with his mother, and when she tried to change from his mother to his lover, it destroyed who he thought he was," Edith said. "Does that make sense?"

"That was exactly the way I saw it, too. That poor kid," Denise said. Denise knew there was more to it, but she was in no mood to talk shop.

"Did he quit bothering you, Denise? I remember you said he had followed you around Center City once."

"He hasn't really bothered me since then," Denise told her, thinking of the black birds and the scarecrow on his paper, the way he stared at her in class.

"That's good," Edith said, looking into Denise's eyes as though she were searching for something—*the truth, perhaps,* Denise thought.

There was an uncomfortable moment of silence between them, and then Denise said, "It was good to see you, Edith. I really have to run. Good luck in your new job! Let me know how it goes." She didn't want to talk about Lenny. She wanted to forget he existed.

"Thanks, Denise. Good luck to you, too."

Denise walked away, her lighthearted mood slightly dampened. She turned around to look back at Edith, who was still standing there, looking at Denise. Denise smiled and waved; Edith waved but she didn't smile. She looked sad, like she was saying goodbye to someone for the last time.

53

Bang...bang...bang...

Joe sat up straight in his bed, awakened from his dreamless sleep by a knocking sound. He hoped he had been dreaming; he hoped he hadn't heard the sound at all. He sat there listening intently, not moving a muscle. He expected Adam to show up at his bedroom door again, complaining about the knocking in that alien voice.

He half hoped it was those creatures that had come knocking, so he could blow them to bits. He was angrier than he was scared; he was sick to death of those things playing their wicked games with his life.

He reached up and knocked himself on the head. *What in the hell are you thinking, old man? Your old brain is conjuring up some real crazy things.* He was so confused. *Am I senile or am I sane?* he wondered. *Is all this craziness a product of my imagination?*

Last time he had ended up convincing himself that the knocking sound had only been the wind, but that explanation left so many questions unanswered. It had been very late, and things that go bump in the night did have a tendency to make one's imagination act up, but his imagination didn't create the paw prints he had seen in broad daylight the following day.

Bang...bang...bang...

There was no mistaking those three knocks in a row. They were calling him down for a duel. He could feel his heart beat faster and his muscles tense. He remembered when he was in high school and Richard Bayliss had challenged him to a fight over a girl—Emily

Caruthers. He would never forget the way he had felt then, the way he had actually felt the blood racing through his veins. His body was like a volcano seething with molten lava, and when Richard had thrown the first punch, Joe had erupted, punching blindly, but on target.

He believed in destiny, because nothing could fit so right as his life had fit him. If he died that night, he would have only one regret: digging up those cursed bones.

Bang...bang...bang...

If he could just ignore it; but the man who was left in his feeble old body couldn't do that. He wouldn't be able to live with himself if he ignored it; but then, if he confronted it—whatever *it* was—maybe it would take his life from him.

Bang...bang...bang...

If he didn't go down, they might come up. The basement door was locked from the outside, but he was sure they could find a way in. He didn't know why they were bothering to play this game; supernatural creatures could do just about anything—walk through walls even, or so he believed. He wondered what they were after? Were they getting their kicks just from scaring the shit out of him?

He didn't think that was the case. They wanted something, and he was going to give them something: a gunshot to the head. But what would a gunshot to the head do to a supernatural being? If they were supernatural, then why would they leave footprints and why would they need to feed on a young Amish man.

Quit stalling, old man. You won't figure it out if you live to be one hundred and fifty. Joe sat up and put on his slippers. He walked quietly over to the closet to get his gun. He seemed to be moving in slow motion, biding time. Every sound seemed amplified—Marie's breathing, the creak of the floorboards beneath his feet; every object seemed dark, looming, and menacing—all the things that had been so reassuring, so much a part of his world for so many years.

He glanced at Amy's door as he passed; no shadow of a wolf's head there tonight. The wolves were too busy knocking on the basement door.

Bang...bang...bang...

All right, I'm coming, he wanted to scream. He wondered why no one else could hear it. But he knew the answer: it was meant for his ears only.

He walked slowly down the stairs; he was in no hurry to meet the enemy. He was certain they would be there—this time; and in his mind's eyes a thousand gruesome images teased and taunted him.

Joe thought about the bones he had dug up, and how, at the beginning, he had entertained the idea that a man and wolf were buried in the same grave, but there were only two skulls, and neither was that of a man. The bones had once formed the skeletal structures of two creatures that defied description; to describe them would be to confirm their existence, and Joe shuddered at the thought of doing that.

It's time to acknowledge the monster.

Instead of providing the sense of security that usually came with a light in the darkness, the night lights that Marie had installed around the house only served to emit an eerie glow, causing every beloved object to cast ominous shadows.

The ticking of the grandfather clock, the hum of the refrigerator, and the gentle hush of cold embers settling in the fireplace—all sounds that were usually soothing and comforting, now served to cause the hair on his neck to stand at attention and make him sorely aware of his solitary condition.

Bang...bang...bang...

He wasn't going to let them get away that easily this time. He stood in front of the basement door, waiting for them to knock again.

Bang...bang...bang...

That was them all right; he could smell them standing there behind the basement door as it rattled on its hinges when they hit it—a musty odor, like a dirty, wet dog, long dead.

Joe walked as silently as possible into the kitchen, and then, after wrestling with the deadbolt, he snuck out the back door. He was going to lock them in the cellar, and then sit back and decide what to do next. Although he had fantasized about what he should have done the last time they paid a visit, he wasn't as brave as the person in his fantasies.

The night was black and strangely noisy despite the absence of wind: from the cluster of trees immediately behind the house came the hooting of an owl—a very big owl from the crackling sound it made as it settled in among the branches; he could see a small, dark form, probably a raccoon that had come hunting for the garbage can, run into the woods as he approached; and his own beating heart sounded as loud as thunder in his ears.

A dark shape suddenly swooped down out of the sky.

Joe dropped down on one knee and pointed his gun at it; but it was only a huge black bird, cawing at him as if in warning. Joe experienced a fleeting sense of deja vu at the sight of the bird, but he realized that it wasn't deja vu at all, but a memory of someone else having an encounter with a similar bird: Denise and the children met with a bird when they were coming to live at the farm. He understood at once that the bird was indeed trying to signal a warning, as it had probably been trying to warn Denise not to come to the farm on that fateful day he had dug up the bones.

You're sharp, old man.

That memory triggered another in his tired mind: there was another bundle of bones in with the bones of those creatures—a small bundle of bird bones. The bird was another soul that he had set free of the dark confines of its tomb; but he intuitively sensed that the bird meant them no harm, and unlike the evil beasts that sought to end his days on earth, the bird was sent to help him.

He crept around to the west side of the house where the cellar door lay like a coffin lid, sealing in the dead come to life. It was locked. He walked around the house trying to see if the windows were secured; but it was too dark to see much of anything. He would have to get down on his knees and try each of the windows to find out, and he wasn't about to do that.

Or was he?

He knew they were in there, and if all of the windows were secured then he would know: he would know that they could pass through stone and glass and wood—anything; and he would know that it was a game—a deadly game in which he was their pawn.

He took a deep breath and crawled slowly, hesitantly, up to a basement window. He felt suddenly cold and vulnerable in his thin pajamas. A coat of armor would have been more appropriate attire.

The window was locked, and the two boards, forming an X and nailed into the wooden frame of the window, were secure. He had boarded up the basement windows after they had found the Amish boy.

If something as strong as the animals that had killed the boy wanted in, he was sure that they wouldn't be deterred by the boards; but like a small yapping dog that could be killed with a kick to the head, the sound of the boards being broken would alert him to an intruder.

The next window he crawled up to was locked and the boards nailed securely into place. How was he going to explain his muddy pajamas to Marie? *I was crawling around in the yard last night, dear, trying to determine how those creatures entered our basement.*

What if one of the creatures burst a taloned paw through the window and...don't even allow yourself to think about it, old man.

The third window was locked and the boards nailed securely into place. He thought about going back inside to get his flashlight, but he was afraid of what he might see if he could see what was down there. What he imagined them to look like was enough to make him swallow his tongue.

He could feel eyes burning a hole into the back of his head; someone or something was watching him from the orchard. He almost turned his back on the window he was checking, but instead he rolled quickly away from it, so that there was nothing behind him but the cold stone wall of the house; he didn't want to turn his back on those windows for a second.

All he could make out in the darkness were two eyes that were blacker than the night that surrounded them, shining with a brilliance that could only be described as unearthly, as if hellfire blazed behind the two dark orbs; the eyes belonged to a sinister shape that resembled a man in a cape, but Joe could see from its oily brilliance that it was the immense bird.

The bird gave him a false sense of security; even though it gave him some backbone, some feeling that someone or something was on his side, he knew that nothing could protect him from his fate, only delay it.

He continued checking windows until he was sure that every last one of them was secured.

Why didn't they just come up to his room and rip his old rickety heart right out of his chest? He began to laugh at the absurdity of the situation; his laugh sounded hollow and maniacal. He wouldn't have believed the nightmare if he weren't living it.

He went back into the house, locked the deadbolt on the back door, and approached the basement door.

Bang...bang...bang...

Why could no one else hear it?

He reached out for the basement door, touched it, and jerked his hand away as if he had touched a hot stove. He reached out again, pushed the bolt up...then over...and then opened the door. He jumped back, pressing his back firmly against the wall to steady himself, and aimed his gun. But there was nothing there to shoot.

GAILA SWINDELL

54

Denise drove along the deserted highway faster than she should have. The clock on her dashboard read three a.m. Once she entered Cooks County, civilization ceased to exist: the people in that part of the world were all boarded up inside their houses by nine o'clock; traffic lights turned off their red and green, and their yellow bulbs blinked non-stop until dawn.

She was tired of driving half way across the world to see her lover, but she wasn't ready to leave the farm. In the back of her mind she didn't know if she would ever be ready. It had nourished her through her prolonged post-Donald blues, and she had grown attached to it. Now, with the remainder of spring and the entire summer spread before her, she could think of nothing better to do than spend her time on the farm, perhaps recapturing some of her lost innocence. Denise knew that her father wanted to send her and the kids packing, and she had promised they would find a place soon, but now that the kids would be out of school and she would be home to care for them, she hoped he might change his mind.

She had even started entertaining fantasies of Bruce moving out there with them and starting a practice up in Cooksville; and she could take a teaching position at one of the smaller local colleges. It was a bit much to throw at everyone all of a sudden, especially when her parents were having so much trouble caring for the kids. They were going to worry themselves to death. She planned to break it to everyone slowly.

She was sure they would all fight her at first, but then, after an untroubled summer...

She hated waking calling her mom's cellphone and waking her parents at that hour of the morning. She wished they would quit worrying about what had happened to that Amish boy. Her intuition told her that the thing or things that had killed the boy had either gone far away or were dead.

Her father always made her feel so guilty for getting him up out of bed so late at night. He would come out with his pajamas and slippers on, his shotgun under his arm. He always squinted in through the car window at her, grumbling under his breath about the time; and she would feel like a guilty teenager again, coming in after curfew with the smell of alcohol and sex hanging on her like a stray dog.

Beeejeeeemm...What in the hell is that noise? The car's engine seemed to lock up all of a sudden in mid motion, as if she had thrown the car into neutral at seventy miles per hour.

Beeejeeeemm...beeejeeemm...

Great, she thought, suddenly not so happy about being the only person on the road; there was no one around to offer help or give her a ride home. She turned down Route 30, which led to the farm.

"Come on, just three more miles and we're there," she told the car.

She had never noticed how dark the road was. There wasn't a single light or a single house on that long stretch of road between her and the farm, only a seemingly endless expanse of forest. She pressed her foot down harder on the accelerator, hoping to get home before the car died completely, but that was a mistake.

Beeeejjjeeeeemmmmm...beeejjjjeeemmm...beeejjjjeeeemm...

The car lurched and coasted, lurched and coasted, lurched and coasted, and then it just died.

"Great!" Denise screamed. She tried to start the car. It winded and purred and sputtered, but it would not start.

Laying her head down on the steering wheel, she felt her eyes sting with tears, but the tears wouldn't come. She thought about Bruce, about lying in his arms, him stroking her hair. Now, she wished she had fallen asleep there, sitting next to him in the car.

She had three things going for her at that moment: she wasn't in the inner city, it was spring and not winter, and she had only about three miles to walk. A pang of regret gripped her stomach as she remembered her father trying to force her to keep a gun under her seat.

She wished she had taken the tiny handgun he had offered her; the road was long and dark and unnervingly quiet.

She thought about curling up in the back seat until the sun peaked its glorious head over the horizon, but that was even scarier: she pictured trolls peering in at her through the windows of her car as she slept, drool dripping from their black lips and down their hairy little chins, as they gnashed their sharp, pointed teeth.

She pushed the button on her dashboard that opened the trunk, pulled the keys from the ignition, and put them into her pocket. She jumped out of the car and ran around to the back of it; she brandished the tire iron in her hand like the most dangerous of weapons.

Denise started down the road in a jog, beginning to hyperventilate in her fear. It was dreadfully dark, and the trees loomed large on either side of the road. She was almost happy that the moon and stars were hidden behind a thick cover of clouds; at least she didn't have any shadows to contend with.

She kept her head and eyes moving, imagining wild beasts, madmen, and escaped convicts in the bushes. There was something else that frightened her, something hidden in her memory, too terrible to remember. Some defense mechanism wouldn't allow her to remember what it was, and she didn't try too hard to override that mechanism.

Get hold of yourself, woman; there's nothing to be frightened of. She felt her paranoia lifting, her body and mind relaxing.

Someone was calling, "Mommy!"

What was that? she wondered, thinking she had to be mistaken.

"Mommy!"

There it is again.

"Mommy!"

Denise heard it, once faintly, twice distinctly: a voice crying "mommy" from the woods.

It wasn't the voice that disturbed her so much as her reaction to it: she was drawn to the voice. Some maternal, instinctive longing inside of her heart, inside of her womb, pushed her toward it. She found herself walking closer to the edge of the woods where the voice was coming from.

"Mommy!"

Such a plaintive voice, tired and lonely. It inspired no fear in her...only a longing to find it, comfort it. *Could it be the ghost of that child? What was his name...Jeffrey Abrahm?* Another memory flitted through her head like an elusive bird; but she could not catch it. Something about the boy, something she knew.

Lately she had found her memory clouded; there were doors in her mind that could not be opened. But she didn't mind; life was easier without those memories.

Where was the voice? She needed to hear it to find it. Was it the boy?

"Mommy!"

But the voice was older, gruffer. It was like a magnetic force, pulling her toward it.

Trancelike, she wandered down a path that led into the heart of the woods, the voice urging her on. What if it was some abandoned or lost child? It was her duty as a mother to find it, care for it.

"Mommy!"

Oh, she thought, *the poor baby, lost in the woods. I must find it.*

"Mommy!"

She was no longer afraid. The path was even darker than the road had been, but she felt safe there, the darkness enveloping her, hiding her, stroking her skin with its black velvet breath. It was as though she had walked the path one hundred times before, in a dream, another lifetime. The trees were suddenly friendly, pointing the way toward the voice—or voices: there seemed to be two voices, one slightly raspier than the other.

The path was dangerously overgrown: slippery, dew-covered, gnarled tree roots slithered across it like snakes; jagged rocks protruded sharply through the hard earth; but Denise made her way easily over the obstructions.

"Mommy!"

The moon broke free from its cloudy prison and cast a shower of light over the path. Up ahead under a grove of pines, Denise could see him: a young boy lying on a carpet of pine needles.

She ran to him. He was crying. "You poor thing. What are you doing here?"

He looked up at her with hungry eyes, swallowing her with his gaze.

"Are you okay? I heard you calling for your mother."

"You're my mother," he said, reaching for her.

She took him in her arms. "Oh, no, honey. I'm not your mother. But I'll help you find her." He looked so familiar. "Do I know you?"

"You're my mother," he said again.

"Come on. I'll take you home. Can you walk?"

"I'm cold," he said, reaching up to take her hand.

"Oh, you're frozen. Let me warm you up," she said, sitting down next to him and pulling him onto her lap. He smelled of raw earth and decay, fetid and foul.

Denise sat with him until the gray-blue light of dawn descended. She forgot the world and would have been content to rock him and sing to him for hours longer, it gave her so much satisfaction to comfort him, but his temperature would not rise, and crept into her heart and chilled it.

"Come on. We'd better go now," she said.

There was a rustling in the trees, something moving. She looked around but didn't see anything.

"Are you alone?" she asked.

He stood up. "No."

"Who's with you?"

"Your children," he said.

"My children are home in bed, sweetheart. Come on, let's go. Take my hand."

He took her hand and began to follow her. Something sharp ripped through her light jacket and bit into the flesh of her arm. She pulled her arm away and screamed; she turned quickly to see the boy smiling at her with blood dribbling down his chin, his skin the blue of death. "Mommy," he said. With sudden clarity she recognized the boy: he was dead; he was Jeffrey Abrahm.

Denise pushed him and her hand ripped through his chest. He fell to the ground and—like a dog—snapped at her leg with his teeth. She screamed and ran. The path split into many, and she panicked; she was lost. She took the path that led straight ahead, the dead boy's voice right behind her: "Mommy!"

She felt she must have been dreaming; this couldn't possibly be happening to her. Denise stumbled and fell, her head just missing a massive oak tree. She got up and began running again. She twisted her ankle when her foot came down the wrong way on a sharp rock, but she kept going, crying with pain and fright. It seemed like she would never get out of those woods. *What was I thinking? How could I have been so stupid?*

Denise fell again just as the path met the road, her hand hitting something cold and hard: it was the tire iron; she had dropped it on her way into the woods and never even missed it.

She ran all the way home, never once looking back.

The next day, she would have sworn the events of the previous evening were a dream, had it not been for the perfect indentation of a human bite marking the flesh on her right forearm.

55

"How much longer do we have to wait?" Nunny asked.

"We've waited over one hundred years, a few more months isn't going to kill us," Cecil whispered.

They sat huddled in the crawl space, gazing down through a crack at Denise with a mixture of wonder and a boundless, desperate yearning akin to lust. In the spell of their reverent watching, there was nothing that could divert their attention, except on occasion when one of them would forget about his brother's presence, and step into his line of vision, causing a short and silent scuffle to take place. Nunny would often reach out in the darkness to pinch his brother's ear to quiet Cecil's incessant wheezing; this would cause Cecil to wheeze even louder in his anger, and the two would struggle to control their stormy tempers.

They weren't going to risk announcing their presence; they wanted Denise to love the old house, not fear it.

"What do you long for, Brother, more than anything else?" Nunny whispered.

"The smell of her hair, and the scent of her breath, which I'm sure will be as sweet as mother's was. And you?" Cecil asked.

"I long for the cool touch of her hand on my brow, and the whisper of her voice in my ear. She is the most lovely of creatures, and we shall be proud to have her as our mother," Nunny told him.

"Most certainly, Brother," Cecil wheezed, "most certainly."

"We'll do everything we can to keep her here with us forever. Soon she will be ours."

GAILA SWINDELL

56

Amy put on her sweater before she went outside, as her grandmother had instructed her to. She wondered why older people always thought a sweater was necessary, especially when it was warm outside.

"You'll be out there playing, and the sun will go off behind a tree or a mountain, and before you know it that sneaky old draft will come sneaking under your clothes and you'll get a chill, and then you know what will happen," her grandmother had told her.

"What will happen, Grandma?" Amy asked like she didn't know.

"Don't play dumb with me, young lady; you know darn well what will happen. You'll catch a spring cold, and those are the worst kinds of colds to catch because you'll be stuck inside the house, resting in your bed, when the day is just as beautiful as can be," she told her.

Amy walked outside, letting the screen door slam behind her, which caused her grandmother to let flow an uncharacteristic stream of angry words that followed Amy out into the heavenly, blossom-scented air. The words seemed to hang heavily in the air, mixing acidly with the sweet, languid breeze, and making Amy extremely suspicious of the day, causing it to have a strangely forbidding edge.

She had heard her brother stirring early that morning; she had the funny feeling that he was up to no good. Her logic told her that he was too far gone; like an apple, its skin beginning to bruise and rot, its tart flesh long eaten away by worms, Adam no longer looked the part of the sweet-dispositioned child he used to be; he now, unwittingly, displayed his rotten interior: Amy could see it in the thin film of sweat that would appear on his forehead when they competed in any game; in the evil glint of his eye when he thought she wasn't looking; and in the pitch of his voice—quavering and high. His vocabulary had changed drastically: he spoke as if from a different era—Jenna's era.

The wolf head shadow on her door made her chuckle in its absurdity: she found it ridiculous that a mere shadow of a ghost had once frightened her, now that she lived in perpetual fear of her own flesh and blood. She understood to some extent how Jenna must have felt: to fear one's own kin, to fear one that you loved, was the ultimate hell.

Amy walked through the orchard, happy to be free to wander alone. She had feared that her grandparents would never let her go outside alone again, that they would force her to stay in that house until the day her mother moved them to the suburbs.

The thought of her mother was like a fingernail scratching a blackboard in Amy's head: they were never going to leave the farm; she could see it in her mother's glassy faraway look whenever Amy asked her about moving. If only they could get away, then the evil season of Jenna's monstrous children would come to an end.

She wanted to show her mother the diary, show her the books about Indians that she had read at the library, tell her everything she knew, but she was afraid. Fear was her only motivator, but it was also her only obstacle: she was afraid of what would happen if she told them, and afraid of what would happen if she didn't.

Now that she believed Nunny and Cecil were influencing her mother, she was afraid of her too. Her mother was not acting like herself.

Amy didn't know where to turn, what to do. She was hoping the walk in the orchard might clear her head, make room for answers; it was good to escape from the stifling air within the stone walls of the house.

Her grandfather would help her—if she could get up the nerve to talk to him about it. When they moved to the farm he had seemed so young, so spry; now he seemed older, feebler, gruffer. But just the idea of talking to him about everything shone like a ray of sunlight in the darkness of her heart.

She walked for some time, feeling her mood lighten as the morning turned toward noon, the sun moving slowly to its highest point. But this lightheartedness didn't last long.

All of her confidence, all of her good feeling, was destroyed in an instant when Amy looked up to see Adam sitting in a tree, the shadows of bitter ghosts flickering across his tortured brow.

"Would you like to play a game, Sister?" he asked in a voice that was old as the woods that surrounded them.

57

Joe walked around double checking the locks on the doors and turning off the lights. They had lit only a small fire that night, and he was happy to see that every last ember had died out. He never liked to go to bed with even the tiniest twig still smoldering.

As he walked up the stairs and past Amy's bedroom door, he thought about going in and checking on her. He didn't want to chance waking her if she had already dozed off; he could always talk to her in the morning. She had acted strangely all day, following him around, watching his every movement. She looked worried and anxious about something. He wished he could be closer to Amy—to everyone in his family—but the recent circumstances kept him distant from everyone, or so it seemed to him. He was preoccupied all the time; he sometimes felt he was living in a world that existed only inside his head.

He looked over at the crack under Denise's door to see that she had finally turned off her light and gone to bed. She had been grading final exams for what seemed like a lifetime. He was happy that the semester was finally over; Denise would finally have more time for herself and the children—and finding another place to live.

Joe's body and mind were weary; he felt older than the earth, and he knew that he had seen more than most people would ever see in a lifetime: he had seen the paw prints of demons in the earth's fertile soil and smelled the rotten stench of the undead.

Marie was already asleep; he could hear the sound of her breathing, slow and rhythmic. He took off his clothes, folded them neatly, and put them in a pile on chair next to his dresser.

He had a sudden urge to pack up all their belongings and get his family out of the house. He wondered how Marie would react if he told her he thought the house was too much for them, that he wanted to move to a condo. He could always say that he wanted to be closer to Denise and the kids once they moved away—but by then, anything could happen.

Ever so slowly and quietly, he opened the old bureau and pulled out a pair of pajamas. They smelled so sweet and clean. He put them on, luxuriating in their softness against his skin, and crawled gently into bed so that he wouldn't disrupt his sleeping wife; the minute he laid his head down on the pillow he was asleep.

Bang...bang...bang...

Bang...bang...bang...

Joe was dreaming that he was in the car with Marie, driving down the road. They were at a red light when he heard someone banging on the car. He looked around, but there was nobody there. The light seemed to stay red forever; the knocking continued. He thought about running the red light, and Marie must have read his mind: "Don't you dare run that red light, Joe Rodman," she said to him, "the police could be hiding anywhere." She looked younger in the dream.

He remembered a ghost story he had heard and proceeded to tell Marie: "Did you ever hear the story about knock knock street?"

"No, I haven't," she said, acting like she didn't want to hear it.

"Once there was an old man who was crossing the street on a dark and rainy night. When he had reached the middle of the street, a car came barreling down the road out of nowhere and killed him. While the old man lay dying, with the car still on top of him, he knocked on the bottom of the car. After the accident, people who drove down that street on dark and rainy nights would hear a knocking sound underneath their cars."

He paused and waited for a reaction from Marie. "It isn't very scary now, but it was when we were kids," he said.

Bang...bang...bang

The banging sound was coming from underneath them. Marie began to cry and scream. She clutched onto Joe's arm. "Go ahead and run the light, Joe; it's the ghost of the old man. Just drive, Joe!"

Joe looked at the light; it was still red.

Bang...bang...what in the hell? Now Joe was awake—groggy, but awake.

Bang...bang...bang...

Would they never let him rest? *Not until it's me buried in the dirt.* "God damn it!" he whispered in the darkness.

This is it! I'm going to kill the sonsofbitches!

He jumped out of bed with a nimble spryness that surprised him. He went into the closet and pulled his shotgun down off the shelf. He was going to shoot them back to hell even if he had to go there with them.

He practically ran down the stairs, not noticing the fire that was ablaze in the fireplace. His mind was intent on one thing: killing the monsters that were terrorizing him and his family. He would not let them win.

Bang...bang...bang...

The door was bending outward from the force of whatever was pounding on it. Joe touched it; it was hot. He could smell them; they were there.

He pushed the bolt over, and when he opened the door and saw the creatures that were standing there grinning at him, looking like nothing he would have ever dreamed even in his worst nightmares, he clutched his chest in agony, his heart going haywire for a moment before it stopped dead. Joe fell to the floor, defeated.

GAILA SWINDELL

58

It was a cool and overcast May day. The cemetery was empty except for the small group of people who had come to pay their last respects to Joe Rodman. People stood staring blankly at the coffin, or with their heads bowed in silent prayer.

Denise was angry at the flowering trees, feeling that they were mocking her with their gaiety. They were reborn with the spring, and her father was dead. He was just not there anymore and never would be again. She wanted to open the casket that lie next to the gaping hole in the earth, take her father out, and shake him to life. She squeezed her mother's hand as hard as she could, and her mother returned it with an even harder squeeze. *He should have had another twenty-five years of life,* Denise thought; *he was only sixty-five.*

She wondered why he was going down to the basement, gun in hand, in the middle of the night? They supposed he had heard a prowler and was going down to check it out. But why didn't he wake anyone else? And what caused him to have a heart attack? The doctor said that it was probably fright that caused the heart attack, but what had he been afraid of? There were no signs of anything or anyone breaking in. Maybe it had been fear of the unknown, of walking down those basement stairs to confront something he could only imagine.

Denise looked over at Amy who was holding her grandmother's other hand. Amy gave Denise a firm look with a little tight smile that said, "Don't cry Mom; I'm here for you." She was such an old soul. She had cried her eyes out the first day that her grandfather was dead;

then she'd told them that they needed her to be there for them, so she would stop crying, "at least for now," she'd said.

Amy had received the visitors to the house and taken their gifts of food and kind words. She had answered the phone and kept the house neat and clean, ordering her stone-faced brother around.

Adam stood to Denise's left, limply holding her hand. He had not openly shed a tear for his grandfather. He had stayed in his room most of the time, so Denise supposed he had done all his crying alone. He seemed to be in shock, walking around like a robot, speaking in a monotone, showing no emotion whatsoever.

Denise hadn't heard the poems that family friends were reading while she was deep in thought. Joe was not a religious man, and when asked what kind of funeral he wanted, he had always jested, "Let them read poems or something. I won't know the difference; I'll be dead." It was the only thing they had to go by, and so poetry it was.

The man that was reading, Ed Gordy, had worked for Joe in the orchard to earn money for college. Ed's father had died when Ed was fifteen years old, and Ed had always thought of Joe as a father figure. Ed had always had a crush on Denise, but she had seen him as more of a brother than anything else. He was now a high school English teacher. When Denise called to inform him of Joe's death and ask him to read some poetry at the funeral, Ed had begun to cry and asked Denise if he could call her back. Twenty-four hours passed before Ed called back. He said that he would feel honored to read at the funeral; that he would write something special.

Denise pulled herself out of her reverie to listen to Ed's words: "...today they put his body into a dry wooden box and lowered it into a cold row in the earth; but no matter, for the seeds of his soul were planted in the garden of our hearts, and there he will bloom forever."

59

They weren't leaving, that was all there was to it. It was as though a little voice had come to her in the night and said, "Stay. Your mother needs you."

Denise looked at the clock; it was six-twenty a.m. She got out of bed and put on her robe. She tiptoed quietly into the bathroom and grabbed her toothbrush. She would brush her teeth downstairs; she didn't want to wake her mother. She went down to the downstairs bathroom and brushed her teeth and washed her face.

She had not eaten in three days, and her stomach was screaming, "Feed me." She wanted healthy things. She would make Greek omelets with toast.

She looked in the refrigerator and the cupboards for some of her mother's homemade strawberry preserves. There wasn't a jar in sight. *That means you'll have to go down into the basement.* No one had even opened the basement door since the police had left after the investigation.

Denise broke some eggs into a bowl. She chopped up some spinach, tomatoes, and onions. She hunted around for feta cheese; they were getting low on food. Later, she would go to the Farmers' market—if it was a day that it was open. She had to look at the calendar to find out what day it was. The last few days had passed in a blur. Life had seemed like a dream since the morning she had been woken from a deep sleep by her mother's blood-curdling scream. Denise must have gone through the details of that wretched morning a thousand times in her head. She had sat straight up in bed, thinking she heard the scream in a dream, and then the painful reality of what her mother's sobbing meant hit her like a falling tree.

It all seemed so unreal. And now here she was chopping vegetables. *How can he be gone?* She started to cry. *Get hold of yourself, Denise. You don't want anyone to come downstairs to find you crying.*

The basement. She had to go down into the basement and get the strawberry preserves. She searched for something else to spread on toast—apple butter, marmalade, honey—but there was nothing. She was afraid to go down there. It had never been one of her favorite places, but now her skin crawled at the thought of it. What if she opened the door and saw whatever her father had seen—*if* he had seen anything at all?

She walked over to the basement door, knife still in hand, and pushed the bolt over. She had her hand on the doorknob and was about to open the door, when she heard someone call, "Mommy."

She walked away from the door to the foot of the staircase that led upstairs. She didn't want the kids to wake her mother. They didn't usually call to her from their rooms unless they were sick. She heard it again, a faint voice calling, "Mommy."

But it wasn't coming from upstairs; it was coming from the basement.

For a moment she thought maybe Amy or Adam had wandered down into the basement; but then, why would the door be bolted from the outside. An image of Adam locking Amy down in the basement came into her head; she ran to the basement door, hesitating only for a second before she opened it, and bolted down the stairs.

Denise had never realized how many light bulbs were down there: there was one practically every ten feet. But they served only to half blind her with their brightness; it was like going from a dark room out into the bright sunlight.

"Amy," she called.

"Mommy."

It was so faint that she could have been imagining it. It was probably just something rubbing against something else, producing a sound that sounded like the word "mommy." It definitely wasn't Amy; her intense anger at thinking Adam had locked Amy down there subsided and changed into guilt for thinking he would do such a thing.

Denise slowly walked around the basement, looking into the many closets and small storage rooms. Junk was all she found—old stuff. *What in the hell is that doing here?* In one of the closets she found some rocks covered with cobwebs. She wondered why they had not been thrown out, why they were there in the first place. She started in after them, but at the last minute decided to save their disposal for another day; in a few minutes she would have hungry mouths to feed. After her mother was feeling better, she would get her to commit to throwing away some of the junk that was stuffed away in every corner of the old house.

She stretched her neck to see farther into the dark closet; maybe there were some old treasures in there.

"Mom," a voice behind her said, while something touched her arm.

Denise screamed, swung around, and stuck the knife that she was holding into the closet door, missing Amy by a hair's breadth.

"Mom, we're staying until you decide what to do," Denise said, watching her mother pretend to enjoy the omelet. "I can't leave you here alone."

The kids didn't say anything. Adam's face brightened at the prospect of staying on the farm, and Amy's looked like it was going to drop off. Denise shot her a glance that said, "save it for later, kiddo."

"Cut it out, Denise," her mother told her. "I'll be fine. Now you go on and live your life. You're going to lose that Bruce if you don't hurry up and marry him. I can tell he's getting impatient."

"I've made up my mind, Mom. We're here to stay," Denise told her. "Now, eat!"

"I don't have the energy to argue with you, now, but you can be sure I will later," Marie said. Her words seemed to trail off into a whisper; her eyes were staring out the window, out into the orchard; her mind was somewhere else.

"You know, I keep thinking that any minute now your father's going to come walking in from the orchard," Marie said, still staring out the window. "I think I'll go up to bed, now. You leave the dishes, Denise. I'll come down in just a little while to clean them up."

"Don't be ridiculous," Denise said. "You go upstairs and rest. We'll take care of everything. Is there anything I can do for you, Mom? Hey, why don't we all go for a ride in the country later on? We could stop at the market and get some things for dinner. It'll take our minds off everything."

"Thanks for the nice breakfast, Denise. We'll see how I feel later on," Marie said, squeezing Denise's hand and giving her a tired smile.

Denise looked at the calendar. Her father had been dead for three weeks, but it seemed much longer. She was distancing herself from the event in order to cope with it.

She was beginning to fear that her mother's will to live had disappeared. Marie had stopped taking meals with the family. She would only come out of her room to go to the bathroom. Denise finally decided to confront her mother. She was afraid she would die of malnutrition if she didn't. Her mother's bedroom door was closed, as it always was lately. Denise knocked softly.

"Come in," was her mother's faint reply.

"Hi, Mom. How are you? Can I get you some lunch?" Denise asked.

"No, thanks, Denise. I'm still working on that English muffin you brought me earlier." She motioned to the muffin, but didn't look at it or Denise. She seemed to be looking inside her own head.

Denise noticed that only one bite had been taken out of the muffin. If her mother would meet her gaze, maybe then Denise could beam some life into her.

"Mom, you've got to get on with your life. I know Daddy's death was hard for you to bear, but, my god, you can't just wither and die," Denise told her. "Look at yourself in the mirror! You look like you're starving to death. Please, Mom! The kids are worried sick about you, not to mention how worried I am. It's bad enough that Daddy's dead, but now, to have you lying in here dying on me. If you won't think about yourself, then think about me! I'm surprised at you, Mom."

"Then move the hell out, god damn it!" Marie screamed. "I'm not asking you to stay. I just want to be left alone to die. Don't you see? I've been cheated! Why...Joe was only sixty-five years old—and in perfect health! What in the hell happened down there?" Marie began punching the pillow next to her, and then fell onto it and started to sob. "Why did he have to die?"

"I'm sorry, Mom," Denise said, leaning over and taking her sobbing mother in her arms. "I feel like I've been cheated, too. It wasn't time for him to go. But we have to go on! I need you, and the kids need you."

"I'm sorry, too, Denise. I just don't know if I can be there for you or anyone any longer. I just don't have the will to live anymore. I don't have the strength."

Those were the words that Denise both feared and hoped for: even though it brought Denise physical pain to hear those words, she knew that her mother would recover if she would only begin to talk about her feelings.

She would leave her with those words, to think about the selfish foolishness of their meaning. She hoped that the next time she came to see her mother, Marie would open her heart and be healed.

Denise awoke to the clanging of pots and pans; the sound was coming from the kitchen. A bolt of fear ran through her body, making her sit upright. She looked at the clock: eight a.m. *Someone broke into the house and is looking for money,* was her first thought; when she realized who was making all the noise, she felt like getting up and dancing.

Her mother was back.

60

Adam looked out the window one last time. He could see his mother and Amy walking through the orchard. His grandmother was at the market.

He walked quietly into his grandmother's bedroom. His grandfather's things were still there: the old bottle that held his coins sat on the floor next to the desk; his clothes hung neatly in the closet; and his silver dish full of loose odds and ends still sat on the dresser.

This was a good sign. It meant that what he had come for would probably still be there.

He wasted no time, but went straight into the bathroom attached to his grandparents' bedroom. He opened the medicine cabinet and scanned the shelves. His breath quickened when he didn't see what he had come for, but then he saw the glint of the blade behind a neat row of pill bottles. Right where Nunny and Cecil said it would be.

Adam studied the pill bottles for a minute so that he would be sure to put them back exactly as he had found them, their labels facing outward. He moved them aside, carefully took out the razor, and then put the bottles back in place.

He took the razor into his own bedroom and hid it under the mattress, pushing it as far into the middle as his short arm could reach.

His mother was going to Florida. She hadn't told anyone yet, but Nunny and Cecil knew. He would get rid of his sister and grandmother while his mother was away; he would take care of his mother when she returned—if she returned.

He couldn't wait to be rid of them all; then, he would live there on the farm with his best friends for the rest of his life. They would never leave him, and they would never hurt him. They'd promised.

61

Denise finished packing. She pulled the crumpled list from her pocket and checked off the items she had packed.

"Denise, you just about ready?" her mother yelled from downstairs. "I've got a snack here for you to eat on the way."

"Be down in a minute, Mom."

She gave the list a twice over, and then tried to shut the suitcase.

"Amy...Adam, would one of you please come here and help me? On second thought, would both of you please come here and help me?" she shouted.

"I told you not to take everything in your closet, Denise," she heard her mother call up the stairs.

Amy scrambled into the room, an open book in her hand, while Adam dragged along behind her. Something didn't look right about him. *He looks...he looks like he's crazy again,* a voice said somewhere in Denise's head. *Shut up and go away,* she told the voice.

"Hop on," Denise told them, pointing to the suitcase.

Amy sat on one side, Adam sat on the other, and with tremendous effort, Denise managed to shut the monolithic piece of luggage.

"You're going to Florida carrying that? Where did you get that old thing, Mom?" Amy asked her.

"I found it in the attic. I wasn't about to travel all the way to Philadelphia to get our luggage out of storage."

She took a long look at her children. She was going to miss them terribly; she almost couldn't wait for the trip to be over. She was going away for Bruce's sake: if she didn't do something to show him she loved him, she was sure she would probably lose him. He had displayed an angry side when she suggested he come spend his vacation on the farm.

"Denise, you're going to miss your plane!" her mother yelled from downstairs.

A sudden urge to cancel her trip overcame her. She hated the thought of leaving. She stood there thinking it over, her hand clutching the handle of the suitcase.

She was beginning to feel like her dependency on the kids and her mother—and even the farm—was becoming abnormal. She just never wanted to leave, not even to go shopping or see Bruce. She was even thinking about refusing to teach the fall term. She didn't know if she could stand to be away from her home and family. She reasoned it was probably a reaction to her father's untimely death.

"Mom, are you all right?" Amy asked.

"I'm fine, sweetheart. Perfectly fine."

Amy didn't like being alone with her grandmother and Adam. She felt vulnerable. The constant whispering she heard around the house didn't help matters. Her grandmother said it was just her imagination. *Why does everyone attribute every weird thing that happens to the imagination?* Amy wondered. And what had scared her grandfather to death? His imagination? They had to be in denial or losing their senses to think *that* was the only force working in the old house.

She couldn't wait for her mother to come home. She would tell her everything—even show her the diary; it was the link to the past that helped to explain the present. Amy was angry with herself for not doing it a long time ago. They would probably be out of that house by now if she had acted earlier; but then, she guessed, if she had told them long before, she would be the only one out of the house—in some asylum for crazy children.

Amy regretted not having told her grandfather what she knew when she had the chance. She felt somehow responsible for his death. She thought that if she would have told him about the diary and her bizarre experiences, he might still be alive. She pictured him bundling them all into the car and taking them away from the horror of it all.

Adam was stranger than ever. He never showered, brushed his teeth, or combed his hair. She looked out her window to see him sitting in one of the apple trees. He was almost hidden in its full head of green leaves. That was where he spent most of his time; every day he would pick a different tree to sit in. Amy sensed that he was waiting for something; it made her nervous to think about what that *something* might be. She made it a point to always know where Adam was; she wanted to be able to see him coming at all times.

62

July 10, 2011

Sheila Delenko looked long and hard at the box of breakfast cereal in the cupboard; she had no desire for food. She closed the cupboard, reached down into the cupboard at her feet, and pulled out a bottle of scotch. She opened the bottle, careful to hold it over the counter, so if it fell from her trembling hands it would hit the counter instead of shattering on the floor.

"This is the true breakfast of champions," she said, pouring the golden liquid into a tall glass. Her hands were shaking badly, and the scotch splashed onto the counter top as she poured. She bent over and licked the precious liquid off the counter like a dog. She was going to need every bit of the stuff when Lenny came home. It would give her the courage to finally reveal the truth to him: he was not their real son; he was adopted. Maybe the truth would convince him to be her lover. There was nothing that she wanted more.

Sheila had felt guilty only once, in the beginning, but had quickly reassured herself that there was nothing wrong with her sexual attraction to Lenny; after all, he wasn't her real son. She had never wanted kids in the first place and was actually happy when she found out that her husband was sterile. She went along with the adoption for his sake; he had always wanted a son—at least that was what he had said. Sheila knew that he what he really wanted was something to keep her home and faithful while he was away on his business trips.

Yes, she thought, *when Lenny comes home, I'll tell him the truth.*

The Florida sun penetrated Denise's skin, warming her frozen core. Every so often a cloud would pass over the golden orb and give her eyes some relief from the glare. The ocean was smooth and calm, but its lull couldn't quiet the storm raging inside her stomach, inside her heart.

It was only nine a.m., but the sun felt like noon—hot. Denise and Bruce had come early to see the sunrise; drinking mimosas at breakfast made them want to lie there all day.

Even in sunny Florida, she could not escape the black bane that had followed her from Pennsylvania. There was a darkness that loomed in her peripheral vision, a horror that lurked there, crouching like an animal in the night. She could laugh, sun, eat, drink, and make love, but the darkness was always there, waiting in the recesses of her mind.

A nightmare that she could not escape—even under the merry eye of the tropical sun—had again entered her consciousness. As much as she didn't want to think about the nightmare, she found herself going over it again and again. It always began with her taking lilacs to her father's grave.

Row upon row of tombstones lined the aisles, some ancient, the epitaphs worn off by time and the elements, some brand new with finely etched inscriptions, elegantly carved, eloquently phrased.

She glanced at them as she passed, trying not to walk over any grave. The name on one of the new tombstones caught her eye. The inscription read:

Sheila Delenko
Born July 5, 1961   Died July 10, 2011

She wondered why the name sounded so familiar. She pushed aside the roses that covered the rest of the inscription:

She Loved her Son Too Much

"Oh, my god, Lenny!" Denise said. "Lenny, why did you do it?" she asked. *She loved her son too much.*

She suddenly felt lonely and afraid. It was so cold there among the slabs of granite. She continued on her way, weaving in and out of the aisles of death, feeling a strong sense of foreboding as she drew close to her father's grave. She started to turn back, but she buried her face in the lilacs and kept going.

She could see that something was wrong with his gravesite. A mound of earth was piled next to his tombstone. She wondered why they had dug another grave so close to her father's. Maybe they never finished filling in the earth over his casket. She thought that was careless of them.

The closer she came to the grave, the more her anger turned to horror. She ran to the grave. Three freshly dug graves, and three tombstones, covered in tan muslin, were next to her father's grave. The entire plot had been reserved for her family.

Denise found herself walking toward the tombstones even though she wanted to run from that evil place. *It's a dream,* she told herself. *It's only a dream.*

She ripped the muslin easily from the first tombstone. It read:

Marie Rodman
Born February 12, 1946   Died July 10, 2011

Denise felt like her soul had been ripped from her body. She wanted to throw herself into the gaping hole in the earth and die there, but some masochistic feeling urged her on.

She ripped the muslin from the second tombstone. It read:

Amy Miller
Born April 8, 2000   Died July 10, 2011

Denise began to sob convulsively. "My baby," she cried, "my sweet, innocent Amy."

She couldn't bear to look at the third tombstone, for fear that Adam's name would be etched in the cold stone.

An icy cold hand seemed to grip her by the spine and force her to rip the muslin from the third tombstone. It's gleaming, polished granite surface was blank.

Denise began to scream and sob, her heart breaking. "Tell me," she screamed at the sky, "tell me who that stone is there for!"

"That's up to you, now," someone said, but she looked around to find no one. "Denise, wake up," someone was saying. "Denise, wake up."

She opened her eyes to find herself on the beach, with Bruce leaning over her looking frantic.

She'd fallen asleep and had the same nightmare she'd had the night before.

Denise and Bruce didn't say much on the walk back to their condo. The sun had sapped all their energy.

"I don't think I'd want to live here. Would you?" Bruce asked her.

"It's too hot for me—and too lazy. I wonder how many of the people that live here spend every weekend lying on the beach, frying in the sun?" Denise said.

"Probably quite a few. I feel like I have skin cancer already," he said.

Denise chuckled at Bruce's sunburn. "You look like a lobster."

"Well, look at you," he said, pointing to her legs.

Denise's skin was bright red, and it felt very tight. She brushed the sand from her feet as well as she could and entered the condo.

"Then we agree on something: living in Florida can be very unhealthy for both your skin and your motivation," she told him.

Bruce followed her in and slammed the door behind him.

"What's wrong, now?" she asked.

"What did you mean by 'Then we agree on something'"? he asked.

"I'm sorry, Bruce. I don't know what's wrong with me, lately. Our relationship just doesn't seem to be working...and I know it's my fault, but I don't feel in control of the situation. There are other things that are more important...right now."

"If you'd just tell me what the problem is, and what's so important that it's going to ruin our relationship, then maybe we could work things out."

Denise picked up her cell phone and acted like she hadn't heard him. She dialed her home number and waited as the phone rang back in Pennsylvania. Her mother answered just as she was about to give up hope that anyone was home.

"Hi, Mom. How's everything?"

"Just fine. How are you two doing? Are you enjoying that Florida sunshine?" Marie asked her.

"Yes, I am...but I miss you guys a lot. What are the kids doing?" Denise asked, relieved to hear her mother's voice.

"Amy went out to read poetry to the animals, and Adam was up in his room the last time I checked. He's a weird one, he is."

"What do you mean, Mom?"

"Oh, he's just acting moody again, even more since you left. I think he just misses you."

"Oh, Mom, maybe I should come home." Bruce shot her a look that could kill.

"Would you cut it out!" her mother said. "It's perfectly normal for a child to get moody when his mother goes away. He'll be fine, Denise."

"I feel guilty leaving them there while I'm down here having a...a great time." The truth was that she was having an awful time with her nightmares tracking her like bloodthirsty hounds. Every time she looked over her shoulder they were there, nipping away at her sanity, her happiness.

"Don't get me angry, Denise," her mother said. "You shouldn't feel even the slightest bit of guilt for taking a trip with your fiancée. The kids will manage!"

"Mom, you sure have changed since Daddy died."

"Well, it's about time, don't you think? When life deals you some tough blows, it just follows naturally that you get tougher. Hold on a minute, I'll go get Adam."

Denise waited a few minutes.

"Denise, he must have gone outside. He's been spending a lot of time in the orchard. I don't see him anywhere," Marie said.

"All right. Tell the kids that I love and miss them very much."

"I will."

"I love you, Mom. Thanks for everything."

"I love you, too, Denise, and you're very welcome."

The day was hot and bright and beautiful. Amy skipped through the orchard, tagging each tree as she passed.

She carried a book of poetry. She pictured herself sitting in the middle of a bevy of creatures, all of them listening intently while she read poetry aloud.

Suddenly, from the direction of the forest, someone called her name: "Amy!"

She continued walking, pretending the voice didn't bother her, but in reality, it had caused the tiny blond hairs on her arms to stand up.

She came to a grassy ridge just outside of the orchard, bordering the woods, and turned quickly, hoping Adam wasn't spying on her. She was too slow, though, and only caught the curtain in his bedroom window falling into place and the blue of his shirt moving out of view. At least she knew where he was.

She hoped he wasn't coming out to bother her. She wanted to be alone with her book and all of nature.

Lenny stood in front of his house staring at the windows. If his mother looked out the window at him, that would be another sign that he was a messenger of fate. He had to do his duty.

He stood there stock still for at least fifteen minutes, until, finally, he saw a hand draw back the curtain and his mother's face in the window.

He felt good. His mind was clear; his goal was set. Finally, his mission would be completed.

Amy scrambled down the grassy ridge and went back into the orchard; in among the trees she would have a better chance of staying hidden. She tried to put Adam's spy tactics out of her mind. Watching her from his window was a sick thing to do, but then, Adam was a sick boy.

The madness of it all rang in her head like a maniac's laughter. In her anger at Adam, she could feel her face turning bright red. *What is wrong with him? How dare my mother leave us alone with the little monster!*

Crunch!

What was that? Amy wondered.

There was something in the trees behind her. She saw a streak of bright blue, and then it was gone.

Adam was wearing a bright blue shirt the last time she saw him.

"Adam?" she called out. "Adam, is that you?"

She heard a rustling in the trees. Something was approaching.

"Adam Miller, if this is your idea of fun, you're a sick person!" she shouted.

Amy backed up against a tree, deriving some feeling of security from its solid strength against her back.

An image of the decapitated rat flashed in her memory; it was so vivid the rat could have been right there in front of her, its limp body squeezed of blood, lying in a bloody pool of feasting insects. She didn't want to die like that...not like that.

Something huge and black swooped down out of the tree in front of her. It was the raven, and it was coming right for her. Amy put out her hands to protect her head from its sharp talons, and although the bird flew right into her, she felt nothing. She had always guessed that the raven was Mina's ghost, but now the guessing game was over. The reality of what she was experiencing suddenly struck her: *this isn't a horror novel; this is the real thing.*

The bird hovered in the air for a moment looking straight at her; it waved its head toward the house in a gesture that said, "go thataway"; and then flew in the direction of the house, passing through the trees like they weren't there.

Out of the corner of her eye she saw the jet of blue in a tree, again, but just as before, it was gone in a flash.

Amy was confused. *Is Adam a ghost, too?* she wondered.

She couldn't just stand there like a fool. She wanted to do what she thought the bird was telling her to do: run for the house. But it was so far away she couldn't even see it. She would never make it. The barn was her only hope of refuge. *Refuge from what?* she asked herself.

"Amy!"

Refuge from that—whatever it is.

She broke away from the tree, running toward the barn as fast as her legs would go. The few feet in distance seemed like a mile; her own breathing sounded like a train in her ears.

"Amy!"

"Wait till Mom gets home," she shouted between gulps of air. "You'll be sorry, Adam Miller."

She suddenly felt silly using Adam's name. It was not his voice calling her; it was a voice straight out of a dungeon in hell.

The gleaming metal padlock on the barn door was not sympathetic to her cause. She pulled on the door with all of her might. Something moved behind her; she turned and caught just a glimpse of something large and brown as it disappeared into the woods. She thought it was probably just a very large ground hog, *but maybe it was...Nunny and Cecil.* Her mind was trying hard to stay rational while her body did just the opposite: she pulled on the weathered boards of the barn door until her fingernails ripped and her fingers bled.

She looked back toward the house; she would never make it. She looked out toward the woods; the small overgrown field that separated the orchard from the woods suddenly seemed to go on forever. They would hunt her down like a frightened mouse if she went that route. The barn was the only answer, but it was useless to her if she couldn't get in.

The three hex signs affixed to the barn loomed down at her; they were powerless against what stalked her. They were an afterthought and not an original part of the barn; her grandfather had bought them and secured them to the wall. She wondered why. She heard her grandfather's voice as clearly as if he was standing next to her: *The Pennsylvania Dutch claim those signs help to ward off evil. But evil isn't something that just comes around looking for you.*

"Yeah, Grandpa. Well, people are fools to believe that those stupid signs can help them...and you were a fool to think that evil won't come looking for you. Look what happened to you!" she shouted.

Calm down, girl, calm down. Think clearly. Amy began to laugh, a high, thin laugh that sounded nothing like her own. A figure rose out of the high grass in the distance. Amy shaded and strained her eyes to see it. She wanted to scream, but the sight of it ripped the air right out of her lungs. It was one of the same creatures she had seen in her dreams, part man and part wolf. It was Nunny or Cecil. It looked straight at her and appeared to grin. Amy fought to stay conscious, to control her breathing.

It was precisely at that moment that she knew she didn't have a chance.

Lenny walked through the front door of his house. His mother pounced on him like a jungle cat, waiting for its prey to saunter innocently under its nose.

"Lenny, I've been waiting for you all day. Where have you been?" she asked, looking a lot like a hefty Elizabeth Taylor in a green silk gown that Lenny could see right through.

It wasn't a pretty sight. She stood close to him, the smell of her perfume and her alcoholic breath mingling to produce a toxic fume.

"I was at school," he answered.

He walked toward the kitchen and then, stopping in his tracks, he turned and headed toward his room. He rarely ate anymore; the kitchen was usually where his mother sat, staring into space with her bottle on the table, a glass in her hand.

"Aren't you going to eat? Lenny, you're going to die of malnutrition. Why, just look at you! You don't want to get so skinny that you start losing your muscles, now, do you?"

"I don't give a flying fuck about muscles right now, so leave me the fuck alone," he told her.

"Why do you treat me this way? What's wrong with you, Lenny?" she sobbed. "You always used to be such a good boy, and now...now look at you. You look and act like there's something wrong with you."

"And you used to be a good mother. Now, you walk around here in front of your own son dressed like a whore," he said, pointing to her sheer gown, fighting his desire for her. He wanted her and hated her so badly he thought he would go up in smoke.

"You don't know the whole story, Lenny. I've wanted to tell you for so long, but I was afraid to hurt you," she started. Her garish eye makeup dripped black lines of tears down her cheeks.

"And you want to tell me now?" he asked in mocking disbelief. "I think you've waited a bit too long to tell me. If it waited this long, it can last forever." He turned and started out of the room.

"Wait, Lenny, you have to know! I have to tell you!" she shouted.

"Nothing matters, don't you see? Tonight is the end of the world," he told her, feeling himself slipping into the void, over the edge. "It has to be that way because you set the dream in motion. You tempted fate, and now you'll pay for it."

Lenny could see that his mother was totally bewildered, but he didn't care. It was time; the dream was waiting in his head, waiting to become a reality.

Denise felt guilty telling Bruce that she wanted to go for a walk on the beach without him. But she desperately wanted to be alone, to think without interruption.

Bruce had pressed her to reveal her nightmares to him: "Denise, I'm a psychologist. Trust me; maybe I can help you."

"I don't want to talk about it, Bruce."

"Just tell me one thing: are your nightmares about your father?" he had asked.

"Please, Bruce. Really, it's nothing. I can't even remember," she had lied.

"Why do you put this distance between us? Why won't you confide in me?" he had shouted. He looked like he would explode. Denise had never seen him so angry, and that's when she had left him there.

She had run across the street and down the path to the beach, ignoring Bruce's calls for her to come back. The warm sand had felt good under her feet. It had been cooled by an early afternoon thunderstorm. She felt good to be alone, to think in peace.

The events of the past year hovered over her head like a swarm of bees, taking every opportunity to fly down to sting her. Be rational, she told herself; it can all be explained. .Denise walked into the condo.

When she returned to the condo, Bruce was sitting on the balcony reading the newspaper, a glass of wine in his hand.

"Did you have a pleasant walk?" he asked, not turning to look at her.

"Very nice," she said.

"Well, are you feeling better? At least you can tell me that much." He turned in his chair to face her. His brows drew together and his mouth opened as if he was about to say something, but no words came out.

"I went for a swim," she said, answering the question in his eyes.

"I see that. Fully clothed?" he asked.

"Fully clothed," she answered. "I'll go take a shower. Why don't you think about what you want for dinner?"

Bruce looked at her like he was afraid of her.

"What's wrong?" she asked him.

He shook his head as if he were seeing something he didn't quite believe and wanted to make sure he was awake. "Nothing," he said. She could see he was trying to act like everything was fine. "I already know where I want to eat. Let's try that Crab House."

"Sounds good to me," she said.

Denise took a shower—her third one that day—and put her clothes on. Bruce was still reading on the balcony.

"Denise, I got a strange email today from a friend," Bruce called into the room. "Did you know that they thought Paul picked up a hitchhiker the night he died?"

"Why did they think that? Paul wasn't the kind of guy who would pick up a hitchhiker."

"Well, they found some animal hair in the backseat of his car. The police thought the hair was from a dog. He says Paul didn't have a dog and neither did the girl he was dating in Pittsburgh. Kind of weird, huh?"

"Did he say what color the hair was?" she asked.

"Grayish," he said.

Denise heard the words as if in a dream. Her mind filled with images, one after another: the hair on her clothes when they first moved into the house; the hair in Adam's bed; the hair in the nest of her clothes in the attic; the wolf creatures dancing in the orchard, the moonlight illuminating their silvery-gray fur; the tufts of canine hair found next to Elam Riehl's body. It dawned on her that Adam was somehow associated with the creatures. Suddenly, she knew with a conviction that made her heart shrivel that Adam had something to do with Paul's death. The tombstones in her dream: one had her mother's name written on it, and the other had Amy's. *The dates, what were the dates of their deaths? July 10, 2011.*

"Bruce," she screamed, "what is the date today?"

"What's wrong with you?" he asked, a look on his face that said she was nuts.

"Answer me, goddamn it!" she screamed even louder.

"July 10th. What is your problem, Denise? You're really acting strange!"

Denise ran into the bathroom and vomited, while Bruce looked on wide-eyed. She flew out of the bathroom and threw some things into a bag.

"I'm sorry, Denise. Don't leave!" he said, holding her arm.

"Please," she said, jerking her arm away. "I'm sorry, I have to go. It has nothing to do with you."

"Denise, this is insane. You can't leave! What did I do?" he looked almost as crazy as she felt.

"Where's my cell?" she said, searching through her purse until she found it. She pulled it out and looked at it. "Shit! It's dead. You must do one thing for me," she told Bruce. "Call my mother, and tell her to find Amy and take her away from the house, as far away as she can get. Tell her that Adam means to kill them."

"Denise, please! Sit down and tell me what's going on!" he shouted. He was frantic, but she was hysterical.

"I don't have time right now! I must get home to stop him. Just call my mother, please!"

That was the last time she ever saw Bruce, standing on the porch of the condo, his heart broken, watching her drive away.

Amy ran to the other side of the barn, where there were several small windows at its base. The stone foundation of the barn was at least two feet thick. Each window opening was covered—from the inside out—with a glass-paned window, then with a wire grate, and finally, with horizontal wooden pegs stuck into holes bored into the thick sides of the window opening. Her grandfather had made sure that nothing would enter the barn—at least not through those windows.

Amy ran from window to window, searching for one that looked penetrable. Each one was reinforced with the special triple protection plan: window, wire grate, wooden pegs. She approached the final window with very little hope in her heart. She didn't know for sure what it was that was hunting her; she didn't know if the barn would protect her from it; but she did know that it was her only possible place of shelter until someone came to rescue her.

She looked at the last window, straining her eyes so hard to see through its dirty surface—and so devoid of hope—that for a moment she didn't notice that it didn't have a wire grate. Her heart soared with hope for a brief moment: maybe she would survive after all.

Amy tried unsuccessfully to pull the wooden pegs from the holes; she wondered how and why they had put them in there in the first place. She finally resorted to kicking them. She cried out; the big toe of her right foot felt broken. She had to continue kicking; a broken toe could be fixed...she dared not let her mind think about what body parts couldn't be; images of the Amish boy and the decapitated rat hovered like phantom actors just behind the curtain of her thoughts, waiting for their turn to make an appearance.

The old wood was weak, which was a good thing, because so was she. One peg broke loose, and then the others followed, one after another like dominoes.

Her next obstacle was the window, its frame sealed over with a century's worth of paint. It wouldn't budge. She punched the frame with the side of her fist, trying to jar it loose. It still wouldn't budge. She cried out in pain at her ripped fingernails, her bleeding, splinter-stuck fingers. Finally, with a burst of adrenaline triggered more from anger than from fear, she kicked a hole in it.

Something moved in the trees behind her; she turned expecting to see Adam and his furry friends, arriving just in time to gobble her up before she made it into the barn, but they were nowhere in sight. The full grass in the field moved in waves in the afternoon sun; someone or something had just passed through it, cutting a dark furrow through the perfect green.

Amy kicked out the rest of the glass in the window and crawled in and brushed herself off.

"If I get out of this alive, I'm going to kill you, Adam Miller," she said. She was sure her grandmother would call the police if she didn't show up for dinner—if, she thought, her grandmother was still alive.

Lenny was napping face down when he woke up to a hand on his back. It was his mother: he could smell her.

It was time.

"Lenny, wake up," his mother slurred.

The position he was in made it easy for him to run his arm down under the blanket and mattress. He winced as he felt the razor-sharp edge of the blade cut into his knuckle.

"Lenny, you awake?"

He wrapped his fingers firmly around the wooden handle.

"Lenny, I have something to tell you. You have to know. It will explain the way I've been acting."

Lenny slowly pulled the knife from under the mattress. He held it there under the blanket for a minute, calmly, feeling as though nothing out of the ordinary was about to happen.

"Lenny, I'm not your mother. We adopted you when you were a baby," she said. Those were the last words to leave Sheila Delenko's lips.

Lenny pulled the knife out from under the blanket. "Lying whore," he screamed, plunging the knife into the exact center of his mother's heart.

He rose from his bed and put on a sweatshirt. He walked over to the phone, sat down, and dialed 911.

"911 emergency," said the voice on the other end.

"Yeah, this is Lenny Delenko over at 1874 Birch Street. I just killed my mother."

"Is this some kind of a joke?" the voice asked.

"No, it was an act of fate," Lenny told the voice.

"We'll send a car right over."

"Thank you," Lenny said.

He pulled a crumpled piece of notebook paper from out of his pocket and dialed the number that was written on it. But there was no answer at Professor Miller's house. He hoped the police would let him call her later; he hoped she was still alive to receive his call, although fate dictated that she was dead the moment he cut into his mother's heart.

From his chair at the window, Lenny saw the police cars coming. He walked quickly to the medicine cabinet in his mother's bathroom, peeking in at his mother lying dead on his bed as he passed.

The medicine cabinet contained rows and rows of bottles filled with pretty pills. They were knocking at his door. They were pounding now. He heard glass shatter.

Eeny, meeny, miney, mo...Darvon, Valium, mix and match. Swallow big, Lenny, he thought, swallowing several handfuls of pills as quickly as he could get them down.

He walked calmly out of the room and down the hall. The police were in his bedroom, gathered around his mother's body. He thought it strange that they all looked so happy to see him.

Amy was lying in the hay, deriving a momentary comfort from the soft cushion of prickliness, when suddenly she felt something wet on her foot. She looked down to see that her foot was covered in blood. Her once white sneaker was now bright red.

She wiped some of the blood away, wincing in pain as her hand grazed pieces of glass that were still stuck into deep gashes on her ankle. She hadn't even felt them in her haste to get into the shelter of the barn. Slowly, she pulled out the wedges of glass, the smell of blood filling her nostrils; the pain was so bad she had to bite her tongue to keep from screaming. She could feel her breathing becoming shallower as she began to hyperventilate; she grabbed a handful of hay and pressed it to her nose and mouth, using its fragrance to mask the smell of the blood. She tried to inhale deeply, but her lungs were already fully expanded and brimming over with oxygen. Her breathing was getting shallower by the minute. *Think, Amy, think—what to do.* There wasn't a paper bag in sight, and she didn't want to start singing—

something her doctor had told her to do in such a situation—because she would make herself easy prey for Adam and his friends. But if she didn't sing, she would pass out, and that just wouldn't do.

"Yesterday, all my troubles seemed so far away, now it looks as though they're here to stay, oh, I believe in yesterday. Suddenly...," she sang.

Amy continued to sing, trying desperately to concentrate on something other than the smell of blood. She looked around the barn, wondering how Adam and his friends would get in, and once they did, where she would hide.

She caught her breath and pushed her face into the pile of hay, inhaling the clean, horsey scent.

Amy heard a noise and looked up at the window she had come in through: a huge wolf's paw was sticking through it. They were coming in after her! Amy looked around frantically for a weapon. She surveyed the tools hanging from hooks on the wall: a shovel...a hoe...a saw...a sickle. She hobbled over to the sickle and took it off the hook. She looked up to see that the paw was gone. Had she imagined it in her fear?

Amy sat back down in the hay, cradling the sickle like a puppy. The thought of using it to kill someone or something made her skin crawl. She imagined the sounds it would make cutting into flesh and bone: solid sounds, like an axe cutting into a tree.

As much as she hated the thing Adam had become, she still remembered him as the little brother she had once loved. If he meant to kill her, then that's what he would have to do, because she would rather die than hurt him.

Lenny sat on the narrow cot with his hand over his nose, trying to filter out the smell of urine that permeated the cell. An elderly man lay on the cot above him.

"Come on and tell me what you in here for, sugar," the man said over and over again, like a broken record.

Lenny wondered if this was a recently introduced form of torture: the broken record method. A cop passed by; Lenny called out to him: "When do I get to make my phone call? I have to make a call right now, or it will be too late!"

"I'll send someone back for you," the cop muttered.

NUNNY & CECIL—A Tale of Terror

Lenny waited for what seemed like an eternity. He figured it had been about an hour since he had swallowed the pills. He had assumed they would let him make a call immediately upon entering the station. But he had been wrong, and soon he knew he would be dead wrong. He chuckled at his little joke, and then frowned long and hard when he thought about what might happen to Professor Miller if he didn't reach her—if she was still alive.

The sound of thick, wide heels on the concrete floor echoed through the crypt-like hallway. Finally, someone was coming. A burly cop with thick black eyebrows over even blacker eyes appeared at the cell door. He stood there for a minute studying Lenny. His mouth opened and Lenny could actually see the words fly out: "You got one phone call and it better be to a lawyer—a damn good lawyer."

Just in time, Lenny thought, watching the words fly around his head; each one had a funny tail hanging from the last letter. He was beginning to hallucinate.

"I don't..." Lenny started to say he didn't need a lawyer where he was going; he hoped to be dead within the hour. *Soon, I'll be knock, knock, knocking on Satan's door.* He decided that he had better keep his mouth shut or they might catch on and pump his stomach.

A cop resembling humpty dumpty appeared next to the burly cop. He had a pair of handcuffs in his hand.

"Hey, I thought you were off duty," the burly cop said to humpty dumpty.

"I am. I decided to stick around a bit so I could get a look at this animal."

The burly cop opened the door to the jail cell, and humpty dumpty put the cuffs on Lenny. Lenny felt like a freak on display at the circus.

"Come on and tell me what he's in here for, man," the black man said.

The cops ignored him and led Lenny out of the jail cell. Lenny's vision was closing down like the aperture of a camera; he had no peripheral vision. *You have to make the phone call,* said a voice in his head. *It's part of the plan.* His brain felt covered with spider webs.

The narrow, winding hallway went on forever; the smell of urine seemed as permanent as the thick concrete walls. Lenny's legs were rubbery; he was so tired. He wanted desperately to lie down and sleep. *Where are they taking me? The phone call,* a voice answered from somewhere in the fog.

Finally, there was a light at the end of the tunnel. The cops led Lenny into a brightly lit room with people scurrying in every direction. The room was too bright, too loud, and too hectic. The two cops took him into a room where they were joined by a third.

Lenny heard them talking, but he didn't know or care what they were saying. The burly cop unlocked Lenny's handcuffs and pointed to the phone.

"One call, and then back to the cell."

Lenny looked at the number he had written on his hand; it was a mass of squiggling worms. *Your duty,* the voice said.

"Could you..." Lenny wanted the cops to help him dial the number, but he didn't know how to express the thought. His eyes started to close. He had to sleep...just for a little while; then he would make the call.

"You got a problem kid? We don't have all day. If you're going to make a call, you'd better make it snappy."

Lenny held out his hand so that the cop could see the number written there. "Could you dial this number for me, please? I don't feel so good."

"What the fuck's the matter with you? Dial it yourself!" one of the cops said.

"Hell, I don't think I'd feel so good if I killed my mother," humpty dumpty said, causing them all to laugh.

Lenny was slipping away into the fog.

"Please," Lenny managed to say.

"Give me that thing," the burly cop said, pulling the receiver from Lenny's hand. "Let's get this show on the road."

Lenny held out his hand so the cop could see the number.

"Hey, that's long distance. You'll be charged for this; and where you're going, you won't be making any money," the cop said, dialing the number and then handing Lenny the receiver.

Lenny stood there, listening to the phone ring at Professor Miller's house. He had no idea what he would say if she picked up the phone; but it didn't matter, because no one was answering.

Lenny put the receiver back on the cradle, and then he lay down on the floor and went to sleep—forever.

"Amy...Adam..." Marie called into the orchard. Amy had been gone the entire day; Marie had no idea when Adam had left the house. He was in for a good bit of trouble when he arrived home. *If he arrives home. Don't even think about that kind of stuff, Marie;* her overactive worrier's imagination was kicking in.

"Amy...Adam."

She hoped they hadn't taken the barn door key. *Joe would have a fit if he found...get hold of yourself, woman. Joe isn't here anymore and never will be again.*

Marie often caught herself thinking he was still alive: she would go out to the back door to call him in for supper, and then feeling like an utter fool, she would lock herself in the bathroom for a good cry.

The phone was ringing. It was a tinny jingle from where she stood in the orchard. Marie began a slow jog to the house.

On the fourth ring, the answering machine kicked on. She ran up the back porch steps, letting the screen door slam behind her as she entered the house. That had to be fixed. Maybe Bruce would fix it for them.

Marie picked up the phone and said a breathless, "Hello." She got a dial tone in answer. *Darn it,* she thought. *What if it was someone calling about the kids? What if something has happened to them?*

The phone rang again, startling Marie as she stood next to it, deep in thought. She snatched it up as though her life depended on it. "Hello."

"Hello, Marie," a man's voice said.

"Yes, this is she."

"This is Bruce, Marie. Denise..." he started.

"Is Denise all right?" she interrupted.

"Denise is fine, Marie," he told her. "She's on her way home right now. She'd call you herself, but her cell battery died."

"Did you just call?" she asked.

"No, I didn't."

"Did you two get in a fight?"

"No, not exactly. Denise believes something is wrong there at the farm. She asked me to call you and tell you...tell you to..."

"Tell me to do what?" Marie asked.

"She...she wants you and Amy to get away from the house...away from Adam."

"What? Why would she say such a thing?" Marie asked in disbelief.

"I know it sounds crazy," he told her. "I would have called you several hours ago, but I felt foolish telling you this. Well, I guess you know Denise has been acting odd lately."

"I guess so—very odd now that I think about it. But I put it down to her father dying and all. Why does she want us to get away from Adam?" She was feeling a little sick all of a sudden, and she wished Bruce would come out with it all.

"Well, this is going to sound ridiculous, but she seems to think Adam might try to kill you and Amy."

"What?" she shrieked into the phone in total disbelief; but a thin chill ran up her spine; for some odd reason Bruce's words rang true. "Where would she get such an idea?" she said, in an effort to confirm her disbelief—confirm it with herself.

"I have no idea. It sounds crazy to me too. I know she's been having bad dreams since we arrived here in Florida. I guess she'll explain when she gets there."

"Thank you, Bruce. Thank you for calling," she said. "Goodbye." She hung up the phone without waiting for his reply.

The wind was picking up, whistling through the cracks in the barn's stone walls. Amy could smell rain, hear the low rumblings of thunder in the distance. She looked through a slit in the wall to see a dark wall of clouds hanging low in the sky. She had been stuck in the barn for what seemed like hours now; surely Adam and his buddies would have made their move if they meant to harm her. She wondered if her earlier visions had been hallucinations caused by fear: the paw she had seen in the window could have been the barn cat's paw; the creatures in the grass, merely gentle deer; the voices, only the wind blowing through the trees. That was it: her imagination was playing tricks on her. Any minute now someone would come to rescue her, and soon she would be curled up in her bed with a good book. But she knew she couldn't afford to make the mistake of blaming the events of the day on her imagination; she would be foolish to let her guard down.

Amy lay back in the pile of hay; she picked up her book of poetry, and losing herself in a poem, temporarily forgot about her predicament. Her ears perked at the sound of something scratching on wood, like a dog scratching on a door to signal that it wanted to come in. It was probably just the cat, she thought hopefully. She continued reading, until a familiar odor wafted into her nostrils. Amy put her book aside; she knew the odor only too well: it was the smell of the blood monster in the basement and the shadow on her door; it was the smell of Nunny and Cecil. They were somewhere nearby.

It was time for a showdown. She heard a scuffling noise and looked up to see three dark figures jump—one after another—through the window she had come through.

An electric surge of fear ran through her body. In moments they would be upon her, tearing at her flesh with their jagged teeth, or worse yet, performing some unimaginably bizarre Ipaki mating ritual.

Amy held the sickle tightly in her hand; she thought about suicide for a moment, but her will to live was too strong. *You fool, girl, get up and run.*

Amy looked up at the window where she had come in. She would never reach it.

"Amy!" someone called in a voice that made her hair stand on end.

The barn door was padlocked from the outside, but it was made of wood. There was a saw hanging on the wall near where she found the sickle; she could saw through the wooden barn door. Amy felt incredibly foolish at not having thought about how she would get out of the barn once she had come in. She was trapped.

Amy edged along the wall toward the saw. If Adam and his buddies came after her, she could swing the sickle out in a half circle around her. They would never get close to her. *Wishful thinking.*

The odor was getting stronger, swirling around her head like a poisonous gas. They were getting closer. She could hear someone breathing, deep raspy breathes.

She saw them then, Nunny and Cecil, doing some kind of strange dance—the same dance they did in her dream, stilted and clumsy. They were terrible to see, with their monstrous heads perched on human bodies. Their limbs were those of wolves, but preternaturally long, thrusting outward, reptilian in their movement. They were covered with a matted coat of silvery-gray hair, long in some places and almost bare in others. They were singing a song—a children's song, one that Jenna must have taught them during their short lives. It was "Pop Goes the Weasel." They seemed entranced in their dance, unaware of her presence.

But where was Adam?

Amy felt her way along the wall. She could see the saw hanging from a rusted nail on the wall. A few more feet and she would have it in her hand. The singing was getting louder. Amy wanted to scream, but she knew if she did, something would happen—something bad. She couldn't believe this was happening to her. Sweat poured from her scalp into her eyes, but her mouth was desert dry.

The saw was within arm's reach. Amy moved toward it, but she slipped on something, her leg sliding sideways away from her. It felt like she had stepped on a bucketful of mashed bananas; she gasped as she looked down to see the badly mutilated body of the barn cat splayed out in the hay. If it weren't for the bright orange color of the cat's fur, she would have never recognized it: it was decapitated and split open from end to end.

"Sister, what have you done?"

Amy looked up to see Adam standing before her, his mouth open dumbly, his eyes glazed and round, a straight razor in his hand. He was looking at the cat.

"Pour little kitty," he said, picking up the remains of the cat and holding it to his chest. "I loved this cat, don't you know?"

"What's wrong with you, Adam?" Amy said. "You're insane."

"You bitch! I hate you. How dare you hurt my kitty!" he said, flinging the bloody mess at her.

Amy jumped out of the way and then, instinctively, swung the sickle out toward Adam, striking him in the temple with its pointed end. Blood fountained out of the wound.

Adam turned and ran, screaming. Nunny and Cecil continued in their hellish dance, singing even louder. "That's the way the story goes..."

Amy wasted no time in grabbing the saw and heading for the barn door. She didn't understand why Nunny and Cecil weren't helping Adam. *Oh, but they are.* Something that felt like a steel trap clutched her ankle; she fell, face first, onto the dirt floor. She turned over to see one of the hideous creatures—she didn't know one from the other—holding her ankle between its teeth. Adam was on her in seconds, straddling her, razor in hand. He slashed her shoulder, and as she twisted her body around to try to get out from under him, Adam cut her throat, sending blood spraying everywhere. She lay there, holding her breath, pretending to be dead, for—when she thought about it years later—what might have been up to ten minutes, until Adam and his playmates left the barn.

NUNNY & CECIL—A Tale of Terror

The girl behind the rental car desk was taking her sweet time with the paperwork. It was bad enough that a storm had caused her plane to circle the Lancaster airport twenty times before it had permission to land.

"I'm really in a hurry," Denise said for the fifth time. She would have called a cab, but she knew a cab driver wouldn't drive as fast as she wanted to go. She planned to get inside the rental car and drive home as fast as the car would go.

Denise walked over to the pay phone again and called home. *Why in the hell aren't they answering?* She called her mother's cell phone, but she knew it would prove fruitless: her mother rarely had her cell phone turned on. *Maybe they're at the mall...something ordinary, something normal. Yes, normal.* How nice normal suddenly seemed.

Denise was finding it difficult to think normal thoughts. She was finding it difficult to remember what the word normal meant. For some odd reason, she envisioned a hotel room with plastic orange curtains whenever she thought of the definition of normal; but her mind was playing with her and kept switching into the abnormal mode like a television switching channels: the plastic orange curtains were not hanging in front of windows on the abnormal network; they were on the ground, wrapped around stiff things that looked like corpses.

The girl at the rental car desk seemed unsympathetic to Denise's predicament.

"Aren't you finished, yet?" I have to get home. You see, I think my son is going to kill my mother and daughter. Please hurry!" Denise said.

The girl looked up in disbelief at Denise and pushed the papers across the counter toward her. "Here you go," she said. "Sign there and you're all set."

Denise signed the paper and the girl dropped the set of keys into her hand as though she were letting go of a dirty hanky.

"Drive safely," the girl said, but Denise didn't hear her. All she could hear was the sound of someone screaming in her head, someone who sounded a hell of a lot like Amy.

Marie looked at the clock and then out the window for probably the twenty-fifth time in fifteen minutes. Still no sign of the kids. She was tired from searching the orchard for them. She'd checked the barn, but it was securely locked so she knew they couldn't be in there.

Those kids are in for a whipping, they are. She had strained her vocal cords calling for them. Sick with worry, she held her stomach.

Bruce's words kept buzzing around her ears like mosquitoes: *She seems to think Adam might try to kill you and Amy.* She didn't believe that for a second...or did she? Logic and reason told her it wasn't true, but intuition was telling her something different, something she didn't want to hear.

She would give them fifteen more minutes and then she was calling the police. She didn't want to jump the gun; they were probably so involved in some woodland game that they completely forgot about dinner. Their stomachs would remind them soon enough. They would come flying through the door all sweaty and dirty, saying, "Grandma, we're hungry." But as hard as she tried to believe this scenario would take place, she couldn't. Amy and Adam didn't play together like normal sisters and brothers; besides, Amy was an angel: she would never make her grandmother worry if she could help it. *Maybe she can't help it.*

An image of a human skeleton lying in the dirt kept flashing into her mind. She would follow the image with her eyes, starting at the feet, but then shut the image out before she reached the rib cage. *Remember Elam.*

They never had found what killed the boy; and now Amy and Adam were out there somewhere...*don't even think about it, Marie.*

What would make Denise say what she had about Adam? What would provoke any mother to say such a thing about her son? Marie chastised herself for telling Denise that Adam was weird. Denise's mental health was suffering and she was wide open to suggestion. Still, Denise had to take a huge mental leap to go from thinking Adam was weird to thinking he would murder his family.

Marie couldn't wait to see the kids' faces when she told them their mother was coming home. She had no idea how to prepare for Denise's arrival: she wondered if she should have the people with the straightjacket there waiting just in case. What if Denise tried to hurt Adam? *One thing at a time; you're old, woman, and you can only deal with one thing at a time. Worry about the kids getting home and then Denise.*

Marie got up from her seat at the kitchen table and looked out the window again. She opened the screen door and walked outside. She was thankful that the storm had only threatened rain and then passed over. A cool breeze whipped her dress around her legs; at least it had brought some relief from the heat. From where she stood on the back porch, she could see someone coming in from the orchard. When she could see clearly who it was and his condition, the sight made her skin shrivel around her bones: Adam was walking slowly in from the orchard with a crimson stream of blood flowing steadily from a wound on the side of his head.

Marie ran down the wooden steps and toward her grandson. "Adam, honey, what happened?" she called, and then, although she was afraid of the answer, she asked, "Where's Amy?"

He appeared to be in shock: he looked at Marie as if he didn't know her and seemed unconcerned—even unaware—of his wound. He was covered with dirt and blood.

Marie continued running toward him, but stopped dead in her tracks when she saw what he was carrying: a straight razor—Joe's ivory-handled one.

"How nice to see you, Grandma," a voice said. It had emanated from Adam's lips, but it wasn't his voice.

"What did you say, Adam?" she asked, taking a few steps backward.

Something skimmed her legs as she was stepping backward: it was a large, grayish animal; she could see it out of the corner of her eye. Whatever it was, it made her trip and fall onto the dirt. She looked quickly around, but there was nothing and no one there, except for Adam.

"Adam, you put that thing down right now!" she demanded, trying to sound stern, but the quaver in her voice gave her fear away. She got up and brushed herself off.

Adam suddenly seemed to come out of his trance. He threw himself at her feet and slashed her ankles with the razor. Marie screamed and fled to the house. She didn't know she had it in her to run so fast.

She didn't turn to see if Adam was following, but she could hear someone breathing as if they were running right beside her. She could feel a hot breath on her neck—or could she. Marie suddenly knew what it was like to feel crazy.

She felt like something was right on top of her. She ran into the house and locked the deadbolt with trembling hands; then she ran to the front door to make sure it was locked. As she passed the basement door, something pounded on it and called out, "Marie."

There was no way she was going to open that door...and end up like Joe. She cried out in pain as she often did when she thought of him. So that's what had happened: that's why Joe's big, strong heart stopped beating...just like that. He had opened that door and seen what it was that was now pounding on it; something that had been to hell and back and had a voice like the devil.

It was the same thing—she was sure of it—that had left those monstrous paw prints in the orchard and had decapitated that rat. It was the shadow on Amy's door and the nose-stinging odor that often wafted through the air without evident cause. It was the scratching sounds on the basement door she so often heard while she was cooking; she couldn't remember how many times she had stopped in the middle of preparing dinner to open the basement door and find nothing...nothing but a foul scent.

She shuddered with horror at the realization that it had been living there in that house with them, walking on the same floors, touching their things, watching them. What fools they had all been to pretend that the evil thing wasn't there. *Don't acknowledge the monsters.*

She was beginning to believe anything was possible. Could it be that Adam's playmates, Nunny and Cecil, were not just figments of a lonely boy's imagination? That was too much to swallow all at once, but she didn't have time to chew it slowly.

Marie wanted to sit down to rest, to think about when and how all the bizarre things had begun to happen, but her desire to survive compelled her to walk quickly up the stairs to her bedroom closet. She opened the door, wincing with pain as she breathed in Joe's scent, still lingering there like a ghost among their things. She was grateful that she had been so stubborn, refusing to get rid of his things, especially the shotgun lying up on the shelf. She had never even touched the thing before; she hated guns with a passion. Guns were good for one thing in her mind: death.

She reached up and pulled it down off the shelf. It was cold and heavy. She didn't know what she was going to do with it; she surely wasn't going to use it to shoot Adam. The back of her hand was the only thing she would use on him. If he meant to kill her, then that's what he would have to do, because she would rather die than shoot him.

Marie carried the gun to Denise's room, opened the balcony door, and then walked out onto the balcony. She had a clearer view of the orchard from up there. It was difficult to see in the dim twilight. *Where's Amy?*

"Amy," she called out. "Amy!" She leaned over the rail and looked down around the house. No sign of Adam. There was a tapping sound coming from above her. She looked up at the attic window to the hideous face of a huge wolf smiling down at her. Marie's lungs seemed to freeze in her chest and the blood in her veins turned to ice. The wolf waved a massive paw at her. The gun fell from her limp hands with a heavy thunk, and she fell back against the wooden railing. *It's in the house...my house.*

Suddenly, it was in Denise's room, walking hand in hand with Adam! She looked up to see the grotesque face still smiling down at her from the attic window. There are two of them! The wolflike thing with Adam was up on its hind legs, walking like a man...coming toward her. She had to save Adam! The thing would devour him. She picked up the gun with hands that felt like Jello. She tried desperately to hold the gun steady; her entire body was trembling. She dug her elbows into her ribs and pointed the gun at the monster.

"Get away from it, Adam!" she screamed. "Move away from it now!"

Adam didn't appear to hear her; he opened the door to the balcony and led the thing out.

"Adam, move away from it!" she screamed again.

The thing was six feet tall and resembled a wolfen satyr the way it pranced on massive haunches. Its tongue lolled thickly from between thin, black lips. Its torso was like a man's, but covered with matted gray fur.

Marie steadied her aim as well as she could; her finger squeezed the trigger, but nothing happened. Adam rushed toward her, shouting "No, Grandma!" His body hit hers like a cannonball, propelling her backwards over the same railing she had once so carefully painted. She tumbled head over heels, her body striking the house only once before she hit the ground, head first, her neck quietly snapping.

The stone walls on either side of the rusted iron gate glinted queerly in the moonlight. They looked older than the earth and much older than Denise remembered; many of the larger stones lay crumbled in small heaps on the ground, leaving large gaping holes in the mortar. The thought that she was at the wrong house flitted through Denise's mind: everything looked vaguely unfamiliar, surreal. It seemed she had been gone a very long time.

The tires of her car crunched along the gravel-strewn driveway, comforting her with the sound they made. Suddenly, everything was right again. She was home sweet home. She would never go away again. If her mother and children were all alive, she would never leave again. *But, oh, what a terrible mother you've been.*

Amy would be all nestled in her bed, looking like a woodland elf. And Adam would be happy to see her, but mad as hell that she had gone away. He would punish her with insolence and frowns for a few days, but then he would be her sweet baby boy again. *Oh yes, your sweet baby boy.*

If they were there, alive, nothing else would ever matter to her again. She would never care about another thing. She would devote herself entirely to them until the day she died.

The house was dark; not a single light shone from inside. Her mother's car was parked in the driveway: they were probably all fast asleep. Denise looked at the clock on her dashboard: it was only eight-thirty, much too early for bedtime. The first in a series of snakelike chills slithered up Denise's spine.

One thing was certain: they weren't expecting her. Bruce must not have been able to reach them. If he had, she was sure they would be up waiting for her. The possibility that they were going to surprise her crossed her mind.

Denise parked her car, pushed open the car door, and walked slowly and calmly to the front door of the house. She hoped that if she acted as though everything were normal, then everything would be normal. The lonely sound of metal clanging softly against metal drifted through the cool night air. She wondered what it was that made the sound.

Denise didn't need to use the key that she held tightly between stiff, sweating fingers: the heavy wooden door opened with a push. *That's odd...but if it's open, they must be home! They must be alive! It's a trick,* she thought. *They must be playing a trick. Oh, but you deserve to be tricked; you deserve to be punished.*

They were home! She could hear them singing some childish song upstairs. *Oh, to hold my children again.* She started toward the stairs in a frenzy, but stopped dead in her tracks before she reached the first step. On the white wall abutting the staircase, words were written with what looked to be red paint, the way it dripped down the wall. *Just like the dream*. The message read, "Welcome Home Mommy!" Her head swarmed for a second with a vivid memory of the dream, while a fetid odor filled her nostrils. She reached for the smooth wooden railing to steady herself.

Denise reached out and touched the still wet words and then brought her hand to her nose. There was no mistaking the crimson, foul smelling fluid: it was blood. But whose blood was it?

The singing coming from upstairs grew louder, higher pitched. Denise ran up the stair to Amy's room. The singing stopped.

"Amy," she said. But the bed was empty. "Amy, where are you?" Of course, she suddenly remembered telling Amy she could sleep in her bedroom while she was away.

She threw open the door to her bedroom, the adrenaline singing in her veins. The door hit the wall with a bang and a crack. No Amy.

Denise could feel her breathing getting shallower by the minute. She fought to control it. Her heart was pounding in her ears as she touched the knob on her mother's bedroom door, but not so loudly that she didn't hear the scuffling overhead.

They were in the attic, playing games and singing songs; that explained everything—except that the voices sounded nothing like the voices she knew. Surely her mother wouldn't be up there too. She hoped the kids hadn't given her mother a hard time.

She opened her mother's bedroom door and turned on the light. "Mom," she said, not knowing why she bothered to say the word; there was no one there. "Mom, are you there?"

Denise's feet barely touched the ground as she flew to Adam's bedroom and threw open the door. No Adam.

"Where in the hell are you?" she screamed, running to the attic door and pounding up the steep, narrow wooden stairs.

A single ray of moonlight shone in from the window, illuminating her son, who sat covered with blood in the middle of the floor. Adam's skin was white as death and the side of his head was swollen to twice its normal size. He held a hand of playing cards in his hand; two other hands of cards lay next to him on the floor. He looked up suddenly as if she had surprised him, and Denise gasped when she saw his eyes. It was as though Adam had put up a "Gone Fishing" sign and simply ceased to exist: there was no one home behind the baby blues.

"My baby, what's happened to you?" she cried. She was so happy to see him, so happy that he was alive.

"Mommy," he said, one of his eyes twitching, pulsating, like it might explode.

Denise put out her arms; Adam rose from where he sat and moved slowly toward her. She picked him up and squeezed him to her chest. If he had done what Denise thought he had done, if he had killed his grandmother and sister, she would just accept it, spend the rest of her life healing his sick mind. What else could she do? She needed him. He was all she had left...*if* they were dead.

"Adam," she said, sitting down on the top step of the staircase and pulling him onto her lap. "What happened to your head? Where are Amy and Grandma?"

He bowed his head in answer.

"Adam," she said, putting her hand under his chin and lifting his head so that his vacant eyes met hers. His irises were ink-filled saucers, the pupils lost in the deep blue; it was as if someone had put out the light.

"Amy tried to kill me," he said in a hollow voice. "It's your fault. You left me here with them."

"Adam, just tell me where they are. Everything's going to be okay. I promise!" she told him. "I know it's my fault, and I promise I'll never leave you again. Now, please," she sobbed, "tell me where they are!"

"It's your fault," he said, again. "You left me here with them."

"I know, I know! It's my fault—I know! I swear to you, Adam, that I'll never leave you again. Never!"

She held him in her arms, rocking him gently. Her eyes were clouded with tears, so clouded that she almost didn't see the glint of metal glimmering in the darkness. It was moving toward her, that glint of metal, in the grim form of a straight razor, while Adam shouted, "You can't fool me. I know you'll poison me—just like she poisoned them!"

Just like the dream. It's time to wake up. Only there was no time to wake up: Adam's razor-bearing hand was moving toward her at the speed of death.

She put her hand up to stop its movement; it bit deeply into her hand, spraying blood. She held it there, locking her fingers around it, barely feeling the pain, as she pushed it away with all of her strength, and in the process, pushed Adam—who was holding onto its handle for dear life—off her lap. There was no place for him to go but down, down the steps, head first to the bottom of the steep, narrow staircase.

NUNNY & CECIL—A Tale of Terror

Denise screamed and ran to him, picked up his lifeless body, and held him, trying to squeeze the life back into him. She wailed until she had no voice, holding him, believing that somehow, some way, if she sat there long enough, she was sure to wake up from her nightmare.

GAILA SWINDELL

Epilogue

The traffic had moved slowly because of the road construction. Denise had thought she would be able to miss it if she left at three o'clock, before the rush-hour traffic hit. She had received another bouquet of tulips that day from Bruce. When was he going to get the hint? She wanted nothing to do with him—or any man for that matter.

The speed limit sign read fifty-five; she looked down at her speedometer to see that she was moving at a fast seventy-five miles per hour. *Oh, what the hell,* she thought, and pushed down a little harder on the accelerator. She had to make up for the time she lost in the traffic jam. Two more miles and she would be home. She hoped her mailbox would contain a request for an interview from a local school; she was tired of commuting to Philadelphia. She had mailed her resume to all of the local colleges.

The farm's fieldstone wall and iron gate were there to welcome her. She stopped the car at the entrance, got out, and pushed open the heavy gate. *Don't want just anybody coming through those gates. Don't need any unexpected visitors.*

She got back into the car and drove through the gates, and then got out again to close them. She thought—for probably the hundredth time—about putting a lock on the gates, but she knew that might raise some eyebrows...especially since those gates had been opened wide in a gesture of welcome for the past thirty-six years. Closing them had been a bold but necessary move. So far, so good: no one had inquired.

NUNNY & CECIL—A Tale of Terror

She loved the sound of the gravel crunching as the car moved along the driveway. It was such a homey, comforting sound. Amy and the boys would be so happy to see her. She knew they would be excited when she told them that their father was coming to dinner. Donald was starting to put too much pressure on her to see them. He was in for a big surprise. They had really grown since the last time he had seen them...and they had changed quite a bit too. In fact, they just weren't the same children they used to be.

Denise could see them eagerly waiting for her at the window: Amy smiling and waving, Nunny and Cecil's furry faces pressed against the glass, their tails wagging furiously with glee. *Boy,* she thought with a smile, *is Donald going to be surprised.*

GAILA SWINDELL

Made in the USA
Lexington, KY
04 January 2013